Changeling Press, LLC

ChangelingPress.com

Billionaire Werewolf
Paranormal Women's Fiction
Crymsyn Hart

Billionaire Werewolf
Paranormal Women's Fiction
Crymsyn Hart

All rights reserved.
Copyright ©2024 Crymsyn Hart

ISBN: 978-1-60521-886-1

Publisher:
Changeling Press LLC
315 N. Centre St.
Martinsburg, WV 25404
ChangelingPress.com

Printed in the U.S.A.

Editor: Treva Harte
Cover Artist: Bryan Keller

The individual stories in this anthology have been previously released in E-Book format.

Billionaire Werewolf Ate My Fiancé
Crymsyn Hart

The loss of her fiancé, Greyson, from an animal attack carved a hole in Sadie Matthews, body and soul. She seeks rest and relaxation at an exclusive resort, hoping for a chance to heal. However, things immediately go wrong when the desk clerk refuses to even hand over the key to her room.

Elijah Dane's not the rescuing kind, but something about Sadie drives his wolf crazy. All he can think of is eating her up. After a wild night together, Elijah warns Sadie to stay inside during the full moon. When Sadie runs, he knows he must let her go. Can he get over his insatiable desire for her or will his wolf go to extremes to hunt her down and claim her for his own?

Chapter One

Sadie set her bag down at the counter and waited for the clerk to notice her. The lobby screamed the place only catered to the rich and powerful. *Why the hell am I here? This is not my style at all. Why did I let Mel talk me into this?* A light lavender scent tickled her nose. It took all she had to stop from sneezing. Five containers filled with water and an array of different fruits suspended between the ice cubes were displayed on a table next to the check in desk. Glass tumblers sat by them, glistening under the track lighting. Faint instrumental music played in the background. The environment radiated warmth and a welcoming atmosphere. However, she felt anything but welcome. Something about the place felt a little off. Sadie just couldn't put her finger on it.

A few brochures lay on the counter for outside attractions. Laughter floated down a hallway as the clicking of heels got closer. She rubbed her hands together at the chill from the overly cold AC blowing down on her. Her stomach tumbled as she worried her lip about why she had agreed to come to this place. She felt completely out of place. A group of women wandered by. All were dressed in fluffy white robes, smiling and smelling like they bathed in expensive lotion, all with perfect, glossy straight hair that cost more to maintain than what she made in a month.

"Hello. Can I help you?" The receptionist finally addressed her.

The words caught in her throat as she turned back to the man. His white teeth nearly blinded her. "Checking in."

He gave her the once over with a little smirk. "Name, please."

"Sadie M-Matthews." She fought the urge to run back to the car that dropped her off. Melissa would be pissed because she had arranged for her to come to this special resort in the middle of no-fucking-where. The last hour of the ride all she saw around her were trees. No signs along the road signaled a high-end hotel was off in the distance. Just more trees as far the eye could see. It almost felt like she was entering into a horror movie. Melissa said she needed a week to relax, unwind, drink in the fresh air, and go along with being pampered. Sadie hated the idea.

"Oh yes, we have you right here," the desk manager told her. His eyebrows shot up as he looked at the computer screen and then back at her. "Some*one* decided to go all out."

Her cheeks burned as she studied the marble countertop shot through with veins of gold and flecks of black. The deep mahogany wood of the desk gleamed. Maybe some felt welcome here, but the whole place screamed of opulence and rubbed her the wrong way. *Probably the handiwork of some billionaire who doesn't know his head from his asshole. He planned out this whole thing for his buddies to send their wives while they are out screwing their secretaries.* Melissa had talked up the place, told her she needed a break, and she wasn't going to take no for an answer. Her friend meant well, but there were things Melissa didn't understand. She was still processing what happened. She wasn't ready to do some scream therapy shit and then get a mud bath to help her feel better. "Yeah... well..."

The desk clerk stood up and waved her comment away as he held out a red plastic keycard. "Honey, you got the all-access pass to this place. This one gets you into all the secret places that the regular guests don't get to see."

She went to take the key from him wondering what on earth he meant about some all-access pass when he grabbed her wrist. *What did Melissa get me into?* "This isn't going to open some door that leads me to a sex dungeon, is it?"

The twinkle in his eyes died. His plump lips set in a straight line making her stomach tie into even tighter knots. "With this comes great responsibility. Don't let it out of your sight. Let me give you a word of warning, since this is your first time with us. You might see or hear certain things here. We request you don't make a big scene if you happen upon some of the other guests engaging in something you might not think is normal." He released her hand.

"What do you expect me to find? Someone fucking in the middle of the pool?" Sadie's mind whirled at the information and it raised a few red flags.

"Nothing like that. Ma'am, you do know where you are, correct?" He looked at her like she had four cats sitting on her head.

"It's a place where I'm supposed to relax. Am I missing something besides the 24-karat gold inlay in the ceiling?" She was about ready to say the hell with all this. Melissa would have a coronary, but this was getting ridiculous.

The receptionist sniffed her. Sadie wasn't sure what she had just experienced. It took her by surprise. He actually leaned over the desk and took in another long breath like she smelled bad. His expression turned grim. "Forgive me, I thought... never mind. Let me get the manager out here." He pressed a button on his earpiece and spoke into it. "Mr. Watson, I need your assistance please."

"This whole thing is already paid for. What's the big deal?" She tried to keep her cool. This wasn't the best start to her relaxing week. So far, she was late on getting there because the limo service picked her up late. Then he had a flat tire. Thankfully he had a spare, but it didn't seem like this was going to be the getaway vacation her friend wanted her to experience. She glanced down at her attire. Sadie wore blue jeans and one of the nicer blouses she owned. It might not scream rich, but she didn't look like a slob. Her feet ached. She wanted to sink into a warm bubble bath, drink a glass of wine, and then forget about the rest of the world for a while. If nothing else, shut out the noise in her head and in her heart. "I should be permitted to whatever that little piece of red plastic entitles me to."

"Miss, I am so sorry. There seems to be some kind of mix-up when the reservation was made. We can certainly accommodate you, but I would need that back." He reached across the desk for the keycard but snagged her wrist instead.

Sadie yanked her hand away, making him lose his grip on her. His nails dug trails in her flesh as he tried to get the keycard back. She hissed at the sharp pain, but the man's expression twisted into one of determination. He moved a little quicker and caught her once more. This time his grip locked around her and he tugged as though he would rip her arm out of its socket. *The little guy's not going to get the best of me. I don't think so.* She set her teeth on edge and jerked back as they played tug-o-war over the little red keycard that was supposed to open magical doors for her. "Look, buddy. I'm not giving this thing up."

"Ma'am, it would be best if you did. Believe me." He pulled back, bringing her over the counter until the edge of it pushed into her stomach.

The quick stab made her grunt. This whole thing shouldn't have been such a big deal. Normally, she would have acquiesced and let them upgrade her or whatever they had in mind to rectify the situation. However, this was different. After losing so much, she needed to hold onto whatever she could. Nothing was getting past her, not even this fucktard who kept telling her she couldn't. He dragged her up again. This time she felt her feet lift off the floor. Sadie grasped the other side of the counter and pulled back.

"I want to speak to your manager," she said through gritted teeth. A sting of sweat hit her eye from the exertion.

He took both hands and tried to get the key from her. This time Sadie couldn't hold onto it with her sweaty palms. The desk clerk took one more tug and she lost her grip on the keycard and the counter. The momentum of him releasing her so suddenly sent her flying backward. Her right shoulder, arm, and hip took the brunt of her impact on the tile floor. The plush carpet cradled her head, so it didn't crack open. The desk clerk had sent her halfway across the hotel lobby and left her seeing stars. Sadie took a few seconds to listen to the thunder in her ears and focus on the highly golden lobby ceiling. When she tried to lift her head, the world spun so she let it rest once more.

"Are you okay?" Her eyes focused and she peered into the most startling honey-gold eyes she had ever seen on a man. A closely cropped reddish brown beard accentuated his strong jaw line. He appeared completely upside down and out of proportion, but she realized her vision was still realigning after having her bell rung. "Here. Let's get you off the floor." He offered her his hand.

It took her a second to make her fingers work until she wrapped them into his hands. He helped her up and pressed his palm against the small of her back. The warmth of him melted through the thin fabric of her shirt. As he walked her over to a chair, the pain exploded in her shoulder and hip. "Mother fudg..." She touched her shoulder where she had landed.

"You're hurt."

"Yeah, you could say that. It's because that dipshit over there wouldn't let go of my key."

"Would you like some water?" the stranger asked

her.

Her anger simmered a moment as she beheld the handsomeness of the man again. "Sorry. Thank you for helping me up. Water'd be great." The man sauntered over to the row of water coolers. Sadie couldn't help but admire how his tight ass looked in his expensive black pants. He poured her a glass from the one container filled with raspberries and lemons.

"This one is my favorite. Excuse me for a moment." He handed her the cool glass and went over to the reception desk.

Sadie took a sip. The water helped relax her, both tart and sweet at the same time. She kept her eyes glued to the man who helped her up. He was dressed in a crisp white shirt and black pants. Both looked perfectly tailored to fit his broad and tall frame. Her gaze drifted down to his ass again. A flush went through her as he turned back around and caught her staring at him. She flashed him a smile and tried to forget about how she ached where she fell. Watching the conversation between him and the man at the desk made it interesting. The desk clerk backed away. The expression on his face turned to dread as his eyes flicked between her and the man who was talking to him. It appeared he actually cowered before the one who helped her up. His whole demeanor changed from the asshole who waited on her to a child being scolded.

"Is there some problem?" a middle-aged man wearing a badly fitted gray suit rushed into the lobby.

Her savior guided him over to Sadie. "Mr. Watson, Jake and this woman had a misunderstanding. I only caught the tail end as I came in. He attempted to take something from her and had her across the counter. When he got it, she fell and sustained an injury."

The manager wiped the sweat from his top lip with a handkerchief and then patted his high forehead dry. "I'm sure there's some sort of confusion. If you'll excuse me for a moment, Mr. Dane." Mr. Watson flashed her an uneasy smile. "Ma'am, I am so sorry for your injury, but there has been some misunderstanding."

"Really? Did the *misunderstanding* throw me halfway across the lobby where I hurt my hip, shoulder, and my head? You're lucky I don't sue your ass," Sadie snarled. "I thought I was supposed to coming to an exclusive resort to relax, and not dealing with...whatever the fuck this is." She gestured until the pain forced her to cradle her arm against her chest.

The manager's cheeks reddened, and the veins stood out against his pale flesh. He patted down is forehead once more. Mr. Dane came over and touched the manager's shoulder. "Ms. M-Matthews. I a-assure you..."

"Mr. Watson, I'm sure we can make some accommodations for...umm...I didn't catch you name." Mr. Dane glanced at her.

"Sadie," she said with a sigh and pressed the cool glass against her shoulder. "Sadie Matthews." A piece of hair fell into her eyes that she brushed aside.

"Right, that some adjustments, can be made for her. This place is open to everyone regardless of her... status."

"But sir, she's a...umm..."

Mr. Dane put a hand on his shoulder and flashed her a grin. "She's a patron of this establishment who has paid a great deal of money to be here and not be patronized or hurt by a member of staff because she doesn't fit your preconceived notion of what a customer should be. Don't you agree?"

He nodded absently, but Sadie caught a look of fear cross the manager's features. Sweat dripped off his forehead that couldn't be stopped even though he kept blotting at it. "Of course, Mr. Dane, but what of the others who have also come to blow off steam?"

"I'm sure they'll understand. Now, I want you to make sure that whatever Ms. Matthews accrues here in extra fees, services, or whatever she likes, is put on my account. Is that understood? She'll be treated with the utmost respect by every one of the staff. Believe me, I'll check with her. If I hear she's been handled badly, then I'll take my business elsewhere. Is that clear?"

"Yes, Mr. Dane. Of course, Mr. Dane." The manager paled at the comment.

Sadie figured Mr. Watson would be screwed if he lost this man's business. Whoever this Mr. Dane was, he had a lot of influence. She could practically smell the money dripping off him, but he hadn't been anything but kind to her.

"Good, now go get the keycard to her executive suite, order her a massage, and I'll send my physician to look after her."

"Sir, all the suites are booked and…"

"Then give her mine," Mr. Dane growled.

The manager jumped back from him and went to fulfill his request. The man turned his attention back to her. Sadie took the chance to take in the chiseled features of the man before her. Even through the fine tailored shirt, his defined physique was apparent. *Wouldn't I like to get my hands on that?* She nearly licked her lips as a quick burst of lust came over her.

The image formed of him stepping out of the shower, dripping wet. He would give her a crooked smile thinking about what he would do to her. She shivered at the vision and then shoved it into the back of her mind for later use. *The massage sounds great. Maybe it'll work out the kinks from my landing wrong. His personal physician? Who travels with a doctor unless he's really sick or something?*

"You really didn't have to do all that. Although, I do appreciate your help. I think Mr. Watson was going to shit a brick the way you were talking to him. You didn't need to give up your rooms for me." Sadie tried to get up, but she winced and fell back down into the chair.

"Why don't you let me help you get to your room?" He offered her his hand.

Sadie wanted to do it on her own, but instead she acquiesced and slid her hand into his. Besides, it wasn't every day she had a handsome man escorting her around a luxurious hotel. "Thanks."

He circled his arm around her waist and guided her down the hall behind a silent bellhop who lifted her bag and led them to the elevator. An uncomfortable silence spread between them as the floors dinged by. She glanced up at him and smiled. The warmth of his body made her feel comforted. It had been a while since someone had touched her even if it was a random man trying to be nice. They got off the lift on the fifth floor and walked down the end of the hallway. The bellhop opened the door and they walked inside. The whole room was larger than her apartment.

"This is the sitting room," the bellhop said. "There's a bedroom on either side with a full bar off to the left. Through the balcony is a private staircase up to the roof, giving you a wonderful view of the moon, which will be full in three days. Here is your keycard. Anywhere you see a red badge by a door, pass the card over it, and you'll have as much access as your heart may desire." Mr. Dane tipped the bellhop as he exited the room, leaving her alone with the sexy man who helped her.

"Thanks for all of this. I really do appreciate everything."

"You're welcome. Like I told Watson, get whatever you want. It's on my tab."

She shook her head not believing this was happening to her. "Look, Mr. Dane --"

"Elijah."

"Elijah, thank you again for all of this, but I can't help feeling this is all too good to be true and that you're going to want something out of all of this. It's clear you're used to getting your own way. I'm way out of my league being here." Sadie waited for the other shoe to drop. This place was the lap of luxury and getting settled in might not be such a good idea. She glanced at the red card. *Where is this going to get me into? Will I walk in on some orgies? Will I find lavish feasts or someone trying to kill one of the guests? Or piles of money?* The piles of money were a long shot.

Elijah chuckled. "You're right about that, Ms. Matthews. I'm very used to getting what I desire. I suspect you're not used to having something handed to you without giving something in return. This is not one of those cases, I assure you. Whoever paid for your stay here made a bit of a mix-up. Can I assume you and your friend don't often travel in the same circles?"

She sighed. He was trying to be nice. This man was used to making billion-dollar business deals and being at board meetings or going to galas with pretty women on his arm. She glanced down at her hands. Her nails were chewed. She was curvy, not like the walking pixie sticks she had seen gracing the covers of the magazines in the lobby.

The doctors wanted her to lose weight. She'd been trying, but after everything she'd endured, she found more solace in ice cream and her favorite chocolate. Melissa had tried to get her to go to yoga or workout at the gym, even offered to hire her a personal trainer. She merely wanted to fill the hole torn in her soul. Melissa's idea was for her to go to the resort as a retreat where she could break out of her funk.

Maybe if they had scream therapy she could use it to get out her anger and heartache. Even if that happened, she didn't think Elijah Dane would be the one to pull her from the darkness. Unless maybe she could have the same scream therapy with him in a different sort of way.

"No. We don't travel much in the same circles, but we're good friends. She booked me here to help me get over some stuff."

He patted her hand and got up. Someone knocked on the door. "I think that'd be the masseur and Kala. She's my physician."

His mention of Melissa and her being complete opposite ends of the social spectrums was correct. They had met in college in the same sorority house. They pledged the same year but became fast friends, as though they had known one another since childhood. When Sadie learned her friend was rich, it made her feel a little uncomfortable. As the years went on, she got used to her friend offering to help Sadie out once and a while. Most of the time she declined, but the past year, Melissa had nagged her about getting over the tragedy that overshadowed her life. Sadie relented and she ended up here.

Elijah Dane opened the door and in walked a woman dressed in a smock who carried a table and waited to be told where to set up.

"Why don't you set up in the bedroom? She'll be there in a minute," Elijah told the masseuse.

The other woman, Kala, was dressed in a long flowing green dress and had shiny, coal black hair that hung down to her waist. The rich green of her dress brought out her eyes. Her smile was as bright as her personality as she slung her arm around Elijah's shoulder in a quick hug. "Hello, Eli. I wasn't expecting to be summoned so quickly."

"Forgive me. There was a need. I'll explain later. I was hoping you could use your magic on Ms. Matthews here. After her massage, of course."

"Of course," Kala glanced at Sadie, but she could see the questions in the other woman's eyes.

"Good. Well, I'll leave you to it, then. Sadie, I hope you feel better. It was nice to meet you."

"Wait, isn't there something I can do to repay you for

all this?"

"Have dinner with me and we'll call it even." He winked at her and ducked out of the room, leaving her alone with Kala and the masseuse.

Chapter Two

Elijah strolled back down to the lobby thinking about the encounter he'd had with Sadie Matthews. He'd heard her confrontation as he stood in the entryway. Her determination not to give up the keycard moved him. He understood that part of her because it was his fortitude that had gotten him to the top of his business, made him billions, and also the leader of the largest werewolf pack in five states. Once the tug-of-war started, he realized what was going on. She had somehow gotten the exclusive package that only other shifters could obtain. From that deduction, he assumed her friend was a shifter. If that was the case, then Sadie didn't know. He wondered if they traveled in the same circles. What kind of a shifter was her friend? Did he know her? Did her friend know how irresponsible she was being sending her to a mainly shifter retreat? The human could find herself mixed up with a hungry tiger and find herself dinner. It was normal policy for any shifter to accompany their humans. He walked back down to the lobby and tapped his nails on the counter as no one sat behind the desk.

A flustered Mr. Watson rushed back out and patted his forehead with his handkerchief. "Mr. Dane, i-is there something else I can help you with?" His lip quivered.

The stench of the man's fear turned his stomach. From the stink of him, he detected the hint of a bird shifter under all that perspiration. His wolf growled and wanted to snap his jaws around the scrawny man's neck. "Who paid for the Matthews reservation?"

"Sir, I-I'm sorry, but I can't give out that information for privacy s…"

He held in a growl and forced a smile. "Dennis."

"David, actually."

"David, I don't want the address or credit card information, just the name to see if I know who it is. We all know this retreat caters specifically to shifters and sometimes their human companions. No mortal comes here as totally unaware as Ms. Matthews is of what this place really is. Whoever sent her here must have had a motive. I'd like to find out who it is and see why they were so irresponsible." He put his hand on the man's shoulder and felt the bird shifter trembling. "I know you were looking out for her welfare before. I apologize if I overstepped my bounds, but the situation could've been handled a bit differently by your employee. I wanted to be sure Ms. Matthews didn't feel the need to file a lawsuit because of the injuries she sustained from the fall. I'm sure you understand that."

The manager nodded. "Yes. Yes, of course. But you see --"

He gave the man a gentle squeeze trying to calm him down. "I know it's against company policy, but this person has been completely irresponsible. Since this person clearly isn't looking out for the welfare for Ms. Matthews, don't you think that someone has to? You don't want to find out that she's been hurt on your watch because she walked into a feeding circle. You know how it can get."

Mr. Watson paled. "That was an accident and we've never had…"

Elijah put a finger to his lips. "I know what happened because all the owners were told."

"Mr. Dane, I didn't know that you were *one of the owners*. You bring in so much business… I'd never presume."

"Calm down. I'm not going to eat you. That incident's behind us, which is why we have the red card for those who need a little bit more excitement in their stay. Do you think you'd be willing to share the information, knowing I want to be sure that Ms. Matthews is safe since my interest as an owner is also a valid point? Really, you wouldn't be breaking any rules.

I'd never mention this to anyone. Maybe even make sure your name gets put in for a raise. We need good people like yourself keeping an eye on protocol here." His wolf paced in the back of his mind as it felt the day growing longer and wanted to get out and run. The smell of the human woman lingered in the lobby. With each inhale, the sweet scent of her blood lingered on his tongue. *She must have scraped something in her fall because I didn't catch it before. Then again, I was focused on making sure she wasn't hurt. The frustrated desk receptionist was close to changing right there. The young one didn't have the control that an older shifter had.* It was clear the pup struggled with his condition. Elijah sensed his fight. If he had transformed, then nothing would have been able to save the human woman.

"I'll get you the information right away, Mr. Dane, and thank you." The manager rushed behind the desk and started punching buttons on the keyboard.

Elijah waited as he thought about how the woman would react if she discovered who was actually waiting on her. He had to figure out a way to keep her in her room when the conclave happened at the height of the full moon in three days' time. The entire resort should have been reserved with no extra rooms for outsiders. Five other pack leaders from the surrounding states were coming with their delegations as well as most of their packs. The entire resort with the cabins could house over a thousand souls, and others were camping in the campgrounds around the forest. When the resort had been conceived, they'd had to find a spot where there was plenty of forest and where there wasn't a lot of human development. This had been the best place available out of the tracts of land. It catered to all kinds of shifters, rich or not, but it gave the ones in the city a place to go if they needed it. And it also provided other services. He sighed at the thought about those other services and checked his watch. He had an appointment to meet with the counselor in less than an hour.

"Here it is," the manager announced and handed him a sheet of paper with a name and phone number on it.

"Thank you, David. I do appreciate it. Tell me, is the young man who was waiting on Ms. Matthews okay?"

"I'm sure he's not. I fired him. He's in the back getting his things."

"Will you go in the back and get him, please?"

"But you said… the way…"

"I know and I was being rash. Please, make sure he gets a few paid days off and keep him on the payroll. I'd like to talk to him. Would you mind?"

"I'll go see if I can catch him." He walked back to get the desk clerk.

Elijah glanced down at the number and the name the manager had handed him. He didn't recognize either but that didn't mean anything. He pulled out his phone and tapped in the numbers. It took a minute for the line to connect since they were out in the middle of nowhere and the cell service could be shoddy.

"Hello."

Once he heard the voice, a frigid chill came over him that even silenced his wolf. Very few beings did that to him. Dane tried to stop the cold from seeping into his voice, but the memories of their time together slid along the outskirts of his memory. "Hello, Narissa -- or should I call you Melissa these days?"

"Elijah Dane. Your voice isn't one I've heard in almost twenty years. How are you?" she purred.

"I'm fine."

"I bet you are. I've heard among the grapevine you've made billions."

"Yes, but we both know that you took a few of those stock tips I gave you. Is that why you're calling? Because you needed a bit of advice?" The sarcasm in her voice made him want to reach through the phone and rake his claws across that smile he knew was on her face.

"I'm not calling you about that, Melissa," he emphasized. "I was calling about your friend Sadie Matthews."

"Sadie? Is everything okay?"

He was nearly convinced she actually cared for the human. "You paid for an exclusive week for her with all access to the resort, knowing it was close to the full moon and she could get hurt. If she was your friend, you wouldn't have sent her into danger."

"Now you hear me, Elijah Dane. I don't give a fuck who you are, but you stay away from Sadie. I sent her to the resort because I knew she'd be well looked after. You have no idea what she's been through. She doesn't need the likes of you butting into her life," Melissa roared on the other end.

"You actually care about this woman?" Elijah couldn't stop the surprise he felt. Something must have changed since the last time he saw his ex.

"Elijah, it's hard for me to believe you're calling me because you're worried about a human. That'd be a first. How did you get my number anyway?"

"It doesn't matter how I got your number. I'm calling to tell you that you should phone your friend and tell her she needs to leave. There's been a mix-up and you've arranged something else for her."

Melissa laughed. The trill of her giggle still set his nerves on edge. Only she knew how to push his buttons even over the vast distance of years. "I'm not doing that. Let me repeat again, she needs to be there to get away."

Elijah swallowed his growing rage. "There's a conclave happening over the next five days. The full moon is at the height of it. Do you understand what that means?"

"Oh shit. I didn't realize."

"No kidding, you didn't realize. Do you think you can get her to come back?"

"You don't know Sadie. She's as stubborn as they come."

"Wow, you really consider her a friend. That's a first."

"It's a long story. Look, I'll call her and think of something. However, once she's dug in, she won't change her mind. You have no idea how long it took me to get her to agree on this trip, let alone the appointment with the grief counselor. If I can't get her to leave, will you keep an eye on her to be sure she stays safe?"

It was his turn to laugh at the suggestion coming from his ex. "I have other things to do than babysitting your pet human."

"I'll make it worth your while."

"Really? How would you do that? It's not like I need the money."

"True, but I'll owe you a favor. You know coming from me that means something."

He scratched his chin at the proposal. One of her kind even suggesting doing anyone a favor was like someone offering him a million dollars tax-free. The manager reappeared with the young desk receptionist behind him. Elijah motioned for them to come over and wait. Mr. Watson backed away while the young wolf shifted, waiting impatiently for Elijah to get off the phone. "Anything I want?"

"Within reason, of course. No wishing for other wishes. We can discuss parameters later. This is only if Sadie won't leave because I have a feeling she won't."

"Fine. I'll do my best to look after her and make sure she doesn't get hurt."

"Thank you, Eli."

He hung up and focused on the young wolf before him. "What's your name?"

"Jake, sir." He cleared his throat and stood up straighter.

He's gotten control of his emotions. Maybe there's hope for him yet. "How long has it been since you've first changed?"

"Only a year. Mr. Watson said you told him not to fire me. Why?"

"Because I don't think you meant to hurt the woman who checked in."

"I didn't, but she didn't want to take no for an answer when I tried to get the key back from her. Rules say because she's human, she has to be accompanied by another shifter to get into the restricted areas. I didn't realize at first she wasn't like us. I began to lose control and..." He hung his head.

"Who is your pack master?"

"I don't have one. I haven't been accepted into a pack. The one around here doesn't accept those who were bitten. My aunt works here and got me the job. She hoped I might feel a little more comfortable being around other shifters. Her husband and she are mates, so she was accepted. I went camping in the woods close to their house with my cousin. He lost it and bit me. Their pack doesn't want me even though I'm her nephew."

He laid a hand on the younger wolf's shoulder. He understood how the boy felt. Elijah had fought his way up from the bottom to get where he currently was. "Jake, I get that you've had a hard road so far. I have a proposition for you. If things work out, then I can put your name in with my pack and see how they feel about you joining. Mind you, I'm not the only one deciding this when it comes to adding new members when they were bitten."

His eyes widened. "Y-you would do that, Mr. Dane?" He lowered his head, showing his subservience.

"I would, but you need to keep an eye on someone

for me while the conclave is here. If you see her getting into some trouble, come and get me no matter what I'm involved with. I'll make it worth your while for the time you'd be taking out of your day."

"What do you want me to do?"

Elijah glanced at his watch and saw he needed to get to his appointment. "I want you to keep an eye on Ms. Matthews. Keep your distance so she isn't spooked. With all the other shifters around here for the next few days and everything culminating in the hunt, I don't want her to get caught up in it. Someone could get the wrong idea that she's on the menu. I'll make it worth your while."

"You don't have to pay me. When do you want me to start?"

"I need to set up a dinner with Ms. Matthews. Can you do that for later tonight and then let her know? Say around seven. I should be free by then. In one of the smaller restaurants with plenty of privacy before everyone gets here. The Verge is a nice spot. Make sure no one else is in the restaurant. I don't want the other pack members getting the wrong idea."

"Of course, I have the perfect idea. Should I let Mr. Watson know about this arrangement?"

"I'll mention it to him. If you can bring Ms. Matthews down at that time, then we should be good for the night." He stuck out his hand and waited for the other man to take it. A moment later, Jake gave him a firm handshake.

"I won't let you down."

Elijah watched as the younger wolf hurried off to do his bidding. He walked over to the manager and explained to Mr. Watson what Jake was doing for him and about making sure the restaurant wasn't booked up.

"I'll make sure to cancel any reservations and move them. Is there anything else I can do for you?" Watson asked.

"Nothing. Thank you." Elijah checked his watch. He was going to be late for his appointment. He crossed the main campus of the resort and let the perfumes of the forest tantalize his wolf. The life in the woods pressed upon his senses. He yearned to give into the sounds of the rabbits breaking the underbrush and the deer who were stirring to feed for the night. Instead, he gathered himself and knocked on the nondescript door to a smaller cabin. It was so well hidden that if he didn't know where it was, he wasn't sure he'd be able to find it. This also worked for his benefit because he didn't want the rest of his pack knowing he was coming here. Some would construe it as a weakness even though the ones closest to him understood. They struggled with it, too. He was about to knock again when the door opened.

"Cutting it close, Mr. Dane," the therapist said. She was no more than four five even in heels. Her gray hair retained a few streaks of brown in it. Her wide eyes reflected even the weakest light as the sun set behind the trees.

"Forgive me, Mistress Maran, I was conducting some business about the coming conclave."

"Lying doesn't suit you either, Elijah. Don't do it again. Now come inside and sit down. I don't need you wasting my time," she snapped and closed the door behind him.

Elijah took in the small cottage that served as the woman's office. It was all tidy and had more of a new age vibe with dried herbs hanging from the ceilings and plants everywhere making it into some lush tropical paradise. She sat in the chair across from him. He had been here before, but it had been a long time. He thought he had it under control, but the compulsion remained. Smelling that women's sweet blood only ignited his hunger. Something about it made him want to take a bite out of her, which would be a bad idea. The last time he'd lost control was eighteen months ago when he'd been in the forest with a friend and they'd been hunting. After the incident, he came to the resort for a week to get his head screwed back on straight from the guilt that plagued him. The counselor had helped him then.

"Any reoccurrences since the last time I saw you?"

"No, but I can feel it creeping up on me again. Most of the time the techniques you gave me help stave off the compulsion. It might be the upcoming stress of the conclave, but it's there and I want..." he shivered at the thought of sinking his fangs into the sweetest meat. His wolf salivated at it. He kept himself as disciplined as he could so he wouldn't lose control. That control was one of the things that had kept him as pack leader for so long. The others trusted him to keep a level head even when his animal wanted to do other things. Unlike so many of the other wolves, he didn't let himself partake in the succulent flesh unless things got the better of him. He prayed that wouldn't happen now. The only human in the place was Narissa's friend and he had vowed to keep her safe. It would look bad if he ate her. He didn't want the wrath of his ex on him.

"You deal with temptation every day. We all do, being in the human world. You can't deny what the animal inside you wants to hunt."

"I don't deny the hunt. Every full moon, I run. Sometimes I run every night to take my mind off of things. I have enough deer on my property that it satisfies the need for meat. However, I want to sink my claws into flesh and tear out the beating heart with my teeth as my muzzle digs into a ribcage. The warm blood. It's saltier than any other animal." His teeth shifted, and he felt the hunger come into his nature. He ran his fingers over his pants. The material caught on his sharpened nails. Elijah steadied himself, thinking only of his obligations. He couldn't give in no matter how much he yearned to.

"The first thing to do is admit you have a problem. The second thing is to face it. The third thing is to gain control of the compulsion. You've done the first two. It appears you're working very hard on the third. You deal with humans all day long in your business transactions. I'll bet some push your buttons, but you don't wolf out and tear their throats out no matter how much you might wish it. Why is that?"

"Because it's one of our oldest directives. We don't show ourselves to the mortal world unless absolutely necessary. We blend in, reminding ourselves we are human and animal."

"Sometimes we have to give into that impulse because something triggers it."

"If I remember correctly, the last time you told me I had to turn my craving inward and make peace with the beast. I don't have any beef with the wolf. We get along well enough."

"Both are true. We need to find the balance in the man and the beast." She dug into a folder at her side and pulled out a pad. "I have this number for someone who runs organized hunts. You might find it stimulating. I've been recommending him to clients."

He took the number. The last time she hadn't seemed against him feeding on humans, but she hadn't condoned it either. "I'm not sure this is a good idea." He handed her back the number. "I'm trying not to keep hunting humans. I want to get away from it even if they are tasty. The last one was delicious, but the only thing that stopped me from going after the woman was her wails. It brought me back to myself."

"That shows you have a conscience. Good for you because that means you know you want to change."

"What do you suggest, then?"

Her smile got a little bit bigger than her face. The light caught her eyes as it reflected off her pupils. "Maybe your wolf will calm down if you find a mate."

"I doubt that's going to happen."

She shrugged. "You never know. It might be trying to channel its impulses into something that it understands because you haven't had the chance to find the one you're supposed to be with. Maybe you should try to have more... let me put this delicately... relations."

Elijah growled. He didn't want to think about finding a mate. His life couldn't accommodate it. With all the pack business, the conclave, and along with his regular businesses, sometimes he wondered how he had time to breathe. Having a woman in his life would only complicate things. "I don't think me hooking up with women and screwing all night long is the answer to keep down my compulsion."

"Really? Since the last time you feasted on human meat, how often are you engaging in female companionship?"

"Why don't you just ask me if I'm fucking a lot?"

"It's only a suggestion. Great way to burn off energy."

He shifted a bit and glanced at his watch. They hadn't been chatting more than twenty minutes, but time was ticking by. His wolf growled and wanted to make its displeasure known to the therapist, but he kept it in check. "Fine. I'll think about it. Is there any other advice you want to give me or am I free to go?"

"We have another forty minutes to discuss things."

"I thought you were supposed to be the expert on helping shifters with special issues," he snarled, feeling the compulsion to shed his human form and run in the woods to appease the agitated wolf. Maybe he could outrun the urge. He closed his eyes and tried to calm his nerves when he caught the scent again of the human woman. Elijah glanced at his shirt and inhaled again. This time he the aroma of blood made him almost lose it. He flicked his tongue over the spot and tasted blood. It was the barest splatter, but it made his stomach rumble. The image of the woman flashed in his mind. Her jeans hugged delicious curves. Her full body and luscious breasts stirred his appetite. Elijah could feel himself sinking into her and knowing how she would taste.

"Mr. Dane." The sudden snap of pain brought him back from his fantasy.

Elijah rubbed his cheek where the therapist had slapped him. She might have been short, but she sure could pack a punch. He never quite figured out what kind of a shifter she was, but she was a strong little thing. "What was that for?"

"Whatever you were thinking about, you were about to lose yourself. I think you underestimate how close to the edge you're hovering. You need to reconsider this conclave or running the days before the full moon so you can drive the urge out of you. What triggered this? Can you tell me? You have monumental control over your beast. I've heard how you deal with things in the boardroom. Nothing gets by you. Talk to me about this. That's what I'm here for. Even a strong alpha like you needs someone to trust. Even if you can't hear the drum yet, you have to be on the lookout for it because something special is coming."

"Drum? What are you talking about?"

The therapist smiled. "Nothing -- an old saying among my people. When we find our mates, we hear the drum of their heartbeat first. Some know by smell, for us it's sound. The drum means something special is coming. That your mate is near."

"Okay... I'm not hearing a drum and I'm not looking for a mate."

"You made that clear. What has you so agitated?"

Elijah inhaled again. The perfume of the blood bloomed in his nose. "It's nothing. A human woman got into an argument with the desk clerk because her friend booked her into the wrong suite. She ended up falling and getting hurt. I helped her out and must've gotten a speck of blood on me."

"Do you normally help women like that?"

His wolf slid back into the recesses of his mind, but Sadie's image was burned in his memory. "I stepped in because I overheard the argument. It was better for me to intervene so she wouldn't think about suing the retreat. None of us want that."

"Ahh, I take it, then, she had no idea this place caters to shifters."

"No. Her friend made the reservations with all the bells and whistles. I spoke with her earlier, the friend that is, and Ms. Matthews isn't aware her friend is a shape shifter. She sees the world for what she believes is in it."

The therapist's lips pursed. She shuffled a few papers and glanced at something. "That name sounds familiar. Ahh... yes. She has an appointment with me later tomorrow. It's good to know she's oblivious. I don't normally work with regular humans unless there's an exception."

"You know who made the reservation for her, then, and who her friend is." Elijah wondered how far Narissa's influence reached.

"I am aware of who she is. And yes, she made the appointment. I find this rather interesting -- you and Ms. Matthews meeting and how it's triggered your hunger."

"It's stress from the coming meeting. I have no plans to eat her. I promised Narissa I'd make sure no harm came to Ms. Matthews while she's here. I'm good for my word. As you said, I have to overcome this compulsion and I'm a little on edge. She compounds the situation. She's an unmarked human among hundreds of werewolves over the next few days. I have to make sure she doesn't walk into danger or end up being hunted down by another pack."

"Then mark her as yours."

He scoffed. "I don't want that responsibility and I don't need another human playmate. I have enough of those."

The therapist stood up signaling their time was done. He checked his watch. Fifteen minutes remained of their time. "You're an honorable wolf. If you promised to keep her safe, then you will."

"Any advice for my little problem?"

"I already told you. You've acknowledged it. You're channeling that energy into vigorous sexual activity and running when you can. The fragrance of her blood might have triggered your beast, but we both know you won't act on it. There isn't any kind of drug that can curb that kind of craving. Once you taste flesh, you can't go back. That's why I pride myself as being a vegetarian."

"I never would have figured that."

Chapter Three

Sadie rolled her shoulders. The scent of spearmint and eucalyptus lingered in the air. Her muscles had released from the massage. Kala pressed her fingers along her shoulder blade ever so slightly. That hurt a little bit, but it felt wonderful.

"You've really been holding the tension in your back," Kala said as she worked her some more.

"You have no idea," she murmured.

"I have some idea if you came here to get away from everything."

"I appreciate you stepping in to do this. Mr. Dane said you were his physician. I didn't expect you to be the one giving me the massage."

"That stupid woman. I don't think she expected you to be so hu -- sensitive."

She shrugged. "I didn't think so either, but she was pushing so hard I couldn't bear it. I don't know how to say thank you. I really needed this."

"It's not a problem. I'll bill Elijah later. I do have a medical degree, but I prefer Eastern techniques rather than Western ones. Like using energy and massage along with herbal remedies to align the body. One has to be right with their spirit so the body can heal." Kala's fingers moved into her neck and fanned downward until Sadie moaned.

"How long have you worked for Mr. Dane?"

"Longer than I care to admit. I hardly think of it as working for him. We have a mutual respect for one another and a relationship."

"Ahh." Sadie could completely see the beautiful Indian woman being with him. They were both exotic and she fit perfectly on his arm.

"Ahh." Kala laughed. "It's not that kind of relationship. We've been friends for a long time. He's not my type anyway."

"Really? He's tall, easy on the eyes, got a smokin' ass, and probably more money than God," Sadie sighed.

The physician snorted. "Do I detect a bit of jealousy?"

Sadie felt her cheeks warm. "I didn't say that. He's nice to look at. Sorry, I shouldn't be saying that since he's your friend and employer."

Kala's fingers moved lower down her back and caught her side. Sadie flinched when she hit a certain spot. "I apologize if I hurt you. Those are horrible scars."

"Yeah, I was attacked by a wild animal a year and a half ago. My fiancé and I..." His screams echoed in her ears. Sadie shied away from the woman and felt her muscles stiffen up. The emotions crept up her throat as the crippling grief threatened to overtake her once more. This was the reason why Melissa had made the reservation. She even set up a meeting with the counselor on staff. Sadie didn't feel like spilling her guts to a complete stranger. Melissa understood how losing Greyson had devastated Sadie.

"Those must have been pretty deep. Did you have any muscle atrophy from them? Did they hit any major organs or bone? Sorry, I don't mean to pry. I'm curious what happened."

"I tried to get to my fiancé, but the beast was already..." She swallowed back the fear that still haunted her dreams. "I screamed and got its attention. I turned to run when it came after me. It got my back and..." She shifted and moved the sheet showing how the claw marks went from her side and then over her right buttocks down to her left calf. "The doctors were surprised that it healed so fast and I didn't have any permanent damage from the attack."

Kala trailed her fingers over the scars and then moved her fingers into the muscles until Sadie whimpered. "I'm sorry. That must have been very difficult to deal with." Someone knocked on the door. "I'll get it."

Sadie pulled the sheet up close to herself and tried to sink back into the relaxation she felt before. Kala came back in with a confused look. "Elijah's asked you to dinner tonight at seven in the Wolf Lounge."

"You look surprised."

"It's not like Elijah to mix business with pleasure. Then again, I was perplexed when he asked me to check in on you."

"I think it's because I asked him if there was some way for me to thank him. He stepped in on my behalf with the manager because of a disagreement downstairs. One of the employees tried to take my key card back. I fell and hit my head and my shoulder."

"That makes more sense. I'm sorry if I brought up a painful memory before. I was curious about the scars."

She waved off the doctor. "It's okay. I'm here to deal with it. That's why my friend sent me up here. I have an appointment with the grief counselor tomorrow night, too."

"If you need me, I'm in room 509. Also, if you want to talk about anything. I know we just met, but Elijah isn't going to be needing me unless something catastrophic happens. If you want to talk, that is."

"Thanks. I appreciate the massage."

"You're welcome. Enjoy dinner tonight. He won't bite, by the way." Kala gathered her things and left the room.

Sadie glanced at the clock. She had time to kill before meeting Elijah for dinner. Her memories threatened to drag her under, but she got up and decided to take a long soak in the bath. The tub was the size of a small swimming pool. Sadie slipped into the warm water and her cares fell away.

She opened her eyes to someone frantically knocking

on the door. *Shit.* Sadie climbed out of the tub, since the water had gone cold. She put on a robe and hurried to the door. Outside stood the desk receptionist. She crossed her arms over her chest and saw his panicked expression. "Excuse me, Ms. Matthews. Mr. Dane wanted to know if you were still coming to dinner."

"Please tell Mr. Dane I'll be down in fifteen minutes. You're not going to push me again, are you?"

"No, ma'am. I'm sorry about that. I'll let Mr. Dane know you're coming."

She closed the door and thought about having dinner with a handsome man who was clearly loaded. Nothing in her luggage screamed, "Let's have dinner with a millionaire." Sadie dug through her bag and came out with a black blouse and a pair of black pants. She quickly wrestled her hair into submission and went down to the lobby. The same desk clerk waited for her. He kept glancing at his watch. The longer she looked at him the more she noticed how uncomfortable he looked. She kinda felt sorry for him. When he looked up, he seemed relieved and motioned for her to follow him. Sadie went down the hall behind him until they came to the restaurant. Candles blazed on empty tables. The light smell of vanilla hung in the air. Elijah sat in the corner staring at his phone. He scowled, but the way the light hit his hair she could see the red and gold strands. He had changed into jeans and a black fitted shirt although he seemed more at ease in his suit. She took in a breath and stepped into the restaurant. His head shot up and his gaze locked to hers. Those intense eyes made her stomach quiver. She tried to push the feeling away, but the emotions stuck in her throat as she remembered the feel of his hand on her back. As she got closer, his expression changed to a puzzled one. It was so quick she wasn't sure she saw it because he also appeared hungry.

"Sorry, I'm late."

He glanced at his phone and sighed. "I was expecting you an hour ago. I'm afraid I can't stay much later."

"This was your idea. If you didn't want to have dinner with me, then why in the world did you suggest it?" She pinched her nose to stop her anger flowing over her. "You know what. Forget it. I don't need this." Sadie turned around to leave when he grabbed her arm.

"Don't leave. I'm sorry. My plans keep getting messed up tonight. I shouldn't have taken it out on you. Will you stay? You did want to repay me for helping you."

The way he asked her in almost a whisper for her to stay made her stomach curl in on itself. Sadie wanted to hear him utter her name because it made her legs shaky and her heart beat a little faster. She took a minute to gather her thoughts. This man shouldn't have her so flustered. The last time she felt her stomach twisting in knots was when Greyson had first danced with her. She thought he was the sexiest man alive back then and he wanted her. Elijah had a shit load of money and women to hang off his arm so nothing would ever happen between them. *It's dinner. Nothing else. This week I'm here to relax. If I don't have a good time, Melissa'll kill me. I know she wants me to move past what happened, but it's not that simple after seeing what I saw.* "I'm hungry and I'm already here."

Elijah pulled the chair out for her as she sat down. Sadie glanced around for a menu when a waiter rushed out and handed them a sheet printed on heavy paper. He hovered. She shifted in her seat and studied the waiter who seemed as nervous as the desk clerk and the desk manager was around Elijah. *What is it about him that makes everyone so uncomfortable?*

"What can I get you?" His hands shook.

"I'll have the grilled chicken and the asparagus with the house salad."

Elijah didn't shift his gaze from her as he spoke.

"Steak. Rare. Baked potato with the Caesar salad. Water to drink." The waiter left so they were alone in the restaurant.

"I'm surprised that you didn't order my food for me. It almost seemed like you were going to."

"What's that perfume you're wearing? I didn't smell it on you before."

"I'm not wearing any."

He leaned over the table and inhaled. His nose twitched. He closed his eyes as though he savored the smell of her. "You're wearing peppermint and something else."

She chuckled. "You must be picking up on the oil that Kala used when she did my massage. She was great by the way. Even gave me a clean bill of health."

"It suits you." He pulled away when the waiter came back with their salads. She ate in silence as Elijah kept snatching glances at her. He downed the salad and his phone went off again.

"You might as well answer it. Don't let my being here stop you from conducting your business."

"Why are you jumping on me after all this? You were the one who wanted to have dinner with me to thank me for being so magnanimous this morning." His phone went off again and he slammed his fist down on the screen. "Shit."

The server brought out their meals. Sadie pushed hers away. His cell rang once more. Her stomach churned and turned sour. He might have invited her to dinner, but he was doing it to placate her. *This whole thing has been a mistake. Melissa had a great idea, but this isn't worth the hassle. I can't do this. I'm better off going home, burying myself in the sofa and binge-watching Highlander. Greyson always liked that show.* "I thought you were a nice guy underneath all the expensive clothes and intimidating people, but I guess you're just like the rest of them. Another stuck-up asshole who thinks his shit don't stink and who expects people to bend to his will. You might be a big shot, but I don't play the kiss-your-ass game. Thank you for your help earlier, but you can keep the offer for paying my tab." She threw her napkin down and got up.

She made it halfway across the room when she noticed the desk clerk blocking her way. Fear hung on his face. Sadie glanced behind her and at the same time Elijah spun her around. He caught her hand as she was about to slap him.

"Running away from me is not a good idea right now," he growled. The look in his eyes was wild, the gold dancing in the candlelight.

He inhaled so loud she could hear it. Sadie tried to pull away but, his grip tightened on her wrist. Before she could tell him to let her go, his mouth found hers in a hungry kiss. Surprised by the sudden of smashing of lips on her mouth, Sadie froze. When she didn't kiss him back, Elijah grabbed a handful of her hair and kissed her harder, nipping at her bottom lip. A swirl of emotions went through her in those few seconds. *Why in the hell is this guy kissing me? Do I let him kiss me? Oh God, he tastes and feels so good. What do I do? How can he be such a jerk and then this? Fuck…* Sadie lost herself.

Elijah sucked on her bottom lip until she felt the quick jab of his teeth. He pressed his hand against her back and moved his mouth on hers like he was about to devour her. No one had kissed her like this before. *Is he growling?* Sadie returned the kiss until her head cleared and she broke away from him. She backhanded him with all the force she could muster, and it felt like her palm had hit a concrete wall.

"What the hell was that?" She cradled her hand against her chest as she also tasted blood. The redness was evident on his bottom lip.

The wild look in his eye hadn't left. It looked like he had almost checked out. Elijah stepped toward her again. Gone was the cool demeanor and replaced with a man she almost didn't recognize. The way he looked at her was as if he wanted to eat her. If he had been an animal, she would have run, but her fury ignited at him kissing her without her permission. Heat ignited in her belly until she found her voice.

"Mr. Dane, I don't know what's gotten into you. I'll chalk this up to temporary insanity or something. Thanks for dinner, but leave me alone for the rest of my stay here. Good night." Sadie walked out of the dining room and left him standing there. She didn't know where she was going, but she didn't want to be cooped up in her room. The blood taste didn't leave her mouth. When she touched her lips, she could see it was still bleeding.

Sadie felt her eyes begin to tear. She patted her pockets and realized she didn't have her phone on her. She walked through the halls of the resort and went outside to clear her head. *I'm not going to cry over this. Maybe I'm the butt of some kind of joke.*

It was so different than her neighborhood. She didn't live in the city, but the train went by her house at all hours of the day. After a few deep breaths, the stillness calmed her. She wanted to escape the whole day. Sadie kept on walking down a stone paved path that wound into the forest. She didn't care where she was going as long as it was away from him. Marker lights led her way. The farther she got, the dimmer and less frequent they became. The trail came out into a garden with a bench nestled next to waterfall that flowed into a pool.

"Come and sit. I'm not going to bite." The woman on the bench motioned her over. Her eyes seemed rather large even behind the glasses she wore.

"Thanks. I didn't mean to disturb you."

"You weren't."

Sadie settled next to her and listened to the tinkle of the water rushing over the stones. It did help to relieve the stress that she felt. "This is a nice place."

"Yes, I come here often to relax. Here, dear. You have a cut on your lip. The woman handed her a tissue.

"Thanks." Sadie dabbed at the place where Elijah bit her.

"Are you okay?" the stranger asked.

Sadie shook her head. "I don't know. My friend sent me up here to pull me out of my slump. Getting up here was a nightmare and then settling in. And now... God, I don't know what I was thinking with him." This time the torrent of tears she'd been holding back came out as the damn burst and spilled over her cheeks. She wiped them away and took a deep breath so she wouldn't get carried away.

"You wouldn't happen to be Ms. Matthews would you?"

"I am. How did you know that?"

The woman adjusted her glasses. "I'm the counselor here. We have an appointment tomorrow afternoon. I understand that your friend scheduled the time for you. We can speak now if you wish instead of tomorrow. Would you like to talk about whatever is bothering you?"

Sadie rolled her eyes. She didn't want to delve into what happened to her with Elijah. "It's been a night. I'm not sure I want to --"

The therapist patted her knee. "We don't have to talk about it. I was concerned, that's all. You were crying. I didn't know if you might've been coming out here to do something to yourself."

A laugh slipped out. *Harm myself?* That was the farthest thing from her mind. Although in the first couple of weeks after losing Greyson she didn't know how she would exist without him. Melissa brought her through the funk she had sunk into then. "No. I'm not going to do anything that drastic. I haven't been that depressed in a long time. I got into a small scuffle with someone."

"Tell me what brought you here. I mean to the

retreat."

"I lost my fiancé in a violent animal attack eighteen months ago. We'd gone camping. I was sleeping, but he stayed up to do something. I woke up to his screams. When I went out, it had its muzzle in his stomach. Half of his throat was gone. When I screamed and tried to get away, it attacked me, and then it... stopped."

"Did you see the animal?" the therapist asked.

"No, just the eyes. They still haunt my nightmares. Another camper found us. I woke up in the hospital. I don't really remember anything after that."

"The grief of losing someone is always hard to process, but to lose them that way is horrific. I surmise the heartache and the guilt has stuck with you. Maybe the question of why it picked your fiancé over you. Survivor's guilt."

Sadie nodded. All of that sounded about right. "I've seen some psychiatrists before. They gave me advice and told me it was normal after having something traumatic happen, but I can't seem to get past it. I've tried. Melissa, my friend, has helped. It was so random. The police said it was a mountain lion or a rabid dog. It was no mountain lion. The scars on my back. The doctors said they are from a large bear, which is insane. I need answers. It would've helped if they found his body, but they never did. I had nothing of him to bury. So, doc, am I crazy? Going to prescribe pills or another session?"

"I think you're perfectly sane, grieving and going through the motions as best you can. Let me ask you something? Did the animal bite you?"

"No. It dug in with its claws and pulled me toward it. I --" For a moment the phantom pain sliced down her back once more. The therapist touched her and she nearly jumped out of her skin.

"My dear, I didn't mean to frighten you, but I think you might want to finish whatever discussion you were having earlier that caused the little tussle you had." The therapist pointed toward the opening of the garden.

Elijah stood in the moonlight staring right at her with the same hungry look in his eyes.

"I don't think that'd be a good idea."

"Did Mr. Dane do something to hurt you?"

"Not exactly."

"Ms. Matthews, can I talk to you, please?" Elijah asked her from across the pond.

The therapist got up. "I think you might want to talk to him alone, unless you feel threatened. If that's the case, then I'll gladly stay. I know Mr. Dane, and he's always been a perfect gentleman."

"Is he one of your patients?"

"No, he's one of the owners of the resort."

Sadie rolled her eyes. *Fucking great. That explains a lot.* "Wonderful. No, I should be fine."

The psychiatrist patted her on the knee one more time. "If you need to talk, I'll be in my office tomorrow for our appointment."

Sadie wanted to say something else as she left, and Elijah walked closer to her. The shrink stopped and said something to Elijah that made him argue with her, but the woman put a stop to it. From his expression, whatever she said made him even madder. Sadie got a little happier because someone wasn't afraid to stand up to him.

"Come over here to accost me again? I should call the police and have you arrested for sexual assault," Sadie growled.

Elijah held up his hands and kept a distance between them. "Whoa. Let's not get too hasty. I came out here to apologize. I shouldn't have kissed you. I got a little flustered and overwhelmed with what's going on. But you kissed me back."

"You bit me, and I did not. You surprised me. I'm not in a headspace to be kissing complete strangers."

"Can I sit?"

Sadie scooted over until the metal arm dug into her side. "Sit. Get whatever it is off your chest, and then we don't ever have to talk again."

Elijah sat next to her as she tried to ignore his body heat and the intoxicating scent of him. "I'm sorry, Ms. Matthews. I didn't mean to bite you."

"Why did you kiss me?" She wanted to know what was going through his mind at the time his lips connected with hers.

He opened his mouth, and then closed it again. He ran his fingers through his hair and sighed. "The smell of your perfume got the better of me. I've been under an extreme amount of stress. I got carried away. I apologize. I didn't mean to get so rough. Will you forgive me?"

Her lip still throbbed. He looked at it.

"Did I do that?"

"You did."

Elijah took her hand. She nearly pulled it out of his grasp until he kissed the back of it. She held her breath as she tried to read this guy. He was telling her he was sorry and that he was stressed out, but not before he pressed his lips to her wrist. He flicked his gaze up at her as he licked her skin, almost daring her to pull away. Elijah trailed the tip of his tongue up over her fingers and sucked on one. Sadie shivered and heard her heart drumming in her ears. She tried to be angry at him again, but what he was doing to her made her so damn hot. Elijah sucked on her middle finger nibbling a little with his teeth as he dragged them upward over her flesh. She whimpered and let out a breath, trying to get back in control from the weird turn her night had taken.

"D-do you make it a habit of sucking on strange women's fingers?"

He took in her finger again before releasing it with a pop. Elijah drank in a few breaths as his eyes glowed. It had to be a trick of the light. "You taste good. I wasn't expecting that, and you make me so hungry. I could eat you up. Come back to my room with me and I'll make you howl."

What in the holy hell is going on? Sadie shook her head not able to answer because this whole situation was bizarre. Her entire being told her to go his room, but she had to be rational. She didn't know this guy from Adam and having a one-time fling was not on the agenda. It took everything in her, but she pulled her hand away. She stood up and put a bit of space between. "I don't think so. Goodnight, Mr. Dane." She dashed away as fast as she could because if she didn't, Sadie knew she'd take him up on his offer.

Chapter Four

Elijah resisted the urge to go after her. The taste of her blood and her flesh lingered in his mouth. It took all his willpower not to pin her to the ground and take her right there. When she didn't come down to dinner, he nearly went up to drag her down. Who would stand him up? People jumped at the chance to be around him. As pack leader, people obeyed him. The same in business. People listened to him. Jake went to check on her and apparently, she had fallen asleep. It eased his anger a little, but while he waited, his phone started blowing up about the conclave.

Three of the rival pack leaders were having second thoughts about attending. Treaties had been signed. It was all petty squabbles and he was getting tired of being the mediator. Waiting topped with the ever-growing frustration put him on edge. His hunger for human flesh sat on the back of his tongue. He'd hoped the therapist would have some magical answer to his appetites, but all she came out with was nonsense about hearing a drum and channeling his hunger into physical activity. He'd already been doing that even though he didn't want to admit it. He'd been spending more hours working out and sleeping with any woman he took an interest in. It wasn't bad. Elijah had the looks and the money, and most human women were attracted to that. He'd fucked so many women in the past year that he'd lost count. He needed something -- someone -- to burn his energy out on.

Sadie's scent lingered in the air, a mixture of her blood and the oil Kala had used on her skin. It made him want to taste her. Hearing her moan made him need her more. The blood was so close to the surface of her skin. Elijah could have nicked her again and let the sweetness trickle down his throat. He nearly lost it when he smelled her desire for him. Her heart raced and the flutter of her pulse against his tongue made his wolf hunger to tear a hunk of her flesh. It created an intoxicating feeling. As he fought against the urge, the offer to bed her slipped out. For a quick moment, he saw her surprise and her true answer. Then her rationalities kicked in.

His wolf shifted under his skin, drawn by the whisper of her blood. They needed to merge and become one of the same mind. He pulled his shirt off and felt his body already transforming even as he tried to get his pants and shoes off. Bones cracked. Fingers shortened and widened to make room for the weight of bone and fur. Hair pushed out from under his skin. The beast needed to sink its teeth into something. Elijah fumbled with his other shoe and kicked it off before his knees buckled and he collapsed onto all fours. The wolf emerged.

It lifted its nose to the wind and detected the odor of the human. The drive to taste her almost overcame his reason. It remembered the smell of her attraction for him, mingling with the taste of her flesh and blood and that trumped the notion she would be a meal. The wolf recalled his promise to protect Sadie. Once they became one animal, he had the instincts of the beast and the reason of a man. He felt the tug to go after Sadie, but first he had to taste blood. If it wasn't hers, then he needed something else. As he raced deeper into the woods, he felt something snag on his back foot. He stopped and noticed he still wore a sock. He tugged off the material and let it drop to the ground.

He caught the scent of a deer. He licked his lips and set out to have his dinner.

* * *

Elijah wrapped the towel around his waist and went to answer the door. After running and bringing down the deer, the edge had been taken off, but the memory of Sadie lingered. But it was late and sleep called. He had to be up early to start greeting the guests coming in for the conclave. The hollow sound came again on the door. He grabbed the knob and yanked it open, only to find Kala standing outside. Her smile turned inward into her cheeks. She dragged her nails down his chest and stepped inside. Her fingers snagged on his towel, but Elijah caught her wrist before she could pull the fabric away.

"You made it quite clear on the way over here you wanted some company tonight," she purred.

"I changed my mind," he growled, not in the mood to play with the cat shifter.

She slammed the door shut. "It's that human woman you pawned off on me earlier, isn't it?"

Elijah walked across the room and scrolled through the text messages on his cracked screen. Several were from his second in the pack letting him know things were in order for the visiting pack leaders for the conclave. "I didn't *pawn* her off on you. I was helping to stave off her filing a lawsuit against the resort. Having you examine her was the most logical step. I didn't need her drawing attention to this place. Especially right now. Is she okay?"

Kala shrugged. "She's fine. A few bruises from where she fell. Nothing serious. Maybe they'll enhance the scars on her back."

"Scars?"

"From some animal attack. All I really heard was blah, blah, hunting accident, something… something. She'll be fine. All I could think about was that hot body of yours. Come here, wolfie." Kala draped her arm over his shoulder liked she owned him.

He shrugged her off and went back over to the door. They had been on and off for a while. They had fun together and he did retain the tiger shifter as his physician. Neither of them had time for a relationship. Something about the way she assumed he was hers irritated him. He held the door open. "You need to leave."

She pouted. "You're not playing fair."

"Kala, I might've brought up spending the night together on the way over here, but this thing between us has never been exclusive. I think it's over."

The tiger shifter hissed. "I know that. God, I can't believe it. You have a thing for the human. Her stench is all over you." She pressed her hand to her nose like she smelled something foul. "I did what you asked because I thought we had something good going here." She reached back to slap him, but he caught her hand.

A soft growl came from his lips as the wolf surfaced. In a fight, Kala was bigger than him by a hundred pounds if they shifted. However, she wasn't an alpha. She stepped away and lowered her head a moment in an instinctual reaction before she bared her teeth. "Once this conclave is over, we're going our separate ways."

"Fine with me." He slammed the door and leaned against it feeling the heat of his anger flash through him. A headache pounded in the back of his skull, hammering with a beat he didn't recognize. It almost sounded like a drum. The counselor's words popped in his mind. *She is not my mate. I simply want to fuck her and eat her.* He tried to calm himself, but the wolf remained agitated. It clawed at the confines of the fleshy cage they shared. He tried to pinpoint what had it riled up, but the beast didn't want to communicate. He rolled his shoulders until his neck popped, trying to feel a little more settled into his own skin. He felt electrified even after the run. Elijah shut the lights out and went out onto the balcony. A few lights burned in the windows. From his vantage point, he couldn't see Sadie's room. A small breeze wove through the night and he caught her strong bouquet from above. *She's on the roof deck.* He went back in and donned shorts and a robe. He took his card and swiped it over the red keypad to the door that opened up to the stairwell that led up to the roof.

Sadie looked out over the forest. The wind caressed her hair and stirred her scent once more. Elijah breathed it in and found it even more intoxicating. *He desired to feel the warmth of her skin along his.* The wolf agreed with him. He didn't understand it, but he licked his lips and needed to satisfy the hunger raging within him. However, he didn't want to scare her again and drive her away.

"It's a beautiful night, don't you think?"

She turned around and backed up a step until she was up against the edge. The wire railing thrummed from the contact. "Stalking me now?"

"Not at all." He held up his red key card. "Gives me access to all the special areas, the same as you."

"Right and you happened to know I was up here." She leaned against the railing.

Elijah was about to answer when he heard something snap. Sadie let out a yelp and tried to get her balance. He lunged forward and grabbed her arm, pulling her back onto the roof. Her body pressed against his as her arms wrapped around him. Sadie shook and gasped from the fright. Elijah felt his hunger stir, brought on by her fear. The look in her eyes and from her body was an open invitation. The world stopped as it had at dinner earlier. This time he leaned in to see if she would pull away. When she didn't, Elijah pressed his lips to hers in a light kiss. Sadie responded to him until she stiffened. Elijah needed to keep her close to him, but he released her. Feeling even the small space between them made his heart race. No woman had ever driven him this crazy before. Sadie was not the type he normally went for.

"T-thank you. That's the second time you saved me."

"Couldn't have you plummeting to your death on my watch." He tried to push past what his body and beast wanted. His mouth watered at the perfume of her desire.

"Mr. Dane."

"Elijah," he corrected her.

Blood flushed her cheeks. Her firm nipples pushed against the fabric of her shirt. She hadn't moved away from him. That gave him some hope. "Elijah, I think I should go back to my room."

He trailed his fingers along her skin, enjoying the silky texture. "Do you really want to?"

"It would be for the best, don't you think?"

"Probably. But what if I don't want to let you go?"

"Why are you doing this? You could have anyone you wanted. Why me?"

He swiped his thumb over her lip and felt the place where he bit her earlier. If only he could answer that question truthfully. *Because you smell scrumptious. Because I want to lick the skin from your flesh and bury my muzzle into your entrails. Because I want to fuck you until you scream my name.* And even with all that, there was something underlying he couldn't put his finger on. "Because I want you. Right now. No strings attached. This one night. Let me make you howl. Is that such a bad thing?"

Elijah licked his thumb and came away with the tang of dried blood. His wolf scratched at the edge of his mind, wanting to merge with him so it could taste her, too. They might have been one being, but times like this it felt like they were two. "There's something about you."

He glanced into her eyes and saw her disbelief. The heat between them sparked, but it was so close to blowing out. Whatever it took it have her, he would do. The wolf surged forward and pushed him to his knees. Something he'd never done before anyone.

"What are you doing?" she asked.

He took her hand, resisting the urge to suck on her fingers and nip the way he had before. If anyone saw him in this position, they would question his leadership, submitting to a human. "I'm on my knees before you, begging you, to come to bed with me. One night. No pressure."

She laughed. Her fingers threaded through his hair. Elijah bit his tongue to keep from groaning from the pleasure. "I'm not your type. But..."

Elijah pressed his lips to her stomach. He slid his hands along her full thighs and underneath her T-shirt. He glanced up at her but didn't see her saying no. Longing burned in her eyes. "Is that a yes?"

She touched his brow and nodded. "Yes." The whisper was so soft it almost got lost in the wind that pulled the answer from her lips.

He stood up and kissed her until she had to pull away. Elijah couldn't lose her once more. He caught her up in his arms and held her. "Your room or mine?"

"Mine's closer. You know... are you going to carry me down all those steps?"

He shrugged. Lifting her was nothing. She wrapped her arms around his neck and held onto him. He shifted her weight and grabbed his key so he could open the door and then go down the steps. Sadie rested her head against his chest. He took a moment to feel the complete satisfaction of having her in his arms. They made it down the stairs to the landing of her bedroom.

"I need your key to get in."

"Let me down so I can do that."

Elijah reluctantly set her back on her feet as she fished out a key. She pressed it to the mechanism, twisted the handle when the light blinked green, and it opened. Sadie took his hand and invited him back into her suite. The intoxicating aroma of her filled his nose. The hankering to have her rushed back. He pulled her to him. The weight of her body along his drove him mad. He tugged at her T-shirt, trying to not rip it off her, but she stepped out of the tangle of his arms.

"What?"

"Slow down. If you want me so bad, then you need

to take a chill. I --" She crossed her arms over her chest and moved away.

With each step she was withdrawing further into herself and he was losing her. He could feel it. Melissa's words came back about Sadie seeing the therapist. Something had happened to her. Something inside Sadie was broken. She had lost someone. "Forgive me. I got a little carried away."

"It's been a while since I've done this. I wasn't prepared for you or any guy. I don't have any protection."

Shit. He didn't either. Shifter females didn't have to worry about protection unless they were in heat. "It's okay. I'll be careful and there's so much more we can do." He slid his hand through the leg of her shorts to be rewarded with her wet folds. Elijah pressed his thumb against her clit and fondled her. She sucked on her lip as her expression grew from apprehension to pleasure. He delved a little deeper and slipped his finger inside her. Sadie's knees wobbled. A soft moan came from her lips. He stopped manipulating her clit and removed his robe. She nearly shied away from him. However, Elijah took her hand, guiding it to his firm cock. Her fingers closed over his length through his shorts. Delight spiked through him that nearly made him come. He had to keep it together so she wouldn't see his true nature. He couldn't wait until they were skin against skin.

"It's been a while since I've handled one of these."

"Like riding a bike."

Elijah stepped out of his shorts. Sadie's mouth dropped at seeing him fully exposed. A little look of fear came to her, knowing he might want to use it on her. "Your turn."

She pulled her T-Shirt off and held it over her front. "You know this was a mistake. I --"

"Are beautiful." He took her fingers and uncoupled

them from the fabric. Elijah took in her marvelous body as she shimmied her shorts off. His mouth watered at the sight of all her marvelous flesh to taste and nibble on. *She'd be a good midnight snack.* The urge to bite into her came back as his hunger for flesh made his teeth shift. Instead, he took her breasts in his hands, as he flicked his thumbs over her nipples.

Sadie trailed her fingers over the lines of his abs and caught the grooves of an old scar. Her touch made him look up and see the tears lingering in her eyes.

"What's the matter?"

She shook her head and sat down on the bed. Elijah grabbed a tissue from the bathroom and sat beside her. "No. Fuck. I'm sorry. I'm screwing this up."

Elijah brought her hand back to his stomach so she could touch the scars he got when he was younger, challenging the pack leader. "I got these because I was stupid and thought I could handle myself with a feral animal. The doctors said I should've died. I learned from my mistake and turned my life around." It wasn't a complete lie. After the pack leader gored him, he made sure he would keep the scar as a reminder. The doctor who bandaged him up had used the tiniest bit of shaved silver to line the wounds. In large doses silver was lethal to werewolves, but if even the tiniest amount got into an open wound their healing ability couldn't wipe away the scar. It didn't pain him, but it left him with a reminder to be ready for all things. It gave him the drive to not be beholden to anyone. He swore to himself then he wouldn't bend a knee to anyone.

Sadie wiped her eyes and turned her back to him. Four parallel lines carved into her flesh ran along her back and the across her buttocks. He traced the lines and saw they fit his fingers perfectly. "I was in an animal attack eighteen months ago. The thing killed my fiancé, Greyson. It clawed me when I tried to get away. It flipped me over and stared at me. I don't really remember what it looked like, but those eyes, glowing in the dark like some haunted creature from the depths. For some reason, it spared me. I've been struggling to hold down my job and my friends all think I'm crazy. Melissa's the only one who believes me. She sent me up here to relax. God, you must think I'm a mess. Naked. Crying with a smoking hot guy about to have sex with me, and then I lose it."

Elijah picked at the story. The last time he ingested human was a year and a half ago. He didn't really remember much about the night. He never did when the craving came over him. The smell of the two people in pack territory caught his interest. He started off on the hunt and the wolf took over. He recalled the sweet taste of the meat and then the scream of a woman. That was had drawn him back to his humanity. Pieces started to fit together. His stomach turned and he wasn't sure he could keep down dinner. A cold chill ran over him as Sadie turned back around. The way she looked at him, the longing and sadness still in her eyes, Elijah understood what he had done to this woman. He had taken her away from the man she loved and wounded her in a way beyond anything he could fathom.

She touched his leg. The warmth brought him back from his thoughts. "I guess this whole thing kinda turned you off to being with me. I understand." She reached for her shirt, but Elijah took her arm, doing his best not to hurt her.

He forced a smile. His attraction to her hadn't changed. *I have to do everything in my power to undo the wrong I've brought upon her even if she is unaware of it.* "No, Sadie. I'm glad you confided in me. Let me take your mind off your scars and what brought you here. If you still want me."

"Yes."

Elijah kissed her again. The taste of her lingered on

his tongue and got him hard again. He cupped her head and eased her back down on to the bed. He trailed his fingers over her learning her full curves. Sadie kissed him a bit harder, pushing her tongue against his mouth, unsure and teasing. Elijah kissed her neck and drawing in the skin at the hollow of her throat. He found her slick curls and dipped his fingers into her well. Sadie broke from the kiss and arched her back off the bed. Encouraged, he took in one of her nipples while he worked her clit slowly, building the bliss in her. Her pert bud on her breast only grew harder the longer he played his tongue over it. He moved two fingers inside her pushing against her inner walls when she moaned again.

He flicked his tongue over her slowly as she widened her legs. Elijah moved lower until he knelt on the floor. He slid his hands under her thighs and dragged her forward. He marveled at the sweet pink petals of her pussy. Sadie whimpered when he pulled away. His wolf pressed upon his mind, yearning to join with him. He tried to swat it away. The wolf didn't want to feast on Sadie's flesh, it wanted to eat her in another way. Elijah pushed it away and yet it lingered on the outskirts.

He sucked in the skin on her inner thigh. She squirmed around and giggling as he went higher. "Am I doing something wrong?"

"No. Tickles."

Elijah tucked that fact away for later. He gripped her hips and plunged his tongue along her folds. Sadie strained against him to rise up, but he held her down. She cried out, rocking her hips into his face. The sweet taste of her washed over his lips. The wolf wanted to delve deep within her, to twist its form until it was wrapped around his human form to pleasure the woman. It wanted to sink its fangs into her and claim her. As she groaned again, Elijah thought he heard the drumming when he realized it was the hammering of her heart. Her nails dug into his head. His cock throbbed in time with her breaths.

"Oh, yesss," she squealed.

Elijah didn't stop even as her moan sent tremors of satisfaction down to his core. His wolf wanted out to rub against her flesh. It wanted her hands in its fur. This was not the time for it to come into his lovemaking. He licked her sweet folds once more when she pushed him away.

"Are you okay?" he licked his lips, tasting her tang that was spiced like cinnamon.

"I can't go another round like that. At least not right away."

He broke out in laughter. "Well, I can certainly give you some time to catch your breath."

"I'm sorry if I --" She put her hand on her chest and then sat up.

He kissed her. "Never apologize. Go do what you need to do. I'll be here waiting."

Chapter Five

Sadie stared at herself in the bathroom mirror. Her cheeks glowed red and she was out of breath. A handsome, naked man lay waiting in bed for her. He didn't mind that she broke out into tears when she saw his scars. They resembled hers but were slightly different. *I certainly read him all wrong. He came off as an asshole, but he's just rough around the edges. And he doesn't mind my body. It seemed he enjoyed it.* She thought about his hands on her. It had been so long since she'd been with another man, she didn't realize how starved she was for sex. At least the orgasm didn't come from a green vibrator she had nicknamed Hulk. Her legs had stopped shaking and she could breathe again. She slipped out of the bathroom and peered around the corner to make sure he hadn't vanished. Instead, he reclined on the bed, leaning on his elbow and looking in her direction. His golden eyes glowed in the soft lamplight. All his muscles were clearly defined as though he had been chiseled out of stone. The only thing to mar his perfection was the scar down his torso. It had a faint silver sheen to it.

"Come here, beautiful." Elijah patted the bed.

Her cheeks burned at the compliment. For a quick second, she was reminded of Greyson stretched out on the bed as though his ghost was superimposed over Elijah. *Greyson would want me to go on with my life and not dwell in the past.* Sadie sat on the edge of the bed and traced the line of his body, feeling his muscles bunch underneath her touch. She caressed his calves and the fine hair that covered his legs. He quivered when she brushed his nipples all the while avoiding his erect cock. The size of it made her a little uncomfortable, but she always prided herself for trying something once.

"You look a little nervous. Did I break the mood?"

"I think I'm the one who broke it and no. I was marveling at how a guy like you would end up sweeping me off my feet, literally."

"You mean because you're curvaceous and you assume all my companions are model types."

She shot him a hard look. "Like they aren't?"

"Okay, you got me there, but there's something about you that drives me wild." Elijah claimed her lips in a slow kiss and pulled her down on top of him.

The gesture made her toes curl. Excitement sparked in his eyes. She could feel the attraction between them. She had felt it at dinner when he nearly wanted to eat her. "What is that exactly?"

"You smell scrumptious. You taste even better. I could eat you up."

"Didn't you do that already?" She slid her down his throat as his beard scratched her nose. Sadie took in the earthy taste of him mixed with the salt of his sweat. She nipped at the meat of his shoulder and Elijah whimpered. They rolled over so he was on his back and she straddled him. He grabbed both her ass cheeks and squeezed. She kissed him a little lower until she came to his pecs. She took a one of his nipples into her mouth and teased it with her tongue. Elijah dragged his nails along her back. When he touched her scars, she jumped. The heat between them hadn't lessened, but she suddenly felt self-conscious.

"Sorry," he apologized.

"It's fine. Instinct I guess," she murmured. *Get your shit together. He's not some monster.* Sadie concentrated on how he felt. The way his hands caressed parts of her. His hard cock rubbed against her inner thigh. He didn't make any move to push her further than what she wanted. *He either has the control of a god or he's about ready to blow.* Sadie sucked in his nipple and bit down.

Elijah's hips thrust upward. He closed his eyes and his face strained. Sadie kept an eye on his expression and did the same on the other side this time using all her teeth. He seemed to like it rough.

"Sadie, stop. Please, or I won't be able to --" Elijah tumbled with her on the bed until he straddled her.

The look in his eyes had turned wild. It was the same look when he kissed her at dinner. He grabbed her wrist and kissed it, pulling on the skin as he worked up her arm and came to the crook of her neck. Elijah pressed his teeth into the flesh. Joy singed her nerves in a way she'd never experienced before. He pushed his teeth a little harder into her skin. Fuck what they had said earlier. She needed him inside her. She wrapped her legs around his waist, slid her hand between them, and grabbed his shaft. Elijah groaned again. This time he took another mouthful of her breast and bit down. She'd have marks in the morning, but she didn't care.

"Elijah, I need you."

Hearing his name made him look up. The untamed look in his eye retreated. A moment of panic flashed across his face. "Sadie, I --"

She didn't give him time to say more. Sadie thrust forward until he was inside her. The feeling of him filling her made her breath hitch. It almost seemed they were made for one another. She hadn't figured it before, but Elijah flashed her a puzzled look.

"Please."

He started a slow rhythm between them. Each time he never completely pulled out but lingered on the edge of her pussy so he rubbed along her clit. She slipped her arms around his neck trying to keep the same dance going. He lifted her up, so they see one another, a tangle of limbs. She touched his face and kissed him. His bottom lip caught on her teeth until she tasted his blood. *Fair is fair.* This spurred him on as he mashed their lips together. The pain in her lip blossomed once more as the wound reopened and their blood mingled. Elijah broke the kiss and entered into her one last time as he came. Sadie was almost there but needed a few more strokes as he eased her down back onto the bed. He nuzzled the place on her throat where he had bitten. The waves of the orgasm crashed over her and she came.

She settled down beside him and stared up at the ceiling. An errant spider web blew with the fan that had kicked on. The taste of his blood lingered in her mouth. Part of her wanted to taste more of it.

"I got a little carried away. I hope I didn't hurt you."

"No. You didn't break the skin so it should be fine."

"It'll leave a mark."

She shrugged. "No one will notice under my clothes. I guess I got into it, too. I bit you. You seemed to enjoy it. Like it rough?"

He chuckled. "I like it a little rougher than you know." He kissed the spots where he had bitten earlier, sending renewed bliss through her.

"You do that, we might have to go another round."

He let out a long sigh and walked his fingers over her stomach. His lips met hers in a lingering gesture that made her lose all sense of self. Sadie wrapped her arm around him to pull him back down on top of her, but Elijah shook his head and got off the bed.

"I can't stay. I should get back to my room. This was fun."

Sadie nodded. *Of course, he can't. He didn't promise me a relationship, just a moment to be together and for him to make up for being an ass.*

As Elijah dressed, she felt the chasm between them widening as though their encounter never happened. "Yes. Fun."

"Hey, I'd stay, but there's a convention starting tomorrow. Some of the guests are coming in early and I need to be there to greet them. Actually, I was surprised you got a room. The whole place is booked."

"Business, right. I forgot for a minute that means

more to you than anything else. This whole seduction thing is your way of me not suing this place and you for everything that's happened to me."

"Sadie, don't be like that. I wasn't expecting you when I came up here, okay? I'm sorry if I hurt your feelings because that wasn't my intention. This wasn't about getting you to not sue. I'm not that crass. I enjoyed this. I enjoyed you, but --"

"Once you walk out the door, you'll forget this ever happened. You're going to give me the cold shoulder for the rest of the time that you're here. I get it. Can't tell your business buddies you had a fling with the fat girl down the hall." Her temper rose. She didn't think he could be so shallow, but she should have seen it coming.

"I don't want this to end this way, but if you're going to get all pissy, then fine. Don't get in my way while I'm here. I'll be sure that everything you need here is paid for that already isn't taken care of. I'm good to my word. Good night, Ms. Matthews." Elijah grabbed his clothes and walked out the door.

It had all gone downhill so fast she didn't know how it had happened. They were in bed together and it was good. *Fuck. It's my fault. My temper got the best of me. Melissa always said it would get me into trouble one day. I'm not going to run after him and beg. We're both adults. I should've known it wasn't going to go anywhere, but damn.*

The emptiness of the suite reflected the emptiness inside her. For a brief moment, he had filled the space between her nightmares and the aching grief that encompassed her. He made her feel alive again. She laid back in the bed and smelled the lingering scent of him on the sheets. Frustration made her scream into the pillow, but she accepted her fate and told herself she would do what he asked. The place was big, and she could easily find things to do to keep her busy.

* * *

Sadie glanced at her phone and saw it was past noon.

She got up, showered, and then looked at the menu for room service and ordered a large meal. When it was delivered, she didn't care what it was, but she made sure to give the waiter a generous tip. As she ate, she found herself thinking about Elijah. The way the light made his eyes a golden color. The faint silvery sheen of his scar. The way made her feel when he touched her.

The food stuck in her throat. As she set the tray outside, a small group of gorgeous people stopped talking and glanced at her, staring as though she were on the menu and certainly didn't belong at their precious resort. At the end of the hall, she noticed the desk clerk from the night before sitting in an alcove with his gaze trained on her room. *Fucking Elijah keeping tabs on me. What the fuck?*

She nearly stepped out and said something to him, but the people in the hall looked at her once more. The hair on the back of her neck rose. Something about them made her want to bolt her door and never come out again. Melissa had once made her feel this way, but they had become friends. Melissa always told Sadie she was worth something, no matter how she dressed or what she weighed. She had to stand her ground. Sadie straightened up and met the gazes of all those who were looking and waited for them to look away. All except one man did and he sneered. She glanced at the clock and saw it was close to her appointment with the grief counselor. If she didn't go, Melissa would find out, and she'd never hear the end of it.

Sadie grabbed her key and made her way into the lobby. People mingled everywhere. Most everyone was dressed in suits or designer clothes. She wove through the throng and wandered deeper into the complex, looking for the therapist's office. No signs pointed the way to the counselor's office. After wandering a while, she found herself lost. A few cabins were sprinkled in here and there. Well-lit trails wound into the forest like the one she had followed yesterday. This one led her to a larger pond surrounded by a row of high hedges. Nestled in the corner were a hot tub and a row of saunas from the steam coming off the small wooden buildings. A couple of women dressed in robes walked by her.

They giggled and said something. Sadie turned back around. "What did you say?"

The women turned back. The blonde snickered. "I said 'Oh look there comes dinner. I bet she'll be tasty.'"

"What the fuck does that mean?"

"That's so cute, Shay. She's totally oblivious. She does smell good and I'm hungry. Surely, no one will notice," the brunette crooned.

They began to circle her. Everything in Sadie told her to run. She swore she saw the flesh on the faces shift. It rolled around their eyes as though they were hiding another face behind them.

"What do you think you're doing?"

The brunette licked her lips. "You smell good. There's enough for both of us. What do you say, Lorraine? We can hide the remains in the woods. Gnaw on a few of the bones afterward." She grabbed Sadie's arm, yanked her close and ran her nose along Sadie's throat. She struggled to get away, but the grip was like iron -- the way Elijah had held onto her.

"Let me go. You guys are insane." She couldn't believe they were talking about eating her. *What kind of a convention are they having here?*

"I say let's go for it, Shay." Lorraine licked her lips.

Sadie was about to yell for help when Elijah came strolling down the lane with an annoyed look on his face. He was dressed in a business suit that was cut to fit his form. Her mouth drooped for a moment and her mind flashed back to the night before. She wanted to say something to him, but the murderous look he shot her kept her quiet. Like she shouldn't be there. Once the ladies noticed him, they squeezed her between them.

"Hello, ladies. I see you found my friend."

Sadie glanced at the one on her left. Shay. The look on her face was priceless.

"F-friend? I had no idea."

Elijah held out his hand to Sadie. She looked at it and then back at him. His expression hardened as he stepped closer, almost commanding her to take his hand. It was better than the strange women eating her. "Sadie, I was looking for you all over."

The other woman let her go. A spark raced through her once she took Elijah's hand. She regretted everything she'd said the night before. "Walk with me back to the hotel." She held her breath as he pulled her closer to him in a protective grip. "Ladies, I expect you'll let others know that Ms. Matthews is my guest, and not on the menu."

"Of course." They lowered their heads like they were bowing to him.

Elijah kept his hold on her until they were halfway back to the hotel. She heard more people coming and Elijah pulled her into a corner. He growled as she stepped away from him. "What the hell was that about?"

"You have no idea what position you've put me in. It's bad enough I have the desk clerk watching you to make sure you don't get into trouble, but you walk right into it. If Jake hadn't raced back and pulled me from my meeting, you'd been in a lot of trouble with those two."

"I'm so sorry I interrupted your meeting. I could've handled myself. Why the hell do you have your lackey following me around?"

"For this specific reason." His voice sounded as though he snarled a little bit. His eyes glowed golden in the light. She figured it was a trick or maybe something that happened to him when he was angry or aroused as they had the night before.

"For two psychos deciding to go all cannibal on my ass? Come on, what kind of a hotel is this?"

"Why don't you ask your friend?" he snapped back.

"What's that supposed to mean? Melissa wouldn't send me any place where I was going to get hurt. Wait, do you know her?" Sadie asked.

Elijah's eyes narrowed. "There's a lot about Melissa that you don't know. Call and ask her about it."

Sadie's head spun. Melissa had never mentioned she knew a sexy millionaire. Then again, Melissa didn't invite her to her lavish parties because it wasn't Sadie's crowd. Whatever questions she had about Melissa knowing Elijah, they could wait. He had rescued her from those crazy women and all she was doing was digging into him. Sadie bit back her rage and took in a deep breath. Having to function and interact with people without the heavy grief weighing on her was something she still battled, but she had gotten used to faking the emotions. Right now, she replayed the night they shared. It might have been his way of making it even between them because he had saved her, but it meant more to her than she realized.

"Elijah." She put a hand on his arm.

"What?" he snapped.

She pulled away, almost feeling as though the question was a slap to the face. "Nothing. Just thank you. Whoever those women were, you got me away from them. I'm sorry if you telling them I was your friend, put you in an awkward position. I got lost going to the therapist's cabin. This place is like a maze. They happened upon me and assumed I was some kind of snack. I-I don't take well to remarks said behind my back, so I confronted them. Look, you're a busy guy and don't need my baggage. So thanks. That's all." She forced a smile and resisted trying to touch him again although every fiber of her wanted to.

The hard line of his mouth softened. "You're welcome. I need to get back to oversee a few things. My schedule is pretty booked because of the conclave." He squeezed her arms and looked at her. "If I asked you to do something, would you do it even if it sounded crazy?"

"It all depends on what it is."

He touched her cheek. "Tonight, and the next two nights are the full moon. Will you stay inside your room and order room service? No matter what you hear."

"I didn't come here to be held prisoner in my hotel room."

"I know. Look, I'll get you a complimentary week at a later date if that's what you want. But please, would you do this for me?"

"I --" she wanted to know the reason behind his request. Before she could answer, his lips met hers and swallowed her words. His smooth hands touched her face and wound through her hair. She pressed into him and tried to tell herself this strange attraction was between them would burn away. His lips mashed harder until the sharp pain made her pull away. "You sure like to bite," she teased.

His expression paled. "I-I'm sorry. I didn't mean to."

"Mr. Dane, there you are. The others are getting a bit antsy for you --"

Kala had found them in the alcove. Sadie caught the look that passed between them and knew there was more to their relationship than Kala had let on. Elijah's expression returned to one of strictly business. "Please, do as I ask."

He left her alone.

Kala shot her a murderous glare as she went after him. Sadie didn't know what to make of the encounter. The first thing she needed to do was talk to Melissa.

* * *

Elijah sat at the table with the other pack leaders as they went over the conclave itinerary. This gathering would conclude with all the clans hunting together. The pack leaders would sign a treaty that would allow them to crossover into one another's territory. They were now going over the logistics of inter-pack or interspecies mating. Some pack leaders were against it. Others didn't accept those into a pack who were bitten. This meeting was to smooth out some of the differences between the large packs in the area and set rules that would keep things friendly between them. He was trying to bring his society into the modern age instead of hanging on to the antiquated ideas the older pack leaders still clung to. Even with all the responsibility, he couldn't get Sadie out of his mind.

He'd hated to leave her the night before. Elijah almost sneaked back up to her room, but he had to stay focused on why he had come here in the first place. Their tryst was only supposed to be a one-night thing. Her lips on his throat. Her mouth on his. The way they fit together as she rode him. In the middle of the opening discussions with the pack leaders, Jake had told him about what was going on with Sadie. That enraged him more.

Damn woman gets herself in more trouble. His anger kept him alert and on the move to her as fast as he could. Sadie didn't know how much danger she was in. Those women would have dragged her off into the woods, eaten her, and not cared about the consequences. They belonged to a pack that hunted humans. They had given him the reverence of pack leader, but it seemed that they didn't believe Sadie was under his protection. Getting into an argument about her staying put at night made him crazy. *Why doesn't she just listen to me?* He let slip that she needed to talk to Melissa. Everything about Sadie threw him for a loop. Her scent drove him nuts, and he couldn't stop from wanting her. Seeing her angry fueled his own passion and his wolf's as well. It wanted to fuck her even though they were fighting. Then they were kissing, and he couldn't stop thinking about their bodies together.

"Elijah, are you with us?"

He blinked and then focused back on Gregor. He was five feet, but muscular and a powerful wolf. He had been alpha to the Pine River Pack for eleven years. His reddish hair had shots of silver in it. He led one of the more progressive packs and was his friend. "Yes. Sorry."

Gregor shot him a look that meant they would talk about it later.

"Gentlemen, forgive me. I've had my attention divided between you and some business. Let's get back to the treaty. We were outlining the laws of the conclave." Elijah clicked his pen and perused the document before him as they went over it line item by line item until they could agree on everything.

Chapter Six

He swirled his drink as he sat at the bar. The sun set outside giving a beautiful hue of colors across the horizon. His wolf nudged against as it felt the moon rising and kept bringing back Sadie's scent and the feel of her. He downed the rest of the drink and got another one. Anything to drown out that damnable woman from his mind. There was nothing special about her and yet she infatuated him.

"Shouldn't you be going easy with the run tonight?" Gregor sat down next to him and sipped on a beer.

"I can't get her out of my head. Her taste. Her blood. The hunger for her." Elijah murmured low enough he hoped only the other pack leader heard him.

"Is this the human Kala was telling me about? The one you had to rescue from Shay and Lorraine. That's why you left the meeting."

Elijah took another swig of his bourbon as the burn went down his throat and pushed the wolf away so he could think straight. "Yeah. At first, I wanted to eat her. Maybe fuck her before I ripped open her chest. She smelled so good and her blood is intoxicating. She's stubborn and won't take no for an answer. Now I don't know what I want to do with her."

Gregor chuckled. "Sounds like you've met your match."

"She's *not* my mate." He crushed the thick glass in his hand. A large shard lodged in his palm. Gregor plucked it from his flesh. "Fuck." Elijah grabbed a handful of cocktail napkins to stop the bleeding.

Gregor took his arm and steered him outside onto the deserted patio. "You have to pull it together. Even if this human has you all riled up. We've been working toward this for over a year. You can't let her get into your head. Man, if you'd only eat her, then it'd all be over. Can't you cover up her being here? Why is she here anyway? I thought this was a no-human zone while the conclave was going on."

"It was. She wasn't planned on. I promised Melissa I'd watch over her."

"Melissa?"

Elijah plucked the wad of napkins from his palm and examined the gash. A pink line marred his palm. The wound be would be gone by morning. "Narissa."

"Shit. What is that bitch doing with a human?"

"That's what I said. She didn't get into it and asked me to watch over Sadie. There's something else." Elijah had been playing over in his mind the night they had gone out for the hunt and found the two humans camping on their land. Gregor had been with him and they both had feasted on the male human. Sadie must not have seen him.

"What is this something else?"

"Do you remember the hunt that started all this? Those two campers that we came across."

Gregor smiled. "Yeah, that man we got was delectable. You were the one who stopped all the fun when that female screamed. Got her good with your claws, though."

Elijah thought back to that night and the taste of the blood. Her shriek echoed in his ears. It knocked him out of the wolf's consciousness. He remained in wolf form, with his claws sunk into the female. He had flipped her over and was about to close his jaws over her throat, when the look in her eyes and her yells stopped him. She reached his humanity. Elijah retreated and brought Gregor with him. Once that happened, he recalled licking her blood from his claws. *Oh fuck! Now I know why she smells so good.* He looked at his splayed fingers as his attraction to her sank in.

"Yes, I did. Fate has brought us back together. She's the one I attacked."

"Well, that's fucked-up, but it does answer why you're drawn to her. Guess the wolf wants another bite."

"Has to be it."

"You don't sound so sure. Did you fuck her?"

"Yeah, but there's a story behind it."

"Whatever the story, does she know what you are? What could happen if she gets caught in the middle of a hunt?"

"She had no clue about anything."

"I find that amazing that she's oblivious to all of it. Surely, she bears scars from where you clawed her. How did she escape not changing?"

"I don't know, but it happens. I never bit her. The majority of those who are bitten transform. Some who are clawed do too, but she didn't. I don't know."

"Whatever it is. You'll keep your promise to watch out for her, but you know Shay and Lorraine are going to talk about your human friend. Some of the other pack leaders might not see it favorably. Don't let this fuck up what we've worked for."

"I don't intend to."

"It's already fucked-up that one of the pack leaders didn't show."

Elijah shrugged. "We knew going into this that it wouldn't be easy. Those who showed up? I take it as a first step. The Shadow Clan have always been a little standoffish. I've only met their leader a couple of times. From what I remember they take stock in mythology more than the other packs do."

"Fuck 'em. We can do this without them."

"Yes, we can."

"Good. Get her out of your head and let's get ready to run. The moon is full and I'm about to burst out of my skin."

"You go ahead. I'll be along in a few."

Gregor slapped him on the back, thinking their talk

had solved all his problems. It only made Elijah think more about Sadie and what she meant. *Is my craving for her a remnant of the past when I tasted her blood? Or is she my mate? Others have found mates by scent immediately and falling all over them like love at first sight, but I don't know.* His hunger for her hadn't retreated. He still wanted to taste her flesh and feast on her while he fucked her. On the flip side, he couldn't get her out of his mind. He glanced at his watch and there was an hour before he had to meet his pack. Elijah shoved his hands into his pockets and rushed over to the cottage he had stopped at yesterday. The door opened and the therapist came out wearing a brown silk robe, her big eyes already bigger under her glasses.

"Mr. Dane, is there something you need? I don't have long."

"I know and I apologize, but I needed to talk to someone."

She sighed. "Come in."

He went into her office, but he was too riled up to sit down. He rattled off what he had been battling with in one long breath.

"Mr. Dane, if you don't sit down, I'll eat you myself." Her eyes shone in the light.

He perched on the edge of the couch. If she said she would eat him, then he had reason to believe her. "Sorry. I don't know where to go with this. Is she my mate? Is this hunger for her some residual appetite from tasting her blood?"

She scratched her chin. "What does your wolf say? What does it want?"

"It wants to eat her."

"Are you sure about that?"

"I-I think so."

"Hmmm... sounds like you really don't know and that's a problem with you young people these days. You don't make it a habit of actually talking and bonding with your animals. You share the same body, but do you share the same desires? You aren't talking to one another. You think all the stories of becoming one are hogwash. Turn your back on legends."

"I'm not here to talk about shifter mythology. I need to know what to do."

"Talk to him and put stock in the old stories. The stars are shifting and showing something special is coming. We are all going to be surprised when it does."

"What does that mean? It has nothing to do with Sadie."

She shook her head. "Mr. Dane, does it hurt when you shift?"

"Of course, it does. Everyone goes through the pain."

"I don't."

"Impossible."

"Impossible?" The woman took off her robe. Her form slipped to the ground and coiled into a large snake over ten feet long. As it swayed its tongue flicked out and touched his chin. Within those oddly spaced dark eyes, he could see the intelligence of both creatures within the copper skin. "Is this still impossible?" the snake hissed.

The therapist had altered her shape faster than anyone he had seen before. "No."

"Then I suggest you speak to your wolf and find out what it wants."

"How?"

"Find a quiet place and meet him in your mind."

"Thank you." Elijah felt the tug of the moon. He darted out of the cottage and ran toward the forest where he would meet his pack.

The moon rose above the trees. A howl split the sky. The call to hunt. Elijah couldn't stop the wolf from coming forward. He answered the call and let the beast take hold.

* * *

Sadie went up to the rooftop balcony. It gave her a great view of the sky and the full moon. She couldn't see far off into the distance because of the treetops, but she thought she saw someone running off into the woods that looked like Elijah. A chill ran over her. What he'd said about Melissa got her wondering.

She dialed her friend's number. It rang a few times and then she heard the familiar voice come on for her voicemail. "Hi, it's Sadie. I need to talk to you. Do you know an Elijah Dane, by chance? He said something I needed to ask you about. Call me back when you get this."

She hung up and sent her a quick text to reinforce the fact she needed to talk. Sadie kept checking her phone, but Melissa hadn't answered her back. The night got a little colder, but she felt right at home. Something about the moon overhead and the peacefulness of this place calmed her for the first time since the attack. She hadn't been camping since Greyson's death. Inherently, she knew monsters didn't lurk in the woods and that what happened to them was a fluke. The doctors told her the odds were like one in two million to get attacked by a bear. But it wasn't a bear or mountain lion that mauled them. She wasn't exactly sure what it was.

Even with those odds, Melissa couldn't convince her to go back out into the forest, or even behind her mansion to camp out.

The idea for her to come to this place was growing on her. Some parts of it had been relaxing so far. It was also very frustrating because she couldn't figure out Elijah. The whiplash of his emotions grated on her nerves. First, he made love to her. If it was going to be a onetime thing, then okay. Today, he kissed her again. His attitude about keeping her safe made her wonder if he really felt more for her than he let on. She wasn't exactly sure where her feelings fell on the subject of him either. A part of her was growing to care for him. He was sexy as hell. She lost sense of herself being around him and then he said something that pissed her off. Then he warned her about staying inside for the next three nights.

"What's going on with this place?" She checked her cell again and still hadn't heard from her friend.

Sadie went back into her room and looked in the folder the hotel provided showing its layout and saw they had an outdoor swimming pool not too far from the sauna and hot tubs. *Fuck it. I can't stay cooped up here, no matter what Elijah warned me about.* She changed into her bathing suit, grabbed a towel and her robe, made sure she had her keycard, and stuck her head out her door. Sitting at an alcove at the end of the hallway was her protector. *I can't believe him.*

She racked her brain and then remembered the stairway that went up to the roof. It also went down. Once she was outside a zing of excitement went through her knowing she was free.

For a packed hotel, the place was empty. She wove along the concrete paths and found the Olympic size swimming pool. It was cool once she took her robe off and set everything on a large beach chair. Faint wafts of steam floated off the water. Sadie slipped into the warm water and enjoyed being alone. After doing a few laps, she got into a rhythm from end to end, and then ducked under the water. When she came back up, she felt the weight of exhaustion pulling on her limbs. She had been so keyed up before. She rested at the corner of the deep end when a loud howl made her jump.

It's only a dog. Wolves don't live in the forest here. A chorus of howls answered the one back. *Okay. I'm done. Maybe that's what Elijah meant about staying inside at night. It's gotta be. Shit.*

She got out of the water and tried to calm her hammering heart. She was about to put her robe on when something growled near the entrance to the pool. A large wall of hedges surrounded the area providing some privacy. Blocking her escape was an animal that stood four feet tall and built like a wolf on steroids. Everything in her froze as she stared at the wolf. The animal snarled, showing her that it wanted her for dinner. She stepped backward and narrowly avoided one of the beach chairs. The wolf jumped over three of them and lunged at her. Sadie grabbed a smaller lawn chair and held it before her, trying to fend off the beast. Another growl came from her other side. A second wolf with a sandy coat bared its teeth. They looked at one another, grunted, and then growled, as though they were talking to one another. Sadie backed up and tried to find a way out. The sharp edges of the chair cut into her skin. "Nice doggies. You really don't want to eat me."

Their smiles got bigger and showed off more teeth as though they were laughing. Strings of drool hung from their mouths and their eyes glowed. The image of what haunted her dreams. Sadie tried to find a way out, but her mind was suddenly thrown back to that night where she had lost Greyson. Those eyes shining in the dark. Echoes of pain from the scar on her back rode her spine and across her buttocks. Sadie tried to move, but the terror of that night overtook her. They advanced. She pushed farther into the hedge, tripped, and went down to her ass. She tried to speak but couldn't. One of them wrapped its jaws around her ankle. The teeth sunk into her flesh. It was then she found her voice.

"Elijah," she screamed. His name was the first thing that came to mind.

The one wolf nudged the one who had its mouth around her ankle. The one looked at its companion and growled. The other snapped at her. Sadie glanced between the two of them. "Please don't."

All she could hear was her heart drumming and

Greyson's screams as those eyes burned in the darkness. The two wolves argued amongst themselves over her. They seemed distracted and Sadie found a little bit of courage. She threw her towel at the one who had its teeth around her ankle. The cloth landed on the animal's face. It shook its head and released Sadie. The towel remained and distracted the other one. Sadie darted around them. She made it as far as the edge of the hedge when another wolf with dark brown fur -- even larger than those two -- stepped out in front of her with its sides heaving.

She backed up. The other two wolves behind her had a pissed-off look in their eyes. This was the end of her. She didn't want to end up as dinner with one of their muzzles buried in her intestines as with Greyson. Terror fluttered in her stomach. She whimpered as her ankle buckled and went to her knees, all the fight drained from her. The two wolves snapped at her again while the gray one dragged its claws along the top of her right thigh. Sadie screamed at the pain. Blood welled up and spilled onto the dirt. The larger wolf pinned the gray one down by its throat until it quieted. He turned to the other one. It lay down before him before it scampered away.

"Please don't kill me. Please." The dark brown animal poked her cheek with its wet nose before he licked her cheek. She sobbed. Her eyes remained on the wolf. It moved from her face to her leg. It inhaled as though it savored the scent of her blood. She tried to pull away, but more blood came from the wounds. He dragged his tongue over the claw marks. She expected him to chomp on her leg, but instead he kept on licking until the blood stopped. *He's toying with me.* It bumped its head against her shoulder and then gazed at her as if saying it wasn't going to hurt her. Those eyes burned in the darkness of her dreams. She nearly screamed until something happened. The hair receded and the face flattened into that of a man who looked like Elijah.

"Try not to move. You're still losing blood. I have to get you some help."

"Elijah?"

"Shh. Stay quiet. I'll get you back to the hotel."

Elijah picked her up. Searing agony flayed her nerves and black dots swam in her vision. Elijah looked down at her, but all Sadie saw were the golden eyes from her nightmares.

* * *

The next time she opened her eyes, Sadie found herself lying in bed with her leg bandaged from her knee up to her thigh. She hissed in pain when she tried to sit up.

"Lie still or you'll pull your stitches." Kala sat on the bed.

"Stitches. Then it wasn't a hallucination. Those monsters were real."

"Yes, those monsters are real." Elijah walked in wearing nothing more than a pair of jeans and glistening skin. Sadie heard the hardness in his voice and the steely look in his eyes. In that instance, he looked dangerous. All the grace he had from walking was that of a predator. His eyes were trained on Sadie. "Kala, leave us."

"I'm not some servant you can order around."

"Then go see if Lorraine is all right. She's in need of medical attention."

Kala glared at her and then at him. "Fine. But remember what I said." The walls shook when the door closed.

"What did she say?" Sadie asked.

"What do you care?"

She touched the bandage and smelled peppermint and something earthy. When she moved, Sadie could feel the tears in her leg, but they didn't hurt as bad as they first did. She glanced at Elijah. Even as a beast, he had saved her. He had licked her wounds and injured the other wolf. He had told her to stay inside, but she didn't think monsters lurked in the shadows. How her world had been blown.

He paced the hotel room. His fists were curling and unfurling as the veins in his temples throbbed with unspoken rage. Sadie could feel the tension in him taunt as his muscles. Yet when she looked at him, she could see the wolf. The same eyes that glared at her. The same hands that could have clawed her, but instead they had driven the other wolves away. He walked by the bed and she touched his arm.

He growled and pulled away. "Monster. You said it yourself."

"Will you sit down so we can talk about this?"

"What's there to talk about?"

Sadie gritted her teeth as he started pacing again. She forced weight onto her injured leg as she stood up. One step and then a hobble. Another step and a shuffle until the world tilted and she caught herself on the edge of the bed. A warm hand grasped her arm. Elijah's expression had softened some. He guided her back down to the bed. Sadie rubbed her hand along his beard before settling on his cheek. "You're not a monster."

"But I am."

He ripped the bandage from her leg, dropped to one knee, and began licking the blood. His eyes never left hers. Each time his tongue moved over a wound, the lines on her legs weren't as deep as they had been before. Whatever stitches Kala mentioned seemed to have already dissolved. Either he was healing her or whatever Kala had put on her wounds was. Sadie wound her fingers through his hair. With the feel of his tongue on her leg, somehow it aroused her. Questions brimmed in her mind. She needed to know what he truly was.

"Why?"

"Why what?"

"Why did you save me? Why not let the other wolves eat me?"

Elijah stopped licking her thigh. "Your blood stirs my hunger. I want to rip into your thigh and taste the meat of your flesh. My wolf enjoyed it as well as being inside you." His eyes had a wild look to them as he lost himself.

Sadie drew him up to the bed. "What of the man? How is this all possible? You're a werewolf. Is that the right word?"

He trailed his fingers over hers and up her arm as though learning the lines of her body. "I'm the leader of my pack. The largest in five states."

"You must've gotten into a lot of fights to get to be leader."

"More than you know. My pack respects me. The leaders of the others here admire me. Although after what happened tonight, I don't know. All because of you. I told you to stay inside."

"Sorry. I got bored. I never wanted to ruin whatever you got going here. Look, I swear I won't tell anyone what you are. No one would believe me anyway. Why did you save me?"

"Why did you call for me?"

Sadie didn't know what to say. "It just came out." *How can I tell him the thought of not seeing him again was almost worse than the thought of death?*

She touched his lips and he snarled. Her emotions choked her up. She should be cowering in fear because of the wildness in his gaze, but instead she kissed him. Their lips met and it felt right. She couldn't explain it.

"No, Sadie. No. You're leaving tonight, and then whatever this is between us goes away. I can't think with you around. I need to concentrate. I have a life beyond this place, and you aren't a part of it." Elijah shook his head so though trying to break himself from a spell.

"Melissa is coming up here to pick you up."

"I'm not leaving until I get some answers."

He chuckled. "Why are you so damn stubborn? Why don't you do as I ask?"

"Family trait. I'm not one of your employees or… or one of your pack you can expect to bow to your whim because you walk into a room. This whole retreat has been fucked since the start, but I met you and…"

"And I showed you favor so you wouldn't sue my company. You're nothing to me. Human. Nothing more than food for the beast with a decent amount of meat on your bones. You aren't even a good fuck."

Sadie slapped him as hard as she could. "You go too far. I know what you're doing. Saying all that hurtful stuff to get me to leave, but I know that's not how you feel."

Elijah got into her face inches away from her nose. The anger pouring off him could have ignited the room. "Fine. You've seen through me, but here's the truth. The only reason I had a hankering for you was because I tasted your blood before. That night when you were camping and tried to run from me. I dug my claws into your back and flipped you over."

Sadie didn't want to believe him. "You're lying."

Elijah snickered as his voice got low and guttural. The expanse of his face changed, deleting the man she thought she knew, replacing it with something between wolf and man. His chest grew broader and his nails sharpened to claws. His teeth were all jagged points and his eyes glowed. He ran his nose along her neck and nipped at her throat so she could feel the pressure of those teeth. "I'm not. You still smell so good. I bet you'll taste even better than your boyfriend when I had my muzzle buried in his guts. You never saw my friend who was chomping on his leg."

"Elijah, stop it." Sadie didn't want to believe him, but

in his eyes she saw the truth. The past suddenly washed over her again. She was brought back to that night with Greyson being eaten alive. The pain of those claws in her back. The impact of the air being knocked out of her lungs when the beast flipped her over. Those eyes looming over her in the darkness. Those same eyes that glared at her now with malice and hunger. That fear consumed her once more. She backed up farther on the bed. He pounced and pinned her down against the pillows. His face still changing and lengthening as he went more beast. "Elijah."

"What if I give you a head start? How fast will you run? I'm hungry from tonight. One." He backed away from her.

"What are you doing?"

"Two."

She tested the weight on her foot and could move it. She tried to go back to Elijah, but he growled at her. "Don't do this."

"Three." She grabbed his robe and made it out of the room.

"Four. Run, little piggy. Run."

As she pressed the button for the elevator, Elijah burst out of the room, grinning like he would attack her. The elevator doors opened, and she walked smack into Melissa.

Chapter Seven

Elijah rolled his shoulders as his bones settled back into place. He went behind the bar downstairs and grabbed the nearest bottle of bourbon. He took a swig and then another until half the bottle had gone. The next thing it exploded out of his hand. The remnants of it were ripped away and he was shoved into the wall. Hands choked off his air. He focused back on the face in front of him and saw Melissa.

"You have no idea what you've done."

"I didn't have a choice," he stammered.

"I told you to make sure she was safe. Then you go and scare her out of her mind!" Melissa yelled at him. Other wolves gathered around. One of them was the pack leader from one of the rival clans.

"Let me explain."

Her eyes narrowed. At that moment he was ready to give up everything because of what he had done. He hated himself. He knew going against his word with Narissa would bring consequences. Other wolves advanced on him, but she said something to them that made them back off. Fear went through their faces, even the other pack leaders'.

"Why should I?" She released him so he could speak.

Elijah rubbed his neck. "Because I -- I fucked up. I was the one who ate her boyfriend."

"Fiancé."

"Whatever. Her significant other."

"Fucking great." Narissa poked him in the chest. "Finish this shit here and take some time. You need to make restitution to her and to me. Do you understand?"

He bowed his head. Doing so would show the other wolves that he deferred to this woman. Considering what she was, she could kill him with a slice of her claws. She might not look like much, but she was something formidable under all the flesh. "I understand. Sadie. Will she be okay?"

"I don't know. Physically, probably. Mentally, you really messed her up. She was just starting to come out of her funk."

This time he growled. "You're the one who fucked up by letting her come here. She needed to go somewhere else. At least you should've told her what you are and the other shifters, Nari."

"I was going to, idiot, when she got back."

"What is she to you?"

"She's special and that's all you need to know." Narissa walked out of the bar.

The silence was broken by Marcus coming back over to him. "If this is how you deal with the meetings, then I'm not sure I want to be a part of this conclave. First the human and then the woman."

He shook his head. "Narissa is not just any woman. She's *byjin*."

"Never heard of it."

"I hadn't either until I dated her a while back. She's a Fairy shifter. You don't want to piss her off."

"A Fairy shifter. What's so scary about that? Where is she hiding her wings?"

Elijah nearly laughed at the question. By looking at Narissa, no one would never know she was anything but an ordinary human. "Ever had your balls frozen like solid ice? Or get stuck between forms for a week? She's five times stronger than any alpha I've ever met. Don't underestimate her."

Marcus didn't reply. "Looks like you pissed her off with the human."

"Yeah, it was her human. It's the reason I went after Lorraine. Once she told me the human was here, she asked me to look out for it." Elijah tried to explain away his connection without losing respect with the pack leader. Marcus seemed to buy it. He couldn't let his mistakes fuck up the conclave.

"I'm going to have to discuss this with the others. I understand why you attacked Lorraine, but... I can't say what the others will do. Whether you believe it or not, I want this to move forward. I think we need it." Marcus put his hand out to Elijah.

The shifter was a little shocked because he thought the other pack leader would be one of the hardest to convince. He took his hand and shook it. "Thank you. I want this, too."

"No more fuck-ups. You know Herb will want restitution for Lorraine being injured even if he doesn't believe your story about the woman, but I can back you up."

"I'm okay with whatever needs to be done." Elijah felt confident the whole thing would work out after all. Even as he tried to think of the conclave coming to a favorable end, all he could think about was the look on Sadie's face when the horror took over. It sent a buzz through him because he wanted to hunt her.

It also hurt his heart. The two sides of himself were at war. He ached to feel her body against his and inhale her sweet scent. The taste of her. For now, he had to push that away and focus on the rest of the weekend and seal the conclave.

* * *

Sadie heard someone knocking on her door. She curled up on her couch and pulled the blanket closer to her chest, not wanting to deal with whoever was there. For the last two weeks, Melissa had been trying to bring her out for dinner, but she didn't want any of it. Thoughts of that night with Elijah ran through her head. She couldn't make sense of them and yet she could. The knocking started again. When she didn't answer it, the door opened. She jumped up to see Melissa standing on the other side holding a pizza and a small cheesecake in the other.

"Okay, I'm sick of you ignoring my texts and my calls. We're going to talk about this." The door closed behind her.

"Go away, Mel."

Her friend sat on the couch next to her and set the food on the coffee table. "Sorry. Not going to happen. I'm not going to take it anymore and I miss our girl talks." She opened the pizza box and held it out to Sadie.

Chicken pesto with gorgonzola cheese, spinach, and Italian sausage. Her favorite. Her stomach grumbled about the pizza, but she turned back toward the television that had some horror movie playing on it. Once the echo of howl came on the screen, Sadie stiffened and reached for the remote, but Melissa grabbed it and turned the volume down. "Turn the station please."

"Not until we talk."

"What do you want to talk about? How you sent me away to some resort where werewolves would try and eat me? How do I know you're not going to eat me? You never even said you knew Elijah. Did you know he killed Greyson? Did you send me there to see how I'd react?" Sadie felt her anger rising at her friend, but also at Elijah. It hadn't simmered, but other emotions lingered she couldn't sort out. They tugged at her heart to think about how they fit so well together and the absence of him made it hurt all the worse.

"Hon, I never would've sent you there knowing what was going on. The place is normally great and well... I didn't tell you about Elijah because how was I supposed to know you were going to meet him there? I didn't know he attacked you and Greyson that night. You're like a sister to me. When Elijah called and told me what was going on, I made him swear to make sure you didn't get hurt. He's the reason you're not dead."

"Mel, he threatened to eat me. He was hunting me.

His face… it wasn't human or animal. The worst thing of all is he enjoyed it." She hugged herself as the movie flashed to a scene where the monster shifted from human to wolf. The image of Elijah licking her leg and becoming human before her set in her mind. The sight of him had made her fear, but the tenderness in his eyes made her heart ache. She ran her fingers over the scars on her thigh.

"If he hadn't done that, then the other wolves would've known you were open season. He staked his claim so no other would come after you. He was keeping his promise to me."

"Sounds great. So he saved me and admitted he wanted to eat me all in one conversation." Elijah had kissed her with a hunger she now understood. He made her body sing in ways no man had ever done before. The dread of him lived within her, but so did the longing to hear him whisper her name again. She was pissed and afraid of him with more emotions rolled into a Gordian Knot inside her stomach that only got more complicated the longer she thought about him. She glanced at her friend, but things were different now. Sadie knew there were other beings in the world. Which meant her friend was one of them. "Are you going to tell me what you are?"

Her mouth turned into a half smile. "I'm really not supposed to tell anyone."

"Bitch!" Sadie kicked her friend.

"Now that's the girl I know. I've missed her."

"I've missed you too. Now that I know about werewolves, are you going to tell me there are Fairies and vampires roaming the woods?"

She handed Sadie a slice of pizza. "Eat this and I'll tell you anything you want to know. No more secrets."

"About damn time." Sadie took a bite, feeling a bit of the tension fade between them. "What are you?"

"I'm a Fairy, but I can shapeshift into a wolf. I was

bitten by a wolf shifter many years ago. Running as a wolf was how I meant Elijah."

"Great so you're a shapeshifting Tinkerbell?"

Melissa poked Sadie in the calf. "I'm not Tinkerbell. Don't be a bitch."

She suppressed a giggle. "I'm going to start calling you Tink."

"You do, I'll turn you into a rat."

"No, you won't, because no one else can put up with your ass." She glanced at the television. The werewolf was falling in love with the heroine, but the film didn't have a happy ending. It made her think of Elijah being there and she longed to feel his touch one more time.

"Are you okay?"

She shook off the sadness and looked back at Melissa. "Yeah. Fine. Why?"

"I'm such an idiot. You're in love with Elijah, aren't you?"

"Of course not. How could I be after everything he's done?"

Melissa grabbed her hand. Her eyes narrowed and she had a faraway look to her eye. Sadie felt a warmth flash that hit the center of her chest. "Oh, sweetie. Do you want me to call him for you?"

"No. Promise me you won't. It doesn't matter anyway. It was a passing thing and what I feel is not love. It's a crush. We shared a moment before he went all feral and it's stuck in my mind. That's all. He made it perfectly clear he wants nothing to do with me."

"All that was a show to scare you. I told you that."

"I know and I understand on some level, but before that? We're too different. I'm not going to turn into a werewolf, am I? That mean bitch bit and scratched me."

"I didn't sense the taint of it in you before when Elijah mauled you. I don't sense it now either. You're rather lucky. Most of the time the virus is conveyed by bite, but sometimes it can be transferred by scratches if it's deep enough. Both times you were gotten pretty good. I'd say you were more than lucky. Actually, I'd say you're rather unique. I think it's one of the reasons I was so attracted to you when we first met. You kinda have this glow. You're special."

"Great. I'm radioactive."

"It's nothing like that. You have this feeling about you. You know like some people are drawn to others. I felt right at home with you. For a long time, I thought about telling you what I was. Then you were attacked. I knew if I told you then that it'd freak you out even more. I didn't want to lose you. Call me selfish."

"Melissa, I like you for you. Is Melissa even your real name?"

"Actually, it's Narissa. Most everyone calls me Nari."

"Nari. I like it. Now that I know, where do we go from here?"

Melissa handed her a fork and a plate with the cheesecake. "We eat until you're sick, and then we watch bad horror movies like we did in college. Tomorrow we go shopping for a dress."

"Why do I need a dress?"

"Because I decided I'm going to have a party to introduce you to all my friends."

"Hun, I don't think that would be a good idea."

"Why not?"

"Because I'm not like you and I'm not filthy rich. You're always so put together and I'm... a lot curvier than you. Besides, I don't have wings to flit around with."

"Sadie, I'm not taking no for an answer. Doors will open for you. Your life is going to change. So what if we can't wear the same tops. Once you've been marked by the Fae, then your life will change."

"Are you proposing to put a bull's-eye on my forehead?"

Melissa's hand began to glow. "I'd never hurt you. This gives you an added layer of protection so no more werewolves will think of you as dog food. No vampires will snack on you. You get the idea."

"Are you some kind of Fairy princess?"

"I am, actually. Although I have one hundred brothers and sisters and with my tainted blood, I'm not welcome back home unless it's official business."

"What do you mean?"

"There aren't many shapeshifting Fairies. We can cast glamours to make ourselves look like other things, hide our true appearance, but we don't actually turn into anything else. However," she rolled up her leg and pointed out the faint bite scars on her leg. "I was bitten by a wolf when I was very young. The bite infected me enough and messed with me so I was able to turn into a wolf. It also made me an outcast among others of my kind. Here I am."

"Do you miss your family?" Sadie asked.

She shrugged. "I've made my peace with it a long time ago. I can go back when I want. I don't spend lots of time there. Enough about me, though. Unless you have more questions."

"What does this mark do exactly?"

"Besides take you off the menu, it might make you a little bit more attractive to the opposite sex."

"Mel, I don't need to get laid."

"Forget it. Don't worry about it. Have fun and see what happens. It doesn't make you my property or anything."

"Good, because I don't plan on being claimed on your taxes."

"Enjoy what comes. What kind of dress are we going to get you?"

Sadie forced a smile, but her mind wasn't on the impending ball or the cheesecake, but on Elijah and if she would ever see him again.

* * *

Elijah shuffled the papers together about the new merger he'd planned. His mind didn't linger on business. It hadn't been since he drove Sadie away. But he did it so he wouldn't lose face among the other pack leaders. From the fear on her face he had damaged whatever chance he had at...whatever had disappeared. He didn't even know what it was. The taste of her blood lingered on his lips and the timbre of her voice stirred his passion. It took all his concentration to not think about her. Business needed to take precedence and not her lips or the sexy curves. The wolf raked its claws along his flesh. The last time he shifted it almost seemed the wolf didn't want to come out, it was so painful.

"Mr. Dane, this arrived for you."

He glanced up as Gretchen came in with a stack of files. She set them on his desk and handed him a black envelope trimmed in gold. She flashed him a smile. He didn't return it and took the envelope. "Is there anything else?"

She trailed her finger along his hand. "I thought maybe we could..."

He pulled his hand away. Elijah had made the mistake of sleeping with her almost a year ago. She kept trying to reignite the nonexistent spark between them. "That will be all, Gretchen. Thank you."

She gave him a tense smile and left. His wolf nudged the inside of his mind that it wanted out. He rolled his shoulders. It pushed back and wanted to be known. The action reminded him of the conversation he had with the psychologist about talking with his animal. *Maybe that's what the wolf wants.* Elijah opened the letter and got a whiff of floral perfume. Narissa. A moment of dread hit him. It was an invitation to an old-fashioned ball on the night of the full moon.

He tossed the invitation aside and didn't think about it. He had other things to worry about. Business was more important than flitting around with a Fairy ex-girlfriend. Elijah studied the most recent spreadsheet to see where the numbers looked the best at the next company he was going to buy.

Chapter Eight

Elijah stretched his legs. His wolf had grown grew increasingly irritated at him. Clearly it wanted to communicate something. Elijah thought about what the therapist said about having no pain when it came to shifting. He looked up at the moon and it was nearing full. He sat in the grass feeling the blades against his flesh and closed his eyes. He felt silly as he sat alone under the stars, but after taking a few breaths he let instincts take over. The clean air along with the mixture of other forest scents enticed his wolf. In the back of his mind, the animal shifted. He pictured himself in a green glade like the place he was in and tried to see his wolf standing before him, visualizing the great beast. The shadows drew themselves together into the shape of his animal. It stared at him with golden eyes. He sensed its presence in a separate way than he ever had before. He was so used to having it meshed with his personality that feeling that sharp aloneness made him wonder what he would be without the wolf.

"You got me here. What do you want?"

Its golden eyes sparked, and stared into his soul even though it was already part of him. It didn't have the power of speech, but it knew how to communicate. The scent hit him first. The sweetness he recognized associated with Sadie mixed with the earthly perfume of cinnamon and vanilla. The taste of her blood flooded his mouth. He coughed at the sensation as it choked him.

"Sadie. I get that you want to eat her."

His wolf gnashed its teeth. As it moved, he could make out the three silver lines on its chest that mirrored the same scars on him.

"Okay, you don't want to eat her. Then what do you want her for? She's human. She's nothing." Even though the words came out, he knew that wasn't true. She was something and the wolf was telling him that.

The beast sat back and let out a forlorn howl. To hear it brought tears to his eyes. It sliced through his heart until he could feel the emptiness and the wanting. It wanted someone to share its life with. The howl echoed in his mental landscape, but nothing answered it. It needed more than the pack to bring it life. Sadie's smell hit him again and the sound of her voice. It was muffled to him, but he could hear it as she cried out and the wolf turned it into a howl. Elijah listened to what the wolf imagined her response to be and he could feel the joy of his bestial companion. The sound died away. When he opened his eyes, the wolf was gone.

Before him was a word written in the sand of his mind. *Mate.* He could feel the beast back with him again. It wanted Sadie as its mate. It was telling him that she was the one even if he didn't want to believe that. Elijah never envisioned being with a human. It meant she would have to become one of them. He didn't even know if that were possible. And then there was the whole idea of what he had done to drive her away. The beast growled again in his mind giving him another warning. He had to do what it wanted. He was a pack leader. If he couldn't rely on his wolf, or trust it, then how could others trust him to defend their territory?

"All right. All right. I get it, but there's a possibility that she won't want us after what I did."

A ripple of pain moved through him that snapped him out of his meditation, giving him the answer he needed. Fix things between them or else his wolf was going to do more harm. Elijah dusted himself off and went back in the house. He had to figure out a way to get back in Sadie's good graces. Elijah grabbed his phone and dialed the one person he dreaded.

"Hello."

"Narissa, it's Elijah."

"What do you want?" Her unhappy tone didn't

make him feel any better. Having her pissed at him could be dangerous. He hated to admit she was one of the only creatures he feared, and he had broken his promise to her to protect Sadie.

"I need to talk to Sadie. Please."

"Didn't you bother to get her number before you scared the shit out of her and drove her out of the resort?"

"We both know why I did that. The others would've pounced on her if I hadn't." He choked back the disgust he had at the thought of seeing Sadie hurt. Part of him had enjoyed her fear, but he understood now that was on him and not the wolf.

"You seriously fucked her up. She's gone back to having nightmares. She's too stubborn to talk to me, but I can tell. I hope the conclave was worth it."

"If you can give me her number, then I'll talk to her. I need her. Please, Nari."

"You almost sound desperate enough that I believe you. I'm not giving you anything."

"Fine. I'll have someone dig into her background and they'll get me the info I need."

"You can try, but you won't get it. She's marked, under my protection. If I don't want you to find her, you won't. Sadie's special, and too good for you. Goodbye, Elijah." She hung up and he stared at the screen. She wasn't going to make this easy.

If Sadie is under her protection, then she must know about the resort and Nari. And I'm totally screwed.

* * *

"What do you mean you can't find any information on her?" Elijah growled. This was the fourth private detective agency he'd hired to find a simple phone number and address for Sadie.

"I'm sorry, sir. Keep the money. Whoever this woman is you're looking for, she's protected. Not even our shaman can penetrate the aura around her. When he gets close all he hears are drums. You must have pissed someone off. My best psychic went blind for three days and went on about the same drumming. Good day, Mr. Dane."

He nearly threw his phone across the room, but he had to keep it together. Meetings were stacking up on his calendar. He slammed his fist onto the desk, sending folders onto the floor. It made him feel a little bit better, but the wolf didn't like how his search for Sadie wasn't going well. It grew more difficult him to shift. He'd tried to communicate with it again, but it made him uncomfortable in his own skin. Elijah sighed and picked up the scattered folders. As he did, he noticed the black invitation to Narissa's ball. Sadie should be there. His wolf wanted to go to the party. It wanted to see their mate.

* * *

Elijah straightened his tux as he got out of his limo. A long line of guests waited outside the sprawling house. The scents of all different kinds of shifters tickled his nose. He recognized a couple of the other pack leaders he knew from the conclave. They nodded at him and turned back around. His stomach sank the closer he got to the door about what he would say to Sadie. *Will she even talk to me?* He made it to the door and handed the invitation to the bouncer.

"You're not welcome." He gave Elijah back his invitation.

"What do you mean I'm not welcome?"

"Our lady has told us you're not welcome, wolf. Go back to your pack."

Elijah wasn't going to argue with the Fairy bodyguards. *Narissa isn't making this easy.* He backed away from the entrance. The line of people glanced at him, but he didn't make a big deal about it. Instead, he walked around to the side of the house. Security guarded all the entrances. Narissa must have figured that he would come to get at Sadie. He recalled the back way into the house that was mostly covered by the forest. He glanced at the moon overhead and the fullness drew him, but he had never felt so disconnected from the wolf. Even his senses seemed dull. He walked into the darkness, sticking close to the road until he was far away from the property and stepped into the woods. His footsteps ricocheted off the trees and the underbrush making him sound like a herd of elephants. Elijah made it to the property boundary and tried to cross the threshold, but he was pushed back.

Narissa, I'm going to kill you. Maybe it was only leaving him out and not his wolf. He thought about his beast and didn't hear it. He calmed his mind and reached out to his other half. *If you want to get to Sadie, you have to let me shift. We have to come together so we can claim her.* His mind was made up. He wanted her as much as his wolf needed her.

* * *

Sadie stood out on the balcony taking in the night. All the different people in the house pressed on her and she wasn't sure she could take the attention. Ever since Melissa put her mark on her, she'd been given ten job offers, had six different men ask her out, each stunning in his own right. She had gone out with all of them at Melissa's insistence, but she wasn't feeling it. Her heart remained stuck on Elijah even after everything. Something about him kept pulling her back to him.

"Why aren't you inside? I have tons of people looking for you." Melissa came out, a vision in a flowing blue gown.

Sadie straightened and shrugged, not used to the tight material of her black dress. It accentuated her breasts and then flared out from the waist. "I needed some air."

"You okay?"

"Fine. It's a lot to take in."

Melissa hugged her. "It's all for the best. Come back in when you're ready."

"Thanks."

Melissa left. Sadie slipped her shoes off and walked farther into the garden away from the noise. As she got to her favorite spot, she sat down and listened to the whispering fountain. She thought of the night Elijah had saved her, appearing as the wolf. It frightened her in the moment but now she yearned for him. Melissa tried to keep her occupied, but it didn't do any good.

"Why are you crying?"

Sadie jumped up and looked over to see Elijah, naked, standing in the shadows with his golden eyes glowing. "Why are you naked?"

He walked toward her with the same grace she remembered when he stalked her before. The sight of him brought back the dread and she retreated from him. He held out his hand. "No. Peace."

Sadie stopped and tried to understand what he meant. He wasn't acting like himself. The way he moved his head and kept his eyes trained on her, it was almost like he was more of a canine. "Why are you here?"

"Sit." He pointed toward the bench again and took a seat. It didn't seem he cared about him being unclothed. He gestured for her to sit by him again. She came over slowly and sank back down. Elijah reached for her hand, but she jerked away from him. "Please."

She slipped her hand in his. He closed his eyes and moaned. She tried not to let herself get caught up into feeling of how right this was. "Elijah, why are you acting so strange?"

He opened his eyes and pressed his lips lightly to her wrist. She shivered as the caress and the pleasure it brought her. "Wolf. Not the man. Will never upset you.

Love."

"Love? How can you love me after what you did? Don't you know how you hurt me?"

His expression was pained and a low growl came out. "Not me. Man." He held her hand over his heart. "Mate."

"Mate? Isn't that presumptuous since we barely know one another and the night we spent together..."

His lips connected with hers before she could finish her sentence. He broke away and nipped at her throat. He bit harder when she pulled away. "Mates." He came toward her again, when she put a hand on his chest.

His kiss didn't have the passion in it. It was soft and yet insistent. It pushed the remaining terror from her until she kissed him back with a hunger of her own. Her mind spun as she tried to make sense of this strange turn of events. "I understand. You're his wolf. You might feel we're mates and you love me, but he did and said some things I need to work out with him. Can I talk to him please?"

He ran his fingers over her face. "Beautiful." He closed his eyes and when he opened them again, she could see the slight difference in his face. "Hey, Sadie."

"Hi, Elijah." The tension between them returned. "Can you tell me what's going on?"

"My wolf is rebelling against me. It's been after me to talk to you. You're a hard person to find now that Narissa, I mean --"

"I know who you mean. Why does your wolf think we're mates?"

"Because we are."

"Hardly. You fucked up any chance of us ever being anything. What you did made my nightmares return ten times worse. I can barely sleep through the night."

"I'm sorry. I got carried away. I only pushed you away to keep you safe."

"I know why you did it, asshole. Melissa explained a few things to me about herself and werewolves."

He placed his hand on her knee, and as right as it felt, she nearly jerked away. "You're afraid of me."

"I can't help it. I don't want to be, but..." Elijah dropped to his knees and screamed. His whole body rippled until she could see the flesh change from fur and back to flesh. She clutched his shoulders. He lunged at her and growled, knocking her backward. When he realized what he had done, the pain on his face stopped, but it was clear he was still suffering.

"Stop. Whatever this is, stop."

"Hate us," he forced out.

She realized it was the wolf and they were fighting internally. She lifted his chin and looked into his eyes. "I don't hate you." Sadie kissed him.

He stopped and kissed her back, lying on top of her. He raked his fingers through her hair, pulling it from the pins that held her hairdo together. His nails pressed into her thigh.

"I smell desire. We mate."

"No. We don't. Let Elijah come back, please. For us to mate, he and I have to talk. You can't butt in when you smell something you don't like. You have to let him and me figure this out. Do you understand?"

"Yes."

"No more pain."

"No."

"Thank you."

Elijah hung his head before he looked back up at her. He seemed defeated and not the proud man she knew. "Thank you. We've been at odds since the resort. The pain makes it hard to concentrate. It listened to you. Please, let me make it up to you."

"Sadie, are you coming back in? Elijah, how did you get in here?" Melissa found them.

"We were talking, Mel."

Her face darkened with anger. "I made it perfectly clear you weren't allowed. Get out before I make you regret it."

Sadie stood up. "Mel, I want Elijah here."

"Sadie, he hurt you. I won't let that happen again."

"You don't control me."

"Don't I? I gave you my protection and threw this party together for you. Haven't you been enjoying the other men you've gone out with, the change in your lifestyle?"

"Other men?" Elijah asked.

"Yes. It's not like you made it easy, so don't get all possessive either. Mel, Nari, whatever. You're my friend. I told you I didn't want all this. You're doing this for you and not me. Oh, let's show off the poor little human who needs my help. Both of you think you can bend me to your whim. Narissa, I love you for being you and not this uppity Fairy princess shit. Elijah, tell your wolf I'm not going to be humped or join it as a mate until we do things on my terms. Excuse me. I'm going home." Sadie walked out of the garden, past all the guests, grabbed her things, and drove back to her apartment.

She got into the shower and felt the tears coming that she had been holding back. Seeing Elijah had jarred it all lose at how much she missed him. The crippling feeling made her double over from being so close to him and then losing him once more. She might have understood the wolf, but it was the man who drove her crazy. After a month and a half, he came back to apologize. *A motherfucking month and a half. That asshole and he expects me to be all happy to see him.* The yo-yo of emotions left her exhausted. She climbed into bed and let the night take her.

She woke up with golden eyes lingering in her dreams and someone pounding on the door. She stumbled to the door and looked out to see Elijah. "What?"

"Can I come in? I brought a peace offering." He held up coffee and a box.

She stepped aside and glanced at the clock. Nine in the morning. She felt like she hadn't slept at all. Elijah came in and set everything down. "Talk." She wobbled on her feet and Elijah caught her. His warm arms and his scent made her head spin. She nearly lost her resolve and kissed him.

"Are you okay? You look…"

"Like hell, I know."

"Tired. Didn't you sleep?"

She took a sip of the coffee and realized it was a mocha with a little bit of peppermint. "I slept, but not well. Ever since you nearly ate me, I can barely make it through the night. How did you know how I liked my coffee?"

"Nari. It's her way of apologizing as well as telling me where you live."

"Why is that an apology?"

He touched her hand. "Because I've been trying to find you for over a month. Nari made sure to keep your privacy hidden so no one could find out and I never got your number. She even barred me from the party, but as the wolf, I was able to get in. She realized she made a mistake. I know I did and I've been paying for it. My wolf and I came to an understanding. He wants you, though. It's difficult to keep him in check when I'm around you. He fears you're afraid of him."

Sadie sighed. "I am and I'm not."

"You're safe with us."

She was so tired even after sleeping. She sat down. He slid closer and wrapped his arm around her. "Why are you even into me?"

He dragged his fingers through her hair. She rested

her head against his chest and listened to the sound of his heartbeat and found it soothing. "Because we fit. It took me a while to understand that when my wolf knew it all along. He knows you're our mate. I think he knew that first night when I attacked you. He heard your voice and tasted your blood. It's why I stopped back then, although I was too stubborn to realize it. You may not believe me, but I want you. I'll do anything to prove that to you."

Sadie heard what he said, but the warmth of his body and the steady thumping of his heart lulled her off to sleep. This time she didn't think there would be any nightmares.

Chapter Nine

Having her in his arms like this was the most satisfying thing he had ever experienced. He dared not move in case he woke her. Half an hour later, though, she started to shake. Her heartbeat sped up, and the aroma of her fear bloomed in the room.

"Shh, it's okay," he murmured. Elijah touched her face and tried to reassure her. He held her closer when she thrashed against him. He understood why Narissa was worried about her. Elijah kissed her forehead and held her until she calmed. Once it seemed like she was okay, he got up and explored her apartment. Plants filled the corners. Shelves overflowed with books. Pictures of her with another man stirred his jealousy, but he understood this was her late fiancé. Elijah covered her up with a blanket and checked his phone. Several messages showed from Narissa, but he didn't want to talk to her. After Sadie had stomped off on the both of them, she'd grudgingly given him Sadie's address, phone number, and a few tidbits as to what her favorite things were, but that was all. The rest he had to figure out on his own. He glanced at her again and felt shame knowing he had caused this. Elijah scrolled through his phone until he found the number he was looking for.

"Hello, Mr. Dane, how can I help you?"

"I'm sorry to bother you, but I needed to ask a favor. Do you remember Ms. Matthews?"

"Yes, very nice woman, for a human. What's the matter? Have you finally realized you're mates?"

"You knew?"

"It was very obvious, at least to me. Are you calling for some relationship advice?"

"Not exactly. I told you I had attacked a couple and I was still craving the human meat."

"Yes."

"One of them was Sadie. She isn't sleeping very well.

Any advice on how I can help her get over this so she can sleep?"

"Is she afraid of you, or the wolf?"

"I don't know. Maybe. She says she isn't, but the attack was quite violent, and she did see me eating her fiancé."

"That would pose a problem. It sounds like her nightmares are being caused by Post Traumatic Stress. Have her talk about her nightmares. Maybe confront their meaning and how you work into them. She can write them down. Maybe even have her play some video games where she can take out her inner aggression on the characters and not on you. The most important thing is for you to be there for her. Help her find a place that's relaxing. I find the pond here at the resort quite calming. Reassure her that everything is all going to be all right. Have her call me if she needs to talk about it. I would hate to prescribe her drugs, but that's something we can look into. Maybe some peppermint or calming teas before she sleeps. Go slowly. Even though she's your mate, she needs time to adapt to the idea of being with you. She still has a flame for the one you killed and blames you, I bet. And whatever happens, know she's a special woman."

He sighed. "Thanks. I appreciate it."

"No problem. How is communicating with your wolf going?"

"Better. We've come to an understanding."

"Wonderful. Goodbye, Mr. Dane."

Elijah hung up and looked back over at Sadie sleeping on the couch. He wanted her to trust him. His phone dinged. More texts from Gretchen about business he needed to take care of. The urge to take care of business got the better of him. He went into the other room to make some calls. At the moment, he couldn't leave Sadie until he made things right with her.

"Gregor," he called his friend.

"Elijah, is everything okay?"

"I need some advice."

"Shoot."

"How did you get Bev to go out with you?"

"What's up, man? You have no problem with women."

"My mate, she isn't sure about us, and I need her to be. I --"

Gregor started to laugh. "Elijah Dane needs my dating advice? That's funny."

"It's not funny, Greg. I can give her the world, but that's not her. She doesn't care about... stuff. She doesn't know if she wants to be my mate."

"Bro, calm down. If she's the one, then woo her. Bring her flowers. Take her places she likes, get her to know the wolf. Love her, man. If she's the one for you, then she'll come around. There isn't much you can do. It's a relationship. It's not magic. You meet and do your damnedest to make sure the woman wants you. It's not all about instant chemistry like you read about. You gotta work for it. Love her. Is this the human you were hell bent on scaring out of the hotel?"

"Yes."

"You have your work cut out for you. Good luck." Gregor hung up, leaving him with a whole lot of questions.

He dialed Narissa's number. "What do you want, Elijah? Sadie finally come to her senses about you?"

"No. She's sleeping, for now. What's her favorite food?"

"It's not duck or venison. She's not into gourmet meals. She likes chicken and pasta. Steak and vegetables. Pizza. She doesn't eat a lot of fried stuff. Does that help?"

"Yes. Thanks." He hung up and then checked out her fridge. Empty. He went online and ordered some food to be delivered from the local grocery store.

An hour later, the food arrived. He checked and Sadie still slept. He began to cook, hoping that would help to ease her trepidation of him. Cooking relaxed him and it let him pass the time until he heard Sadie stirring. She walked into the kitchen.

"You're still here."

"You sound surprised."

Sadie drank some of the cold coffee while she woke up. It took all his concentration not to pull her into his arms. She leaned back against the counter and ran her fingers through her hair. A shiver of yearning speared him seeing the expanse of her skin. He gripped the counter and looked down. She was beautiful and he'd never truly seen it before. Her dark hair fell in slight waves over her shoulders.

"Are you okay?"

"Yeah, I was marveling at how lovely you are."

"You keep saying that."

"I mean it." He went toward her, but then stopped.

"Elijah."

He couldn't take hearing his name on her lips any longer and not being able to touch her. Elijah scooped her up and sat her on the counter. He slid his hands along her neck and cupped her face until he kissed her. Meeting her lips was like coming home and completed something inside him. Sadie moaned as he worked his way from her luscious mouth to her supple neck and nipped.

"Elijah."

"Yes?" he murmured.

"The chicken is on fire."

It took him a moment to snap out of his stupor and smell the smoke. "Fuck."

Sadie giggled as he turned around and saw the chicken was aflame. He turned the faucet on and took the sprayer to stop the fire, only it whooshed the flames higher. "Here, let me." She pushed him out of the way with her hip and covered the frying pan with a larger pan. The flames leapt out trying to escape, and then they died down. The room was left smoky. He looked at the ruined meal and sighed. "I'm sorry about all this. I wanted to make you dinner to show you that I meant what I said."

She looked up at him with those deep brown eyes and all that he was drained away. *I've been such a fool.* Sadie bit her lip and touched the side of his face. He caught her palm and kissed it. The fire had sparked something between them or burned away a barrier. Something in her had changed about how she felt toward him. It might not have been love or forgiveness for all he had subjected her to, but it was something. She slid her hand down his shirt and undid a button. His chest tightened with anticipation.

"Sadie, I didn't come here for that. I only…"

This time she kissed him lightly. The feel of her lips and her body along his made it feel like he was home. It broke his heart that he had never felt like that before. He realized what he had been missing and what his hunger was all these months. It wasn't for human flesh, but for her.

"I know. Look, I can't say that I'm ready to be your mate, and all that entails. I don't want to get furry every full moon, but I know I love you. I've been trying to rationalize it all and I can't. I thought it was lust, or fear. Maybe a combo. Your wolf is adamant we need to be together, but maybe we can go slowly. I know it's you under the fur, but I'm not ready for all of that yet. Can you respect that?"

"Yes. Although I might have to be away from you at the full moon, if you don't want any of that. The pack will eventually demand you take a place at my side as a wolf. I'm a pack leader. There are expectations. Do you understand?" He didn't want to chase her away at the idea she would have to join him.

"I understand, but how about you both promise we get to know one another first? I don't mind if we end up in bed, but no shifting or biting. It's a deal breaker if you get any hairier than you are now."

"He may want to come out and eat you," Elijah nipped her finger but didn't break the skin.

"I don't know about that."

Elijah trailed his hand along her thigh under her nightgown and cupped her warm sex. He slid a finger along her slit under her panties and found her clit. He was rewarded with a throaty gasp. "What if I made him promise to be gentle?" He went to his knees and spread her legs. He gripped the flimsy material of her panties with his teeth and tugged until they tore. Sadie groaned when his tongue found her clit. Her breathing came in short pants and firmed his cock. The wolf growled with satisfaction at the tang of her. Elijah flicked his tongue over her bud as she pressed herself into him. It took all of him to keep pleasuring her instead of sinking himself into her pussy. He slowed his strokes as she moved her hips faster.

"Elijah."

He nearly lost himself as the wolf took control of his body to flick its tongue along her folds and taste more of her before pushing his tongue inside her. He almost fought for control back, but he felt the wolf. It didn't want to hurt Sadie, only tantalize her. That meant it heard her about taking it slow and wanted to obey her wishes. He had never known his wolf to back down for anyone. He went back and forth between her clit and her pussy, teasing until her nails pressed into his scalp and she was crying. This was how she needed to be treated, revered and pleasured, kept safe and loved above all else.

"S-stop. I can't... Elijah." She gripped his shoulders for support.

He licked his lips. "I love how you taste. How you say my name when you come. Let me treat you as a queen. Say you'll be mine."

"Aren't I already?"

* * *

Elijah asked her to be his and all she could do was say yes. All her emotions were rolled into a ball, but she trusted him. She wanted him in her life because he filled a part of her that remained empty. The way he'd looked at her ever since he got to her apartment and the night before at the party had been what convinced her. He hadn't stopped looking at her even when her hair was all over the place. She hadn't brushed her teeth and she was in the tattered nightgown she'd had since college. He didn't care about any of that. Elijah kissed the inside of her thighs and sucked on her skin. He pressed his teeth into her flesh but didn't break the skin. The little bit of pain made her want him inside her all the more. It drove her hunger to taste him and feel his skin sliding along hers. Elijah fanned his hands along her stomach, brushed his fingers over her breasts. She pulled her nightgown off and tossed it to the ground.

"Come here." She led him back to her bedroom. He tried to kiss her again, but she held up her hand. His expression turned into a sad puppy that had been scolded. She glanced around the room and saw something that gave her an idea.

"What did I do?"

"Nothing. But it's my turn." She pulled his shirt from his pants. "Aren't I allowed to want you, too?" She cupped his cock and flashed him a smile. Elijah finished undressing. His dick pointed at her ready for her. She pulled his belt from his pants.

"What are you going to do with that?"

"Put your hands behind your back."

"Sadie, I don't think that's such a good idea."

She heard the trepidation in his voice. Narissa told her Elijah was an alpha, the pack leader, and dominant male among the wolves. Everyone had to defer to him when he made a decision. He was used to being obeyed. But she wasn't about to take orders from him now. He didn't move. She grabbed one of his arms and felt the fight in him to give up his control to her. Sadie kissed his back and felt him relax some. When she stood on tiptoe and bit the curve of his shoulder, a shudder went through him and made him loosen up. She took the advantage and tied his hands behind his back. He was strong, she knew, and figured he could break out of he wanted, but he stood still.

Sadie ran her hands over his back, learning the bends of his flesh and ass. She took her time, enjoying how he quivered under her touch. Sadie wrapped her arms around his sides and pressed herself upon him. She planted kisses along his neck and touched his chest. He tried to move his hands and touch her, but she stepped away. Sadie guided him over to the bed.

"You're not making this very easy," he growled.

"That's the point. If you want this to work, then you have to know I'm not going to bow to your every whim."

"If you become like me, then sometimes you might have to."

She shrugged. "We'll see. Right now, you're not bossing me around. Lie down on the bed."

Elijah flashed her an annoyed look but sat down on the bed. Sadie reached between his legs and fingered his balls. He arched his back but kept his gaze on her. He tried to shimmy closer to her, but she went to her knees and took his firm shaft into her mouth. He jumped and nearly choked her, but she grabbed hold of him and eased him back out. She wrapped her tongue around his length and teased him. She dragged her teeth along his sensitive skin and around his spongy head.

"Sadie…" He nearly howled her name.

She enjoyed his struggle against his tied hands. Sadie slowed until he thrust his dick into her, trying to make her go faster. She pulled it out relishing the power she wielded over him. He moaned and pumped his hips upward. The salty essence of his pre-come lingered on her tongue. When she looked up, his eyes were glazed over with pleasure and she was ready to feel him inside her. Sadie straddled him and dragged her fingers over the silver scars. She could feel the slight roughness of the metal mixed with the flesh. She took one nipple into her mouth and stroked his shaft with the other hand.

"Enough."

"I don't think so. I'm not ready yet."

Elijah growled. Before she knew it, she was on her stomach with Elijah behind her. His hot breath blasted on her neck. His fingers ran along the lines of her scars. It brought back images of her being attacked. "No. Stop. Please."

"What?" The mood broke and she wound into a ball. "What did I do?"

"You can't do that." She tried not to let her voice get shaky or feel scared knowing he wasn't going to hurt her.

"Love, forgive me, I got lost in the moment." He lay down next to her and stroked her unmarked back. He kissed her shoulder and her throat. "I'm sorry. I didn't mean to hurt you."

"I know. It was a flashback."

"I'd never mean you harm." Elijah kissed her. "Do you still want…"

Sadie returned the kiss and twined their hands together. *He's not going to hurt me. I need to remember that.* Her pulsed slowed as she took a few calming breaths. She still needed him. The desire hadn't left. "Come here. Slowly."

"Of course."

She wrapped her leg around his hip. Elijah entered her and hit her clit. His eyes never left hers as they moved together. Sadie could feel as he dipped inside her, inch by excruciating inch. Heat seared her nerves. She tried to hold onto to her sanity. He claimed her lips once more and gripped her ass until they moved together. He broke the kiss and moaned. He rested his forehead against hers.

"The wolf wants to claim you, Sadie." His face shifted.

Sadie stretched as she was building to the climax of their lovemaking. "No. If you love me as you say, then you won't bite me. I'm not ready for that." She cried out as he thrust into her again.

Elijah stretched out his neck. "Bite me. Hard."

As his fingers dug into her shoulders, she knew she had to do this to appease his wolf. She bit into Elijah's throat until she tasted blood. He cried out as she licked his wound. Elijah hit her clit once more and she also came. They collapsed on the bed still entwined. He kissed her shoulder and nibbled on it a bit more.

"I'm sorry. He wants you more than I can control. I know what we said, but he does have a mind of his own. Biting me shows that you've claimed us. I think it'll placate him for now." He pushed the hair from her eyes.

"What does that mean exactly?"

He kissed her nose. "It means you won't seek out any other mates. Like you said before, you were mine. This cements it a bond between us. You tasted blood. You tasted our essence. Just like I tasted you the first time I kissed you. I didn't mean to scare you before. Being tied up like that, I lost it. I'm not used to not being in control."

"I noticed."

"Maybe we can try it again where we don't get carried away."

She laughed. "I'm not sure that can happen. I've missed you more than I thought I did. I'm still trying to work it out from the past. You ate my fiancé. It took me a long time to get the strength to get out of bed. Greyson was my rock and then having nothing left, not even to bury. It messed me up."

"I know and I'm here to work it out with you. After all, I'm the cause of it. I'm so sorry."

Sadie snuggled against him and kissed his throat. She loved the taste of him. "I know." Elijah wrapped her in his arms and held her. When she was with him, all was right in the world. He would protect her from any danger and help her through her nightmares. Together, the future held so many possibilities. Even if he was a billionaire who ate her fiancé. She couldn't hold that against him forever, could she?

Hungry Fur You (Billionaire Werewolf 2)
Crymsyn Hart

Sadie Matthews thought she had it all figured out with her sexy werewolf billionaire, Elijah Dane. However, she's bitten by another wolf who thinks Sadie is her rival. Waking up from her transformation, Sadie finds herself in Luke's cabin. Sexy as hell, it's all Sadie can do to keep her paws off him because she knows Luke is her mate as well as Elijah. What's a girl to do with two smokin' werewolves?

Luke never expected to find a mate in the middle of the forest. When he first catches Sadie's scent, he knows he'll do anything to have her. But first, he must return her to Elijah, then deal with dissension in his pack.

Can both men satisfy Sadie's new desires? Will she give in to the beast inside? And can Elijah and Luke see eye to eye when it comes to sharing their new mate?

Chapter One

"How's Elijah doing?" Narissa asked.

Sadie looked up from her meal and tried to hide her smile. The last year had been a whirlwind. Her relationship with her werewolf lover had been rocky at first, but it had evened out as they both got to know one another, and their boundaries were set on how far she could go. "It's good."

"Good. You look happier than I've seen you in a long time."

"I wasn't the one who disappeared for six months."

"Didn't have a choice. There was some upheaval in the Fairy realm. Time runs differently there. I needed to get things back in order."

"Everything okay over there?" Sadie asked. Now she knew her friend was a Fairy, she could ask her all kinds of questions. For years, Narissa had kept her true self a mystery. When they'd met in college, she'd introduced herself as Melissa.

"Nothing for you to worry about. I'm not sure even why they called me back since they don't like I'm of mixed blood."

"It had to have been important. Want to talk about it? We've always shared everything."

Narissa poked at her food. "I know. I never told you everything before because I didn't know how you'd deal with it."

"I can deal with it. I'm dating the werewolf who killed my fiancé. So spill."

"Most Fairies don't exist in this realm. We broke from the humans long ago. Those who do -- we keep ourselves closed off. I'm not the only shifter among the Fae. It seems a couple of them have gone missing. They thought I might know where they were."

"Did you find them?"

Her friend pushed her plate away and a look of

disgust soured her expression. "We found parts of them. They were dissected. They had the stench of humans. The Fae don't think it's an isolated incident."

"That's horrible."

"Indeed. Enough about me, I didn't come to talk to get you down. I've been trying to get in touch with you, but it's crazy. New job. New place. I told you my protection would bring you good things."

"Yeah, you did. It makes Elijah jealous. It's kinda funny to watch when we're out and random men come up to me."

"Wolves are protective of their mates, but you haven't let him make you furry yet."

She sipped her wine and glanced at the calendar. Elijah was out of town until after the full moon. "I'm not there yet."

"When do you think you'll get there? He's not going to let you stay human forever. Wolves have a long lifespan."

She held up her hand to silence Narissa. "I know. We've already discussed it."

"Do you have an idea when you might let him turn you?"

"Will it be hindered by your mark?"

"Not at all, it might make you stick out a little bit more. I can't take it back. Besides, I want to be sure to throw you an epic party when you get all hairy. Then we can hunt together and I don't have to be so dainty with you."

"I'm sure you'll be happy about that."

"I'm happy that you're happy. I mean it. You're working for a company that's mostly shifters."

"Yeah. They shut down for the full moon so it makes it better."

"What does Elijah say about you working?"

"Like he can control me."

Narissa gave her a hug and kissed her on the cheek. "Make sure you keep doing that because once he thinks he can bend you to his will as an alpha, he won't stop."

Sadie returned the hug. "Don't worry about that. He knows that I'm not going to bow down to him in any form."

A plant rustled next to them and a tall man stepped out from behind it. The texture of his skin appeared to be a blend of bark and flesh. He leaned in and said something to Narissa. She paled.

"Shit. I gotta run. Not sure how long I'm going to be. Gotta go back to Fairy. You two should use my place. Bye, hun." Narissa waved and popped out, leaving a faint trail of glitter.

Sadie cleaned up and sat down on the sofa, wishing Elijah were with her. He had taken to working from home with her. When it came to the pack, he rarely discussed that part of his life. Her decision not to become a wolf hampered their relationship. Sometimes she felt like the dirty secret he kept hidden in the closet. She glanced at the moon and felt the pull of it herself. Being with him, she had begun to understand the power it had over the shifters.

Maybe I am ready. They both knew it was coming and a condition of their relationship. It always surprised him she hadn't already turned from the two attacks she had already endured. First, Elijah attacking her two years ago when he killed her fiancé, Greyson, and ate him. He had tackled her and clawed her back. He claimed the wolf realized she was his mate then, but he didn't know it until later. The second time she had been mauled by a wolf in another pack, but Elijah rescued her.

His wolf grew more insistent that it wanted her to join him. Sadie loved him beyond measure. It didn't matter he was a billionaire CEO of a large company or controlled the largest pack in five states. All she wanted was him. However, each time during their lovemaking, her fear that he would bite her arose. The strain had started to show on their relationship, forcing a distance between them. Tonight he and the pack would all be gathered at the resort. Sadie had never been happier except for the growing tension between her and Elijah. He wasn't about to let her go, and she loved him too much to lose him.

At the very heart of the matter, she was afraid. Afraid she would become a bloodthirsty beast that wanted to feast on innocents. She didn't want that to be her. She couldn't imagine bringing the fear and the hurt to someone the way it had happened to her losing Greyson. Her fiancé would want her to be happy. Sadie didn't know if he would understand shape shifters and Fairies. He would encourage her to take charge of her life and not live in fear. The way he always did. She'd been putting the decision off for so long, it had become the ugly beast in the room. Her stomach tightened in anticipation. Sadie grabbed a bag and threw some things inside it. She couldn't wait to see the look on Elijah's face when she got to the resort. Her resolve tightened.

There wasn't any going back.

Three hours later she arrived at the resort. Sadie parked her car, grabbed her bag, and walked into the place that had changed her life. Even though it was late, the same young man who had given her a headache the first time she had been there was behind the desk.

"Good evening, Ms. Matthews."

"You remember me?"

The other man smiled. "Yes. It's because of you that I have a position with the pack."

"That's wonderful." That was something she didn't know. "Is Elijah here?"

"Mr. Dane is out with the rest of the pack. Does he know you're coming? It's not really safe for you to be walking around the grounds tonight."

"I'm here to surprise him. Can you let me into his room?"

"I'm not supposed to."

"Trust me. You really want to."

He glanced around and then nodded. "Okay. Come on, but we have to be quick. It wasn't me."

"Of course."

The clerk brought her up to the penthouse suite where she had stayed before. It happened to be Elijah's room. He opened the door and then let her in. She dug into her purse and handed him a tip. "For your trouble."

He shook his head. "Can't. It wouldn't be right, considering who you are."

"Thanks, but really. You could get into trouble."

"Okay. I appreciate it."

He closed the door and left her alone. Elijah's strong scent blanketed the room. It helped to calm her nerves. She didn't know how he would react to seeing her. Her stomach roiled. She wanted this to go smoothly. Sadie freshened up in the bathroom and sat on the bed in a nightgown she had bought for a special occasion. She glanced at the clock. Three-thirty in the morning. The only thing keeping her going this far was the adrenaline. The longer she sat there, the more she fought to stay awake.

Her eyes opened when a howl split the room. It instantly brought her back to the night Elijah first attacked her, but she shook that off, knowing he wouldn't hurt her. A chorus of others joined in. She peeked out the window to see dozens of wolves racing off, back into the woods or to their hotel rooms. She set herself back up on the bed and smoothed her nightie. The door clicked and Elijah laughed. Then she heard a shrill giggle. Her heart ran cold. She got up and went into the living space to find

Elijah naked and kissing another woman. Her hands trailed over his back and his cupped her ass. Sadie swallowed a sob. *This is what he's been keeping secret from me.* The woman broke away and growled. Elijah glanced between the two of them. The woman lunged at Sadie. She yelped and slammed the door before the woman could get to her.

"Who is that human?" the woman spat.

"Denice, you'd better go."

Sadie tried to keep it together. Showing fear to the wolves only made her an appetizer. She swallowed her dread and opened the door, not even able to look at Elijah. "Yes, *Denice*, you'd better leave."

"You let a human give you orders, Pack Master?"

"Denice, let's continue this discussion tomorrow."

The woman glared at Sadie while she kissed Elijah and he pressed against her. Sadie bit her lip to keep from losing it until the wolf smirked and sauntered out. Elijah turned to her with a venomous look.

"Do you know what you've done, you bitch?"

Before Sadie could even think she slapped him as hard as she could. "You don't ever call me that. I don't care who you are or what wolf thing I fucked up. You're supposed to be my mate and I'm yours. You told me that was sacred among wolves, a bond that couldn't be broken."

He rubbed his jaw. "What is pack business is none of yours. Mate bonds are sacred among wolves, but you're *not* a wolf. She is wolf and we are to be mated."

This was not the man she knew. Something was going on with him. Maybe it was one of the reasons the rift between them had widened. She took a deep breath and felt a calm come over her that hadn't been there before. The butterflies in her stomach flew away, leaving her clearheaded. "Why do you think I came up here, genius?"

She gathered her things and got dressed again. Elijah stood in silence, but he didn't move from the doorway. "Let me by. I'm tired and you're being a dick."

"Prove it."

"Prove what?"

"That you wish to be mated, truly as a wolf."

"You want me to cower before you, *Pack Master*? Bare my throat to you after what I just saw? I don't think so. My coming here should be proof enough of how I feel -- felt -- about you. This person is not the man I fell in love with. I know I've been reluctant to change, but you *know* why. I've never gone behind your back with another man. All bets are off." She pushed past him and this time he moved aside.

She made it to her car and then the emotions overwhelmed her. The man she loved had made it perfectly clear she meant nothing to him because she was human. *Fine. If that's how he feels, fuck him.* She wiped her eyes and gripped the steering wheel.

"Sadie." Elijah knocked on her window.

"No."

"I can explain. Please, I love you…"

She gunned the engine and headed into the night, hot tears burning her face. She didn't care where she was going, as long as it was away from him. As she drove through the dense woods heading back to civilization, Sadie thought she heard a series of howls around her. *I'm tired and freaked out.* A streak of silver dashed before her car. Sadie slammed on the brakes and jerked the wheel. She held on for dear life as the car went across the road and flipped over into a ditch, landing right side up.

"Oh shit. Oh shit," she whispered as she realized she was alive. From the light of one headlight she could see the steam coming from the engine. The car was toast. She slowly tried to move everything. Besides feeling like she'd hit a brick wall, she was okay. She undid the seat belt and scrambled out of the car as her ankle buckled. Warmth flowed from her forehead. Sadie hobbled up the embankment and came face-to-face with a gray wolf. She tried to back away, but another wolf blocked her way. The gray wolf smiled. Sadie felt like they had met before. The shifter shimmered and grew back into a woman.

"Denice." She blurted out and felt the pain in her chest from where the seat belt had cut into her.

"You remember me."

"I really don't have time for this."

The other woman chuckled. "Have time? Sweetie, you're going to have all the time in the world. You wanted to play at being with a wolf, now you get to truly be one." Denice shifted back into a wolf in the blink of an eye.

Sadie tried to get away, but the other wolf snapped at her from behind. Before she knew it, a great pain clamped around her leg. Denice met her eyes and then crunched. Sadie screamed. The wolves howled and ran off into the darkness. Denice had broken her leg with the bite. It wasn't the break that worried her. A sudden burning pain shot up her body and ignited every part of her into agony. She thought she heard the rambling of an engine, but blackness took over and she followed it down.

Chapter Two

Elijah's spirits sank watching Sadie drive off. Her words stung, but what he said to her crippled his heart. He didn't know how to fix what he had done. He walked back inside and resisted the urge to go after her. He had to remain through the weekend with the pack because he had business to finish. Denice was part of that business.

Jake, the newest member of the pack, stared at him with accusing eyes. He didn't need the young wolf's judgment. Elijah grabbed a bottle of bourbon from the bar and took a long drink. The bite of the alcohol didn't do anything to ease the fuckup that just occurred. Sadie had come up and was going to give herself to him. He shut his eyes against the image of her face when she saw him and Denice together. The betrayal in her eyes. Elijah threw the bottle across the room, but the explosion of glass and liquor didn't ease the empty pit in his soul.

"Make you feel better?" the voice of the resort's therapist cut through a bit of his rage.

"Some."

"I take it Ms. Matthews found out about your tail."

"I'm not in the mood for a lecture, doc."

"I'm not here to give you one, just a piece of friendly advice."

"And an 'I told you so'."

The shrink shrugged. "You said it, not me."

Elijah ran his hand through his hair and looked at the strange, small woman. He had sat down with her a few months ago about his problems with his wolf. It had grown impatient with Sadie and didn't understand her reluctance to join him.

"I fucked up. I don't know how to fix it."

"Do you love Ms. Matthews or was it all some elaborate game?"

"She's my mate. I can't breathe without the thought of her."

"Yet you've been going behind her back with this other woman, a born wolf."

"I haven't fucked her in either form, but..."

"You've wanted to because she doesn't hold you back the way Ms. Matthews does, and she is part of some treaty too, I understand. Do you love this female?"

Having a mate wasn't supposed to be this complicated. "No, I don't love this female wolf. Our mating would unite our packs. I don't have to hold back with her. But I love Sadie. She's my other half."

"Then what are you doing here with me? If you love her, go after her."

"I can't. I have to stay here with the rest of the pack. They'll know something's wrong if I bolt. The treaty I'm about to enter into will be null and void. I can't do that. Mating with Denice will unite us and give the pack more territory. It works into the accord we signed a year ago."

The therapist got off the stool and sighed. "Mr. Dane, whatever this resentment you have stemming from your wolf, remember that it's not just him. Sometimes, you have to go against everything you are to get the one thing you truly want. If you love Ms. Matthews, then you should risk anything to claim her. I get the marriage of convenience, but you'd have to explain that to Ms. Matthews also. Did either of you claim one another as a mate?"

"I always refrained from biting her even in human form in case it changed her. I've nipped her from time to time, but nothing serious. She bit me several times and..." Elijah shook from pleasure remembering Sadie sinking her teeth into him. The last time they had made love had been a little bit rougher, but she had initiated it. It aroused him, but left him frustrated when he wasn't able to bite her back. The wolf was irritated, too. It wanted Sadie running through the woods and hunting with it. It made his other half question if Sadie was the right one for them. His life had been turned on its head. He never thought Sadie would be his mate when he first met her. Then the wolf demanded she was. Elijah couldn't share anything about the pack with Sadie because she wasn't pack. It began to drive a rift between them.

It started six months ago when the wolf came out while they made love. It wanted to bite her and fuck her. The look of dread in her eyes and his willpower had driven it back. She apologized, but the wolf had enough of her fear and waiting. It wanted a female to share its life with. Elijah tried to explain. He knew the beast loved Sadie and wanted to protect her, but then Denice came along. She was all wolf and knew how to strut. She came with a deal from the Shadow Clan pack. Mate with her and the two packs would settle their differences and abide by the conclave's new terms for the region. Denice was everything Sadie was not, but Elijah wasn't into her.

Elijah needed some time alone to talk to his beast. He wandered outside and listened to the quiet. It was close to morning, but it was still quiet. He sank into a chair, listened to the chirping crickets and the few birds, and closed his eyes. He relaxed until he could feel the wolf inside his mind and they came to a meeting place where they could speak. His beast stood before him, more of a man than a beast. Seeing the creature this way unnerved him.

"You look different," Elijah said.

"We're becoming one. It makes it easier to take this form. Soon we will be merged completely. We will be of one mind."

"You can certainly communicate better."

"I don't care for this banter. You've come about Sadie."

"She's our mate."

The wolf huffed. Elijah could see the confusion on its face and feel it welling up in his chest at the same time. It was having difficulty processing its feelings about her. "We love her."

"Yes. I feel incomplete without her," Elijah told his other half.

"She is not wolf."

"She was going to be. She came to us to become wolf. We screwed it up. She claimed us. We've tasted her blood. She's our mate. Isn't that how it goes in either form? If you love her, then we don't need Denice."

The eyes of the wolf glowed golden and its form wavered. It huffed and shook its head. "Even bitten to become wolf, she might not be accepted among others in the pack. We can't show weakness. We can't see her hurt. Denice will not be hurt. Will not hate us if she doesn't love us when the deed is done."

Elijah finally understood. "You've been trying to push her away. That's why you don't want to share anything about the pack with her."

"Yes. As I said, we both love her. Denice is the better choice."

"Maybe she is, but I don't care for her. She's not right for the pack. In the end, I think she would try to manipulate us. Sadie is our mate. You and I both know that. We have to give her the chance to see what kind of a wolf she's going to become. Don't you think?"

The wolf ran a hand through its hair mirroring the gesture that Elijah always did. "Yes. Is there still a chance to be mates?"

Elijah sighed, thinking about the damage that had been done. She had seen him naked with Denice, kissing her, almost ready to have sex. The urge had been there to claim the other woman, but it hadn't gotten that far. It never had because Elijah didn't want Denice that way. Sadie had already been through so much. "I don't know, but not if we stay here."

"Then we must get her. Make her understand and

welcome her as wolf."

"Easier said than done."

"But we must make her see. We must make apologies."

"We'll try."

Elijah snapped awake from the mediation when he heard giggling and footsteps. He sat behind a potted plant and listened to the conversation between Denice and another man from Denice's pack.

"Did you see the look on her face?" the big man said.

"It was priceless. She's going to wish she never fucked with me. Who does she think she is?"

Elijah clenched his fists. *They have to be talking about Sadie.*

"Why are you going through with this? You and I are already mated. Don't you know how this makes me feel?" The other man swept Denice up in his arms and kissed her. Denice kissed him back with the same hunger Elijah felt for Sadie. His wolf clenched his teeth. Any affection it had for Denice vanished.

"Nick, I didn't have a choice. Alpha's wishes. Even I can't go against that."

"Where is your brother anyway?" Nick asked, running his hands through Denice's hair.

"He's off communing with his inner beast or some shit. I don't know. He sticks more to the old ways and mythologies than I do. I think we're one of the only packs left that has a shaman."

"You could rule the pack much better than him. He needs to bring it into the modern age."

"Don't I know it. But that's not how it works with us. You know that. Besides, he doesn't know about you and me." Denice kissed his lips.

"If he did, what would he be able to do? He can't stop us from being mates. It's the oldest law among us."

"I know, and I'll tell him. I've never slept with Elijah.

You know that. You're the one who's in my heart, baby."

"But you wanted to. Is he a good kisser?"

"Why don't you ask him yourself, *Nick*?" Elijah stepped out from behind the plant.

Denice paled and dropped from Nick's arms. "Elijah, I didn't realize you were there."

"You and he are mated?"

Nick pushed Denice behind him. "That's right."

"It's good to know. This goes against everything I was told. Your alpha isn't going to be happy about this."

Denice scoffed. "You didn't reveal your human. How's that going to look when I tell your whole pack?"

"Tell them whatever you want. She won't be a secret much longer."

"That's for sure." Denice's grin widened.

"What did you do?" Elijah seethed.

"You don't have to worry about her being human anymore," Denice revealed.

Elijah lost it. He and the wolf both had the same goal in mind, and it was to make sure Denice paid for whatever she'd done to Sadie. Nick lunged at him, but Elijah shoved him out of the way and had Denice by the throat. His vision turned red. All he could think about was Sadie. What did they do to her? Where was she? Was she suffering? The woman he loved had run out of his life, and Denice had turned her against her will. It wasn't until he was pulled off Denice that he came back to himself. Nick had gone for help and come back with Chris, his second, and Jake.

"Enough," Chris said to him.

Elijah put up his hands and walked away, pacing as though he were caged. Denice struggled to take in a breath. "You'll pay for that."

"Elijah." Chris pulled him aside. He growled at his second. Chris bowed his head and looked down. It calmed him enough he could think.

"I need you to lead the pack and watch them. They aren't going home until I can get a hold of their alpha."

"What's going on, Elijah?" Chris asked him.

"They've hurt my mate."

Chris's eyes held his surprise, but it seemed like his second knew something was up. The whole pack probably knew something was up. "About time you admitted that human was your mate. We've all been hoping this bitch wouldn't be your first choice."

It was his time to be surprised. "You knew about Sadie?"

"Sure did. We were waiting to see what you'd do. You're our Pack Master. I've seen you with the woman. She seems strong and she makes you happy. I'll make sure these two don't go anywhere. Go get your rightful mate."

Elijah nodded. He let the wolf take over and raced down the road. She couldn't have gone far. Denice and her mate hadn't been gone that long. He caught the smell of smoke and saw a fire burning. A dark bloom of black smoke came up. Flashing lights lit up the night. He darted into the thick woods so he wouldn't be seen. Sadie's car was in the ditch on the opposite side of the road. The windshield was cracked and the passenger-side door looked crushed. He got as close as he could and caught a whiff of blood. A lot of blood. He tracked the scent away from the car where he detected the aroma of Denice and Nick. He could almost see what they did.

God. What have I done? Where is she?

The wolf didn't have an answer for that. Elijah put his nose to the ground and followed the blood. She'd stopped somewhere along the way and must have fallen because of the impression of her body.

Where did you go?

He caught the trail of another man. He followed it up to the road and then lost both scents. Relief went through him. *Someone found her and brought her to the hospital.* He raced back to the hotel. Elijah felt a bit of comfort knowing that. The drive to be in her arms again and feel as though he were home spurred him on. As he ran, he knew he had to do some major ass-kissing to make up for what he had done. *She has to understand. I wasn't doing it to hurt her. I only wanted to protect her. I swear. I'll do anything it takes to make this right.*

* * *

Sadie opened her eyes but could barely focus. Burning pains shot through her body and radiated to all her limbs. Every time she thought she could fight her way back out of the foggy world she lived in, she was dragged back down. In a small window of clarity, a man hovered over her. His words made no sense and his features blurred. His tone soothed her. She kept surfacing and dipping back down into the strangest dream. The last time she fell into the vision and away from the heat of her body, Sadie found herself in a clearing with the full moon overhead.

The air was still, but she could feel the cool dew on her arms. The sweet scent of jasmine lingered on the breeze. It felt like a real place. Her thoughts lingered on Elijah. She was still pissed at him, but her love for him never seemed to be stronger. The thought of that other woman with her paws wrapped around him and her lips on his fueled her rage. The one who did this to her would pay. A growl came from out of nowhere. The shadows drifted together into the form of a wolf. It was silver in the light with crisp green eyes, not Elijah's golden amber eyes. It kept its gaze on her and the terror died away. The beast approached her and licked her face.

Sadie slipped her fingers through the rough fur. "You are beautiful."

Thank you.

She jerked her hand away and felt a familiar feeling as though she knew the voice.

There's no need to be frightened. The wolf bumped her knee with her head. She could feel the weight of the beast and smell it. *We're now part of one another.*

It all slammed back to her. Denice bit her, forcing her to become like them. "Are you what I turn into?"

Yes. You were going to ask our mate to do this anyway.

She wasn't sure about Elijah. "Really? How do you know after... what he did to us? After what we walked into."

The wolf nudged her with its nose. *I know. Give him a chance. Give me a chance. I know you're afraid. I know all of you are because we're one.*

Before Sadie could answer the wolf, she felt a jolt. The clearing fell away and she opened her eyes. She was in a bedroom. The room was small and wood-paneled with a chest in the corner and a chair. A man had his feet propped up on the end of the bed in heavy boots that still looked wet. He wore a navy plaid shirt, dark jeans, and a hat pulled over his eyes. It couldn't hide the long brown beard that rested on the top of his shirt. He snored. His hand dropped from his lap as his head lolled to the side. Sadie held in a giggle. Then she looked down and realized she was naked. She held the sheet to her body and tried not to move. She felt her head. It didn't feel like she had been in an accident. Something about her body seemed more dialed in than before. Denice had bitten her leg and broken it. She thought about her toes and could wiggle them without pain. Pale scars dappled her leg where Denice had bitten her. It made her regret not sharing this with Elijah. He had told her he would be there for her to go through the change. Instead some stranger had watched over her.

"Your leg was broken pretty badly. You're lucky I set it and your healing ability kicked in."

Sadie jumped when she heard the man's low voice. The tone hit something in her that made her quiver in a way she didn't really understand. He pushed up his hat and stared at her with electric blue eyes. "Thanks for helping me. I-I was in a car accident and hit my head. I really don't remember --" The one rule she learned from Elijah was not to reveal anything about shifters.

He gave her a stern look. "You don't need to bullshit me. I know you're a wolf because I'm also one. Go ahead and freak out now about it. You're a werewolf. Scream, cry, hit something, or whatever. Once you're on your feet, then I can release you back into the wild."

He thinks I'm the victim of some random bite by night or was going to be dinner to some errant werewolves. She pulled her leg back under the sheet. Every time she breathed, something enticing roused her desire. She pushed it away and stared at him while he waited for her to have her hysterical breakdown. "Don't worry. I'm not going to freak out."

She got the slightest hint of emotion from him. It seemed to be surprise, but she wasn't sure. His beard hid so much of his face. "Good to know. You were touch-and-go there for a couple days. The fever gripped you and brought you deep. I wasn't sure you would emerge from the shadows. It seemed something might've been interfering with the bite."

"I bet it was Narissa."

"What is a Narissa?"

"She's my friend and a Fairy shifter. She marked me with her protection so I wouldn't be on the menu for any more shifters."

"Fairies? That might explain a few things."

"What do you mean?"

"Listen."

Sadie listened but didn't hear anything at first. She shook her head. He sighed and sat on the bed. "Close your eyes and use your senses."

She closed her eyes and strained. In the distance, she heard the steady thud of a drum. His heart. The longer she listened, the more she could make out the beats. However, beyond the walls of the cabin, something sounded offbeat and played a tune that called to her. "I hear it, and something else. Chanting. It's faint."

"Chanting? That's not possible."

"There's a man singing. I can't tell. Does that have something to do with the Fairies?" *Now that I'm a werewolf does that mean I could hear into that realm?*

"No. If she's your friend, then maybe you can get her to pick you up. Forget about the drumming and the chanting. It's nothing."

"I have no way to contact her."

He placed his hand on her thigh. Her eyes snapped open. She felt a pull toward him she had only ever experienced with Elijah. The wolf shifted within, urging her to touch him. Sadie didn't fight the other presence of the awakened animal. His earthy scent stirred a hunger in her that she only felt with Elijah. The aroma made her hunger for him. Sadie felt the sudden need to sniff him. Maybe if she licked him, then it would satisfy this sudden desire. She nearly tasted his flesh with her tongue. Instead she ran her nose along his neck. His scent made her body ache.

"Hey, watch it," he barked.

Sadie flinched, but met his eyes. "Sorry. I don't know what came over me."

"Forget it. You're new. Never approach a Pack Master that way or an alpha. It could get your throat ripped out. You have to show respect to those higher than you. Right now, everyone is higher than you because you have no pack and lone wolves aren't looked at favorably."

"Oh, good to know. How do I know someone is an alpha or a Pack Master?"

"You can tell by feeling. It's a knowing once you're around the wolves long enough. You can't disobey the

Pack Master who gives you orders or another alpha unless you're one yourself."

"I'm stubborn and don't like to be bossed around."

His eyes narrowed. "You won't have a choice. Back away."

An overwhelming urge to cower and retreat from him came over her, but she wasn't going anywhere. Pack Master or Alpha. This man was not going to make her do anything. The wolf wanted to listen to this man, but Sadie wasn't going to let being a werewolf change the very core of herself. He wanted her to obey, but she held on. The wolf stepped up, more sure of itself, and gave her its strength, learning to trust her.

"I don't think so."

"Back away." He put more of a growl into it and gnashed his teeth.

The skin on his face rippled so she could see the beast beneath. The more he oozed alpha, the more it felt like a physical force hit her, forcing her back, trying to make her bend to its will. She set her teeth and felt a growl roll over her tongue. As the energy came over her, so did his scent. All wolf. She couldn't help the utter wanting that flooded her. The tension between them sparked something. Before she could understand what was happening, her lips found his in a kiss she had only shared with Elijah. His fingers wound through her hair as she pulled at his shirt trying to get to the flesh beneath. All her senses were dialed into him. He smelled like earth and pine with a dab of cloves. His tongue pushed against hers as she caught his lip between her teeth and nibbled on it, tasting blood. Once the blood hit her tongue, she groaned.

His hands roved over her body, taking her in. She couldn't get to his flesh fast enough and tugged at his pants needing to feel him inside her. He broke the kiss and trailed his nose along her neck the way she had done with him. She shuddered from the pleasure of it and finally understood what it was like for Elijah being with her. Sadie didn't understand the primal need to be with this man she didn't know. Both sides of her knew they had to be with him. He yanked the rest of the sheet back, exposing her. His nails dug into her back, and the pain felt good. He claimed her lips once more in a fast kiss, but ripped away.

"We shouldn't do this." His chest heaved as he stood up.

Sadie felt the wolf slip into her nature. It didn't push her back, but she let it take the lead. She crawled over the blankets and cocked her head. "Is that what you really want? I know you feel it, too."

He shook his head as if trying to snap himself out of the attraction that stirred between then. "You're new. You don't know what this means."

"The body might be new, but I'm as ancient as the trees. You told me to back away. Now I'm telling you to come here. I hear the drum of your heart and know you're from the Shadow clan." The wolf knew what it said was true. Energy flushed through her and it moved outward. Her savior clenched his fists trying to fight her pull. Sweat appeared on his brow as he came back onto the bed.

"Do you truly know what this is between us?" he asked, his voice filled with a bit of awe.

She wrapped her arms around his neck and kissed him slowly as the passion for him grew, and the wolf slipped back a little. The wolf led this exchange and she knew it was right. He moved his tongue along her throat and nipped at her flesh. Sadie groaned. She felt this with Elijah and knew this couldn't be denied. Sadie slipped her fingers through his hair while he undid the buttons of his shirt. She bit him, harder, tasting the sweat and salt of his skin. When she got to the meat of his shoulder, her teeth shifted in her mouth. She ran her tongue over her sharper canines. The wolf waited impatiently for her to catch up. Her savior shifted his mouth to the same spot on her neck. She nipped once more.

"I claim you as my mate." Sadie bit deep into his flesh. The blood rushed over her tongue, and he bit her in response. She licked the wound as his tongue dragged over his bite. Each stroke of that sandy texture made the need for him beyond belief. She pushed his jeans down and this time he didn't fight her. Sadie straddled him and guided his firm cock inside her. He gripped her shoulders, sucking in a nipple until he bit down. She screamed as it felt like every fiber of her body was tuned to this man and how he touched her. She was so close to coming it almost hurt with joy. The wolf reveled in this closeness with its new mate. His smell bathed her as he thrust into her.

Her mate nipped her ear. "What's your name?"

"Sadie. Yours?"

"Luke."

She rolled the name around in her mind as he hit her clit. "Harder, Luke."

He obliged and held her ass as they moved together. "Sadie." Her name came out as a half a howl and she answered it. The ecstasy of their joining rocketed her into another world as they collapsed on the bed.

Luke kissed her stomach and touched her. Her wolf was satisfied with this arrangement. As she trailed her fingers through Luke's chest hair, she thought about Elijah. He had very little hair on his chest. An emptiness lingered without Elijah. It seemed like he needed to be there too, even though she was still pissed at him.

The wolf bumped its head against her mind to get her attention. *He's in for a surprise.*

You said Elijah was our mate, but how can Luke be, too?

It just is.

What was that about him being Shadow Clan and the

drum?

It's hard to explain. I just knew his clan. We wolves all come from various clans to make up the packs. The drums and chanting are something beyond me.

What about him obeying us?

The wolf didn't have an answer for that.

"Hey, where did you go?" Luke asked. The concern in his voice surprised her.

"Sorry. I was thinking about all this."

"Yeah. Pretty fucked-up. I certainly didn't expect you when I picked you up off the road. What were you thinking about?"

"My other mate."

"Your other mate? Who the fuck is that? Don't you think you should've told me before we fucked?" Luke got up and pulled up his jeans. "Shit!" He slammed his fist against the wall.

Sadie jumped. "Do you think it would've made a difference?"

He glanced at her over his shoulder. His icy glare, even though pissed-off, still turned her on. Luke gripped the bedpost. "No. I don't think it would have."

"D-do you...? Never mind." Sadie shook her head not sure how to ask this man a question and wondered if she would sound crazy.

"Tell me." He sat back down again and bumped his forehead against hers. The little gesture comforted her on some primal level. "I'm sorry. I'm... I wasn't ready for you." He kissed her cheek and then her lips again. "God, you taste so good. Smell even better."

She tried not to get carried away with how he made her feel. "Do you hear the wolf inside your head? Is that normal to have it talk to you?"

He smiled. "Yes. It's perfectly normal to have the wolf talk with you. I don't know what you did to me, but no one has ever made me bow to them. I don't know what kind of alpha you are, but you're... fabulous."

She blushed. "I don't know about that. I don't even know really how all this works or what Elijah is going to think. Shit."

Luke backed away. "Your other mate is Elijah Dane?"

"That's right."

"Great. We're fucked."

Chapter Three

Luke stood on the porch of his cabin and sipped on his coffee. Sadie slept in his bed. Their bed. Her scent clung to him and he couldn't get enough of it. He couldn't get enough of her. After they made love, she fell back into a deep sleep. He hadn't wanted to wake her because her body was still adjusting to her new state. At first when he found her stumbling on the road, incoherent, and burning up, he was going to bring her to the nearest hospital. Then he noticed her leg and the scent of the other wolves. Luke had realized what was happening to her. He brought her back to the cabin and cleaned her leg. The scent of the wolf kept growing stronger in her. The responsible thing to do was to make sure she came out of the turn okay. He'd seen bitten wolves get pretty fucked-up sometimes, stuck between states. Some didn't make it at all. Once she woke up, he planned to give her the rundown of who and what she had become. As a Pack Master and Alpha he had to do to make sure the new wolf was safe. Then he would set her out into the wild to make a life for herself.

Whoever had bitten her had done quite a lot of damage. Luke tended her for three days as the fever took her. She kept muttering in her sleep. The only thing he got were two names Greyson and Elijah. He figured they were people close to her. On the fifth day, her fever broke. Luke kept checking in on her, trying to give her some water and smelled the wolf within in her. Her scent enticed him. His wolf was attracted to her, but he wasn't going to make any sudden moves.

When she opened her eyes, he caught the faint green glow that faded away and her eyes became deep brown. Then he tried to control her, so she would learn her place. Her scent amped up and told him everything he needed to know. She was his mate even if he didn't want to believe it. It wouldn't have mattered if she had ten different mates. She was his. He had originally gone to the cabin to commune with his wolf and see if he could contact his ancestors. If they didn't answer, the next action was to go to the shaman. The pack he led was the Shadow clan. Unlike a lot of the other wolf packs, they still abided by the old ways. They had a shaman to help guide them. The wise man had suggested Luke send his sister to Elijah Dane so they could mend fences. Now that Sadie said her mate was Elijah, he wasn't sure what to make of it. Nor was he sure what to make of her. She had heard the spirts chanting and their drums. None besides himself and a few others in the pack heard them from time to time. Unless it was the shaman who communicated with the spirit world all the time. It baffled him.

Luke closed his eyes to talk to his wolf, to see what it thought of Sadie. *"We have a mate."*

A wave of pleasure came from the wolf as it thought of her naked, beautiful, and making him bow to her. *"We've never had a female so powerful. I don't know any pack that has."*

"She's special. Can't you tell?"

He didn't have to answer because he already knew that. *"What about her other mate? He's a rival alpha. How are we going to work that out?"*

His body tensed at the unease of the idea of sharing his mate. Elijah was a powerful man. He didn't agree with some of the conclave provisions Elijah had introduced over a year ago. After all the other packs around agreed to it, Luke consulted the shaman, and he suggested a gesture of good faith to unite their packs. That was where his sister, Denice, came in. If Elijah was her mate, then why was she just turning? Something had to have happened. Luke had to take her back to Elijah, but he didn't want to let her go. He didn't know what the impact would be on his own pack either.

"We'll make it work. The pack might not accept her."

He growled. *"We'll make them accept her. Yes, we have to make sure that she gets back to Dane."*

"How did you know she was our mate?" Elijah Dane had no idea what she was capable of.

"Humans. Sometimes you think too much. I knew the moment I smelled the wolf in her. What happened when she woke up was inevitable. She already knew. You're right. She's something extraordinary. She's amazing. She's also right behind us."

Luke caught her scent. The mixture of vanilla and cloves and something floral -- he wasn't sure. It overwhelmed him, but he could also feel her. The strength she gave off without even knowing it was something he had never sensed in one of his kind before. Her hands slid around his middle and her lips at his nape.

"That smells wonderful."

He turned and handed her the coffee before giving her a kiss. Her lips were full as her body molded to his. When she stepped away, he groaned. Sadie took a sip, made a face, and gave it back to him.

"Not to your liking?"

She coughed. "It's a little strong."

"There's cream and sugar in the house. Although not much. This place wasn't really equipped for comfort."

She leaned against the post. "Where are we anyway? The last place I remember is coming from the resort and then the crash."

"I needed to get away from things to commune with my ancestors, and see if my wolf and I could integrate ourselves and become one."

"Is that even possible?"

"It is. Some don't think so, but I've found the closer we are, the easier it is to shift. It's not as painful."

She sighed. "Great."

"Hey. I'll be there for you when you do. We still have a couple of weeks until the full moon."

"Yeah, but you can't keep me here until then. We have other lives outside this. Shit. I have to call Elijah. He's got to be worried sick. My job. My apartment. I don't know how I'm going to function. Then there's that bitch that did this to me."

"Bitch? Do you remember who bit you? Elijah should be the first one you call. Unfortunately, I don't have a phone here, and there's no cell reception."

Sadie nodded. "I think that's a good idea too. And yes, I remember who did this to me."

"Want to share?"

"Not right now. I'm still processing all this. Do you have an idea when we might get back to civilization?"

"Ready to get rid of me that easily?" Luke felt a bit of irritation from her questions, but he and his wolf didn't want to let her go.

"Not at all." She ran her nose along his throat and inhaled his scent. He shivered at her nibbling on his ear. "Mmm... I can't help how you make me feel. My wolf's feelings and mine. How do you deal with it?"

"I was born this way. The wolf's always been with me. You're right, though. We have to get back to the others. We have lives. Hell, I don't even know where you live. We could be hundreds of miles apart. I don't even know how this is going to work." Luke cupped her cheek and lost himself in her deep brown eyes. He kissed her again and slid his hands down her sides. She squirmed in his embrace.

"I really should call Elijah. We have some things to discuss."

"That doesn't sound like a good conversation."

"I don't expect it to be."

Luke knew the inevitable was coming. "Let me go take a shower and then we can hit the road until we get a cell signal. Although, we're going to have to get you some clothes."

"Your shirt was all that I could find. I didn't think to grab my bag before I stormed out on Elijah, just my purse which had my phone and my wallet."

"I have some sweats you can borrow. You look damn sexy in my shirt. It shows off your gorgeous body."

Sadie's cheeks reddened. "Thanks. I'm not the most -_"

He put a finger to her lips to stop her from saying anything else. "You don't ever have to justify how you look to me. Mates accept one another for who they are. You're beautiful. Besides, I've always had a thing for bigger women. More to grab onto when we fu -- make love."

"Better to eat, I bet."

Luke opened his mouth to say something. An image went through his mind of him sucking her clit as she cried out his name. The wolf agreed they needed to do that soon, but he realized what she meant. "I'm not into eating humans. Some of the packs hunt them. It's never been my thing. I don't ban it like some do."

"Will I have that same hunger?" A look of distress and disgust went over her face.

"It's hard to say. That's something you have to ask your wolf. If you both desire flesh, then you might. I've seen your scars. I don't know what happened to you before the bite, but it's clear you were attacked by another shifter. I take it that's why your Fae friend marked you."

"We've been friends forever and yeah."

He could see she wasn't ready to talk about her past. From the look of pain on her face, she'd lost someone special to her. *The Fairy must have really cared about her to protect her.*

"When you're ready, we can talk about it. Let's get you back to Elijah. I'm sure he's worried sick about you. I know I would be. Don't want him to think your disappearance was planned or a power grab."

"Oh, I'm sure he won't after I'm done with him."

* * *

Elijah scoured the hospitals. His people checked with every doctor's office and medical clinic within a hundred-mile radius of the resort. The police didn't find a body. The cops returned Sadie's things from the car to him because he said he was her fiancé. It wasn't far from the truth. The time without her plagued him. He barely ate and he couldn't concentrate. He kept touching her clothes to remind him of her scent.

"Hey, Elijah. What do you want us to do?" Chris asked.

He glanced at his second. "We have to find her."

"Whoa. Ease up." Chris put a hand on his shoulder. He found the touch to be slightly comforting. It helped to pull his mind out of the bottomless pit it had spiraled into.

"Sorry. She could be out there with a human who has no idea what she is. She could be hurt. She might be... No. I can't think that." The dark thoughts of seeing her body in a ditch drove his nightmares. His hands shook. He saw her lying helpless with her accusing stare. Her mouth opened and all he could hear was her screaming.

"It's going to be okay. She'll turn up. If she's going through the change, then it can take longer with some. I'm sure she's getting oriented. Why don't you get some sleep, take a shower, and eat? We're all here for you."

Elijah never thought he would have such support from his pack. He didn't want his pack to think him weak. He had fought tooth and claw to get where he was. Elijah didn't take no for an answer and wasn't about to back down to anyone. This was out of his control. He needed Sadie back in his arms. Once that happened, nothing would come between them ever again.

"Thanks, Chris. I appreciate what you and everyone

else has done for me."

"You've always had our backs. It's okay to lean on others when you need to. I'll make sure everything is running smoothly. Go get some rest."

Elijah went upstairs to shower and sleep. Food was the last thing from his mind. Exhaustion rolled over him as warm water flowed over his body. It worked out some of the kinks, but it didn't replace Sadie's hands gliding over his body. Or how she felt pressed against him and the smoothness of her skin. The feel of him inside her. He stepped out and dried his hair. As he walked out of the bathroom, a cold whoosh of air lifted him off his feet and slammed him into the wall. The sudden pain sucked most of the breath from his lungs. It felt like a hundred-pound weight crushing his chest.

"What the hell did you do to her?" An angry woman's voice echoed through the room. He struggled to get down, but he was stuck to the wall. Narissa stood before him. Her eyes burned silver-purple and white streaks jetted through her brown hair. Red veins in her face stood out against her pale skin. He had only ever seen her so angry once before.

"Nari, put me down," he wheezed.

She squeezed her hand together and the grip tightened on his throat. "I can't sense her. My guards can't find her. What the fuck did you do to her? She's not at my house. I find out you were sneaking around behind her back with another wolf. Give me one good reason why I shouldn't kill you." Nari was stronger than she appeared. She was Fae royalty, and even though her family shunned her because she was a shifter, she still had power.

"It's not like that," he gasped. Her invisible grip pressed upon his windpipe.

"Tell me how it is!"

Her grasp loosened. "I love her, Nari. You can read

my heart and mind. I'm not hiding anything. I swear. I only wanted to protect her."

Her silver eyes narrowed. The full force of her power slammed into his mind. She rooted around his thoughts like a toddler peeling an orange. He once made a promise to Nari to protect Sadie and he had failed at that. He suspected this was part of her retribution for breaking that oath. A trickle of wetness slid from his nose and he tasted the blood on his lips. Without warning he dropped to the floor. Ricochets of pain lingered in his mind as he tried to catch his breath.

"You're lucky I don't skin you and use your hide to wipe my ass. If she's in any danger, I'll make you suffer in more ways than you can imagine."

He leaned against the wall as his body tried to recover from Narissa's assault. "I didn't want to hurt her."

"And yet -- you chauvinistic asshole -- couldn't wait for her to be ready to join you. You of all people know how hard that decision was for her. You keep her secret like some dirty laundry. Then you go off and make a deal with another pack. Sure, that's *love*."

"You're her friend. What good is your mark of protection if you can't even find her? Doesn't your all-powerful Fairy blood tell you that?" Elijah got into her face and didn't care what it might cost him. She was pissing him off.

"I marked Sadie because she's unique. Haven't you figured that out?"

"Of course she is."

"Not because you love her. Think about how many times she was assaulted. Odds are against her being attacked twice by you and another. I know she tasted your blood and you tasted hers. I'm not stupid. You've bitten her even a little bit and she still hasn't changed."

"What's your point? Sometimes those who are

scratched never turn."

"I gave her my protection because I wanted to be sure no one would take a shot at her. I've always known Sadie was special. Your *mate* didn't heed my warning. She'll pay the price." Nari started to leave, but Elijah caught her arm.

"You can't do anything to her. She's under pack protection until we can reach her alpha. I'm not about to pass judgment on her when it could cause a war. Sadie is the most important thing right now. Find her first and then we can worry about everything else. Please, Nari. I need to know she's safe."

The phone rang. Elijah raced to answer it. He saw a number he didn't recognize, but he had a feeling. Narissa glanced at him.

"Hello."

"Elijah."

"Sadie." Hearing her voice calmed him. He nodded at Nari. "Are you okay?"

"I'm fine, but we need to talk."

"Of course. Where are you? Can I come and get you?"

"Ask her if she needs anything," Narissa interrupted.

He waved her off.

"Tell Nari I need clothes. I don't have any except the ones Luke's given me."

"Luke?" Elijah didn't like the sound of that. "Who is Luke?"

"That's something we need to talk about. I'll be at your place in a couple of hours. Get rid of everyone except the two of you. Understand?"

The tone in her voice was not one he was used to. It had a deeper, commanding edge. "I'll do my best, but I need some of my pack here to watch the two who did this to you. We have the woman who turned you against your will."

"We will talk about it later. Put Narissa on."

Elijah handed the phone over to the Fairy and wondered what their conversation was going to end up being about. Narissa walked away, but her accusing stare said everything. She answered Sadie in nonsensical sounds instead of yes or no answers until she hung up.

"What else did she say?" he asked.

The Fairy flashed him a wicked smile. "You're fucked, Eli. She'll be here in a couple of hours. I'm going to go get her some clothes. I'll be back." The air around Narissa folded and enveloped her until she was gone.

His heart hammered. *Who is Luke? Did he watch over her while she went through the change?*

Elijah dressed and went downstairs to clear out the house, leaving Chris to watch over Denice and Nick. He kept them in the basement cells where he locked rogue wolves during the full moon so they wouldn't hurt themselves when they shifted. The bars were made of silver. Plus, the room was filled with security cameras. Elijah ran his hands through his hair and paced the house.

A cold pinch squeezed his body as the air was sucked from his lungs. Narissa appeared holding a bag full of clothes. She flashed him a grin and set the clothes on the ground. "She's close. I can feel her."

"Great. Is that all you're going to tell me?"

"Yup."

The dim lights of an approaching car got brighter as it came up the driveway. His heart tightened. *What if she rejects me?* An older pickup truck stopped out front. Sadie sat in the passenger seat while another man drove. Elijah tried to help her out of the truck, but she shot him a look that made him step back as though it was some silent command. The wind stirred. He caught her scent. It was not the same one he remembered. He could smell the wolf mixed in with her personal scent. He needed to hold her and beg at her feet for forgiveness. Sadie brushed past him and hugged Narissa. Luke stayed by the truck. Elijah's hackles rose. He pushed past his apprehension and went over to him.

"Luke, right?" This man had brought Sadie back to him. He owed him his thanks at least.

"That's right."

He stuck out his hand. Luke looked at it, but he didn't take it. Elijah forced a smile and put his hand down to take in the other man. His brown beard hung down his chest. He was dressed in a plaid shirt and faded blue jeans with worn boots. Luke was almost a foot taller than Elijah and much broader. An air of power emanated from him. When the wind shifted, he could smell the wolf on this man. Luke sized him up and sneered.

"I don't know what she sees in you."

"What's that supposed to mean?" Elijah growled.

"Fuck off, man. You have no idea what you put her through."

"You come into my territory and say that to me. Boy, you have no idea who you're dealing with. You don't fuck with me!" His wolf came out to warn this interloper off. *The sooner Sadie sends him on his way, the better.* Elijah gathered his strength and stood up straighter, projecting out that he was an alpha and Pack Master. Luke didn't flinch, but he bristled as their auras clashed. This man was at least another alpha and not backing down.

"Are you two done with your pissing contest? If so, get in here," Narissa demanded.

Elijah huffed and a warning growl spilled over his lips. Luke pressed his fists to his sides as he walked by. Elijah felt the unspoken challenge roll off him. He followed Narissa into the living room. Sadie stood by the fireplace with her long hair spilling over her shoulders like liquid chocolate. Narissa sat on the sofa. Luke went over to Sadie, kissed her, and threw Elijah a look saying she was his. Sadie returned the kiss with the same hunger and raked her nails down Luke's back.

Watching the display felt like a kick in the gut. Elijah launched himself at Luke with everything focused on ripping him away from his mate. He charged the other wolf and tackled him to the floor. Elijah clawed Luke's face. Luke shoved him off. Elijah flew backward and hit the chair that slid across the floor. He sprang back up and charged. Luke dodged out of the way. Elijah caught himself on the ottoman and turned back around. Luke smiled, showing his growing teeth. His bulk grew as he took on more of the beast. Elijah felt himself doing the same thing.

"You touched my mate and you're going to pay for that."

"You can try, but you have no idea who you're talking to. She's mine!" Luke licked his lips. "And she tastes good."

The comment sent Elijah over the edge. He went to all fours. He relished the thought of tearing this other wolf to pieces. The fabric of his jeans tightened as his body changed. Rage consumed him. His wolf desired to rip this man to pieces. Then a voice stopped him in his tracks. The words didn't register, but the sound and the power behind it hit him. Elijah he tried to fight the command. The rage remained, but his wolf retreated. He found himself standing up and sitting down on the sofa with no clear memory of getting there. His body responded. Luke sat on the couch opposite him. They both still frothed with anger, but they seemed trapped by whatever directive had pulled them apart. Narissa flashed him a smug smile.

"What did you do?"

She chuckled. "Don't look at me. Told you she was special." She nodded over at Sadie.

Sadie's hands were clenched by her sides. Her eyes

glowed green and her forehead was knotted in concentration. The power -- the vibration -- that emanated from her was more powerful than any other alpha he had come across. Sadie caught herself on the fireplace. The force vanished. He got up and went to go over to her. When she put up her hand, the energy came upon him again to stay away from her.

"I don't need your help. Sit down and listen." She drew herself up and looked at him. Her eyes cooled back to brown again. He sat back down. Luke relaxed into the sofa, but the tension remained.

"Denice made me swerve off the road and flip my car into a ditch. She and another wolf pinned me. She claimed you were hers. She bit me and broke my leg. I don't remember anything after her biting me. Luke found me and nursed me through the fever. If it wasn't for him, I wouldn't be here." She held out her hand. Luke got up and nuzzled her neck as he settled next to her. Elijah noted he stood behind her. "Luke is my mate."

His heart dropped. "Mate? Impossible. You claimed me for a mate." Her gaze stared into his soul and he felt himself shrink.

"Elijah, you pushed me away when I came to you. You never shared anything with me about pack life. You knew how difficult it was for me to agree to the change. I asked you to wait until I was ready. I was getting there. Being a little bit more aggressive in bed. I tried and tried to make you share with me, but you found another female." Her tears broke him.

His wolf howled in despair. He could feel her pulling away. "Can we talk privately?"

"I don't think so," Luke scoffed.

"Please. We can talk about this now," he implored Sadie.

"No. You had your chance before. Whatever you have to say had better be good."

Elijah had done this to himself. She needed to know how much she meant to him. He went to his knees before her and ignored Luke's snicker. Whatever power or strength she had gained in turning only made her more magnificent. Luke uttered a low growl when Elijah took Sadie's hands. He tried to ignore the audience and stared at their hands. Doing this before another alpha would degrade him in his pack's eyes.

"Forgive me, love. I fucked up. I know that, but I didn't want to see you hurt. Some in the pack don't accept those who are bitten. I didn't want to force you into a life you weren't ready for. My wolf pushed you away because he loves you. I know how fucked-up that sounds. He showed interest in another to protect you."

"I thought you were ashamed of me because I was human and how I looked."

Tears stung his eyes. He looked up to read her face. "Never. I love you. We're mates. I --"

"You say that, but you hide me away from the pack. You never claimed me no matter how many times I bared my throat to you. After all the times I claimed you. Empty words, Elijah. Empty promises. How do you think that makes me feel? In all the times we made love, you were never wolf enough to take me."

"I didn't want to risk forcing the change on you. After our history, I didn't want you to hate me. I didn't want you to look at me with disgust and know what I'd done to you. Like the way you look at me now. Believe me when I tell you I love you. I give you everything I am, even my life." He craned his neck to her. "Strike but make it quick. I don't deserve to live for what I've done to you. For all the hurt that've I've caused my mate. My love." Tears escaped down his cheeks as he barred his soul to the woman he loved. He couldn't hold her gaze any longer or feel the scrutinizing eyes of the others in the room.

Her gentle touch glided down his cheek wiping away his tears. When he looked up at her, he saw forgiveness in her eyes. It broke his heart and restored hope to his soul. "I'm not going to kill you, Elijah, but we still have a long way to go. I accept your apology. I do love you. Now get up."

Elijah got up. Nari looked at him with something like pity, and Luke had an arrogant grin on his face. He went to kiss Sadie, but she shook her head. Too soon to be doing that. Instead, he tried to think positive. "I have the woman who did this to you."

Her eyes glowed green and she growled. "Where is she?" The hatred he felt coming off her roused his wolf back into action. He had prostrated himself before the woman he loved and her mate. It was clear Luke came first for now.

"Downstairs, with her mate, in a holding cell. I needed to keep her safe until we could find her alpha."

"Her mate?"

Both he and Sadie looked at him.

"Something you want to tell us?" Elijah asked.

Chapter Four

Luke wasn't sure he heard Elijah correctly. His sister never said anything to him about having a mate. That was the only reason he sent her to meet with Elijah in the first place, so they could form a union between the two packs. The shaman had suggested it as well. Elijah was supposed to be unmated.

"You know her?" Sadie turned to Luke.

"You weren't really in your right mind for me to tell you. The last couple of days we've been in bed more than we've been talking. Not that you seemed to mind," Luke muttered.

Sadie's anger rolled off her. No command came with the irritation that made him obey, but he still wanted to step away from her. However, he wasn't about to go anywhere after the show that Elijah put up. Granted, he never thought he would see the great Elijah Dane down on his knees offering his life to anyone. *He seems genuine about it, but I'm not buying it. They still have to work some shit out.* Luke's connection with her was still new, but he couldn't feel her. When wolves mated, a bond formed between, linking them together. Their lovemaking grew even more passionate. They could speak to one another telepathically. Sense one another's emotions. He ached to touch her and reaffirm their bond.

"Did you two plan this? She bites me. You save me, knowing somehow that you'd be my mate?" Sadie pulled away from both of them. Her disgusted look made it feel like he'd been slapped.

"It wasn't like that. I didn't know anything about Denice and what she did to you. Let's go talk to her and straighten this out."

"Fine. Let's go, because I'd really like to know what the hell is going on here myself. I can't believe this." Elijah left the room and they followed behind him.

Narissa grabbed Luke's arm as the others left the

room. "If you did this to hurt or manipulate her, then I'll make sure you pay. Hell, I'd bet you and Elijah were in this together if I hadn't seen the great Elijah Dane down on his knees. I've never seen him prostrate himself before any man or woman, so I know he's telling the truth. I don't know about you yet."

Luke tried to pull his arm away from her, but she was stronger than she looked. He couldn't get a sense about her and then remembered Sadie telling him about her friend. "You're the Fairy."

"Yeah. That's right. I'm the Fairy. Sadie is my best friend and bears my protection. She's special."

"I know she's special. I could tell that when she came through the change. She's no ordinary wolf. The power she holds over me and him isn't natural. Does that come from your mark?"

"It shouldn't. The first time I met her, I knew there was something different about her. I couldn't put my finger on it. I wanted to keep her safe. Look me in the eyes and tell me you had nothing to do with her turning the way she did. Lie to me and I'll crush you."

He stared at the woman, sensing something familiar that was almost wolf and yet not. The coldness about her should have tipped him off right away she wasn't human. He had never encountered Fairies before. Luke knew the rumors of their powers. They could rip apart minds and shred souls. He didn't want to have her for an enemy. Cold tentacles latched onto his brain. His first instinct was to fight, but he relaxed and let Narissa do her thing. "I knew we were mates the first time I smelled her. She initiated the mating when she woke up. I didn't authorize what my sister did nor did I have anything to do with it. I'd never force being a wolf on someone."

Her eyes narrowed. "Yet you did a few times. It might've been wise to keep that detail about Denice being your sister quiet for now."

He winced as her barbs in his memory went deeper. "Yes. I was younger and thought my way was the best. I was wrong. My sister doesn't share my sentiments."

"Do you love Sadie?"

"You already know the answer to that. Will you let me pass?"

Narissa stepped out of the way, and he caught up with Sadie and Elijah by following his mate's scent through the house. He found Denice huddled up against Nick. His sister perked up when she saw him.

"Bro, you come to spring me? Hey, look it's the human pretending to be one of us. Wait, you don't smell human anymore," Denice smirked.

"What did you do, Denice?" Luke seethed, not sure how he would punish his sister.

The amused look faded. "What are you talking about?"

"Denice, you never told me that Luke Esposito was your brother," Elijah said to her.

"You just forgot. I'm sure it came up," Denice answered.

"All you told me was that the Shadow Clan alpha sent you. I knew Luke was the alpha because he was the only one who didn't show up for the conclave. However, I never knew that you were his sister. You two planned this, didn't you?" Elijah snapped as he came at Luke.

"Whoa!" He put up his hands. "I didn't know anything about this. Just like I told the Fairy. I was away from my pack trying to contact our ancestors and commune with my wolf. As far as I knew, you and Denice were getting along swimmingly. No one mentioned you had a mate, Dane. How do you think I felt when Sadie told me about you? Probably as fucked up as I did when you learned you weren't the only one. Trust me, I have no intention of sharing her with anyone."

"Guys hold up." Narissa stepped between them.

Luke hadn't realized how close to Elijah he had gotten. He took a deep breath and regained his control. He couldn't lose it now. Denice might be his sister, but she had disobeyed pack law and kept vital information from him. "Denice, why didn't you tell me Nick was your mate?"

"Because I knew you wouldn't approve," Denice told them.

"Was he bitten?" Sadie asked.

"No. He wasn't bitten, Miss Know-it-all."

Nick came up to the bars. "I'm a hybrid. Part wolf and part fox. I shift into wolf, but I have fox attributes. In most wolf packs, hybrids are ranked below bitten wolves. We're third-class citizens."

"I've never treated you that way. You're my third. Why do you think I sent you with my sister as her chaperone with Elijah? All you reported back was good things. You never told me anything about his hu -- Sadie." Luke felt betrayed by the man he had grown close to over the years. Nick didn't share his feelings much, and few knew of his mixed heritage. Luke accepted him into the pack based on merit not because of who he was. To him, he was a good wolf.

Nick looked down and he saw his remorse. It was his sister's idea to keep the fact they were mates from Luke. Denice was an alpha in her own right and dominated Nick, but she wasn't strong enough to take Luke on. He glanced at his new mate and saw the hatred in her gaze directed toward his sister.

"Luke, you know we can't deny who our mates are. It's hardwired into us. If I told you, then you never would've sent me here. The good of the pack comes before anything else. Father drilled that into us."

"I remember everything he drilled into us. I bear the scars that I took for you."

"I never asked you to protect me from anything."

Denice gripped the bars and hissed as a wisp of steam came away from her burnt hands. "And you" -- she turned her gaze to Sadie --"you have no idea what you're getting yourself into. I hope you like my gift. You can keep Dane. He wasn't worth it to even fuck."

Sadie swung at her between the silver bars, but Denice danced out of her way. She held onto the metal and tried to get to her. "You never should've fucked with me."

Luke pulled her away from the cell. "Let me see." He was ready to tend to her hands, but they weren't burnt.

"What's the matter?" Sadie asked.

"Elijah." Luke motioned for him to come over and look at her hands.

Sadie tried to pull away and shot him a look. "What is this about? I don't care if she's your sister. She's mine!"

"Calm down. She's my pack and I'll deal with her punishment. That's something you will have to learn, mate or not."

She bit her lip as Elijah took her other hand. "How bad are the burns?"

"What burns?" Sadie asked.

Luke ran his fingers over her palms. They should have been blistered from the silver bars. "No burns."

Narissa also looked at Sadie's hands. "That's impossible."

"Guys." Her voice was filled with concern and a little fear. "What's all the fuss about?"

"Sadie, those bars are silver. Silver burns a wolf. It even affects me," Narissa told her.

Elijah examined her hands as well. "There wasn't any pain?"

The uncertainty in her eyes grew. "What does this mean?"

"I don't know. I've never heard of a wolf who isn't allergic to silver." If anyone else found out she was immune to silver, he didn't know what they would do. "Let's not worry about it now. You're still so new. Maybe you haven't settled completely into your wolf. You haven't shifted yet so it might change then."

Elijah shot him a look that said what he was thinking. It didn't matter if she changed or not, her immunity to silver would remain.

"Yeah. Maybe."

"How about we worry about that later? Luke, you and Elijah deal with the bitch, and I'll bring Sadie upstairs." Narissa tugged on his mate's arm. Luke felt the unease and anger rippling under the surface and the pure hatred she had toward Denice.

"Fine." They left the room.

The next thing he knew, the wind was knocked out of him and his back was against the silver bars of the unoccupied cell. He hissed from the pain of the silver on his exposed skin. Elijah had his arm pressed against Luke's throat. The other alpha growled and gashed his teeth until his eyes glowed amber under the lights. His face shifted as the wolf was in his nature.

"Whatever you're planning with Denice, I want no part of it. Sadie might've bought your story about not being involved in her turning. Did you plan on destabilizing my pack from the inside? Turn my mate to fuck with me and have your bitch claim me as mate so you could declare a challenge?"

"No." Luke shoved him away. His wolf wanted to rip Elijah's throat out. As much as he wanted to give into that urge, it would hurt Sadie. He couldn't risk their fragile ties being severed. It was clear she loved Elijah even if they hadn't cemented the mate bond between them. He rolled his neck and paced, carefully facing the other wolf at all times. "As I told the Fairy, I'm not in on anything."

"We'll see about that." Elijah knocked him to the

floor and straddled him.

Luke put up his hands to block the blow he saw coming. Claws shredded his shirt and drew blood. The coppery scent mixed with his anger drove him nearly to the edge, but he remembered Sadie. He shoved Elijah as hard as he could and scrambled backward. Elijah licked his claws.

"You got this, Luke," Denice egged him on. Nick remained silent.

Elijah came at him again, but he jumped out of the way. The other wolf howled in frustration. This time Sadie's influence wouldn't stop the fight. If this went on much longer, it would be to the death. He had to get through to Elijah.

"If you love Sadie, you'll see past this."

"Of course, I love her. She's mine." Elijah's form shifted until he became a mixture of wolf and man. He grew taller. His teeth sharpened. His eyes glowed as his jaw widened to fill with more teeth. Luke had never seen such a type of a transformation without the other being in pain. He wondered if Elijah and his wolf had become one instead of two separate beings, the same way Luke was trying to achieve this union. It seemed more difficult for him to keep his balance as he walked. Elijah rushed him again, but Luke bent low and swept his legs out from underneath him. The other wolf landed close to the silver bars. Luke grabbed his head and pushed it into the silver.

"If it wasn't for the woman upstairs, I'd gut you and leave your rotting carcass filled with silver so the rest of your pack can see how pathetic you are." Luke pressed his face until Elijah screamed, giving him some satisfaction. "The mate bond has formed between Sadie and me. I would feel her grief and anger if you died. It's only because she loves you that I'm sparing your life. I had nothing to do with my sister changing Sadie. Denice will be punished accordingly." He stared at his sister and saw her surprise. "This can stay between us or we can tell your second, who is coming, that you lost a fight to another Pack Master? Is this worth losing you pack over?"

"N-no. Yield."

Luke gave him one more shove for good measure before he stood up. Elijah stood up with a nasty line of red on his face from the bars. The second came in and went over to talk to him. Luke confronted his sister.

"Good show. You had him. Why'd you let him go?" Denice asked him.

"Because I meant what I said. Sadie is my mate."

"You're kidding. That lump that Elijah is gaga over."

His eyes narrowed. "Watch what you say. You're on thin ground as it is. You know pack law. You don't bring anyone into this life unless they ask for it and know all the facts first. You don't torment humans. And you especially don't fuck with another alpha's mate."

"He never told me. You sent me here even though I had a mate. How do you think I felt?"

He glanced at Nick and felt bad for him. "If you'd told me, I never would've sent you. I would have inquired with the shaman about another way to unite our packs. Unions of this kind have been done before. You work it out. Now you fucked it all up."

"Luke, please."

He had to pass his judgment before the pack so they knew what it meant to break pack laws. Luke imposed his authority upon them so they couldn't disobey. "Both of you will return to our stronghold, await my return, speak to no one about anything. You're not allowed to go anywhere unless it is to hunt for game and that means no humans. Is that understood?"

Nick bowed his head. "Yes, Pack Master."

Denice stared at him as her power flared outward and tried to fight his. Luke held his ground as the wave of strength took him until his sister looked down. "Yes, Pack Master," she whispered.

"Good. I'll bargain a deal with Elijah to let you go." Luke let his influence fall away and left the room so he could find Sadie and Elijah.

Chapter Five

Sadie shook with anger because she wanted to tear Denice's throat out. If she saw the woman again anytime soon, they would get into it. She dragged her hands over her face as the wolf retreated. As it did, she caught the earthy scent mixed with flowers that she knew to be Narissa. Never before had she felt the otherness in the woman and also a deeper sense of kinship than she could fathom.

"It's going to be okay."

She looked up into Narissa's eyes and noticed they changed in the light to silver. "Why are your eyes doing that?"

A small smile curled her lips. "You're seeing behind my mask. What else do you see?"

The image of the woman she knew flickered and then unwound in wisps of shadow and dust revealing a beautiful and ethereal creature. Her skin was pale and threaded with red veins. Her hair was black and not the strawberry blonde she normally kept it. Her eyes were rounded and her face more heart-shaped and elongated with sharp cheekbones. "I see you. Is that because of the mark you gave me?"

Narissa tapped her chin. "I don't know. It could be, but I'm not sure. Not even the regular wolves see me unless I want them to."

"What does that mean? The same with me being immune to the silver."

She pushed a strand of hair behind her ear. "I don't know. Forget about that now. You're a wolf. Isn't that what you wanted? I mean, to be with Elijah."

Sadie hung her head. Her thoughts flashed back to him bowing before her. She didn't know what to say. She was hurt and still angry with him. Her wolf insisted they were mates. Her wolf told her by him offering his life that he was completely submitting to her, something never done by an alpha. It had no answer for why she could force the two men to do things when she asserted her power over them. The sudden surge of emotions was not something she was used to when all she wanted to do was rip Denice's throat out. Violence had never been her way. It also made her wonder about other things when she thought about Luke. She could feel him on the edge of her mind. If she concentrated on him, his emotions flooded her mind. His smell and the feeling of him washed over her. It was almost as though he was right there with her. It made her long to have that kind of closeness with Elijah.

"Yeah, it's what I wanted."

"He loves you. So does Luke. I wouldn't approve of either of them if they didn't."

She rubbed her arms from the sudden chill that gripped her. "I know they do. The whole mate thing is fucked-up. It's like I woke up from the accident, and I smelled Luke. I knew it in my gut. It's the same with Elijah, but…"

"You're pissed at him for what he did to you and your wolf. You have every right to be."

"Yeah. Why did it have to be this way, Nari? I wanted Elijah to go through this with me. Not have it done by some bitch. And she's Luke's sister. How fucked-up is that?"

"What's fucked-up is that you have two alpha pack masters as your mates and you have them licking your feet. I've never seen that. Honestly, I was influenced by your presence, too. You're strong. You need to finish the mate bond with Elijah even if you're still wary about it before that feeling fades away. It can happen. Don't let it."

"Great, so I go in there and jump his bones?"

"You could, but Luke'd be pissed. I don't envy you there. You'll work it out. Look, you got this. I'm going to go now that I know you're okay." Narissa kissed her cheek. "Don't take any shit from either of them. Make them know who is boss in the relationship. See you soon." The air seemed to fold around her, and then she was gone, leaving Sadie to the two wolves she called her mates.

"Excuse me."

The back of her neck pricked when she heard the voice. She turned around and saw another man standing in the doorway. He looked familiar, but she couldn't pull his name from her mind. Her inner beast told her he wasn't a threat.

"Yes. Who are you?"

He flashed her a smile and stepped forward with his hand out. "Chris, Elijah's second-in-command. You're Sadie, right?"

She took his hand and returned the firm grip. "Yes. What can I do for you?"

"Look, I heard what Elijah said to you in the other room. He's had everyone in the pack looking for you. After he heard what happened, he was devastated. I've known him a long time. I've never seen him so distraught. He loves you."

"Why are you telling me this?"

He came closer, palms out and looked down once he met her eyes. "You're new to pack life, but it's clear you and he are mates. I'm telling you because ever since he's been with you this past year, it's the happiest I've seen him."

"You knew about us even though he tried to hide me and was planning to mate with the other woman?"

Chris shook his head. "Denice is a bitch. She deserves what she gets. None of the pack liked her. It was understood the union would unite the packs. All we want is peace. I've seen you together with him. You might not've noticed me then, but I watch his back. I had to be sure you didn't come with any baggage we might have to deal with. Ex-husband. Jealous boyfriends. Criminal history. It happens."

Her irritation grew from being investigated, but she understood he was protecting the pack from an outside threat. "I take it I passed muster. Anything else?"

"Give him another chance. We might be wolves, but we're still human and can fuck things up."

"Chris, why are you bothering Sadie?" Elijah barked.

He smiled. "See you around."

"He was introducing himself."

Both Luke and Elijah looked at her. An uneasy peace seemed to exist between them. Luke was taller than Elijah and bulkier. The pull to go to Luke overwhelmed her, but she resisted.

"Sadie, I need to bring Denice and Nick back to my pack so they can be dealt with for what they did. When I have it sorted out I'm coming back, Then the three of us can work this out." Luke glanced at Elijah.

She felt his uncertainty if she and Elijah could fix their relationship. Luke wanted her all to himself. She didn't want him to leave, but his pack was important. She molded her body along his until she could feel all of him and inhaled his musky scent. His lips claimed hers as his hands slid down her back and gripped her ass. He gave it a good squeeze before nibbling her lip.

"I'll be back soon. My pack will want to meet my new mate."

"I'll want to meet them too and get you under the sheets." She thought of them together and shivered as something of a purr came out of her lips.

"Fuck. Whatever that sound was, I want to hear it again." He kissed her again and backed away before they ended up ripping one another's clothes off right there. She pressed her nails into her palms and felt the sharpened tips against her flesh and saw the blood she had drawn. "I'll see you soon."

Luke stuck his hand out to Elijah. Her other mate gave him a murderous glare, but he shook it. "Take care of her and handle your shit."

Luke left leaving her alone with Elijah. They stared at one another until the silence got awkward. She tried to recall how she first felt about him and the feelings resurfaced, but so much had happened. Sadie wanted to melt into his arms the way she had before, but the rift remained.

"Can I get you anything?" he asked.

"No. I'm good. Thanks."

"Sadie, I --"

"Not now, Elijah. Leave me be for a while, please. Just tell me one thing. Did you ever sleep with her? Did you have feelings for her?"

"No. I never slept with her. It was a union to join the packs. We weren't invested emotionally with one another. Is there anything else you want to know?"

She shook her head. "Not right now. I'll let you know."

He turned with whatever else he wanted to say dying on his lips. He sighed and walked back into the house, leaving Sadie alone. Luke had gone, and she felt the hollow ache in her soul for him. She rubbed her arms and slipped around to the side yard where Elijah placed his garden path which led into a labyrinth. A koi pond was nestled into the corner. A stream meandered around the beds and along the outside of the maze. Elijah had installed this part of the garden for her to help her nightmares and the post-traumatic stress of her two wolf attacks and seeing Greyson devoured.

The path was paved with small stones that had a Celtic knot work design. Sadie started at the outer line and worked her way inward trying to quiet her mind, focusing on nothing more than her breathing and the careful placement of her feet. Halfway through the maze, her wolf lingered the edge of her mind until she finished walking the maze and sat down. Sadie closed her eyes and thought about the other half of her. Having that other presence in her mind didn't freak her out like she thought it might. It gave her comfort knowing she had another part of her that was stronger. Sadie accepted it because it felt right.

"You have doubts about our other mate."

"Don't you?"

"I know all you know and feel the anger you have over what he's done. I don't like the other bitch's scent on him at all. She disobeyed the Pack Master. She'll be punished, but I'd rip her throat out if I could."

"I know, but you wanted to talk about Elijah. Not Denice."

The wolf laughed. *"He offered us his life. He means for us to be united. You must let him into your heart. I say he is our mate because we've claimed him, but the tie that binds us is frayed. You hold the power to mend it. I won't stand in the way if you wish to sever that link."*

"Won't that devastate you?"

"Yes, but we are one heart that you control."

"What about Luke? You chose him right when we woke up."

She nudged her hand with its nose. *"He was my choice and he smelled wonderful. Elijah smells just as good, but he is your choice. You must decide if he's what you want."*

Sadie thought about what the wolf said. She didn't want to lose Elijah, but she wasn't ready to take the step and completely trust him or give her heart to him yet. *"I'll think on it. Tell me why we're not allergic to silver like the rest of the other wolves? Why are we able to control the alphas?"*

The wolf retreated. *"I don't know."*

* * *

Three days passed silently as he and Sadie existed side by side, and it killed him. Elijah felt his heart being torn apart as she slid further away from him. His wolf was restless. He needed to run and let himself move with nature. The moon would be full in a few more days and he wanted to run first with Sadie as his mate so he could introduce her to the rest of the pack. First, he had to cement their union. He bought her flowers. She thanked him, but still remained aloof. He felt pulled in so many directions, but his mind was focused on her.

Elijah paced outside her door. He would crawl out of his skin if he didn't let the wolf out. It wanted to have her hunt with him so it could prove it was a worthy mate for her. He had been worrying the same spot in the floor for five minutes not sure how to approach the subject with her. He was about to knock on the door when she opened it.

"What do you want, Elijah?" Her look told him she seemed as pent-up as he was. Her eyes had green mixed in with the brown making them dazzle. The rawness of her aura rubbed along his.

"I wanted to know if you'd like to come for a run with me."

"Trying to get me to lose weight?" she growled.

"What? No. I mean as a wolf. I thought you might want to hunt. A few days before the full moon I always start to feel restless, like I'm in a cage of my own flesh. Shifting can help burn off some energy or just physical activity. It's the reason I swim a lot or hike when I can. You've been with me when I get like this and we end up in bed. Don't you remember?"

Her lips curled into a smile as she recalled their nights together, but her hardened expression returned. "I recall. Running would be good."

"Great. Come on."

Elijah led her outside where he began to strip off his clothes, feeling the chilled wind on his chest. Her scent engulfed him as she stood beside him. He glanced over as he plucked one of his shoes off, but she wasn't taking her clothes off. She glared at him with her hands crossed over her chest.

"It's best to take your clothes off before you shift."

"Turn around."

"Sadie, I've seen you naked before."

He turned back around, finished undressing and felt the wolf ready to jump out of his skin. It yearned to chase a rabbit through the brush and run beside his mate. He began to jog into the woods when he heard a yelp behind him. Sadie clutched her stomach in pain. He raced back to her to side.

"What is it?"

"It feels like my skin is coming off. Something is clawing its way out."

Sweat ran down her face. Her fingers clawed the stone next to her. She screamed again. It cut him in half. "I can help you, if you let me. Can I touch you?"

Sadie nodded.

Elijah had done this before with other wolves, helping them through their first turn. As Pack Master and alpha he could take control of the wolf and ease their fears. He pulled her into his arms as she screamed again. He didn't know if it was possible with her because she was stronger than he. His claws grew. He cut the material on her shirt. She didn't fight him except to whimper. Her skin burned with the fever. Elijah held her to him and felt her presence against his mind. Their bond was tenuous at best, but she had reached out to him so he responded while he could and tried to let his surprise show because only another pack leader could initiate the communication without being bonded to a pack or a mate.

Let me in. Trust me.

Elijah?

Yes, love. Her fear blasted against him. She had pulled into herself like she had in the past. *Trust me, please.* He felt the wolf waiting to burst forth from Sadie's flesh, but she didn't know how to surrender to it. The first change was the worst. She could get stuck between forms or lost in some feral mindlessness.

You're fighting with yourself. Trying to stop your body from giving in to the wolf. You trust her, don't you?

Yes, but oh God, it hurts.

I know. Don't think of the pain. Think about being free of that, feeling the power and strength of the wolf. He took her hands as she yelled again. Chris rushed in at the sound. Elijah shook his head to let him know he could handle this. His second backed away, but stayed near in case he was needed. Elijah held onto her as her nails sharpened and cut into his palms. Sadie sniffed the blood and licked it. She glanced up at him and something wild lived in her eyes. He felt it in her mind, but her humanity held so she couldn't shift.

Reasoning with her wasn't working. He had to try something else. He held out his hand again so she sniffed and licked the blood. He grabbed her face and kissed her hard. The taste of his blood on her lips drove him wild. Elijah didn't hold back. He bit her lip and forced her onto her back pinning her. It got the reaction he hoped. She growled at him and threw him off of her.

"How dare you touch me!" she seethed.

He motioned for her to come at him. "Come and get me. Show me how mad you are. I chose another woman over you because you were human."

"I'm not human anymore." A loud snap echoed as her back bowed. She bared her teeth and her face pressed out as her form rearranged. She tore at her bra and jeans to get them off.

"Prove it. I see nothing but a pathetic human. Good enough to eat. Only prey for the beast." He backed up as she lunged forward on all fours.

Her spine elongated. Her wolf scent grew stronger than ever. She threw him out of her mind. Elijah couldn't hold back any longer. He slipped into the wolf and snapped at her, making it clear he didn't see her as a threat. It gave her the boost she needed, and her human side fell away. Elijah saw the pure silver wolf with its piercing green eyes shake out of the rest of her clothes and glare at him. The anger coming from her made her powerful and only made him see how much he'd fucked up. Her sight was set on him. Elijah knew he had pissed her off, but it got her to stop thinking about holding onto her skin. He backed away a step and dashed for the woods.

He ran as fast as he could, dodging fallen trees. As he jumped, her teeth grazed his back paw. He looked behind him and Sadie was gaining. He wove to the left and veered off toward the lake. She tried to push him off the trail, but he knew the terrain. He leapt over the ravine where the brook cut through and down to the lake. She landed in the trench while he kept going. Elijah raced to the small beach and waited for Sadie, seeing if she would pick up his scent. He stared down the path she should have come, but didn't see her. She had done so well until that point and… sharp pain cut into his sides and neck. The great weight made him tip as it took him a moment to catch on that Sadie was on top of him. He rolled over to shake her off. She had a good hold on him as her teeth found skin. He yipped and finally managed to twist out from underneath her. Sadie lunged at him again, but he stayed out of her way. He didn't want to hurt her. She was hellbent on hurting him. Elijah stood his ground but made no move to give up dominance. Her lips pulled back from her teeth showing the curved canines. She attacked again and caught the underside of his throat. Elijah reacted, mate or no, he wasn't going to be killed by her. He snapped back and caught the underside of her jaw. He locked his mouth around it and flipped her over onto her back. She might have been powerful, but she was a novice when it came to fighting.

She struggled to get away.

"Stay down."

"Never."

Sadie got her feet again. Elijah snapped back and defended his flank as they both lunged and nipped at one another. She pushed him off. He didn't know how it happened, but he found himself on his back again, unable to move. The sheer force of her will held him in place as the water lapped at his head. His sides heaved as he fought against the control she had over him. He looked into her eyes and the woman he loved didn't exist.

"Sadie. Love."

That didn't seem to have any affect. Elijah let the wolf slip away and became a man again. Her teeth remained pressed into his throat. He turned his head and met her eyes. *"I'm all yours, my love. Take my life. I won't stop you. My beautiful mate, I'm not worthy of you. When I first met you, I hungered for you. When you first whispered my name, I lost my heart. I never wanted to hurt you, and I cut you deeper than I ever realized. Give me one more chance and I'll spend a lifetime making it up to, figuring out how to share you, providing for our children. You are everything I've ever wanted in a woman and a wolf. Forgive me for being an asshole and a bastard."* Elijah felt the tears slip from his eyes as her teeth pierced his flesh. It would be ironic for him to die this way. "Please."

Sadie saw Elijah under her, trembling and crying. His words in her mind brought her back from the anger and the wildness of the wolf. It was the please that brought her all the way back. It brought back the horror of how she felt when she looked into the beast's eyes after he attacked Greyson. The hurt split her heart into a thousand pieces. Luke was now in the picture and she needed him the same way she needed Elijah. They healed the hole in her soul leftover from losing her fiancé. She had to let him in and forgive him. She needed to feel him. Sadie let the wolf move out of her body as she adjusted back to human form. The pain from the transformation wasn't as bad as it had been before. It took a moment and she was human and naked on top of him. Her teeth remained sharp.

"I love you, Elijah, but you hurt me. If you ever hurt me again, I'll rip your heart out."

"Understood," he whispered.

She held his head to the side and sank her fangs into the meat of his shoulder. His blood tasted good and it felt right. "You're mine."

Elijah bit into her shoulder. His tongue dragged over the wound. She shivered as the pain became something more. "As you are, my mate." Once he said the words, she felt something open between them. It was hard to explain it, but she could feel him in her mind the same as she could with Luke.

Sadie licked the wounds she had inflicted on him. Her anger from his actions with Denice lingered, but she understood it on some level even if she couldn't put her finger on it. Elijah guided her mouth up to his and claimed it in a slow kiss that burned her insides. He swiped his tongue alone her bottom lip and trailed his fingers over her flesh in featherlike strokes. It made her whimper and want more of him. She didn't want to wait for him. The need to have him inside her overwhelmed her in a way she hadn't known before. The connection between them opened and she could feel his desire for her. It went beyond the physical. She felt his utter devotion to her, and everything she loved about him was there too. He slipped between her thighs and entered her.

"I need you. I can't --"

She kissed him again feeling the same urge he felt. "I know. Fuck me. Hard."

Elijah rolled her over on the beach. She wrapped her thighs around him as he pumped into her. She met him each time. The look in his eyes grew wilder as she felt the animal in him taking over. Her wolf wanted out too, so it could join in their new union. Sadie felt it meld with her personality. They found a rhythm that was fast and slow. Painful and yet full of pleasure. The heat of the orgasm rose within her. She raked her fingers down his back and nipped at the place she had marked him. Elijah grabbed her hair and yanked on it, exposing her throat. Sadie knew she would never let anyone do this except her mates. Elijah dragged his teeth over the expanse of her neck so she could feel the points. As his breathing increased, he bit her once more. A howl broke out of her lips as she climaxed, and the sound became one with the wild.

* * *

Sadie leaned against Elijah as he massaged her shoulders. She felt like a squished pretzel inside. Her nerves were frayed.

"You need to relax, love." His fingers dug into a spot by her lower back.

"Can't help it," she groaned. She walked a thin line between being anxious and wanting to throw him down and fuck him again. They'd already gotten off topic twice. "How do you know they'll even accept me? You mentioned that some wolves don't accept those who are bitten."

He chuckled. "That was before I knew you were super wolf."

"I'm not some super wolf."

"You are if you're immune to silver and can make two Pack Masters bend to your will."

"I told you I had no idea how I do that."

He kissed her shoulder and trailed his nose along her neck. She quivered in response. "Not all wolves are made the same, even those born to it. Not everyone is an alpha. Some are betas, seconds to an alpha. Some are omegas. They are the last in the pack. It's my job to see the pack is safe. That we have land to run on. That's why I had the conclave last year. I invited Luke to come, but he never showed. We all agreed it'd make it easier to cross pack boundaries and make it safer with one set of laws. Now because of the conclave we can run from the Florida Keys all the way up to Maine and west into Kentucky, Arkansas, and Ohio. It's almost the whole East Coast east of the Mississippi. Louisiana is off-limits unless we make arrangements first. They are a little odd, let's say."

"What about with you jet-setting all over? Don't you run into other shifters or wolves? Nick said he was part fox."

"When I go into another's territory on business, I make sure to make compensation to the local leader through gifts or money. It's all a tax write-off. It's understandable as a human I have to do business and move freely. If I went to roam on another's land without permission or reporting to the alpha, then that's a breach of conduct."

"What if I'd been bitten and didn't know any of that?"

Elijah kissed her throat. "You would've been brought before the Pack Master or nearest alpha who ruled the land. Depending on the pack, you'd be reprimanded and put on probation to see if you were worthy. Or they might kill you outright."

"Wonderful. What about you? Would you have killed me on sight, Pack Master?" She turned and captured his lips.

Elijah groaned as she caressed his cock. He kissed her hard as she worked him and he broke the kiss. "We can't get going again or we won't meet them. They've already started arriving. Can't you feel them?"

Sadie pushed away from him, knowing he was right. They couldn't end up having another tumble or they would spend all night going at it. She took in a breath and closed her eyes. Once she stretched out her awareness, the pressure of the others stirred her wolf. With its strength helping her, she calmed. The thought of meeting the other wolves made her less anxious. She desperately wanted to have Luke by her side as well. Then it entered her mind that she would have to do this all again with Luke's pack. Elijah ran his fingers down her arms.

"It's going to be okay."

Outside the sun moved lower and the howls started outside. Each new voice that joined the chorus sparked something inside her until she wanted to join in the song. More and more sound filled the air. It tingled her spine and made her heart beat a little faster.

"What are they doing?"

"Calling us out. They want to meet the Pack Master's new mate. Don't be nervous. They will love you."

She flashed him a smile, not sure they would love her. They would sense her nervousness and want to eat her. He kissed her quickly and grabbed her hand. Elijah tugged on her as they went outside and she was greeted by a hundred different faces. They were all shapes and sizes. They all shared a connection. She could feel it as she stepped among them. Chris stood off to the side and winked at her as though he had confidence she would do fine. They were all clothed. She expected them to be all in wolf form, but they were all human. More arrived as the others gathered around their Pack Master waiting for him to speak to them. All eyes were on her. The howling stopped as Elijah put up his hands.

"Welcome, everyone. You have gathered here by my request. I appreciate you taking the time to come out. I asked the whole pack to join me here so you could all meet my new mate. Some of you helped me try and find her a few days ago. If I haven't told you how grateful I am, then please know that I am. This is Sadie Matthews."

"What about the bitch from the pack you were supposed to form a union with?" A man stepped forward.

Sadie didn't get a good feeling about him. He looked scruffy and smelled more like an animal than a human. His jeans were dirty. He had bare muddy feet as though he had just run through the woods to get there. She figured he probably had.

"I thought you were supposed to be protecting our pack." A few others started murmuring and shaking their heads. The discourse among the pack grew. Growls erupted through the wolves. Elijah glanced at Chris who gave him a quick shake of his head. Whatever he was thinking, Chris must have picked up on it. Sadie wondered if they were linked on a telepathic level as she and Elijah were.

Elijah held up his hands. "Rocky, it's good to see you."

"I didn't have a choice."

"You're right. You were demoted to one of the lowest-ranked members of the pack after you lost the leadership challenge. I wanted to be sure you were aware of who my mate was."

"She certainly isn't anyone I ever thought our pack leader would choose. You sure she'll even be able to keep up when we run?" Rocky scoffed.

Sadie felt her hair bristle and the wolf pushed against her flesh.

Let's tear his throat out for being disrespectful. He has a following in the pack. Can't you feel it? the wolf whispered to her.

She could feel it and see how a few of the pack members surrounded him as though to protect him from whatever retribution Elijah might seek. Having dissension in the pack was not a good thing. Hearing about the leader challenge made her worry.

"You have no right to say that to me," Sadie growled.

Rocky smirked. "The bitch has a mouth on her. What's that going to do to protect the pack?"

Elijah wrapped his hand around her waist. "Don't let him rile you up. He's just trying to get to me."

She glared at him. "I know that."

He gripped her harder. "You're still new. You don't know the ins and outs of how a pack works."

The wolf got irritated at his comment. Not even her mate believed in her. She was not going to be coddled. A deep strength slipped through her. Sadie could feel it taking root within her. The scent of pine and cedar surrounded her as the wolf moved into her personality until she could feel it becoming one with her. She had felt it before when her two mates were fighting. The longer she was wolf, the more she began to understand this inner strength. Each wolf had a different energy that came off them. Sadie could feel which ones were the toughest. She flexed her fingers and felt her nails lengthening as her teeth also got pointier. The power resembled a clear body of water, but she wasn't ready to peer at her reflection. The vast amount of knowledge waited for her to tap into it along with this strange power that infused her.

She grasped that strength. Her anger drained away replaced by calm. She couldn't lose her head over this one who had been demoted in the pack. She smiled at Elijah. Her love for him swelled. The knowledge that she was supposed to protect him in a fight entered her mind, but there was something else. He had bowed to her. He had offered his life to her and even Luke had bowed to her. She was more powerful. If that was the case, she could rule over this pack. *I'm not ready for that, but I'm not going to stand for Elijah losing face because of this hooligan who thinks he can threaten me through my mate.*

"Rocky, is it?" she asked.

"Yeah. That's right. You think you have such a magic pussy that you can twist our so-called Pack Master around your little finger. You won't be able to do that with me." Rocky smiled.

"You son of a bitch," Elijah muttered and lunged at the unruly wolf, but Chris caught him. Others in the pack looked between them, waiting for their leader to start a fight with someone who didn't deserve it.

"Let me do this. I'll be okay," she told Elijah. *"If he makes a move on me, it will be a move against you. I will not raise my hand to one that doesn't deserve to be even counted among the pack."*

"I don't expect to wrap you around my little finger." She walked down the steps as the rest of the pack cleared a path for her. Some averted their gaze and tilted their heads, exposing their throats to her already showing her a slight sign of respect. Those who supported the other wolf encircled him so she couldn't get close.

"What will you do, then?"

"Make you bow." That ancient power imbued her. She focused it on the wolves surrounding Rocky with the intention of making them move away. Sadie kept her eyes on Rocky. Even those who backed Elijah went down to a knee before her. They didn't even glance up. The fight that some of the others gave her blasted against her, but she exerted a little more pressure until that melted away as well.

"What the hell are you doing? Get up," Rocky snarled at the wolves who followed him.

"They can't answer you," Sadie replied to him.

"Why the hell not?"

"Because I won't let them. They have to learn their place is with their Pack Master. There can't be any dissension within the pack. You're the weak link. You are nothing without this body that protects you."

"You don't know what you're talking about, bitch."

"That's enough with the language. It's called respect. I am your Pack Master's mate, and you will show me the same deference you show him. Is that understood?" She trained all her will on Rocky with the intention for him to be on his knees.

He fought against her, but he was nothing compared to the two alphas she had put in their places before. Rocky tried to fight her. Sweat trickled down his forehead. Tendons bulged in his neck until he dropped to his knees and pressed his face into the dirt. A murmur went through the crowd. She glanced at the rest of the pack members. Fear and admiration lit up their eyes. They had never seen anyone take on Rocky. He was an alpha for sure, but not as strong as Elijah or Luke. He wouldn't be able to hold his own pack. It would disintegrate. The beast inside him cowered. Sadie went deeper, feeling something form between them. Loneliness enveloped her. The wolf yearned for a place to belong. A scene flashed before her eyes of Rocky as a young boy. A beast attacked his parents and bit him. He never reconciled with becoming a wolf. It tormented him until the rage became twisted into something hateful. A few of those around him backed away as she caught the scent of urine. He had lost control of his bladder, and now it caused further humiliation. She knelt down and eased up on her power. Rocky glanced up at her with tears streaming down his face.

"Please," he begged low enough only for her to hear.

Sadie wiped away a tear, feeling sorry for him. "Go inside and get cleaned up. Ask Chris for some clothes. Wait in the study for me. Do nothing else no matter how long you have to wait. Do you understand?"

"Yes."

She let go of her control over him and the power inside her snapped back to where it came from.

"Let him go get cleaned up. He will wait for me," she told Elijah.

"Are you sure you trust him?"

"Yes."

"Does anyone else have something to say to me about being the Pack Master's mate?"

The whole pack remained silent. Sadie turned back to Elijah, waiting for him to address everyone. A smile appeared on his face. "Everyone meet Sadie. As she said, if you have anything to say to her, then you need to do that right now."

No one said anything. Elijah threw back his head and howled. The rest of the pack joined in the song. It reverberated through her body, calling to the wolf in her. All of a sudden, she felt confined in her flesh. Elijah started stripping. They looked at her to follow suit. They had seen she was stronger than the rest. They waited for her. She took up her courage and pulled off her clothes not wanting to show any fear, but clothes had to come off. Heat blasted through her. She embraced the pain and rode the wave until the wolf emerged. They cleared a path for Elijah and her. He nudged her with his nose and then ran toward the woods. The pack soon joined them until the energies of the other wolves melded together, and they became one entity.

Chapter Seven

Luke glanced at the moon and felt the call of the silvery glow. Before he could shift, he had to address the pack. They gathered on their ancestral lands they had been running in since before anyone had come from Europe. His descendants made sure to bite those settlers who wandered on the land and made them join the pack. Luke was a mix of the Native People and the white settlers who eventually comprised the pack. It had grown and shrunk over time. Now it was one hundred and fifty members strong. They respected him. He ran a tight pack and tonight he would remind them what happened when rules were broken.

Luke stood on an enormous stump the size of a small house. They had gathered around it for as long as anyone could remember. A young pup gazed up at him with fear in its eyes. Once upon a time that had been him, but the fright was for his father. One step out of line and the silver-tipped whip came out. The scars of Luke's infractions told the story. Luke challenged his father and won. Rule had run in and out of his family for generations. Having a strong female alpha was rare. One like Sadie who could make two alphas bow was something special. He ached to have her in his arms again and sharing her agonized him. Tonight he would tell the pack about her.

"We gather here to give thanks to the ancestors who allow us to run and be joined together under this great moon. I called all of you here tonight so we can reinforce the bonds we have as a pack and the consequences of breaking those bonds." He nodded to James, his new second, to bring his sister and her mate.

Denice still had the defiant look in her eye. She always did even as a child and he stood up to his father for her. Nick was like a brother to him. He didn't want to banish them from the pack, but Nick had helped his sister and they both had to pay the price. The two knelt facing the pack.

"I sent my sister to the Oak Clan to see if a union between their Pack Master and her could bring us closer. My sister concealed she had a mate, Nick. Their Pack Master also did not disclose he had a mate so there is no blame there. However, the Oak Clan's mate was human. Denice willfully bit his human mate, turning her against her will. Nick went along with this."

Murmurs of disgust and hisses went through his pack. It was one thing to get lost in the moment while hunting, come across a human, with the intent to eat it, and within the confrontation, the human be bitten. It happened in the past and punishment was not brought as long as whoever bit the human tried to find it and explain what occurred. His sister had no intention of doing that. Denice held her head up waiting in silence to accept her punishment.

"They are banished, stripped of any authority or ties to this family. They are lone wolves."

Denice looked up at him. "You're worse than father."

The words hit him, but he brushed them off. He loved his sister, but the pack was more important. No one was above pack law, not even him. Luke steeled his heart and pictured the ties that linked them together severed. Once he cut them, a power rushed out of him that affected his wolves. Luke lifted up his head and howled. The threads between him and Denice fell away like ash in the wind. Before the last thread disintegrated, he sent his love to his sister.

"I'm sorry, sis. It has to be this way."

"Fuck off," Denice roared at him.

The howl died away. The entire pack turned their backs on Denice and Nick. Denice got up and looked forward as she walked toward the forest. Nick glanced back. The look on his face was hopeless. He was not meant to be a lone wolf. All they had now was one another. If they were ever accepted by another pack, it would only be because they had done something to deserve it. Most would see the dark mark on their auras or feel it somehow. As they left pack lands, the rest turned back to him. He felt their sadness. He would never fill the place where his sister had been. The eyes turned to him and all he could think about was Sadie and that was the one thing he had to hold onto and seeing her soon.

"Everyone, while losing any member of the pack is horrible, I have good news. The human my sister turned is also bonded to me. While she is the mate to the Pack Master of the Oak Clan, she is also my mate."

"Where is she?" one of the members asked.

"She is with the Pack Master of the Oak Clan. He has first claim. The first thing you should know, the union planned to bring our packs together has happened. I will bring her back by the next full moon so you can all meet her. Her name is Sadie Matthews. She's remarkable. I hope you all love her as much as I do. I know you feel the pull of the moon. Hunt well, my brothers and sisters." Luke unbuttoned his shirt and dropped it onto the stump. Others were doing the same. He started to shift when he noticed a shimmer of silver among the trees. The rest of his pack raced into the woods to hunt.

The shimmer took on the outline of a wolf. He recognized it as the sending from the pack's shaman. He hardly visited the older shifter unless he needed advice like when he went about Denice. However, this was not something he was used to seeing outside of the rituals of the pack. If this was his sending, then he needed to follow the sending. It led him to a cave he didn't remember ever seeing in the forest. Luke knew every inch of the woods. The spirit wolf slipped into the darkness and the light of its spectral energy lit up the cavern. A drumbeat echoed along the walls. It drew him into the shadows of the hollow. He found a small fire with an older man staring into the flame. This was not the pack's shaman, but he had the air of power around him. His silver hair hung loose around his face. Deep wrinkles told the story of his wisdom. His fingers tapped a drum that drew Luke to sit across from him.

"Welcome, brother wolf. You have heard the call of the drum."

"Yes," Luke whispered not sure how to react to this vision. Everything felt outside of time. It was best he went with the experience, but he also had to worry about his pack and how this would affect them.

"You worry for your tribe. I'm here not to bring them harm," he said, answering Luke's unspoken worries. "I bring a message about the silver wolf."

"I don't know of any pure silver wolves, Grandfather."

The older man smiled at the term of respect. "She is special. She comes to us in times of great need. When unification among all the tribes is needed, healing old wounds, mending rifts, doing what can seem to be the impossible, bringing together all those lost so we become one great clan."

"Grandfather, forgive me, but we exist in a world where we have to hide our nature. Humans and technology have come along that if they knew what we were, then there would be chaos."

The older shaman chuckled as he set the drum on the cave floor. "The ancestors see more than you know. Great tragedy is coming. She is needed among all those who can slip their skins. You are one of the lucky who call her mate."

"Sadie." Her name slipped from his lips. "She's the silver wolf."

"She will need you and her other mates in the times ahead."

"Other mates?"

"Don't worry about that now. You heard the drum right before you met her."

"Yes. I thought it was the Fae. The gateways are thin around the full moon. I've heard them before."

The older shaman nodded. "They too are feeling the struggle and have need of the silver wolf."

"Why?"

"It was not their drumming you heard, but mine. The woman chosen was attacked twice before and marked. The third time it was her choice."

Luke scoffed, not sure what to make of what he was hearing. Even if this older man was a spirit, Sadie didn't choose to become a wolf. "Forgive me, but I know she didn't want to become a wolf. My sister bit her for revenge."

"You sister might have bitten her, but it was her choice to become wolf. She felt the calling and it was time for her. She'll need you and the others to keep her safe. Take the drum. It will call others to her that are needed. You must be brave with her. The silver wolf will need your love and strength for the trials ahead." The old man pushed the drum toward Luke.

Luke didn't know what to make of the spirit shaman's message. What was coming? What was Sadie going to have to be tasked to do? Why did she need his help? He wouldn't abandon her, but there were so many questions. He took the drum and power surged up his arms. "Thank you."

"Don't get discouraged. You have nothing to fear. Don't let your jealousy get the better of you. It will drive a wedge between you when there shouldn't be any animosity. Love those she chooses. Even when you think it is the darkness, there is always light. When the time is right, remember the drum. Let the beat show you the way."

The man before him faded out. Luke clutched the drum. Whatever this visitation meant, Sadie was at the center of it. All he knew was that he had to protect her from whatever was coming. Luke left the cave. When he reemerged, the moon had barely moved across the sky. He made his way back to the stump and waited for his pack to return. It took a powerful spirit to reach across the void and send a message. Sending the drum must have used a whole lot more. Tanned skin was stretched over a thin wooden frame tied together with a mixture of rawhide and some plant made into rope. He didn't need a mallet to beat it. The lightest tap of his fingers and the sound reverberated through his very core. It made him uncomfortable, but also produced a soothing sound that resembled a howl. He tapped it a little harder and it made him shiver in a sensual way. Luke didn't know what power the instrument held but finding out would be an adventure. He tapped it again with more force and felt the ripples of power around him.

"Will you quit it with that damn drum?"

He looked up to see Nari standing over him covering her ears. Luke set the drum back on the tree stump. "Where the hell did you come from and how did you hear that?"

"I heard it all the way in Fairy. I was called back because more bodies have been found. They wanted me to look into it."

"You weren't just in a cave disguised as one of my tribal elders, were you?" Luke still wasn't sure he trusted the Fairy, even if she was Sadie's friend and a wolf shifter.

"I don't do old Native American with magic drum appearing in vanishing caverns. I might be royalty, but even my abilities have limits. That thing has a power to it. I know the sound of those drums because I was drawn to them. It was one of your tribe that bit me and killed my parents. The drums were used by your tribe to call to my people."

"What did my people want with Fairies?"

"They used to eat them." Narissa sat on the stump and wiped a tear from her cheek.

He squeezed her shoulder. "I had no idea."

"It was a long time ago. Forgive me if I don't get to warm and fuzzy around you."

"Yet you encouraged Sadie to become a wolf, and you seem fine with me and Elijah."

"As I said before, I saw something special in her when we met. She never cared about how much money I had or took advantage of it so I knew she was a true friend. And I was right about the special part. I'm not exactly thrilled she turned into a wolf. Although it was headed this way since she was with Elijah. It makes things a bit easier. Now I don't have to worry about eating her."

"That's not funny."

"It is if you knew her better. Look, I'm not here to argue with you. I got caught up in that damn drum beat of yours. I thought the last one had been destroyed a long time ago."

"This didn't come from this world."

"Great."

"Forget the drum. You said bodies had been found. What did you mean?" Luke asked seeing the Fairy in a little bit of different light than he had before. He wondered how much his ancestors and the Fairies were linked.

"There are other, different, Fairy shifters, around. We are rare, but we do our best to blend in. Someone has discovered us. The other Fairies have found bodies. They've been dissected, seeing what makes them tick. My father called me back with a mission to look into who is killing them. I've been a little distracted with that. I haven't been able to find anything. Something is stirring. I can feel it. Whoever is doing this won't stop with Fairies. I went deep into the realm looking for some advice from one of our mystics. She didn't give me much to go on just that she mentioned a silver wolf. Said that it appeared in times of trial. Gave me this to give to her." Nari dug into her pocket and pulled out something wrapped in cloth.

"What is that?"

She unwrapped it. Inside was an engraved silver ring. He picked it up, but dropped it back into the bundle when it singed his fingers. "It's for Sadie."

"What does it say?"

"I asked her the same thing and why I needed to give this to Sadie. I can feel the energy in it like I can feel the magic in that damn drum. What did your guy say who gave you the drum?"

"Sadie's here to bring together wolves and others alike. Something dark is coming and we need to be there for her. I can't be jealous of the mates she has."

"She is here to unite the worlds and heal rifts, as your elder said. At least we know something. We should get back to her. Don't you think so?"

He nodded. "I can't go back just yet. The pack is running tonight and I need to be out there with them. Why don't you come with me?" Luke set the drum down. Narissa put the ring inside the drum. "No one will take it."

"Thank you, Luke. I haven't run in a while and need to stretch my legs." She pulled off her dress.

Luke took in the lay of her body and pale skin as the glamour fell away and he could see her true self underneath. She smiled at him and then quickly went down to all fours. Her bones snapped and cracked as she switched her shape. Standing before him was a golden wolf with red highlights under the moonlight. She was sleeker and thinner than a normal wolf, almost the shape of a fox and the coloring, but definitely her scent was wolf mixed with an off scent he associated with her. He pulled off the rest of his clothes and let the moon overtake him and the call of the wild. Once his feet touched the ground, his worries fell away. Luke threw back his head and howled until his pack answered him back letting him know where they were hunting. He raced off to rejoin them, with Narissa keeping pace with him.

Chapter Eight

"Are you sure you can trust him?" Elijah asked her.

Sadie touched his face and sensed his concern that Rocky would hurt her. She pulled the robe closer that Elijah handed her as she ran her fingers down his face. "I know you're worried, and I understand why, but there's more to him than you know. You asked me to give you a chance when you bared your throat to me."

His expression hardened and his gaze shifted toward Rocky. "That's different and I don't expect that to be made public knowledge."

"Trust me, love. This is the right thing to do."

"He might hurt you. He challenged you outside. I've known him since we were kids. And --"

Sadie kissed him and silenced her mate's fears. He groaned as he pressed himself against her. His frustration rolled through her, but she pushed it away. "And that was in the past. Let me talk to him. You'll hear what I'm saying and if you feel a threat from him, then you'll get my back."

He grunted and then trailed his fingers along the inside of her palm. She needed him to let her do this so he could understand that she was learning to be whatever she was supposed to be and grounding into her skin. He nodded. Sadie closed the door and went into the other room. Rocky tapped his foot. He dragged his fingers over his ragged jeans and dug grooves in the fabric. His shirt clung to his frame from sweat even though he had showered and put on some clean clothes. The hammer of his heart made her ears twitch and gave her a headache. Rocky's eyes snapped open. He gazed at her with fright and he waited for her to pronounce his sentence. She squeezed his shoulder as she walked by him.

"Do you want any water?"

"Anything stronger?"

"Maybe after we've talked some."

He shrugged. "It was worth a shot. Water is fine."

Sadie grabbed him a bottle of water and sat down across from him so she could keep an eye on him. He didn't meet her eyes and kept looking down. She set the water on the floor and then took his hands. He tried to pull away. "Hey, it's okay."

He sniffled and shook his head, succeeding in only yanking one hand out from hers to wipe his eyes. "No. It's not. I'm not even worthy to be in your presence. I'm nothing."

"If you were nothing, then you wouldn't be part of this pack anymore. I'd have severed your link, but I see what's going on. You were bitten when you were younger. You put up a front that got twisted around until you've become as you are now. If you ever did beat Elijah, you wouldn't be able to hold the pack together."

"Are you going to humiliate me even more?" he growled, but there was hardly any effort behind it.

"No. That wasn't my intention before. You pissed me off and I lost control. I'm sorry."

"Why did you order me to wait for you?"

She touched his hand and his pain sliced through her. "Because I know you have good inside you."

"And you can heal me of all my ailments by commanding me? Is that what you propose to do?"

"Not at all. I expect you to work on yourself. I can be there to help you. Your wolf is strong and so are you. I ordered you to stay here to prove a point to you and the others. I couldn't have you doing anything against Elijah."

"I'm not the touchy-feely type who takes well to some female who can make me bow."

"You did more than bow. You know I'm stronger than you and the others who defended you." Sadie wasn't getting anywhere with him. *What am I doing wrong?* She got down on her knees and took his hands.

Once she closed her eyes, the images of his past flew through her mind until she felt the pain of the bite that turned him. The agony of his first shift and how he went feral. He killed the woman he fell in love with. Rocky never thought he would have a mate and wanted something to anchor him into the life he hated. Sadie felt the self-loathing and understood. As she closed her eyes, she felt pushed forward and caught the whiff of a scent attached to Rocky. She smiled when she felt the rush of love that came with it. She didn't understand it, but knew this was the mate he was waiting for.

"You won't be alone for long. The mate you've longed for is coming."

"How do you know that?"

She opened her eyes and felt the scent lingered on her tongue. She breathed out and Rocky inhaled. Sadie touched his cheek and felt the bond between them expand. A loud sob left him. It snapped her out of her trance as well as the weight of his head on her lap. She placed her hands on his head. He looked up and wrapped her in his arms.

"Thank you. Thank you."

She peeled him off her. "You don't have to thank me. You have to have faith. Don't hate what you are anymore. I know that's not easy after all that's happened to you, but try and reconcile with your wolf. It'll help bring you peace."

"How do you know these things will pass? What are you?" Rocky asked.

"Just trying to figure it out like you are."

He took her arm and squeezed it. "But you're more than just a wolf. I can feel it. No one wolf can command a whole pack of alphas and betas the way you did. You're something else. I vow to protect you through whatever comes your way if you'll give me the chance to redeem myself in your eyes and in the eyes of the pack."

"You don't have to do that to prove anything to me. You have to prove it to yourself." Sadie didn't like the idea of him thrusting himself into her life to protect her.

"You have to let me do this. You've given me a purpose. Please, Mistress. I'm yours."

He wasn't going to leave her until she accepted him as her bodyguard. "For me to accept you, I have to trust you. I'm not sure I do right now."

"What can I do to earn your trust?"

"Convince the others who stand with you that you're not going to challenge Elijah and that you back his decisions. If you go against him, you go against me. Understand?"

"I understand."

Sadie guessed he wasn't happy about it. She couldn't have anything happen to her mate. She squeezed his hand and stood up. "Stay here tonight. You can leave in the morning. This is not a request."

Rocky nodded. "Thank you."

"Good night."

Sadie left him to sleep in the bedroom he had gotten cleaned up in. She went back in to see Elijah. He wrapped his arms around her and kissed the back of her neck. She leaned against him taking in his scent and the steady beat of his heart. His presence calmed her, but she missed Luke. Something else that left her feeling hollow.

"What is it?"

"Nothing. Just thinking about what happened in there. I caught the scent of his mate and visions of them together in the future. I shouldn't be able to do that. What does that make me?"

"It makes you the most wonderful, magnificent creature I've ever encountered. You've endured so much at my hands and at the others. You" -- he kissed her throat again and nipped her skin --"are a gift that I'm not worthy of. I don't know what else to say about why you're immune to silver or why you can make me bow to you and make it feel like my brain is mush. I can't understand how you do it. You turned Rocky back to the pack. Whatever you are, it's special and you chose me. I love you."

Sadie turned in the circle of his arms and pressed herself against him. The love in his eyes floored her as well as the trust. She closed her eyes and felt the bond between them. Elijah started to speak.

"Shh."

Elijah quieted. The link between flared open so she could feel his emotions. Images flashed before her about the future. They were a blur, but she caught the scent of another male she couldn't place. Elijah shared the scent with her and the visions. She didn't how she was doing this, but she felt the wolf and the energy within her. It was almost as though she could see it flaring silver. The more she looked into it, the more she could feel the ancient power that came with it. At the center something called to her. She could almost hear a voice and was drawn to it, but she pulled away when she felt the pain come from Elijah.

"What is it?" she asked.

"I can't take whatever you're seeing. It burns."

His eyes were red as though he had some reaction to a chemical. "God. I'm sorry. I didn't know." Sadie laid her hands over his eyes. Cold rushed through her and flowed out of her palms. Elijah snapped back and when he did, his eyes were no longer red and bloodshot. He took her hands and looked at them.

"How did you do that?"

"I-I don't know. Elijah, I'm scared. What's going on with me? This isn't normal."

He touched her cheek and it calmed her some. "It's like Rocky said. You're special."

"What if I don't want to be special? I just want to be

with you and Luke. It took me long enough to be comfortable with the idea of being a wolf. Who knows what this is?"

"Sometimes we have to accept what fate hands us. Whatever happens, I'm here for you. Even Luke will be."

She chuckled. "I know you don't want to share me, but I don't have much of a choice in how that happened."

"You're right. I don't want to share you. The pack recognized you. You don't have to worry about that. They know you will support them. You felt it tonight when you were running with them."

"Yeah. They all made a point to come over and show their allegiance or make some sign of it, even if they were afraid. I don't want them to fear me."

"They will love you. Just like I do and I worship you."

Sadie knew what he said was true because she could sense it, but the part of her that was still angry with him lingered. "I know. I'm going to head to bed. I'm tired."

"I'll be up in a few. I still have some things to go over for the office. We're supposed to close on a few deals." He kissed her again and went to complete this work.

Sadie crawled into bed and felt weary as she closed her eyes. Whatever she had done with Elijah and Rocky had drained her. Once her head hit the pillow, sleep pulled her down into its embrace.

When she opened her eyes, she found herself sitting in front of a clear pond. On the other side stood another woman with a silver wolf sitting next to her. Sadie recognized the wolf as her other half. She didn't feel frightened, but she wasn't calm either.

"Who are you?"

"She is our mother." The wolf looked up at the woman.

The woman gave her a small smile. Her pale golden eyes were filled with love. Sadie never felt more acceptance or understanding than she did now. "Hello, daughter."

"Hi."

"You have many questions to why you possess the gifts you do. Why you are torn between the men whom you've claimed as mates?"

"Yes. I'm grateful for all of it, but I don't understand why I was chosen. Why not someone who was born a shifter? Why am I able to heal or have these flashes of others' lives? Tell them the future. I don't understand. I'm hardly used to my own skin and these other attributes are thrust upon me. Is there anything else? Am I going to be able to fly now?"

The woman laughed and the breeze kicked in. The clear sky darkened as though a storm was blowing in. "No flying, I promise. Much is expected of you. The silver wolf appears in times of great need. You heard the drums and the chanting from the spirit realm with Luke when you first awoke. It was the call of the three realms signaling your arrival. The Fae, the spirit world, and your world."

"What does it mean being this silver wolf?"

"Your answers will come in time. You touched upon your essence earlier than you should. You can't share it with anyone as it will hurt them as it did your mate."

"But I healed him. How is that possible?"

"It's a part of who you are, as are the visions of the future of those you connect with. It doesn't happen with everyone. As was the way you detected the scent of the mate of the wolf from your pack. It brought him hope. You are here to unite the packs. You will understand as you become more integrated with the wolf. When you do, knowledge will come easier for you as well as a glimpse of what is to come. First, you must be whole."

"What do you mean by whole?" Sadie asked not liking the conversation with this being.

The woman's look changed to one of sadness and yet there was still warmth. "I know this is not what you wished your existence to be as a wolf. You became this for the man you loved and then found another one who fit into your life's puzzle. And yet, the puzzle is not complete. You need to keep your heart and mind open. You'll understand as things fall into place. Each piece is going to bring you the strength and the completeness you need."

"How long do I have?" Sadie asked.

The woman touched her face and an electrical charge shot through her. Sadie tried to stay where she was, but she was thrown back into her body. When she opened her eyes again, the sun streamed in and Luke was looking down at her.

Chapter Nine

When Luke stared into the eyes of his mate, his soul was put at ease. Once the pack had come back from their hunt, he told his second about needing to get back. He and Nari drove as fast as they could until they arrived back at Elijah's. He didn't care if he was barging in on Elijah. Luke needed Sadie in his arms to know she was okay, especially after what the Elder spirit had told him. That, along with Nari's information, made him not want to let his mate out of his sight ever again. Sadie had woken up from some kind of a dream. The shock lingered in her eyes. Her arms went around him as she pulled him close. He smoothed her hair and held her, breathing in her scent, calmed him.

"What is it?" he asked.

"Nothing. Just a dream."

"It's more than nothing. You're trembling. I can sense your distress."

"I don't know what I am. I can do things and something is coming. She told me it was coming."

"Who told you?"

"Our mother."

Before he could ask, a scream erupted in the house. Sadie threw back the sheet and rushed out of the bedroom. In the hall, Narissa had backed up against the wall from a man who had a dumbstruck look on his face.

"Nari, what's the matter?"

"Sadie, get this asshole away from me."

"Sadie, is there something I can do to help?" Luke asked.

"Get him away from me," Narissa demanded. Luke pulled the other wolf away from the Fairy.

"She's mine!" The other wolf growled at him.

"Whoa! I'm not here to argue, but the lady asked for some space. I think you should give her that," Luke replied.

Nari hugged Sadie and then pulled her aside. He didn't know what they said because it was too low for him to hear. The other man tried to get back to Nari, but Luke held him. Luke sensed the alpha vibe, but it wasn't strong enough to take him on. "What's your beef, man?"

"She's my mate. Sadie said she was coming. I-I didn't believe her at first, but then I caught the scent from her." The wolf looked at Sadie with awe as she came closer.

Luke didn't really understand what the wolf was talking about except it involved Sadie and he had to be sure she would be safe. Her robe opened and showed off her luscious breasts. It took all his control not to pin her against the wall and make love to her right there with everyone watching.

"Rocky, did you jump Narissa?" Sadie asked.

He dropped to one knee. He took Sadie's hand and kissed it, clutching it like she was the second coming. "You told me she was coming. Forgive me for doubting you."

Luke gave her a questioning look. She shook her head, meaning he would find out later. It seemed like they both had things to say to one another.

"Rocky, it's okay. I understand. Believe me, but are you sure Narissa's your mate? She's... ahh... not a usual wolf."

Rocky glanced at the Fairy and his expression lightened while hers grew darker. "Yes. Just as you are sure our Pack Master is your mate and this one." He gestured toward Luke. "Please, Mistress, you asked me to trust you and I did. Trust me when I know this is true."

Sadie sighed. Narissa had a murderous look in her eyes. It was clear she didn't want this shaggy wolf for a mate. "Okay. I trust you, but Nari is my best friend. Like my sister. You can't just run up on her and start telling her she's your fated one. You have to get to know her. Talk to her. Introduce yourself."

"I can do that."

Sadie turned his head back toward her. Luke felt the force of her will, but it was a light touch. "Let me talk to Nari and the others first. Go get something to eat and go take a walk. Come back after you have a clearer head and remember what I said. Patience is your best bet with her."

Rocky got up, looked at Nari one last time, and then walked away. Fury burned in Narissa's eyes. "He is not my mate, Sadie. What did he mean when he said you told him it was me?"

Sadie squeezed her eyes shut and pinched her nose. Luke went to her, but she put her hands up and stopped them both. "Nari, I can't listen to you now. Luke, all of us need to find Elijah and have a talk."

"Yes, we do," he agreed.

"Fine, where is the pompous pain in the ass?" Nari asked.

"Can you tone it down for now?"

"Sadie, he's a billionaire who thinks he's God's gift to women," Nari grumbled.

"You're still pissed at him for breaking his vow to you about not hurting me. Although it did work out in the end. Come on. He's in the kitchen."

Luke followed behind Sadie and sensed something different about her. She seemed surer of herself even in the short time they had been apart. In the kitchen, they found Elijah standing at the stove making breakfast. An impressive spread of bacon, pancakes, fruit, eggs, and bagels were laid out on the counter and the table.

"You do all this?" Luke snagged a piece of bacon.

"I had some help."

"Thought so."

Elijah growled at him.

"Boys, now is not the time," Sadie scolded them.

A woman wearing a chef's uniform came from outside carrying a large tray of steaks. "I have another batch going on the grill. I'll take over from here."

"Thanks, Jenn. The pack should be coming in soon."

"You make breakfast for your whole pack?" Luke asked, surprised the other wolf was so generous.

"Of course, if we meet here. Not everyone stays the night. They'll be in and out. Jenn helps and I thought you might be hungry, but I wasn't expecting Luke and Narissa. Grab a plate. We can talk in the other room."

Luke's stomach growled. Sadie laughed. It twisted his insides that it took all of him not to claim her. He took the plate and loaded it up with bacon and grabbed a steak, too. The others took food and followed Elijah into the other room. Luke sat with Sadie between him and Elijah. He brushed his hand along her exposed knee and was rewarded with her dazzling smile. He nuzzled her neck. She giggled and touched his leg.

"Later. I promise."

He nodded, feeling like he could hold it together for now. They dug into breakfast until he pushed his plate away. Sadie sat back. "Breakfast was wonderful, but we need to talk. I had a dream last night about this woman who claimed to be the mother of all werewolves. She told me a storm was coming. I was chosen for a reason. She also said that I wasn't complete."

"What do you think she meant by that?" Elijah asked.

Luke shared a look with Narissa. It seemed like a big coincidence he had gotten the drum and she had gotten the ring and Sadie had the dream as well. "I didn't have a visitation, but I had an experience."

Luke told them about his encounter with the elder shaman and the drum. When he was done, Nari pulled out the silver ring and placed it before Sadie wrapped in the cloth.

"I went to speak to an elder deep within Fairy. She told me about a time when a silver wolf led the Fae against an ancient enemy. In order to unite the tribes, she had to turn a few of them from each tribe. They were okay with it at first, but then they rejected all the shifters. That has stayed with the Fae. We have long memories. She gave me this ring." She unfolded the bundle. "It's forged for the silver wolf. All the tribes bound their magic to it in the past as a symbol of being united under her and if need be, to be called up on again."

Sadie picked it up. Luke waited for her to drop it from having a reaction to the silver, but she held it and examined the band. "There are symbols on it."

"Are you sure it's not the one ring from *Lord of the Rings*?" Elijah asked.

Luke broke out into laughter. "Seriously dude, your inner nerd is showing."

"What? I happen to enjoy the movies."

"Whatever." Luke sat back in his chair and shook his head at the revelation.

"Guys, we can discuss movies later," Narissa snapped.

Sadie laughed. "The ring has an energy to it. It kinda feels like a magnet." She slipped it onto her finger. Her whole body shivered.

"Are you okay?" Luke asked. He grabbed her hand and touched the ring, but once he did he was thrown backward from the chair.

"What the fuck was that?" Elijah asked.

Luke shook his head, trying to get the buzzing from his ears. It felt like his head had been shoved into a concrete wall. "What the hell is that thing?"

"It's not meant for you." Sadie helped him up. When his fingers touched hers and the ring, he felt the power of it, but it didn't send him reeling.

"Narisa got the ring and I got something else. Let me grab it." He raced to the truck and grabbed the bag the drum was in. He set it on the table so it didn't make any noise. Sadie drew in a breath.

"You recognize this?" he asked.

"No, but she mentioned a drum that draws everyone together. She didn't say anything about the ring. Although it feels like I'm supposed to wear it. Frankly, all of this is fucked up. I didn't want any of this when I wanted to be a wolf." Sadie slammed her hand down on the table.

The impact made the drum jump and the vibration it made shook Luke. It felt as though he was dunked in cold water. He glanced up at Elijah and it seemed he had the same reaction. All the hair was standing up on his body. The same with Narissa. Sadie didn't seem to be affected. Instead she trailed her fingers along the surface of the drumskin. Each time her fingers came down, it pulled him closer. He could hear it inside him. His eyes closed to a slit as he felt himself slipping into a trance. It wasn't until the drumming stopped that he pulled himself out of it. Luke didn't like how the drum affected them all or what Sadie's role was in whatever this storm was that was coming.

"Please don't do that unless you mean to call every wolf and other shapeshifters around." Narissa hissed.

"Fine. Keep it with you, then." She tried to take the ring off, but it remained on her finger. "Guess this is going to stay with me. Elijah, can you take Luke into the kitchen?"

"Is that an order?" Elijah smiled.

"No, but I need to talk to Nari. Rocky is in the kitchen waiting for me to get done with her."

He wanted to know how she knew the other wolf was waiting in the kitchen for them. However, Luke wasn't about to question it. He was quickly learning that things in the world were not what they seemed. He loved Sadie through the good and the bad. Luke got up and motioned for Elijah to follow him. They left the room and walked down in the hall when Elijah pulled him aside.

"What's the deal with the drum? Are you trying to set her up?"

"Look, Elijah. I know you don't like the idea of sharing Sadie, but I'd never do anything to hurt her. This isn't something I quite know how to handle either, brother. Whatever's happening is all news to me. We both know she can make us bow to her will. She even did it to Rocky. I see the fear in your eyes. What happened?"

The other wolf leaned against the wall and he seemed defeated. "She shared something with me last night. A vision... a glimpse of the future and a scent or scents of another. I saw silver and felt it running through me. It burned my eyes so that when I pulled away I was blind. She didn't do it on purpose. When she realized what she had done, she healed me. I love her, but..."

"You're afraid of her."

He nodded. "How horrible is that to say?"

"It's not horrible. I have the same kind of feeling, but I'm not afraid of her. I'm afraid of what is to come. We have to be strong for her. She's adjusting to this as we are adjusting to her. When the time is right, you have to tell her. For this to work, we have to be open and honest with one another. Even if we don't like one another very much."

"It's not that I don't like you. It's that she chose you, too. I don't like the competition."

Luke clapped him on the back. "I know what you mean. A least we did what we needed to do and united the packs. She one of a kind. Don't let the jealousy get in the way of that."

"I'll try."

"Good. Let's go get Rocky."

"He can't be my mate, Sadie. I've lived for a long fucking time and there's no way. He's..."

"I know, but he *is* your mate, whether you like it or not."

Narissa sat back in her chair, crossing her arms over her chest. "Giving me orders now?"

"You're such a bitch sometimes. I'm not giving you orders. I'm... telling you what I know. How many years did you tell me to trust you? How about trusting me for a change?"

"You're letting this second coming thing go to your head."

"You know better than that. It scares the shit out of me. I'm not ready to be whatever it is that I'm supposed to be. I'm scared, Nari. It's all happening so fast. I was okay with becoming a wolf and then that got all fucked up. I'm scared. Please don't be throwing me under a bus when I need my best friend."

Sadie sighed and felt the doubt rip through her. Hearing her mate's and her best friend's messages about what she was going through and how it all seemed to be connected only made the situation creepier. It wasn't about knowing the wolf was there, it was about feeling something more. Something beyond her. She could feel more of the wolves around her. The drum shook something loose. The longer the vibrations hit her, the more it sounded like a long howl calling out to all the wolves.

The ring amplified the drum until she could almost split worlds. Together the two things were a powerful combination. Yet she didn't know how she knew things. They seemed engrained within her. Like when she stared at her reflection in the dream. Underneath the surface was so many things waiting to reveal themselves. The little pieces of that knowledge didn't all fit together, but when they hit her she knew them to be true. She also knew that her mates were afraid of her and she couldn't stand that.

Narissa put a hand on her knee. "I'm sorry, Sadie. I feel like I might've had a hand in what's happening to you. If I'd never marked you with my protection, then maybe you never would've become this silver wolf."

"It's not your fault. I was mauled by wolves twice and I didn't change. The third time was how it was supposed to be, because I had originally chosen to be this way. Fuck, how do I know that?" Sadie sobbed, feeling as though she was walking the line between loosing herself and sinking into whatever she was turning into.

"It's going to be okay. I'm here for you. So are Elijah and Luke. Give them a chance to get used to all these changes. Fuck, I hate it when you're right. I'll give Rocky a chance. He's not what I expected for a mate. I was hoping for someone from Fairy or a little bit more... I don't know... just not him."

Sadie squeezed her friend's hand as a bit of relief flooded her. "Thanks, Nari. Be gentle with him. He might look all big and tough on the outside, but on the inside, he's broken and scared. He's never thought he could have a mate after what happened."

"What happened?"

"I'm sure he'll tell you when he's ready. Don't reject him because you don't think he's not your ideal mate. Besides, you could have someone else out there for you."

"Is that another prediction, Madame Endora?"

Sadie giggled. "Shut up. I have no idea. Maybe. I'm still going to call you Tinkerbell."

Her friend rolled her eyes. "Can I make a suggestion that might make your mates a little bit more comfortable with this whole situation?"

"I'm willing to take anything to make sure they get along."

"Bring them together."

"They're already here."

Narissa poked her and a wicked smile spread on her lips. "No silly. Bring them into bed together. That way they can't say no to you."

She felt her cheeks burn at the thought of both of her mates in bed with her. "I-I don't know if that's a good idea."

"Of course it is. Just because you have this notion of how sex can be doesn't mean that you had to play by the same rules. You're changing. Change with it. I'm not telling you to get rid of your humanity. You told me to believe you. Then you need to believe in yourself, and that means embracing the sexy creature that you are. I know self-esteem has never been your strong suit, but you got the wolf thing going on. No matter who the man or woman is, they will pick up on that. Own it." Narissa got up and tugged her to come along.

Even with her new skin, it was difficult to embrace the confidence she felt bubbling inside her until she needed to command the pack or force someone to do something. Then she felt like she was in control. She didn't want to make her mates do anything they didn't want to do, but maybe Nari was correct. "Fine. Let's go."

In the kitchen, Luke and Elijah were talking to Rocky. The doors to the patio were open. More than thirty wolves crowded the kitchen as they snagged food for breakfast. Once she entered, they moved out of the way. Some touched her arm, but she didn't feel any negative things from them. Luke looked up and grinned at her. Seeing the smile put a few of her fears at ease. Rocky glanced between her and Narissa. Her friend went over to Rocky. He nearly pounced on her, but she stuck out her hand. It stopped the wolf and puzzled him. She nodded at him in encouragement knowing he fought the urge to claim her friend right there. His anticipation rubbed off on her until she could almost feel his desire for

Nari infuse her pores. He knew that the Fairy was his mate. She pulled herself away from Rocky's consuming feelings and focused on the links between her two mates. They were hers and yet there was something missing. Her wolf nudged her to stop thinking so much and just feel.

Rocky and Narissa went outside. The others of the pack kept looking at Luke because he was from a rival pack. Their hackles were up. The tension in the room rose. They didn't understand why he and Elijah were being so friendly and not trying to run one another through. Sadie slipped her arm around Luke's waist and pulled him down to her mouth. She savored the taste of him until she broke away and then kissed Elijah. Their excitement filled her. Elijah gripped her hips as Luke pushed against her until she became a sandwich. A few catcalls broke them apart. She felt her cheeks burn and Elijah eyed her.

"Can we go upstairs?" She posed the question to them.

"With him?" Both came back at her.

She took their hands and tugged them after her. They made it out of the kitchen, and then Elijah cornered her.

"What the hell is this?" Elijah asked.

Luke stayed close.

"This is between me and Sadie."

"No, I think she made it clear that it's between all three of us, man," Luke growled.

"Guys, this isn't about putting one above the other. You are both my mates. We can't be separate all the time. Sometimes we have to be together."

Elijah glanced at Luke. "Sadie, I don't mind working with Luke or getting along with him. It's like a business deal. Sharing a bed with him is unacceptable."

Luke slid his hand down Sadie's throat and moved her hair away. He kissed her neck until her stomach fluttered. "It's what she wants. I might not want you in bed with me, but I'd do it for her because she asks us to."

A gush of love came from Luke. "You have no idea how difficult this is for me to even talk about. Asking both of you to join me together is... I know it's messed up, but you both accepted me as a mate. I need both of you. Elijah, I know you're afraid of me after what happened last night. Luke, you have doubts about all this. I can't lose you."

"You're not going to lose me, Sadie." Elijah stroked her cheek and she saw his resolve caving.

"Then come upstairs."

"I'll be up in a minute," Elijah responded.

She nodded. It was the best she was going to get for now. Luke threaded his fingers through hers as she led the way up to her bedroom. She felt like all of it was crumbling. Luke pulled her close and held her as a bout of panic set in. He took her in his arms once more and it felt like she would be okay.

"You don't have to panic about this. He'll figure it out. We all will. I don't like sharing you either, but this isn't going to be all the time. If it's what you need, then I'm okay with it."

Sadie laughed. "Good, because you seem to be the only one who is."

"I love you. No matter what you're becoming. I loved you and knew you were mine the first moment I smelled you. You opened your eyes and I was lost. You are amazing. Whatever your journey is, I'm happy to be right beside you walking the same path." He caught her up in his arms and kissed her until her cares fell away.

It ignited her passion. She slipped her hand along his broad chest until she came to the waistband of his jeans. She pressed her hand along the bulge of his dick. Luke broke the kiss and slid his lips down her throat until he sucked in her skin and bit down. Sadie cried out as the pain left her wanting more. Narissa was right. She needed both of them. Never in a million years did she ever think of having a threesome when she was with Greyson. Her heart ached at the memory of him. She tried to push it away, but it twisted her heart up. She pulled away from Luke.

"What is it?" he asked, his voice husky with desire.

"It's nothing."

"It's not nothing. You went from all hot and heavy to sad. Something popped in your mind."

"I was thinking about Greyson."

"Your fiancé that Elijah ate?"

"Yeah. They never found his body. When I was with him, I never would've been with two guys at once. Sorry. This shouldn't be affecting me like this."

He stroked her arm and wiped a stray tear from her cheek. "Of course, it's going to affect you. No matter how much you love a person that love never leaves you. I'm surprised you aren't crying every time you see Elijah after the injustice he caused you."

She couldn't help but laugh. "I love you."

"I love you, too. You can share anything you want with me. I know how much you love me. You're so fucking beautiful." Luke pulled his shirt off. "Come here, hot stuff."

She could feel her cheeks sear at the compliment and then the muscular expanse of his chest. Sadie kissed his flesh. The taste of the salt on her tongue made her wolf growl. Her mind wandered until it latched onto the link between her and Luke. His anticipation and the need for her nearly made her come as the pleasure flooded her. He touched her face as she licked his nipples and made her look up. Sadie sucked in his Adam's apple and found the sweet spot on his neck. Her teeth grew pointier as she thought about them coming together. Luke grabbed her ass and lifted her up. He carried her to the bed as he buried his face between her breasts. The shift in him happened so quickly she barely caught it. The beast settled into him, and it was a smoother transition than she remembered. Sadie nipped down on his shoulder. Luke grunted and then returned the gesture with a harder nibble at the top of her breast. Luke tried to take in more of her breast as he pressed her down into the bed, spreading his entire body on top of hers. She welcomed the weight and needed to have him inside her, filling her so they could be of one flesh. She tried to get at his jeans, but her nails raked his sides instead. He hissed.

"Sorry."

He flashed her a smile showing off his teeth. "I like pain. I don't think we've gotten that far into what we both enjoy. Believe me, I can show you a few things."

"How about we figure that out later? I'm not much into getting whipped." Elijah walked into the room shedding his clothes.

Sadie shimmied out from underneath Luke and wrapped her arms around Elijah. He kissed her slowly, walked his fingers down her back, and slipped his other hand between her legs. She gasped as he rubbed her clit. The thread between them opened and she could feel him against her. She wound her thoughts around his until he could feel her feelings.

"*I love you, Elijah. Whatever this is... what's happening... please don't be afraid of me.*"

He brushed his tongue along her bottom lip. "I love you, Sadie. I'm nothing without you. You complete part of me I never knew was empty. Yes, I'm afraid, but not of you, just what you are becoming and what it means. Forgive me if I came off as a bastard before. I didn't mean it like that."

"No hogging her, Elijah," Luke said behind her. His hands slid down her sides as he pressed against her back.

Her body ached for them. Luke's body was warm along her back and his firm prick pressing into her ass. All she wanted was to feel him inside her. Elijah trailed his hands over her arms.

"Beautiful," Luke whispered behind her.

He kissed her neck and along her shoulder. Each small place he left his brand the imprint of his mouth remained. Elijah knelt before her and trailed his hands along her inner thighs. Sadie squirmed as he reached her panties and tugged them down until she stepped out of them. Luke lightly thumbed her nipples until they grew harder with each small stroke. Elijah parted her legs slightly, kissed her mound of curls, and trailed his fingers along her moist slit. Sadie jumped when he pushed a finger inside her and at the same time Luke squeezed her nipples harder. A small whimper escaped her throat.

Luke nipped her shoulder blade. Each time he released her skin it only left her wanting more. Elijah found a slow rhythm of pumping his fingers inside her pussy that forced her hips outward. His thumb discovered her buried nub and fondled it. Sadie didn't know who to turn her attention to Luke or Elijah because each of them imparted pleasure to her body that roused her to heights she never thought were possible. The world spun out of control the longer Elijah massaged her clit. Luke bit a little harder along her shoulder and then sucked in the skin. Each time he did, the pain mixed with the pleasure of Elijah's manipulations sent her rocketing into another world. If it wasn't for the two of them being there, she wouldn't be able to stand. Her legs shook as the orgasm built within her.

She wound her fingers through Elijah's hair as he flicked his tongue along her thigh. Luke's nails seemed sharper as he turned her face toward him. He captured her lips in a hungry kiss. Sadie moaned into his mouth which only made him kiss her harder, insistent. He sucked in her bottom lip and tugged on it lightly with his teeth before releasing it. It left her breathless.

His hot breath blasted along her ear. "I want to fuck

you so hard, Sadie. I want you to scream for me." Luke took her hand and placed it on his cock. "You feel me, baby?"

"Yes." She wanted to whisper, but the same hunger overcame her that he must have felt because at that moment, an orgasm slammed into her. She dug her nails into Elijah's skull, but he just continued to pleasure her with his fingers. All she knew was she had gone into a world of white and she didn't know if she would burn up or not.

"What about me? Do you want me, too?" Elijah crooned.

Sadie realized that the orgasm had stopped. She floated from both of them and had to catch her breath. Elijah kissed the other side of her neck that Luke hadn't claimed. His mouth didn't burn as much as Luke's, but all his touches lit her up inside. "Of course." It took her a minute to separate herself from the others. When she did, she looked at both men, feeling shy, but when she gazed into their eyes all she saw was love. Sadie had a little bit of courage and walked her fingers down his chest and over his pert nipples. She bit her lip and squeezed one. His eyes fluttered shut and a soft groan rumbled from his chest. She slipped her hand lower and squeezed his balls.

"Fuck," Luke muttered.

"You bet."

"What about me?" Elijah spun her around.

"I wasn't done with Luke yet." Sadie touched the tip of his dick which moved when she did.

"What if I want you first?" Elijah pinched her ass.

"I guess you're going to have to wait."

Sadie took Luke's hand and led him over to the bed. Her heart hammered in her chest. She kept telling herself this was what she had wanted, She sat on the comforter and Luke crawled over to her. He touched her cheek.

"Stop worrying, love."

"I'm not."

He pressed his lips to hers and kissed her slowly, lovingly. "Yes, you are. I can feel it as much as I share the echoes of your pleasure. You are all that I want. That we want."

Sadie nodded and placed a hand on his chest feeling the steady beat of his heart. His heavy musk wrapped around her. Her body ached for him. She needed him inside her. The bed depressed from Elijah's weight. He flashed her a smile. He took her other hand and placed it on his chest so she could feel his heart as well. Both men's hearts beat strong and reminded her of the vibration of the drum.

Warmth spread throughout her body. It settled at the base of her spine and moved upward along all her nerves until her body buzzed. It was an orgasmic feel, but it didn't put her over the edge. It quickened her breathing. She threw her head back and let it wash over her until her clit throbbed with the need for release. It was as though she had been infused with lust. Luke took her nipple into his mouth and sucked on it, biting it. Her back arched and she threaded her fingers through his locks. Elijah took her hand from her chest and led it to his cock. Sadie gripped it and pumped her hand over it slowly.

"Yes, baby," he moaned.

Luke looked up, his eyes clouded with ecstasy. He grabbed her hips and hauled her over to him so that she was straddling him. "I need you. Now."

She nodded because she experienced his craving for her too. It was almost an echo as he had said before, but as it mixed with her own pleasure and Elijah's. It drove her mad. She needed the release that only the two of them could bring her. Sadie guided Luke's shaft inside her. He locked his eyes with her as his thumb found her clit and he massaged her. Sadie squeezed her eyes shut.

"You can't do that if you want me to concentrate…"

Sadie said to him.

He thrust into her and rubbed her a little quicker. Sadie cried out and dug her fingers into the meat of his shoulder. "Who said anything about concentrating?" He drove into her again and groaned. Luke kept her steady while he moved into her slowly and worked her clit until the pleasure burst within her. She had no control as she writhed on top of him. All she knew was that Elijah was behind her. He cupped her breasts and began moving in the same tempo as Luke.

"I can feel you coming, Sadie. Oh God, I can't describe it. But I want more. Don't stop," Elijah begged her.

Luke took control of their coupling and ended his torture of her clit. Her pussy gripped his cock tighter with each thrust inside her. Sadie became a slave to the both of them. All she could do was feel. Her mind stretched along their connection, and it was as Elijah had said. They were sharing one another's pleasure. As each time one of them got closer to their orgasm, the more their minds were blending together and they were sharing one another's feelings.

Sadie had a hard time unweaving herself from their minds, but realized it didn't matter. She could feel Luke moving inside her. She felt Elijah sliding his dick along her ass using the friction between them. Soon it was all too much to even think any more. All she could do was go with the flow of things.

Right at the pinnacle of them being in unison, the world exploded in light. Tremors ran through her body. Her nerves were on fire. Sadie sensed the beast within Luke. It reached for her and she caressed it. When that happened, she came.

Sadie nestled between her two mates, feeling complete. Their love flowed through her as her body hummed from the aftermath of their lovemaking. Elijah snored and Luke grumbled in his sleep. She wished she could sink back into the dreamland she had been in, but something had shaken her from that. The only other creatures in the house were Narissa and Rocky. She closed her eyes and heard their heartbeats together, but they were not close together. It seemed like Narissa got her way and they were separated. She hoped they would get along. Sadie tried to let the warmth of her mates' bodies lull her back into sleep, but something lingered on the outskirts of her mind. A vibration, like a second heartbeat, flowed through her. As she listened, she realized it wasn't another heart, but the beat of a drum. The same drum Luke had brought with him.

It was a rhythm she couldn't ignore. She Sadie grabbed Elijah's robe and slipped it on. Every time the drum was struck, it wasn't painful, but it made her stop. She clutched the wall halfway downstairs. It came again. Once she could continue, she made it to the dining room where they had left the drum on the table. She expected to find the room empty. A man sat in one of the chairs, trailing his finger over the surface of the instrument. His eyes flashed in the dark. A low growl echoed in the room. He sprang out of the chair and went down to all fours.

"Hey, it's okay. I'm not going to hurt you."

"Who are you?"

"I was going to ask you the same thing." Sadie moved a little closer so she could get a better look at this man who had invaded the house.

"I heard that drum. It called me. What did you do to bewitch me?"

"Nothing. What's your name?"

The strange wolf backed farther into the shadows so she could only make out his form. "I have no name. Why do you smell so good?"

She heard him take a breath and sniff the air. "I can't

answer that one. I can help you, but you need to let me know why you're here. Who is your pack?"

"I have no pack. I run alone. I have since I can remember. I've come upon others who…" he growled and shook. His spine cracked and he backed up against the wall. "Can you… can we speak in the kitchen?"

"Of course. Only if I know you aren't going to attack me." Sadie glanced at the open door that led to the patio.

"Whatever has drawn me here still has its hold on me. I've been running for hours since I heard the sound. Can I get something to eat? I haven't had human food in a long time. You lead."

The stranger had her intrigued. Even with only a little light she knew he could see her. She left the room and heard the faint patter of his feet on the carpet as they went into the kitchen. Sadie went into the fridge and pulled out the containers of leftover steaks and bacon. She grabbed the pancakes too and put them on the counter. The wolf stayed in the darkness.

"I can heat up whatever you need."

"No need. Cold is fine. Although, do you have any peanut butter and grape jelly for the pancakes."

Sadie froze. "What did you say?"

"If you don't, that's fine. It's just been a while."

"No. I -- sure there's some around. It's just funny. My fiancé used to make a PB&J with leftover pancakes." Sadie found the peanut butter and jelly and set them on a counter with a knife and some napkins. She leaned against the counter and pressed the button to make a pot of coffee. The stranger sighed.

"Coffee. I haven't had any some in a while. Would you mind?"

"Only if I can put the light on so I can see you."

"Okay."

Sadie poured the coffee and turned the light on. She was ready to set the mug on the counter when her eyes adjusted. Her gaze landed on the wolf in the kitchen. Her heart stopped. The mug slipped from her fingers and shattered. "Greyson."

Feast or Famine (Billionaire Werewolf 3)
Crymsyn Hart

Sadie Matthews wasn't sure what to think when her dead fiancé waltzed back into her life. Not to mention wondering how he would get along with her other two werewolf mates, Elijah and Luke. With all three pulling on her heartstrings for attention, she needs to figure out how they all fit together because her heart can't break into three pieces. Just as she's about to figure it out, danger comes to the wolf packs.

Wolves are winding up dead, and everyone is looking to her to find out who is behind it. With this new turn of events, she needs her men behind her even more. Can she discover who is behind the murders? Will she be able to bring peace between the rising tensions of her three mates?

Chapter One

"Sadie, is everything okay?"

She jumped when she heard Luke, one of her wolf mates. He came into the kitchen wearing nothing more than plaid pajama pants. He slipped his arm around her waist and nuzzled her neck. His beard tickled her skin as he kissed her. It was then he held her closer and growled.

The strange wolf who had entered the house looked up.

"Who is that?" Luke asked.

"I-I'm not sure. I... He looks like Greyson."

The other male stopped eating mid-bite and dashed out of the kitchen onto the patio. Sadie broke loose from Luke's grasp and ran after him, but the fleeing wolf disappeared into the densely wooded backyard. The full moon shone bright silver as it sank beneath the trees. The night would be over soon. She wanted to go farther into the forest, but Luke caught her hand.

"Hey, come back inside and tell me what happened. He'll come back if he's hungry enough. Sometimes strays are drawn by the smell of food or the energy of the pack. They might linger for a day, but they normally wander off. If he shows up in the morning, then Elijah can talk to him. Come back to bed."

Sadie shook her head. "No. He's more than some random wolf. I know it."

Luke sighed. "If he is, then we can look for him in the daytime with Elijah. I missed you in our bed." He slithered his hand underneath her robe and found her patch of curls. His finger massaged her clit and he fondled her breast with the other hand. His desire flared along the mental bond they shared. He trailed his tongue over her throat. Sadie sank into the bliss he evoked in her. The more he worked her clit, the more her thoughts of the strange wolf fell away. Luke squeezed her nipple until her breaths came in small pants. His fingers slid inside her. Sadie ground against his cock as it poked into her ass. "Do you think you can put him out of your mind for a few hours?"

"Oh, Luke."

"What are you two doing down here?" Elijah, her other wolf mate, came into the kitchen. "I think I know what you're doing. Shame on you for not inviting me." Elijah kissed her.

Lust strangled any thoughts of the mysterious wolf that had dashed out of the house. Their emotions mingled with hers until she didn't know where she ended, and they began. As Sadie sank deeper into their yearning, the animal nature of their wolves surged forward. All thoughts of the pleasure they wanted to draw out flew out the window. She needed them.

She raked her fingers down Elijah's bare chest. He broke the kiss as she shoved her hands down his shorts. They had been gentle with her the night before, but the animal yearned for more. Elijah tugged at the belt of her robe. Luke pressed his teeth into the meat of her shoulder.

"Harder, Luke," she urged.

Luke tore her robe from her shoulders. His dick pushed against her ass. The tips of his nails pierced her hips. Sadie growled with joy. Elijah kissed the other side of her throat. The beasts within took control. Their bodies writhed against one another. She kissed his throat and then bit into it. Elijah howled and grunted. She wrapped her arms around him trying to get closer.

Elijah's scent enveloped her. The strong musk of the wolf and the aroma of his expensive cologne made her need him more. Knowing she had him at her mercy -- Elijah, a man who people bowed to and who had billions of dollars -- only made her understand the true power she possessed over him. Over both of them. Luke was an influential alpha. She hadn't met his pack yet, but that would come. For now, this was all there was, the three of them bonding together.

"Sadie, what're we doing?" Elijah groaned.

"You're both fucking me." Sadie pushed Elijah against the wall. He grabbed her ass and picked her up. "Is that a problem?" She bit into the side of his throat. Elijah cried out as he thrust into her.

At the same time, Luke kissed her neck, but his want for her screamed to be unleashed. "What about me?" He nibbled on her ear.

"I didn't tell you to stop. Take me."

Luke worked his lips along the line of her neck and then sampled her throat. Heat raced along her nerves. It felt as though she occupied both of their bodies and hers at the same time. She could taste the blood on her lips, but they weren't her lips. They were Luke's and Elijah's. She could feel Elijah moving into her as her breasts bounced against him. Luke slid his cock between her ass cheeks as he tried to hold himself together so he could pleasure her. Her mind couldn't take all of it. She could almost see the three of them coming together.

Luke kept rhythm with them until they all moved in unison. She twined her fingers through Elijah's hair. Luke scraped his nails along her thighs.

"Sadie, love," Elijah moaned as she rode him.

She pressed her hand against the wall. The joy of sharing with all three of them engulfed her. White heat flooded her mind and a howl burst from her throat. Elijah's and Luke's howls joined hers. All she could feel were their bodies pressed against hers, each out of breath. Elijah eased her down. Both mates held her and their scents mingled with hers.

As she listened to their breathing, another cry sliced the night. A howl she had not heard before. It sent a chill through her. Her eyes opened. Her mates uncoupled from her. Elijah snarled. Something in him snapped. She felt the alpha rush forward as he shoved her into Luke's arms. He shifted and darted into the yard. Luke growled and went after Elijah. *What the holy fuck just happened?*

"It's the other wolf," her other half said. *"The one you thought you recognized."*

The snarling intensified. The wolf rolled through her, and she didn't stop the transformation. She dropped to all fours and raced outside to see what her two mates were doing. They circled a smaller wolf. The moon highlighted the animal's reddish fur, but in the pale light she could see where the wolf was badly scarred. His teeth were bared and his hackles were raised. He wasn't an alpha, but he tried to stand his ground. His ears lay flat against his head. She could see his ribs now and how skinny and scruffy he was. Now she was closer to him, she could smell how enticing he was. *Can't you give me a manual with all this? I can't handle having another man to deal with.*

The stranger snarled. Sadie nipped Luke's leg, but he didn't even acknowledge he had felt the bite. Elijah jumped at the new wolf and pushed him into a corner. He glanced at Luke.

Sadie didn't sense the men, just the animals. They were protecting her. She sighed, not wanting to deal with the pissing contest. Sadie darted between the new wolf and her two mates. She stood her ground. The other two did not want to back down. The wolf in her grew annoyed. Sadie forced her dominance over her two alpha males.

"Back off."

"He's in my territory and shouldn't be here without invitation or announcing himself," Elijah snapped.

"He did. You were upstairs asleep. I invited him into the house to talk." Sadie tried to reason with him. He pushed back against her, but she held her ground.

"You're ours. He has no right to stake a claim," Luke snarled.

"Oh, for fuck's sake. You told me we could look for him in the morning."

"That was before I knew he stayed around to watch us together." Luke gave her the eye and his power pressed upon her.

"Enough of this, both of you." She made them retreat a couple of steps. *"Go take a cold shower and come back when you're rational."*

Her two mates turned and went back into the house, but they fought her all the way. She pulled back her presence as the other the male wolf growled at her. *"They won't do anything while you're here, either. I'm not going to bite. Come back inside and get some food. It's easier to talk as humans and not wolves."*

"They will kill me if I step any farther into their territory. The Pack Master made it very clear I wasn't welcome here."

"I swear to you, no harm will come to you."

"You can't give your word when the Pack Master rules this region."

She laughed to herself. *"I get you're a little apprehensive about this. Didn't you tell me you were drawn by the sound of the drum?"*

"Yes, but that's different. It felt as though I didn't have a choice." He cocked his head to the side and studied her. *"You're different. You made them obey you. No female should be able to do that."*

"Come inside. Sleep in a bed. Take a shower. We can talk this out. They're bristling because you stayed around while my mates and I were getting busy in the kitchen. We were having a private moment and we didn't want to share."

He looked down. *"Forgive me. That wasn't what I meant to do. I smelled your desire and it piqued my interest. I've smelled you before. I just don't know where."*

Sadie didn't want to let her imagination get the better of her. Just because this man looked like Greyson, her dead fiancé, didn't meant it was him. The fiancé Elijah had eaten before she knew him. *"Come inside. Once you're rested and fed, we can talk about it in the morning. I'd really like to go back to bed."*

She transformed back into human. "You coming? Last chance if you want to find out what the drum is all about."

Her robe lay across a chair in the kitchen. She slipped it on and saw her mates glaring at the new wolf with murder in their eyes. The strange wolf returned to human form and lingered at the threshold. He glanced at her and then down again.

A low growl came from Elijah.

She threw him a look, crossed her arms over her chest and waited. "I told him he could stay here without you harming him."

"Fine." She turned her attention to the stranger. "Luke, take him upstairs to a bedroom."

"Sadie, can we talk?" Elijah touched her arm and she jumped. "Are you okay?"

The stranger hurried past them.

"Fine. Why?"

"You're not fine. Something spooked you. You got a little rough in the kitchen. I'm not complaining, but you aren't normally so... forceful." Elijah pulled Sadie to him and kissed her lips, then pushed her hair from her face.

The small gesture helped calm her. He was right. She *was* a little jumpy.

"If you didn't like it, then you should've said something." She didn't like the way he had treated the other wolf.

Elijah didn't release her. "It caught me off guard. When I woke up and you weren't there, I was worried. I heard you with Luke and smelled the other wolf. I was going to say something, but I got a little jealous."

Sadie kissed him. "Nothing to be jealous about. I'm fine. I woke up because I heard that blasted drum. When I came downstairs this stranger was in the house. I thought he was drawn by the full moon and the call of the pack. He said he heard the drum."

"He overstepped his bounds, and so did you. You can't be letting in any stray you see fit and second-guessing my authority as Pack Master. I know you can pull rank on me, but sometimes you have to let me rule. Why did you say he could stay?"

"When I turned on the light, I thought he was Greyson."

Elijah nodded. She saw the understanding in his eyes. "Ahh, love, I know they never found his body. He was dead after I… ate him."

"I know. Give him the night and tomorrow so we can learn more about him. He's been mistreated by most of the wolves he's come across. He said he came miles to get the drum out of his head. Let's see where he fits into all this."

"I can't say no to you."

She poked him in the ribs. "You have before. I promise I'll ask you next time. I don't want the pack to think you're unworthy of leading them."

"We can talk about it later. Right now, you're coming back to bed with me." Elijah swept her up and carried her upstairs.

Chapter Two

Grey opened his eyes and stared at the white ceiling. Fear raced through him as he caught the scent of the two alphas who had cornered him the night before. The instinct to bolt nearly drove him back into the wild. Then he caught the aroma of the female. When Grey thought of her, he thought about the drum and how it called to him. The instrument had given him the promise of a female and the whisper of maybe regaining some of his knowledge along with it.

Sometimes Grey scratched at the surface of his memory. In the early days, it brought pain and blackouts. When he woke up from them, he was never in the same spot. Sometimes it was a welcome relief when the beast took over, so he didn't have to worry about interacting with humans.

He sat up in the bed. The memory of the sound evoked the images of her and stoked his desire. *She's already got two mates. Both of them alphas. She wouldn't look at me. Fuck, I don't even know what I want, but I know I wasn't like this before. I used to be something else.*

A knock stirred Grey from his thoughts. "Come in."

The door opened, and the woman entered carrying a tray. The aroma of coffee made his mouth water. She glanced at him and then cast her eyes back down to the tray. Nothing in her demeanor remained of the assertive female he encountered last night. It was kinda sweet the way she smiled at him and then set the tray down.

"I didn't know what you liked so I grabbed a few of the leftovers. Everything except the coffee is cold. Sorry."

He felt himself return her smile with ease. She intrigued his wolf and had a comforting presence he couldn't place. "It's fine. I haven't slept in a bed in… Well, I can't remember when, honestly. Most of the time I find some hollow to curl up in. I steer clear of pack territory if I can and cities. I prefer the quiet. Can I ask you something?"

"Sure."

"Why did you stick up for me against the two alphas? You could've let them tear me apart."

She pushed the hair out of her face. "Y-you remind me of someone."

"You called me a name last night." He slipped out of the bed until he was only a few inches from her. Grey was about to touch her when another woman burst into the room. They jumped apart from the sudden intrusion.

"Sadie, the guys said you took in a stray."

He glanced at her and watched her jaw drop.

"Holy fuck. Greyson."

"I'm sorry. You have me confused with someone else," he said to her. Her scent was mixed with something else. Grey turned his attention back to Sadie.

"I thought you were dead. Sadie --"

"I'm not whoever you think I am," he snapped, feeling the growl roll over his tongue.

"Narissa, can I talk to you? We'll be right back." Sadie pulled her friend out of the room. Grey grabbed a cold pancake and munched on it. He focused on the conversation to hear what they were saying.

"...I'm telling you. The man outside is Greyson."

"It can't be. He's dead."

"You never saw his body, and they never found it."

Sadie huffed. It sounded like Sadie had cared for whoever this man was. She tried to speak and then another long pause filled the silence.

"Elijah and his friend had their muzzles buried in his stomach and his throat was ripped out. Nothing could've survived the attack. Don't tell me this stranger... I can't."

"Well, you're going to have to. I know how he smells. His scent might have changed a little bit, but for whatever reason, he's alive."

He heard a loud whack and then the woman

marched off. Grey peeked out of the door. He caught Narissa's eye. She came back into the room and walked around him, sniffing him.

"Sit." Narissa sat down on the bed and then pointed to the chair.

"I'm not your dog to command."

"You are whatever I say you are until I can figure out how you're doing it. What kind of glamour is around you so you can pass yourself off as Greyson? I don't need you upsetting Sadie. If you really are Greyson, you have a hell of a nerve coming back here now. She's getting used to her life and she's in love," Narissa scolded him.

Grey didn't move. "I don't know who you think I am, but I'm not here to interrupt anyone's life. The drum called me."

"The drum. Shit."

"Why is it so important?"

"Doesn't matter. Look, what's your name?"

He shrugged. "I don't remember. The bears called me Grey. Everything I was before I woke up as wolf is gone."

She drummed her nails on her leg. "How long have you been a wolf?"

"Almost four summers."

She got up and grabbed his chin, forcing it up as she moved his head around. Grey didn't try and break her grip. This one seemed to have some influence with Sadie. He didn't want to make her mad and jeopardize whatever connection he had with Sadie. Grey winced when Narissa poked at some of the scars on his stomach.

"Where did you get these?"

"I walked into sleuth of bears without knowing it. Their shaman took pity on me and healed me. At least that is what he told me. I have no memory of it."

She trailed her fingers over the uneven marks on his abdomen. "That could be how it happened. I've had a conversation or two with them. They're strange creatures, those shamans. You happen to know where I might find this man now?"

"So you can prove what I'm saying is wrong?"

"No. If you are Greyson, how in the world did you survive? I need to know if someone's fucking with Sadie. She's been through enough and faces... whatever is going to come."

"And that means what?" Her statement intrigued him.

"Nothing you need to worry about. Any idea where the shaman is?"

"It's not like he gave me his phone number. All I remember is he's north of here. Maybe about three hundred miles."

"Okay. That gives me some idea. I'll tell Sadie I'm off."

"Where are you going?" This from another man who stood in the doorway blocking the woman's path. He didn't smell like Sadie's mates.

"Nowhere you need to worry about, Rocky," Narissa said to him.

"Sorry, but now I've found you, I'm not letting you out of my sight." Rocky wrapped his arms around Narissa. She rolled her eyes and tried to step away, but his grip tightened. Rocky claimed Narissa as his mate and he sensed she didn't want anything to do with it.

A pang of loneliness hit him. Sometimes it felt like a mate bond had been ripped from him. Something in his life was missing besides his memories. When Grey tried to remember, darkness descended and his wolf took over, blocking him from his past.

"Fine, but we're going to have a talk about this whole mate thing. This discussion isn't over," Narissa said to her mate.

Rocky kissed her hand. "I know, but I'm not letting

you go. We talked last night and you're remarkable. I can help you. You said something about bears. I know a few. Their holy mystics find a place and camouflage it. Kinda like what you Fae do with your glamour thingy."

"Glamour thingy? What a way to describe it. Come with me. Show me some bears, but I've got to go talk to Sadie before we leave." She turned her attention from Rocky to Grey and poked him in the ribs. "Don't do anything to her or you're going to have to go up against her two mates."

"I don't plan on doing anything."

Narissa walked out of the room. He needed to talk to Sadie and explore this draw he felt toward her. Grey couldn't let it go. He snagged a piece of bacon and wrapped it in another pancake to soothe his hunger. As he did, Luke knocked on the door.

"What now?"

Luke stood in the doorway holding some clothes. "Sadie said you could use something to wear. Elijah's more your size. His stuff is a bit too silky for my taste, but I don't have anything here. I'm Luke." He extended his hand.

He looked at it as he set the clothes down the chair. "Hi. Don't take this the wrong way, but you were going to rip me to pieces last night."

Luke pulled back his hand. "Yeah. I didn't expect you to be hanging around while we were with our mate."

"I wasn't planning on it, but…" Grey shook his head. "…there's something about her. I know she's yours and I don't want to step on your relationship."

The other wolf's face went red. "Don't think you can come in here and take her away from us. She's special. You have no idea. Sadie might've said you were off-limits and we were supposed to be nice to you, but don't fuck with her."

"Thanks for the clothes, man," Grey told him.

Chapter Three

Elijah saw Sadie rush outside while he tried to make himself some coffee. The idea of the new wolf staying in his house didn't make him happy. He tried to make Sadie understand that undermining his position as Pack Master could jeopardize his standing. Although watching her take on Rocky and his supporters and put them in their places made him wonder how much he should worry. It proved she was stronger than any Pack Master he had ever met.

He loved Sadie and didn't want anything to happen to her but hearing the news she was some super wolf didn't sit well. Neither did sharing her, but after he fucked up, he understood why she ran out. Elijah wasn't expecting her to return with Luke. He respected the other wolf, but he was still getting used to the idea of sharing his mate.

He set his coffee down and went out into the garden. Sadie sat at the koi pond he'd installed for her. Elijah slid his hands over her shoulders. She tensed and then relaxed back against him. The link between them opened. Her confusion and soul-splitting grief washed over him.

"What's the matter, love?" Elijah tried to ease the knots from her shoulders.

She slipped her hand over his and grasped it. Tears lined her cheeks. He dropped onto the bench next to her. Sadie hugged him in a strong bear hug like she wanted to meld the two of them together. He stroked her hair, but she quaked in his arms. She looked up at him with troubled eyes.

"I need to know something and I need you to be truthful with me."

"Of course."

"When you ate Greyson, did you leave him alive?"

"Why are you asking me this now?"

"His body was never recovered, but…"

"Love, he was dead when we left him. I had my jaws around his throat. I felt his neck crack. Gregor tore into his stomach."

"The man upstairs is the spitting image of my dead fiancé. Narissa says he *is* Greyson. You and I both know he's dead."

Elijah ran his fingers over her back feeling the place where he had scarred her years before when he hadn't curbed his appetite for human meat yet. "Yes. Even if I bit him, he'd have to remain alive in order to change. Bites can't bring people back from the dead."

"I know. I just don't know what to do. When I saw him…"

He nodded, understanding it would be a shock for her to see someone who looked like Greyson. It dropped into place why she was so protective of the new wolf. She felt something for him even if he was a stranger.

"Why does Narissa say it's him?"

"Because he smells the same to her, but with the wolf thrown in. What if she's right? She said she was going to investigate his story. Why won't she leave it alone?"

"Because she's Narissa, and once she has a bone, she won't let it go. Damn woman. Look, a lot of strange things have been happening lately. This wolf doesn't even know his name, does he?"

"No."

"It seems we have to talk to him to see what his story is. Don't worry."

"I gave him my word he wouldn't be hurt."

He gritted his teeth. Elijah wanted to take a bite out of the man, but he would honor his mate's request. "I won't hurt him, but we have to get to the bottom of this."

"I know, but I can't confront him right now. I need some time to figure all this out."

He stroked her hair. "It's fine. I promise I won't hurt him."

"Thank you."

"What if he really is Greyson?"

Elijah didn't know what the implications would be if this strange wolf was really her fiancé come back from the dead. It could drive wedge between them. Their mate bond had formed and cemented. He didn't think anything could break it, but that didn't mean something or someone couldn't dredge up old feelings. He loved Sadie.

Losing Greyson had been a deep blow to her. Narissa helped break her out of her funk by sending her up to the retreat he owned. She got involved with him. It took her a year to get up the nerve to become a wolf and join him. Then he'd nearly lost her. Luke's sister, Denice, had bitten Sadie and turned her into a wolf in the end. Because of it, Luke banished Denice and her mate from his pack. Elijah admired the wolf for making the hard decision.

"I'll take care of it." He kissed her quickly and then walked back into the house only to hear something hard hit a wall upstairs. Elijah raced up to find Luke cracking his knuckles and a noticeable dent in the thick wood frame. "I don't mind you staying here, but try not to destroy my house in the process."

"Sorry. The new one pissed me off."

He laughed at the statement. "I'm not thrilled about him being here anymore than you are."

"Do you really think he's some reincarnation of Sadie's dead fiancé?" Luke asked. He ran his fingers through his beard. Elijah had seen this man naked and shared a woman with him. It didn't mean he was mate bonded to him, but to hurt him would hurt Sadie, and Elijah couldn't take the chance. Besides, he was grateful to Luke for saving Sadie's life and seeing her through the change.

"I don't know. I was going to talk to him. You get anywhere?"

"He says he doesn't remember anything. Maybe Narissa can get more information about him," Luke explained.

"She's a resourceful one."

"Sounds like you know from experience."

Elijah shook his head. "Water under the bridge. Sadie's upset. She's in the garden. Can you check on her, please? You might be able to calm her down more than I can."

"I'll do what I can." Luke went by him and headed downstairs. Elijah sighed and knocked on the door where the other wolf had slept.

"What now?" the strange wolf growled.

Standing there before him was the spitting image of the man he had eaten, wearing a T-shirt and pants which were too big for him. Faint scars showed around his neck and arms as well. "Fuck."

"Everything okay?"

Elijah caught him by the throat and shoved him farther into the room. The wolf grabbed his hands and tried to push him off. Elijah couldn't think anything past the idea this man had returned from the dead and he would get between him and Sadie. "I don't know how the fuck you did it. But whoever sent you, you need to go back to them and tell them not to interfere with what's going on here. Whatever hell you crawled out from, there is no way you're alive. Either you're some skin-walker, or you're some phantom brought to life. Either way, you're not welcome here. Get your shit and get the fuck out!" He threw the strange wolf into the dresser.

Grey stayed on the floor and looked up at him, his eyes shining in the light. Elijah's inner wolf sensed danger. Grey's face had already started to change. "She said I was safe in this house. Is this how you treat guests?" The words came out garbled. He kept low to the floor, waiting for Elijah to spring.

Elijah laughed. This wolf wasn't strong enough to challenge him, but it would be fun for him to try. "This is my house. Sadie doesn't make the rules here."

The other male's smile widened up into his cheeks. "You should tell her that. She had your balls earlier, and there was nothing you could do about it."

"Leave my mate out of this. Whatever you're here for, get it done and leave us alone. You're nothing more than a shade from her past."

"Your mate is the reason I'm here. Soon she'll be mine. I know it and there won't be anything you can do about it."

The comment drove Elijah over the edge. Sadie wasn't going to be with anyone else except him and Luke. It was bad enough to even include Luke, but Sadie wasn't going to get rid of him. The mate bond had already formed between them. He had felt it when they made love. It almost felt as though the three of them had merged. It made him come harder.

Elijah shook it off and launched himself at the wolf. Grey changed into a half man-half wolf beast and slammed Elijah into the wall. Elijah tried to recover, but sharp nails sliced across his stomach. Pain exploded in his torso. Another swipe came across the top of his chest. It scraped across his ribs. He got a little bit of space between them and pushed the other wolf away. Grey rushed forward again. Elijah stepped out of the way, but not before the wolf caught his side.

He never expected the wolf to be so fast. Grey dove and sank his fangs around Elijah's ankle. Bones crunched. Elijah whimpered as the wolf pulled his leg out from under him until Elijah was flat on the floor. He tried to get up, but the wolf-beast grinned with his intent to gut Elijah clear. Elijah tried to shift, but he was too drained. He didn't know how this man held the in-between state. It was painful and hard to control, but this wolf seemed to have mastered it, making him a lethal fighter. The clawed hand swung down. Elijah never thought he would lose a challenge to a lesser wolf. Sadie's beautiful smile flashed in his mind. He closed his eyes. Sharp-tipped claws grazed his throat. A force washed over him. The pain of it nearly made him black out.

"Stop!" The command rang in his mind.

He opened his eyes. His whole body ached. His mate stood in the doorway with Luke by her side. The horror of what she saw reflected in her eyes until something else came over her. Her face went blank, and yet Elijah could almost see the power coming off of her in waves. The wolf beast dropped and cowered before her.

"No more, please," the strange wolf whimpered.

"You will not harm anyone of my pack or my mates. If you do, you'll be imprisoned in the cells below, and you'll never see moonlight again."

"You swore no one would touch me," he spat.

"I don't care. All bets were off when you tried to kill my mate."

"He's not worthy of you," Grey grumbled.

Luke helped Elijah up. Elijah grunted as the discomfort from his injuries grew. "Come on, let's get those wounds cleaned out."

Elijah leaned on Luke, who helped him into the bathroom down the hall. As he passed he saw no pity in her eyes. The warm and caring woman he loved was not in her. He saw a leader who would stand up to anything. It made Elijah proud and a little scared at the coldness he felt in the link between them.

"What the hell did you do?" Luke asked.

Elijah sat on the toilet while Luke peeled off the remains of his shirt. He got a towel and dabbed at the wounds, hissing in a breath at the pain. "I got a little pissed when he threatened to take Sadie from me. I ouch... hey, watch it."

"Yeah, he presses my buttons, too. You should be healing by now."

Elijah looked at the gashes on his chest. They were closing, but slowly. He figured it was because they were deeper than normal. "Yeah. I'm sure I'm fine. There are some bandages in the closet."

Luke got the bandages and cleaned up his gashes. Elijah winced a few times.

"I take it you didn't get anything out of the wolf to see if he's the one you ate," Luke commented.

"Yeah, too busy trying to stay alive."

"I thought you were better than him with all your bragging about being too alpha and running the biggest pack in five states. Big shot billionaire wants to make it seem like he's in control of everything. Boy, they really don't know you."

He growled at Luke. "You don't know me either. Just because we've... we have Sadie in common doesn't give you the right to judge me. Besides, I wasn't expecting him to hold the beast form for so long. He's adept at it. I've never seen anyone hold it and still be able to control himself."

"Maybe we can learn something from him."

"Not funny."

"I wasn't being funny. I was totally serious. I don't enjoy holding the shape, but it's something to learn about if he sticks around. It all depends on Sadie and what she wants. It's quite clear she's in charge of all of us."

Elijah sighed and stared at Luke, wondering if Luke would accept Grey as a potential mate for Sadie. Greyson or not, he was not going to take Sadie away from him.

"She might be. Isn't it easier to accept she can dominate us?"

Elijah shook his head. "No. I'm not used to accepting it. Although, did you see her and feel the link between us when she was commanding him? It's like she wasn't even there. She was so cold. I don't know if it's the drum, but if she's going to turn into something that doesn't resemble the woman I know, then what's the point?"

"Yeah, Sadie had me a little worried, too. I'm sure it's growing pains and she'll settle into her wolf. There. All done." Luke patted his chest, and Elijah grunted from the quick shot of pain.

"Thanks."

"You guys done being asses?" Sadie stood in the doorway.

He forced a smile. "I wasn't being an ass. He challenged me over you."

She rolled her eyes and knelt next to him. Her smile warmed his heart. The thread between them opened and her love surrounded him like a blanket. She kissed him and the love slid around him. She tasted like vanilla and bacon. The combination was a little odd, but he didn't care. He stretched up to meet her lips, but the pain made him hiss and he broke away.

"Don't you know I'm not going anywhere? I have you two."

"What about him?" Luke asked.

She shrugged. "I don't know. Can we leave it for now? I have too much to figure out. Let me worry about it. I love you both. Do I have to keep showing my love to you?"

"No," Elijah replied. "Maybe." He tried to kiss her once more, but his head spun.

"Are you okay?"

"Yeah. I'll be fine. Just the blood loss, I guess, and the wounds healing."

"I'll go take him to lie down. Just be careful of the new one." Luke kissed her on the cheek quickly and helped Elijah out of the room. When they made it into his bedroom, it felt like he was going to lose his lunch. Once he lay down, he felt better.

"I'm going to get you some water. I'll be back."

"Sounds good." Elijah closed his eyes and tried to push past the dizziness he felt even with his eyes closed, but it just grew worse.

Chapter Four

Luke let out a breath as he walked through the garden following his link to Sadie. He didn't know what to make of Elijah's encounter with the new wolf everyone seemed to feel was Sadie's dead fiancé. He'd seen a few things in his time and knew the shaman of his pack would say something. He needed to get back to the pack and bring Sadie, but he couldn't leave her or Elijah in this state. The others in his pack wouldn't appreciate him bringing the other alpha along with him, but he might not have a choice.

Sadie looked forlorn. Grief and confusion encompassed her. Whatever was going on had to play itself out. Luke felt something greater than all of them was influencing them. It all had to do with the drum, with Narissa's conversation in Fae, with Sadie meeting the Great Spirit who claimed to be their mother. If all these things were coming together, then something grave hovered on the horizon. Some battle Sadie was being prepared to fight. *I'm going to make sure nothing happens to her.*

"Here to tell me the new wolf has to go away?" Sadie looked up at him. The coldness in her tone sliced through him. It seemed she was retreating from him and Elijah. With her being able to force them to do things, he didn't know if she was capable of severing their mate bonds.

He sat next to her on the stone bench and stared at the fat koi as they swam lazily among the water plants. If only life were so simple to exist only in a pool and not have any cares in the world. Luke thought back to all the times he was punished because he stood up to his father and stayed his father's hand on his sister. However, Denice always resented him for that. She rebelled. Always thought she could take control of the pack when it was time. Denice was never strong enough to fight his father's influence as alpha.

Luke had challenged the old man and won control of the pack. In doing so, he had been leading the Shadow Clan for over a decade and trying to undo all the strict edicts his father had imposed for almost sixty years. Sometimes he felt like he was caged, even though he was free of his past. No one could truly be free of his past, just like Sadie could never truly be free of the things that set her on the road to become whatever she was. If having this strange wolf was part of the road she needed to walk, then -- even though he didn't like it -- he would be sure to do whatever she needed.

"No, although I want to. For some reason, he interests you. To send him away would hurt you. Look at it from Elijah's and my point of view. Sharing you with Elijah is hard enough. Then you ask us to consider this other wolf. How do you think we feel? No wolf likes to share his mate."

She laughed and wiped her eyes. "I'm not asking you to accept this stranger as a potential mate. I'm just asking you to leave him alone until I can figure out if he's Greyson or not."

"How is it possible he's risen from the dead? It's obvious you have feelings for him. I'm surprised you're not ready to tear Elijah's eyes out for what he did to him and you."

She shook her head. "It was a long time ago. Sometimes I still have nightmares about those eyes in the dark, but it's gotten a lot better. When I first met Elijah, it felt like he wanted to eat me, literally. Then he came to terms that his hunger for me was as a mate and not to eat me. It took me a while to wrap my head around the idea of me and him being together. It took me even longer to get behind the idea of turning into a wolf. I'm still not happy about the whole Denice situation, but I understood why he did what he did because he wanted to protect me. He loves me."

Luke felt the confusion within her and some of the acceptance she spoke about. Her mind wasn't completely closed off to him. He slid his arm around her waist and drew her close. She rested her head on his shoulder. They sat together for a while with the trickle of the water from the waterfall at the far end of the pond. He inhaled the sweet scent of her hair and let the warmth of her body calm the wolf inside him. This simple moment in time was something he wanted to freeze so he could live in it all the time. There would be no more responsibility for leading the pack. Just him and his mate without the hassle of vying for her attention or her affection. When Luke slid his thoughts along their bond, all he could feel was her love for him. Her wolf radiated it even under her human emotions. Luke savored those feelings.

"With all this going on, I never got to ask you how you are doing," Sadie asked him.

"I fine. Why do you ask?" Luke didn't want to think about his sister at this moment. He wanted to continue to push the world out and freeze the moment with this beloved mate.

"You had to banish Denice from the pack. She's your sister. You have to be feeling something about her absence." She looked up at him with hazel eyes showing her wolf shared her personality. It seemed intrigued by what had happened to Denice. He understood why it would because Denice's bite had awakened the wolf inside Sadie.

"Can we not talk about it?" Luke broke her gaze and shifted away a little. He'd thought he was ready to talk about it. Cutting the ties with his sibling might have been pack law, but it hurt him worse than he realized. He loved his sister. Even though it was pack law to exile a member who had bitten and turned a human by force against her will, it wasn't any easier to cut the ties he had with Denice and Nick, her mate.

He was of two minds because of the conflict. As the Pack Master, he knew he did the right thing and his wolf agreed. But the hole where the link he shared with his sister had been seemed like an empty pit in his heart. Even in the past few years when she had defied him, she still was family. The only family he had left. Now Denice and Nick remained lone wolves and it would be a miracle if another pack took them in. He secretly prayed someone would so she wouldn't be alone.

"Sure. I didn't mean to bring up anything --"

He squeezed her hand. "It's okay. We had a tough relationship, but she was family. I guess this is kinda how you feel when we keep asking you about Greyson."

"I didn't think about it that way, but it's true." She slid her fingers along his jaw and turned his head back to her. Sadie stretched and pressed her lips to his in a sweet kiss. He returned it as her passion infused him. Luke trailed his tongue across her bottom lip.

The images of them together flared through his mind and spiked his desire. He could've eaten her up right until she begged him to stop. Luke's yearning to envelop her was a drive he had never experienced before, and yet in just this sweet kiss it was like coming home. It was like sinking into the knowledge everything would be fine and she would always be there for him. Sadie was an anchor point in his life. A small moan passed his lips as he pulled her to him. Sadie's hand's trailed over his jeans. This wasn't what he came out here for, but he stopped and let her press against his firming dick. Luke kissed her a little harder and tasted her blood.

Sadie groaned and deepened their kiss. Her hands found the button on his jeans. Her yearning to be together overwhelmed him. The feeling almost overtook him, but Luke pulled himself out of her influence and broke off their kiss. "I don't think this is the right time." Luke backed away, adjusting his jeans and tried to think of anything but her naked body to make his hard-on go away.

"You're hurting and I can make it better. This is part of what I am here for."

Luke turned around because he heard the difference in her voice. Her tone had some sort of inflection he couldn't place. The aroma of her wolf permeated the air. This wasn't Sadie, but her wolf talking. Her eyes had turned bright green. The same way they blazed the night she had awakened and become a wolf. Luke could sense the great age of the being housed within his mate. He wondered if the wolf within her had more knowledge than either of them even knew.

"Can I ask you something?"

She tilted her head, the way she would in wolf form, studying him like she didn't really understand the question. "We are mates. You and I share knowledge."

"Do you know why you're here? The drum, the ring, and the vision you had of our mother. Do you know what this coming storm is my ancestral spirit talked about? Is that really Greyson in there? Is all this some kind of a joke to twist us around your fingers? Are you manipulating all this and Sadie with you?" He sat back down next to her.

A flash of pain went across her face. "You distrust us after we have shared ourself with you?"

She started to gather her power to use it on Luke. He realized he had overstepped. He laid a hand on top of hers, hoping the gesture would calm her. "I don't distrust you, but you aren't like any other wolf I've ever come across. You share Sadie's body with an ease many don't have. I'm not even sure she's in there right now."

"She's here. Listening. I told her I was the best to answer your questions. I sensed your hesitation in the shadows of your thoughts. You asked me if I know what's coming. The answer is I don't. I am as new as Sadie is to this union of souls. And yet, there are things even I don't understand how I know them. The way we share this body. It's a true melding of spirits. This meshing is why I can speak so easily and she can use my will to make you do as we wish. This new wolf looks like Greyson. He's what you call a wild card. Sadie has gray feelings about him." She shook her head.

Luke tried to sense what she was thinking, but he got nothing. The wall had come down around their bond again. "I think you mean she's undecided about him."

"Yes. Undecided. She's scared. We are both afraid of what's coming. I'm here for a reason. I am with Sadie for a reason. With you. With Elijah and the other who is to come."

His heart sank. He had a feeling it was already going to be Greyson. "Another mate? How do you expect us to share you?"

Her lips turned into a twisted smile. The gesture was a true mixture of animal and human. He could see the overlay of the wolf in her face as her lips turned up to show off too many teeth and her eyes sparkled. This time she straddled him as they sat on the bench by the koi pond. She wrapped her arms around his neck. Sadie kissed him and the link between them opened. Luke could feel the wolf as the dominant personality at the moment, with Sadie there as well. Sadie pressed herself against him.

This time he let the bond between them bring them closer together until he could feel her lips on his. The pressure of his mouth on hers. They were one and yet separate as the mate bond entwined them into something he never experienced before. Luke lost it when she undid his jeans and guided his cock inside her. She broke the kiss and rested her forehead against his as she rode him slowly. She stared into his eyes and their color dimmed to brown and then back to green. Sadie and the wolf sharing a body. He could feel the ebb and flow of her energy as it changed and merged with his and within her through their bond. Luke slid his hands under her robe and caught her hips, urging her to go a little faster. The agonizing speed she held made it hard for him to hold back. But she drew him nearly to the edge and then drove herself back on his shaft once more.

"Sadie, please," he begged her. She tugged on his beard and made him come back up to her mouth.

"I love you, Luke," Sadie said against his lips.

She threw her head back and howled. The jolt of ecstasy from her singed his nerves and he released. Sadie continued to ride him until the quivers running through her stopped. They were both out of breath from the encounter. When he looked back into her eyes, they had returned to normal. The thread between them unwound until he found his way back to himself, and they were separate entities once more. Sadie slid off him and sat next to him on the bench. Luke held her against him as the waterfall trickled in the background.

"I love you, too."

She trailed her fingers over his face. "We both love you. We're here for you. I can't answer most of the questions you asked. We're figuring it out together. I know I can't fill the hole where your sister was, but let me help ease the pain."

A surge of love overcame him and he felt his eyes burning with tears. He looked away until he regained control. "You already have. Sadie, I'm sorry about before. I didn't mean to come off --" A buzzing in his pocket cut off what he was going to say. He tried to ignore it, but the incessant vibrating made him growl. He got up and answered the phone. "Yes."

"Luke, you have to come home," James said to him, his second-in-command.

"Is everything okay?"

His second took in a long breath, but Luke heard his

hesitation. "They found Denice and Nick."

"They're exiled. Why does it matter if they found them?"

"I understand. If they were still living on pack land, I would've kicked them off, but this is different. I'm not calling to tell you they're defying you. I'm calling because she's your sister and… and…"

"Just spit it out, James."

"One of the pups found her body and Nick's while they were playing by the lake in the meadow. You need to come home, Pack Master."

Bodies? What had happened to them? "I'll leave right away." He hung up the phone and looked over at Sadie. "I have to go."

She nodded. "Okay. Do you want me to come with you?"

"I-I don't know… you have stuff to deal with here."

She ran her hand down his arm trying to comfort him. The words pinged through his mind. Denice and Nick dead. His sister dead. The one person he had shared his childhood with. He remembered her running around in pigtails. All she did was look up to him when they were younger. They had a five-year difference between them. He always took responsibility for her. Even when she got older and snuck out. Even when his father's rage got dumped on him, and he took his father's beating with a silver-tipped whip that was meant for her. Denice always thought she was strong or cunning enough to lead. If she'd ever tried, she would run the pack into the ground. The hole in his heart would never be healed now.

"My stuff here isn't as important as being with you when you need me. I'll get changed and talk to Elijah. Can you give me a few minutes before you head back?" Sadie asked. Her love filled him again, trying to push away the cold and numbness taking over. She wove her arm through his and tugged. Luke followed her back to the house.

"Okay."

Sadie said something else to him. He nodded in response as she dashed off. He slid down in a chair and waited. The words of his second came back to him. They'd found Denice and Nick. If they'd found them, something happened. Denice would have gotten off pack lands. *Something must've jumped them. Maybe it's a power grab from outside. I have to get back and make sure the pack is okay. I've been gone too long.*

When he got back, he would consult the shaman to see what the mystic said about what happened to his sister. His wolf paced in the back of his mind as it absorbed the news about Denice. They played when they ran together as children, and now it also felt her absence. Its fury was more directed at who could have done this to them. Who could have wounded them? It gnashed its teeth in the back of his mind. Denice may not have been pack any longer, but she was still family and whoever did this would pay.

Chapter Five

Sadie went to talk to Elijah about leaving with Luke after the news of hearing his sister had been found dead. He needed her right now even if he didn't want to admit his need. Something inside of him broke when he heard. As she got up to the room, the man who looked like Greyson stopped her.

"Can I talk to you?"

"Now really isn't a good time," she sighed and tried to get past him. He stepped in front of her and blocked her path.

"It's important."

"I have other things I need to worry about besides trying to figure out if you're my dead fiancé come back from the grave. There's been a death. I need to leave with Luke to go back to his pack. He needs me with him. You're safe here. Elijah won't bother you until I get back. I'll make sure to let him know."

Grey touched her arm and then pulled back. "Actually, it's about Elijah. He's been moaning ever since you let him rest."

Her heart dropped. She rushed into the bedroom to find Elijah curled up into a ball, shivering on the bed. His skin had paled. A sheen of sweet slicked his body. When she touched him, it felt like her palm had touched a hot stove. His eyes fluttered open and he gave her a forced smile. All the gashes from Greyson's claws were an angry red around the edges.

"What's the matter with you?"

"I'll be fine."

"No, you won't." Panic set in. "Greyson, go get me some ice, water, towels, anything we can use to wash these cuts. Alcohol, vodka. I don't care go get it."

"Sadie, I'm not sure you should call me that. I don't know if it's my name --"

She looked at him and felt her power lash out so he

would obey. "Go. Damn it! I have to call you something. It's better than 'Hey you'!"

He bowed his head and raced out of the room. She had to keep it together for Elijah. "You've told me wolves can heal just about anything unless silver was put into the wounds like the ones on your stomach."

His breathing hitched as he tried to sit up but didn't make it. "We are. I don't know what's going on. It started after I got wounded by the stray. Something about his teeth and claws are different. I don't know. Maybe it was from him being in the wolfman form. It's a difficult form to keep for very long, but it seems to be something he's mastered."

"How do I help you?" Sadie asked.

"I don't know if you can, but maybe you are the only one who can. You healed my eyes. Maybe you can do the same for these claw marks."

Sadie felt her wolf lingering with her. "*Can we?*"

"*We can try. I don't know if this is something we can heal.*"

"*We can't let him die.*"

"*No, we can't.*"

"*How do we start?*"

"*I'm not sure. We looked inward last time. Let's try again.*"

Sadie nodded more to herself than to anything. She closed her eyes and thought about what happened last time she went to explore the link between her and her wolf. She had gone deep within to find her wolf standing next to a woman who identified herself as their mother which Sadie assumed meant she was the mother of all wolves. Sadie still wasn't sure about that, but she needed to heal Elijah.

She slowed her breathing and found herself walking through her mind. When she came to the pool, what looked back at her was her own image with the wolf superimposed over it. It almost seemed they were one being. When Sadie moved her head, she could see the wolf move a moment later. She thought back to the wolf's conversation with Luke about how they shared many things which was why the wolf could speak, why Sadie could make the other alphas do whatever she wanted. But Sadie was getting the hang of it. It was like flexing a muscle. The longer she used it, the easier it was to access. It didn't do her any good figuring out how to heal Elijah.

She touched the surface of the water. It didn't ripple. "Hello, if you're there I need some help."

The vale within her mind stayed silent. She tried to dunk her hand under the water because Sadie sensed something underneath the liquid. A power or a strength she didn't know how to get to. Maybe it was what she needed to heal Elijah. When she put her hand on the plane of the water to break it, all she was met with was a hard surface.

"Do you know what this means?" Sadie asked her wolf.

It didn't have an answer. The fear she was going to lose Elijah surged through her. If this place couldn't give her anything she needed, then there was no point for her to be there. She banged on the surface of the water again and it cracked.

"Please," she cried again to the silent meadow and nothing happened. She pulled away from the place in her mind and brought herself back to the present. When she opened her eyes, Luke stood in the doorway with a stricken look expression. Greyson pressed a wet cloth to Elijah's forehead.

"Greyson told me what's wrong with Elijah. Sadie, you need to stay here and take care of him. I don't need you to worry about me and coming back to the pack. It's fine. I need to talk with my shaman."

"Would your shaman know what's going on with Elijah? A way to help him? I can't heal him. I can't leave him like this."

Luke scratched his beard. "He might be able to, but I'm not sure he can help."

"The shaman who healed me said I had similar wounds," Greyson told them.

"Would he be able to help?" Sadie asked Luke.

Luke shrugged. "I don't know. Maybe, but can Elijah travel? I have to get back."

"I'll help you with him. It's the least I can do," Greyson told her.

Elijah moaned again, and she could feel he wasn't doing good. They had to get him help soon. "Luke?"

"Bring him, but we have to go."

She nodded. "I'll get ready quickly." Sadie raced into her room and took the quickest shower she ever had. She dressed and threw some clothes in a bag. Her heart hammered as she gathered her wits. She had to hold it together. She couldn't fall apart right now because Elijah needed her. She needed them. She grabbed her bag and met them downstairs. Luke waited for them outside. Chad, Elijah's second, met her at the door.

"What's going on?"

"Elijah's been infected with something. We're bringing him to Luke's pack to see if his shaman can help heal him. Can you hold down the fort?" Sadie asked him.

He paled. "I-I guess so. What do I tell everyone?"

"Tell them we're visiting Luke's pack. He's my mate and Elijah wanted to be sure their relationship was cemented."

"If anything happens to him..." Chad warned.

She sighed. "You'll be the first to know."

Luke waited in the car. Greyson sat in the back seat with Elijah. Sadie slid into the front seat. Elijah's skin had lost a bit more color. Greyson nodded at her and gave her a concerned look. Luke squeezed her leg and they sped off.

Most of the drive was silent as Luke had his foot to the floor. She didn't care if he broke the speed limit. The sooner she got to Luke's pack, the quicker she could get to see his shaman. Luke hadn't told her what was going on, but from what she figured, it wasn't anything good.

They were in the car for several hours before Luke pulled onto a private dirt road. She didn't see any other vehicles at the end of the lane. Greyson began to pull Elijah out when Luke pushed him out of the way.

"You stay behind me and Sadie. I'll carry him from here. Don't say anything unless Sadie or I ask you something. Are we clear?" Luke growled.

"Crystal," Greyson answered.

"Luke, should I do anything with your pack? What should I expect?" Sadie asked as the butterflies in her stomach bombard her going back and forth between the worry she felt for Elijah and the nervousness she felt at meeting Luke's pack.

"Stay to my right and slightly behind me. My pack is used to the Pack Master's mate being silent."

"You don't expect me to do that all the time, do you?"

"No, but follow my lead. Don't go all alpha on everyone in the pack unless someone threatens you. Things are a bit up in the air right now." He adjusted Elijah's weight and then trudged through the tall grass. The scents of the other wolves lingered on the air as they got closer. She stayed behind him as they got to a clearing. In the center was a large stump the size of a car. In the center of it were two figures wrapped in white cloth. Flowers had been set down at their feet. Other wolves had gathered around, kneeling before the bodies, and singing. A man looked up and met her gaze. A zing of power went through her. His brown hair was shot through with silver as it hung down his back. A few wrinkles lined his face.

A different man rushed over. His body language deferred to Luke and yet he also had some power. This was Luke's second. Sadie tried to stay focused on what was going on, but her eyes kept straying to the man who was chanting around the bodies. His gaze kept coming back to hers like he needed to talk to her. Well, she needed to talk to him.

"Luke, I'm so sorry about Denice. We gathered what we could find of them and laid their bodies here until you could come. I've called the pack together just as you would've wanted."

"Thank you, James. Right now, I need to speak with Kade. Will you get him for me?" Luke asked.

His second rushed off to get the shaman. He came over a moment later. "You wanted to see me, Pack Master."

"I need to know if you can heal this man. He's the leader of the Pine Clan. He is also my mate's co-mate. It's a long story. Can you heal him?" Luke asked.

"Bring him into my cabin. I can look at him. You should examine your sister's remains. There are questions. I'll bring them with me," Kade said to Luke.

Luke handed Elijah off to Greyson. Kade walked deeper into the compound. Sadie remained behind with Luke. "Is there something I can do here?"

"Go with Kade. Worry about Elijah. I'll come later." Luke's expression remained blank and she could tell he expected to be obeyed.

She wasn't going to argue with him. Sadie brushed her fingers along his hand before catching up to Greyson and the shaman. Inside his cabin, the scent of dried herbs hit her so hard it made her sneeze. It was dark and difficult for her to see, but she followed the voices and found Kade speaking with Greyson. The shaman was already examining Elijah. He peeled back his shirt and pulled the bandages away.

"Stay where you are."

Sadie stopped and watched from the doorway. Kade pulled something from a bundle by the bed. He put it into his mouth and chewed. Greyson glanced at her, but he remained silent. The guilt she sensed from him made her heart reach out to him. The longer he was around her, the more she was trying to believe this was the man she loved come back from the dead, but she still didn't know how to reconcile with what was right in front of her. It didn't matter right now. She would deal with him when she got through the next crisis. Right now she needed to be sure Elijah came through this okay.

Kade spat out whatever he was chewing and put the wad onto some of Elijah's scratches. He repeated the process until Elijah's body was covered in leaves. When he was done, Kade said something to Greyson. Greyson nodded and took a seat by Elijah. Kade pulled her into the main room. He walked over to a fireplace and threw another log into it. After a few moments, he poked it and sat down. Sadie stood in the shadows.

"Sit down. I've been expecting you."

"Expecting me?" Sadie asked. "I don't even know you."

"I've seen you in visions. It's the reason I suggested Luke send Denice to the Pine Clan. You and she were destined to meet. Your meeting initiated the mating of our Pack Master. He wasn't too keen on sending her at first. It took a little coaxing before he came around to the idea. If he hadn't, then you never would've been."

"You're saying you orchestrated this whole thing and have known what was going to happen? Without even telling Luke what the results of this meeting would be?"

Kade shook his head. "I can only see certain roads. If you hadn't come now, then we'd all be done for. The harrowing has begun."

A cold chill walked up her spine. Whatever this harrowing was, it was the reason she had been called. It was the reason for the silver wolf, but she had no idea what it meant to be this super wolf. "Do you know what I'm supposed to do?"

"No, just that you were coming. Did you bring the drum? And there was a gift from the mixed beings."

"No. I -- I wasn't thinking about the drum. Just making sure Elijah'd be okay and getting here because Luke needed to get here. Greyson thought you might be able to heal Elijah. What did you do to him in there?"

"It's an herbal mixture used to draw out infection from silver. It should draw out some of the metal as well if it's not too deeply embedded in his system."

"Silver? Werewolves abhor it."

The shaman took her hand and touched the ring before he pulled away. She caught the faint scent of burning flesh even from the slight touch. "Yet you wear it and have immunity to it. It's part of your makeup. This was the gift from the mixed breed."

"You mean the Fae?"

He nodded.

"Yes. What about the silver poisoning? Greyson can't have any silver on him. I saw the fight between the two of them. Or part of it. Hell... I..." Overwhelming emotions hit her, and she found herself biting back tears. Talking to this strange man who had a hand in her future made her want to know more, and yet it could mean she would be separated from her mates.

Kade squeezed her knee. "Drink this. It will help you relax. It's peppermint tea. The one you love should be okay. The one who inflicted the wounds is an enigma. He stands in this world, and yet he is very much a part of the other world."

Sadie wrapped her hands around the mug trying to get some comfort in the warmth of the beverage. The smell of it did help to ease some of her fears, but it also left her more confused. "What does that mean? Speaking in riddles is not something I can handle." She lost control of her power and wrapped it around the shaman as the wolf wanted more specific answers. However, when she met the aura or energy of the other wolf, there was nothing to latch onto.

"You can't make me bow to you as the others would. Please don't try it again."

"Sorry. I didn't mean anything by it. My wolf is as frustrated as I am. We're both trying to figure all of this out. I've only been this way for a month. I think. I don't really know the exact time. I woke up and Luke was there. Half of the stuff I know or can do, I have no idea how I do it. When I tried to heal Elijah I wasn't able to. She said that was part of my gift."

"This *she*? Who was it?"

Sadie trailed her finger over the rim of the cup. "She called herself our mother. About the same time, Luke had an encounter with a spirit who gave him the drum. Narissa, my Fairy friend, came back from meeting with a mystic in her realm who gave me the ring. I'm still trying to put the pieces together. One of those happens to be Greyson." She sat back in the chair and felt the weight settle on her shoulders. "The only reason I ever agreed to become a wolf was because my decision not to was driving a wedge between me and Elijah. He knew I didn't want to become a monster."

"You must forgive me. I thought you were older. The silver wolf has been here before. It's helped our people in the past and the mixed breeds. Do you not know this?"

"I can sense my wolf has been here before, but everything that happened is blocked. It's like I can see it just beneath the surface, but I can't get to it. The whole of it..."

"Kade, can I speak to you for a second?" Luke

interrupted them.

Kade nodded and got up. Sadie sipped the tea and went into the bedroom to check on Elijah. Greyson dabbed at his forehead with a cloth. Then he used another cloth to pour some water into his mouth. She went in and sat on the other side of the bed and lifted Elijah's head so he could take the water. His skin seemed somewhat cooler, but he still trembled from the fever wracking his body. She leaned over and pressed her lips to his forehead. She tried to feel the link between them, but it was quiet. It almost seemed as if he wasn't there. It was silent and dark. "Elijah, come back to me."

Luke's thread was laden down with grief along with anger. The dark part of him scared her because he would go off and do something drastic without thinking. She didn't think he was the type to run off without thinking things through, but the crux was she didn't really know Luke very well. She had opened her eyes and basically knew he was her mate from his scent. Her wolf chose him. They made love until he brought her back to Elijah. From there it was more of a whirlwind so they hadn't had a chance to sit down and really talk. She didn't even know his favorite food or his favorite color. They were all just learning about one another. She had been with Elijah for over a year and knew him. Loved him. If she lost him, it would devastate her as much as it had when she lost Greyson.

"You love him very much," Greyson said to her.

She turned her attention back to him. His gray eyes peered into hers and she could feel something between them. She wanted to believe it was the man she loved once upon a time. A place in her heart remained for Greyson. Even if the man before her was Greyson, she didn't know where he would fit into her life. He had no memory of what happened to him before he became a werewolf. Part of him was wiped away and born again once he transformed. Whatever happened to him, it hadn't been easy. He hadn't lived a good life since he was killed, and she did feel sorry for him. She didn't know how her wolf felt about him. Seeing him alive and walking around meant she had to reopen a chapter of her life she'd thought was closed. It meant reliving the grief and the questions of how he had somehow been rescued and maybe even brought back from the dead. The whole idea was unfathomable, but then again so much had happened to her bordered on the insane. Before any of this happened, she never believed in werewolves or fairies.

"When I first met Elijah, he helped me out at this resort he partially owns. It was okay at first and then I thought he was a pompous asshole because everyone was kissing his ass. I didn't realize at the time the resort was for shifters. I never thought they were real. As we got things worked out, he saved my life. He confessed to me I was his mate. I didn't know how to process the knowledge because he was still being an ass. But he apologized again. At the last bit, he confessed he ate my fiancé."

"You forgave him for hurting you?" Greyson asked.

"I did. He stopped from killing me because his wolf realized I was his mate, but the human in him couldn't accept it. The shaman said the wounds you inflicted are threaded with silver. How is that possible? Shifters can't abide silver. Just the barest touch of it against their skin burns them."

"I don't know. The one who healed me must've done something with it."

"Did you know when you fought him how it would end?"

He dabbed at Elijah's wounds. "Yes. I've been in fights before. You've seen the scars. The first time I fought with another shifter, a lion. He attacked me and I blacked out. When I came to, he was dead. The wound I had inflicted where blackened from the silver. I had a sense it wasn't natural, but I also understood when anyone got into a fight with me it would result in something like that if they didn't get it treated. It gave me a leg up when I came across anyone even if they didn't know it at the time. I don't become human much. It's easier to be a wolf, but then I heard the drum. It called me to you. He pissed me off and was going to take you away from me."

She scoffed. "I'm not yours to be taken away from. Others have claims before you. Now isn't the time to be talking about it anyway. Don't presume you can come back into my life and things can pick up where they left off. We're both very different people."

The expression on his face looked as if he had been slapped. "I'm sorry if I presumed. Even if the drum called me to you, your scent told me you were my mate. My wolf knows it. You don't want to admit it. Whatever relationship you think we had in the past, it means nothing to me. I know I'm beneath you because I'm not an alpha. I'm painfully aware of that," Greyson stated plainly. He threw down the cloth and walked out of the room.

Her anger welled up and it was combined with her wolf's. It didn't enjoy being put on the spot. Greyson declaring her his mate didn't come out of left field, but she couldn't reconcile it. It was all too new. She threaded her fingers through Elijah's and kissed them. She tried to stay focused on him, but the memory of that fateful night when she and Greyson were attacked flitted through her mind.

* * *

Camping had never really been her kinda thing, but Greyson enjoyed it. This particular weekend, Greyson had gotten her up at four in the morning for the five-hour drive. They got in the car and he started babbling about a great place his friend told him about. It was in the middle of nowhere. She nodded as she barely heard him. Once they hit the highway the blur of the lights and the motion of the car made her fall right back to sleep. The next thing she knew, Greyson was shaking her awake because they had stopped and needed to hike the rest of the way into the wilderness. It took her a moment to shake off the sleepiness. When she did, Greyson was bubbly as ever though he had driven and gotten up before her.

"Are you going to be able to wake up enough to get to the campsite?"

"How long's the hike again?" She yawned while she got her pack out of the trunk. Greyson helped her adjust it.

He rubbed her arms to help get her going and then flashed her his epic smile. It always made her feel better no matter what obstacle was in her way. He always told her she could do anything she put her mind to. "It's a couple of hours if we make good time." He pointed to the map which to her looked like a bunch of squiggly lines on top of a big blob of green and blue. She let him plan everything and grabbed a corner of the map as the wind kicked up and nearly tore it out of her hand. Something about this place felt off. Sadie couldn't put her finger on it, but it felt like they were walking on someone's grave. Her instincts said they should leave. It didn't feel like a place they should be.

"Are you sure we should be here? I don't have a good feeling about this place. We're in the middle of nowhere and on private land. I can read a map to know this isn't part of a state forest," Sadie said to him.

"No one will ever know that we're here. Bass came up here and no one ever caught him. He said he thought he might have even seen a Bigfoot. Think about it. Maybe we can find one up here."

"Bigfoot or not, let's go somewhere else. Please,

Grey."

He folded up the map and stuffed it into his pocket along with the compass. "Don't worry. It'll be fine. Come on. Have I ever led you down the wrong path?"

She poked him. "There's always a first time."

Greyson chuckled and kissed her quickly. "Let's go. Daylight's burning."

"Fine."

They trudged through the woods, going higher and higher until they came to the campsite. She thought back to the first time he had seen her. She didn't think that was possible, but he wooed her. He sent her flowers and chocolate. Greyson took his time gaining her trust, and then it all seemed like a Fairy tale. He never minded her curves.

They made camp for the night. Greyson dug a fire pit and lined it with some stones. They had a fire going and cooked hot dogs. They snuggled and roasted some marshmallows as it grew dark.

"Didn't I tell you this was going to be okay?" He hugged her and pulled her closer.

The night air had grown cold, but he and the fire kept her warm. She rolled her eyes and hated to admit he was right. "No, it's been great. No Bigfeet."

"No."

Sadie yawned as she watched the fire dance. "Why don't you go in the tent and get some sleep? I have plans for us in the morning. There's this great waterfall Bass was telling me about not far from here. He said the pool is wonderful. I was thinking we could --" He nipped her ear and then sucked on the sweet spot at the curve of her throat.

She giggled and twisted away from him. "Not fair. You're sending me to bed and then not coming in to finish what you've started."

"You're going to fall asleep before I get in there.

Besides, I have to stay out here and watch the fire until it dies down a little bit more. Then I'll come to bed and wake you up. How does that sound?" Greyson kissed her and trailed his tongue along her lips.

Sadie pulled him close, showing him how much she expected him to keep his promise. "You'd better." She stretched, feeling her sore muscles from being still for so long. She climbed back into the tent, slipped into her sleeping bag. The cloth-covered blowup pillow wasn't the best, but once her head hit it, she fell into sleep.

The screams woke her.

At first she thought it was an animal in the night, but then she realized it was Greyson. Fear held her in place until she got up the nerve to look out into the campsite. The light from the full moon shone through the trees. Something -- some kind of beast -- stood over him. Its golden eyes looked up from its prey focused on her.

She felt the scream building in her throat until it made it to her lips and...

* * *

"Sadie, can you come outside?"

She blinked, the memory falling away as she looked up from Elijah. She wiped her eyes and realized she had sunken into the recollection of the night she lost Greyson. Luke stood in the doorway. Their connection remained closed, but it was obvious he needed her. "Sure."

"Are you okay?"

"I'm fine. Don't worry about me. I'm here for you." She touched his face. "What do you need me to do?"

He trailed his fingers down the lines of her tears. "He'll be okay."

She nodded. "I hope so. Your shaman said it was silver poisoning. Somehow Greyson has it in his claws and his teeth. It shouldn't be possible, but it seems to be."

"We can figure him out later. I saw him walk into the woods. Kade went after him. Will you come out and meet my pack?"

"Of course."

She followed Luke into the middle of the clearing. About two hundred wolves had gathered around the stump where the bodies were laid out. Luke slung his arm around her waist as they walked toward them. The other wolves looked upon them with awe. She could see the adoration in their eyes and feel their sadness. They were all in mourning even for a member of the pack they had disowned.

"You've gathered here because of my call. James has reached out to others to let them know about Denice and Nick. I know I exiled them from the pack. If circumstances were different then I would not be before you or preparing them for a pack burial. Something or someone killed my sister and her mate." He pulled back the sheet covering the bodies.

Parts of the corpses were missing. Together they might have made up one body. Denice's head remained, but they had taken Nick's. Sadie looked away, but forced to herself to look back and keep the contents of her stomach down. The wounds were done with surgical precision. The wind stirred. She caught the scent of something metallic. The sun glinted off a fine mist stirring in the air. Screams started as the dried blood on the sheet moved with the breeze. Luke hissed. Sadie lunged forward and moved the sheet back over the bodies. Those closest fell to the ground covering their faces or other parts of their body.

"Quick, everyone get into the water. Get into a shower. Anything to wash off the silver," she said to them. No one seemed to notice. The power of her wolf latched on and made her able to control all the other wolves. She felt the blanket go out from her like an energy wave. "All of you get to water now. Those who aren't hurt, help them." The others in the pack didn't question her but acted as if they were in a trance. Luke fell to his knees as his hands covered his eyes.

"It burns."

She pressed her forehead against his. When she thought about how she could heal him it was the same thing when she tried to patch up Elijah. Nothing happened. *Please. Please. I have to be able to help them.* Sadie helped Luke peel his fingers away from his face. His eyes and his face had been burned in splotches from the fine silver. She couldn't see him suffer.

"You're trying too hard."

Kade's voice was behind her. She glanced at him and saw Greyson lingering on the outskirts of the clearing. Greyson had a defeated look on his face and something about him sulked. Something had been said between him and Kade. He would have to wait until this crisis passed.

"What do I do?"

"May I?"

She nodded.

Kade guided her hands to his temples. "Close your eyes and think about the stillness. You see the lake and the reflection of yourself, but you're pounding on the water to crack it for your power. It's not under the surface. It's here." He pointed to his heart. "Think about how you love them. How you and the wolf are one. Things within you are trying to come together."

"That doesn't give me anything to go on. I tried it with Elijah and nothing happened."

"The first time you were both connected, whatever happened between you was on instinct. You healed him because you loved him. You love our Pack Master. Just embrace that."

Sadie tried not to close off her mind and to feel nothing else except the love she had for Luke. Her panic nearly encompassed her again, but she pushed it aside. Sadie thought of the first time she saw Luke. He had smelled so good. She knew he was the one for her. That feeling overtook her and the link between her and Luke flared open. She grasped at the coolness and let her lips touch his. Luke kissed her back. Her fingers slid along his cheeks. He hissed, but it seemed like it was working.

"Sometimes the easiest way to find your way is just to feel it and not to force it," Kade explained.

Sadie hardly heard him because she had broken the kiss. Her eyes remained closed, but through the link they shared, she could feel Luke's pain and discomfort.

"Sadie," Luke moaned. The silver was still eating away at him. The others in the pack would have the same thing happening to them as well.

"Shh," Sadie whispered. She concentrated on how to be the balm. Power flowed out of her and filled in the dark spaces she felt in his face where the silver worked on his system. Sadie worked on pushing out the silver out until he coughed and pulled away. When she opened her eyes, he had been healed.

"How did you do that?" Luke asked.

It took her a moment to catch her breath. She wanted to say something, but Kade answered for her. "It's who she is, Pack Master. It's what the silver wolf is for. I'm afraid I have to steal her from you." Kade pulled Sadie away from Luke. "Can you help the others?"

"I think so."

"Good. You are a gift from the Great Mother. We are so thankful to have you here. If you can take care of the others, then I will go back to your other mate."

"Will he be okay?"

"I can cure his illness. You can cure them." He motioned to the other wolves who were coming back.

"You can't burn the bodies. More silver will be dispersed. It's the reason why they were dumped by the water. Whoever did this hoped the water would be infected and the silver ingested."

"How do you know all this?" Kade asked.

Sadie shook her head as the words just came out. "I don't know."

A young girl stood before Kade. Her pale face was also burned. "She'll help you. You can trust her, Jasmine."

"Hi. This might sting a little, but I can make it all better."

Chapter Six

Greyson watched as Sadie healed those who were hurt. Once they had all been cured, Luke guided her back into his cabin. The other wolves didn't seem to notice him as they all dispersed and didn't seem to even worry about him being there. Luke must have said something to him. Without anywhere to go, he felt alone. Greyson sighed. It would be easy to slip back into wolf form and turn back into the wilderness. But he couldn't get Sadie out of his mind. The wolf wanted her, but he was too afraid to approach her.

"The look on your face says you've heard the drum and you can't get the woman out of your head." The shaman patted him on his back.

He jumped and nearly growled at the other wolf. "She wants nothing to do with me, or she thinks I'm something I'm not or I don't remember. It's the damn drum. I wish I never heard it. I'm surprised I didn't come away with callouses on my paws from the distance I ran in order to find her. I'm not good enough for her." He raked his hands down his arms and didn't feel the pain until the shaman grabbed his wrists and held them.

"Give her a chance to come to terms with what's going on. You're a part of her puzzle. Have you ever tried remembering your life before?"

"Why do you care about me? What's the point?"

"Come with me. Did you bring the drum with you?"

Greyson nodded. "It's back in the truck. I grabbed it before we came up."

"We can get it later. We'll need it." Kade headed back toward his cabin.

Greyson wasn't sure why the shaman was interested in him. The man had been nice to him even though he was clearly an outcast among them. He would never truly have anywhere to go among any of the shifters. He might have been one of them, but with the silver in his blood he would always be an outcast. Greyson stood at the threshold of the shaman's cabin. He almost turned away. Then a deeper instinct told him he needed to stay here. Sadie would need him even if he didn't understand or if she never accepted they were mates.

"Are you coming inside? It's your choice to leave or not. If you do, I can tell you the woman will come apart. You're part of her life's journey. I can help you rediscover who you were before you took on fur," Kade said to him as if he was reading Greyson's mind.

He brushed his hair out of his face. It was longer than he normally had it. An echo left over from the man he was before. His wolf nudged against his mind to go into the hut. It wanted to fill in the black hole of his memories. "I'm not sure I want to know what was before."

Kade nodded. "I understand, but we can't run from the past. You might not have chosen to be what you are. It's obvious someone put some thought into how you were put back together with the silver running through you. Come inside the circle. We can start when you're ready." Kade walked into the bedroom to check on Sadie's mate. Greyson could smell the other wolf, and he didn't smell the sickness in the air as he had before.

Greyson studied the circle of stones on the floor. He didn't remember them from before when he walked out. Then again, the cabin seemed out of place when he stood in the middle of the doorway. Energy played against him like a thin film of water he passed through. Life had to be simpler than it was now. Turn and run back into the darkness and see if he could make a life for himself. Or make a go of it with the two alpha males and stake his claim with Sadie. Take the chance to feel her body against his. *What if I don't like what I was before? What if I was a dick? Suck it up. It'd be nice to sleep in a bed and belong to someone and not be off on my own all the time.* Greyson slipped into the circle. The door closed behind him. The air grew heavier. Kade stepped into the circle. A clap like thunder deafened him. A sheen of silvery energy closed around them as it followed the stones. A sudden chill went down his spine. He got spooked and tried to leave, but the energy of the circle he hit like a concrete wall.

"It won't let you leave until this is done."

"Until what is done?"

Kade shrugged. "You were the one who sat down. It'll show you whatever you need to know. I'm only here to be the guide. "

"How can it know what I need to see? Aren't you going to give me some herbs or blow smoke in my face?"

The shaman chuckled. "You've watched too much television. That's not how it works. These stones are older than you or I and have spirits of their own. They once lingered in the other world of the Fae and were brought here as a gift. They used to help us cross into their realm, but now that's closed off to only a special few."

He gritted his teeth not sure he believed the baloney the shaman fed him. However, it did appear he was trapped in the circle until this thing played out. "Fine. What do I do?"

"Close your eyes and think back to the last thing you remember. When you get to the point where you think you might black out or the wolf is about to take over, then open your eyes and see what you need to see."

"What about you?"

Kade sat with his legs crossed and his hands resting, palms up on his knees. "I'm part of the decoration. If all goes right, then you won't even know I'm here."

Greyson closed his eyes and tried to relax. He cleared his throat and let his mind wander back to when he first woke up. Faces surrounded him. Ones he had never seen before. He didn't understand them at first. All their language was garbled. It felt like he was outside himself and getting reoriented with how things worked. His thoughts were cloudy. Everything about his body was pain. It felt like he was burning from the inside and being torn apart and put back together all at the same time. A tremor ran through him as he tried to push past the memory.

As he stretched back farther, he felt the wolf on the edges of his vision. It started to turn red. Something ripped at his throat. Greyson rubbed his scars. He never recalled how he had gotten them. The pain intensified. Spots floated in his vision. He tried to pull out of the vision. When he opened his eyes, the circle had fallen away. Kade no longer sat in the circle. Instead, a campfire flickered near him. He could hear the crackling of the wood in the pit. The crickets were chirping in the distance. He could smell the wood burning and the dark smoke filled his nostrils.

Greyson focused and he heard someone rustling in the tent a few feet away. When he unzipped the tent, he saw Sadie huddled in a blue sleeping bag that had seen better days. A dark green one lay next to her waiting for someone to join her. A pang of loss went through him as he stared at the sleeping woman. This was an echo of a past he didn't remember. And yet as he watched her slumber, the love he felt for her overwhelmed him. His wolf held the same sentiment. This was some proof they had been together in the past. It frustrated him further because the little details to cement his memories of a life before awaking as the wolf remained out of reach.

Sadie turned and murmured in her sleep. He smiled and marveled at her beauty. Every fiber in him knew they were meant to be together. They hadn't set a date yet for the wedding. Greyson shook his head as the flash of memory overtook him and then flitted away. The log popped in the fire and he turned back from the tent. Flames dimmed and it seemed darker. Some time had passed because the moon was in a different position in the sky. Bright and full. The tent was closed. He poked the fire with a stick, not recalling how he had gotten back to sitting. Greyson felt the weight of sleep tugging at him. It would be good to turn in and snuggle up to Sadie. He had plans in the morning to take her skinny-dipping by the pool and watch her glistening form as she stood under the waterfall.

He had promised to wake her, but the day's trek had gotten to him. Greyson shook his head and tried not to get caught up in the memory. Whatever power the shaman had over him took its toll. Greyson tried to fight it, but when he looked at the tent again and thought of Sadie and the possibility of a life with her, then he knew he had to ride it out.

A twig snapped behind him. He turned and peered into the darkness but didn't see anything beyond the perimeter of the light from the dying fire. He'd left his flashlight in the tent. *Just a deer or raccoon looking for food. Nothing to worry about.* He stood up and was about to pour sand on the remnants of the fire when he heard a growl. A shiver of primal fear took him over. It took him a moment to regain his composure. Nothing could happen to Sadie.

Greyson took a step toward the tent when another growl came. Out of the darkness two golden eyes appeared. It took him a moment to register what they belonged to. The shape of the muzzle and then the body came closer to the fire. A wolf, larger than a Bull Mastiff and built like a lion. It pulled back its lips showing off the curved canines like small daggers. Its gaze flicked between him and something else. Greyson looked behind him and noticed the other wolf. It was a little larger than the one in front of him. They had him cornered. The fire was about out. He glanced at the tent one more time. He dashed from the campsite, but one of the wolves caught him around the neck and brought him down. Greyson screamed as he stared into those golden eyes. He yelled again when the other one struck his torso. He tried to take in a breath. It all grew cold and his last thought was of Sadie.

Greyson found himself standing over his body watching as Sadie rushed out of the tent. The wolf that took him down turned his attention to her. She screamed and tried to get away. Greyson tried to stop the wolf, but it went right through him. The animal mauled Sadie's back, flipped her over, and then stopped. He didn't see what happened next because he felt himself fading. The world went gray and he drifted away.

Faces. Blurs came in and out of focus. A steady beat drew him back until the world wasn't as gray but filled with colors. The tempo almost talked to him, telling him something important. He tried to understand it, but the phrases never made sense. He drifted, felt pain, felt burning in his limbs and in his head. Soon the pain took over and the drumming faded away, but deep down he knew he would remember the language of the drum.

He opened his eyes and found himself staring at a man with blue eyes whom he didn't recognize. His lips moved first and then the words registered later. "He's awake."

He drifted again and when he opened his eyes again, Greyson found he could move and breathe. Everything around him seemed more alive, and yet he had no idea of how he had gotten there.

"You've rejoined us. For a moment, I didn't think you'd come back from the nether."

"Where am I? Who are you?"

The man smiled. "You're the grey one. Your name before was Greyson. We've brought you back and made a few adjustments."

"What're you talking about?"

The old man patted his hand and then tapped his nails. "Had to use silver to bind your flesh and spirit. It will be needed later when she comes."

"When who comes?" Greyson asked as he weighed what the man said about his name. He tried it a few times on his tongue and decided he liked it.

"Never mind. It'll all make sense when it needs to. Listen for the drum and you'll know her. But for now, you'll need to rejoin the others. The bears will fix you up. They already know about the modifications."

"Where am I?" he asked again, but the face of the man was already growing dim.

"A step between here and there. Don't worry about it until you need to," the man answered his question. "Just know we fixed you up."

The man faded completely and the next thing Greyson saw was the familiar face of the bear shaman who had fixed him up. He knew this memory and came back to himself. Kade appeared before him, and Greyson found himself sitting in the circle of stones.

"Welcome back. Did you find your answers?"

"I think so. You didn't see any of it?"

"Not all of it, just the last part, about binding your spirit into your flesh with silver. I understand now why you are the way you are. Only one being could perform that magic and because they did, it means you also play a part in this."

"What kind of being could bring me back from the dead?" As Greyson said it, he realized he truly had been dead from the wolf attack. He hadn't wrapped his mind around the idea he had died and been brought back to life.

Kade sighed and offered Greyson a hand to get up. "Fairies."

Chapter Seven

Luke rubbed Sadie's shoulders. She tried to get some feeling back in her body. Healing all those in the pack left her drained. Luke comforted her the only way he knew how, by being close to her. It still came off as a shock his sister was dead and someone had done this on purpose. Whoever it was, they had no love for shifters because they had turned Denice and Nick's bodies into weapons. They couldn't bury them on pack land and they couldn't burn them.

She felt tired and wrung out and she couldn't help her thoughts from going back to Elijah and Greyson. She feared for Elijah, but had to trust Kade. Greyson insisted she was his mate. She didn't know if that was the case and didn't have time to process it.

Luke stopped when someone knocked on the door. He answered it and Kade walked in. Greyson lingered in the doorway. Luke came back over to her. "I have to go with Kade and speak with the other elders of the pack. Will you be okay? They may want to question you about what you did today."

"I'm not going anywhere."

Kade stepped over to her. "Greyson said he left something in Luke's truck. Would you mind going with him to retrieve it?"

"What is it?" Luke asked.

"The drum," Greyson replied.

"Why do you need that damn thing?" Luke growled.

She got the sense Luke didn't want her alone with Greyson. "It's fine. I need your keys." She held out her hand.

"It's unlocked."

She gave him a quick kiss and headed toward the door. She saw the look Luke gave Greyson, but she ignored it. Sadie went outside and Greyson followed her. They didn't talk. She kept her attention focused on moving forward and not on the man who trailed behind her. "You're allowed to walk with me."

He caught up to her and walked beside her. "You like caramel sauce on your ice cream and you add a spoonful of peanut butter to it. Your favorite flavor is fudge swirl. We used to go to the place on Elmwood because they had the stupid statue you liked of the raccoon shoving its face into a banana split."

Sadie wasn't sure she heard him correctly. Only Greyson knew that small detail of her life. If he knew, there was a good chance this truly was the man she'd planned on marrying. She stopped and studied him. He looked the same as he did before, but something in his eyes seemed different. "How do you remember?"

"I'm right, aren't I?"

"Yes," she said softly.

He shrugged. "I sat with Kade. He helped me recall a few things about how I became what I am. I saw you in the tent when the wolf attacked you. It spared you."

"It did." Her old emotions for him swirled within her heart. She couldn't deny her love for him, but knowing this was him opened up a can of worms.

"Do you know why?"

She didn't know if now was a good time to have this conversation. She kept walking toward the truck, not sure she wanted to answer the question. *What would he do to Elijah if he found out?*

Greyson grabbed her arm. She turned around and growled. He backed up and put his hands up. "Whoa! You don't have to get all bitchy about it. I was asking a question."

Sadie turned around and looked at the man who used to be her fiancé. She took in a calming breath and tried to calm her raging emotions. "Sorry. It's been a hell of a day."

"It has."

"I'm sorry if I snapped. Did you remember anything else?"

Greyson's forehead creased. "I'm not sure. Fractures of memory." He took a step forward. "I do remember this." He rested his palm on her cheek and brushed his lips across hers.

Sadie wasn't sure how to react. It was such a familiar feeling. She wound her arm around his neck. Her body molded to his. When she took in a long whiff, she could smell the familiar scent she had snuggled up with at night for so many years, along with the aroma of the wolf. It brought back all the memories of them together. Her wolf was leaving the decision up to Sadie on how this was going to play out. Being a wolf had changed his body so it was leaner. "I remember this, too." Sadie returned the kiss and then rested her head on his chest listening to the beating of his heart. Greyson held her. The dam held in her emotions cracked. The tears she cried for the hole in her soul and the loss of his presence all rushed back again. She spent a year and a half in mourning before she met Elijah. Greyson hugged her and kissed the top of her head. The feel of him felt like home. "I missed you."

He lifted her chin and swiped her tears away. "I missed you, too, even though I didn't know it. I've always felt something wasn't there, but I didn't know until I saw you. I meant what I said about you being my mate. Regardless of our past history. I know you're it for me."

She took in a breath and calmed down now that her old emotions about Greyson had run its course. She felt clear-headed as though some weight had been lifted off her. "Grey, I have Elijah and Luke now. I don't know if there's room in my life for *three* men. I'm still trying to wrap my mind around dealing with them."

He brushed his lips against hers once more. The soft caress sent chills down her spine. "I'm not going anywhere, so you have to get used to me being around. I'll do whatever it takes to be in your life. Besides, I have nowhere to go. Why not stay here and keep you safe?"

"Am I in danger?"

"Sorry. I shouldn't have said anything. It came up in this vision quest with Kade. Whoever put me back together mentioned I had to protect someone. I'd know her by the sound of the drum. They bound my spirit to my flesh with silver. It's why I'm able to hurt the other shifters with just a scratch. It brought me back to you."

Sadie nodded, not sure how to process the revelation. Someone had known about her being special before she ever met Elijah. *Did Elijah know, too? No, he couldn't have known. He was as surprised as me when he learned who I was and what he did. I have to get back to him.* She needed some time to think. She unlocked the truck and saw the drum in the back seat. Once her fingers slid over the surface, a sense of urgency filled her.

"We need to get back to Elijah and Luke. Something's coming."

"How do you know?" Greyson asked.

"Just do. Come on." She started off with the drum in hand. Greyson fell in step next to her. She could tell he wanted to talk, but she couldn't focus now. They got back to the pack. The first thing she did was check on Elijah. She set the drum next to her as she sat down. Elijah wasn't breathing as heavily as he was before. His color looked better. The leaves, or whatever the remedy was, seemed to be working. Her hands itched as warmth entered them. This time she went with the healing ability. Sadie felt the silver poison in his veins. She focused on their link and where the wounds were festering. She forced her healing ability into those lines and moved the silver from his veins. The leaves took on a silvery sheen as they absorbed the metal. Sadie pulled back and felt winded again. A surge of energy filled her as it flashed up from the drum. Elijah took in a deep breath and his eyes opened. A small smile spread on his lips once he saw her.

"Hey, beautiful."

Sadie brushed the hair from his face. "Hey, yourself."

Elijah's gaze moved from her around the room and settled on Greyson. "What's he doing here?"

She placed a hand on his chest to calm him. Even in his weakened state, she could feel the agitation of his wolf. "It's a long story, Elijah. He's going to be around for a while."

"A while? What does that mean?"

"I'm here to protect her," Greyson replied with a smug smile on his lips.

Elijah growled. Greyson nearly swiped at him again, but Sadie put up her hands. "Enough from the both of you. Greyson, go see what's up with Luke, please."

"We're not done talking," Greyson said before he left.

"What's he talking about?" Elijah asked.

"How about we talk about this later when you're a little stronger?"

"How about you don't change the subject?" Elijah grumbled.

"Greyson claims he's my mate."

"He's come back to haunt me. How can he even claim to be your mate? Isn't two men enough? Aren't I enough for you?"

Sadie sat beside him. Their bond flared and she could feel his insecurity. She trailed her fingers down his jaw and felt the stubble of his beard coming back. He knew she preferred him without it. "Elijah Dane, billionaire who could have any woman he wants, is worried I'm not going to want him anymore?"

He threaded his fingers through hers. "That life is

behind me. I want no one else but you. Is this something you wanted? Your dead fiancé to replace both of us?"

"I never wanted any of this. I just wanted to be with you. I wasn't expecting Luke or to see Greyson again. You know how long it took me to choose to become a wolf. Do you really think I wanted to throw a wrench into all this?"

"No. Sorry. I know how much you loved him and after what I did to him... Have you told him about who I am and what I did?"

"Not yet. There are other things I thought were more important. Luke's talking to his shaman and the elders in the pack. Someone poisoned his sister and her mate with silver. I had to heal all those who were affected by it."

"Heal? When did you become a healer? Where are we anyway?" Elijah asked.

"Luke brought us back to his pack. We needed his shaman to heal you. Hence all the leaves on you." Sadie began pulling the leaves off his wounds.

"Great. Let's go find him. I --"

"Sadie, they want you outside. Luke said it's important and to bring the drum." Kade dashed into the room and gestured for her to come out.

"I'm coming with you." Elijah got out of bed and stood up. He grabbed onto Sadie as he wobbled on his feet. She held his hand and could still feel him recovering from the silver poisoning. Sadie wrapped her arm around him, took the drum, and walked out of the cabin wondering what was so important they needed her.

Chapter Eight

Luke listened to the elders. They wanted to meet Sadie and understand what she was. They didn't want to take his word or what they had seen with their own eyes. She had healed those who had been poisoned by the silver. He wasn't sure he believed it either, but he had felt her do this. He wanted to put his sister to rest, but didn't know what they were going to do to with her and Nick's bodies since they were laced with silver. This was a deliberate attack on his pack.

Kade came back with Sadie. Greyson lingered on the outside of the pack. Luke didn't like the wolf. Something was off about him. However, he had the sense he was important which was why he let him remain. He wasn't expecting to see Elijah walking behind her. As they came closer, Luke noticed the other alpha stumbled. He wasn't back to his old self, but he was sure he was getting there.

"This is the one?" Cedar asked him. She wasn't there when the silver had infected the others.

Luke nodded. "She is my mate. The spirits have given her many gifts."

"I wouldn't expect her to be the one who was chosen," Justice said to him.

"We can't choose the things like this. It just is. Wasn't that something you once told me?" Luke asked the older wolf.

Justice grunted.

"We shall see why she's so special. I saw her heal the others, but I'm not sure. I don't believe she's not in on this." Hector rubbed his chin as they came closer.

"What was so important?" Sadie asked.

Luke held in the smile as she stared at them. He could feel her power and her confidence as it came off her. "The elders wanted to meet you. They think you might have been in cahoots with those who are trying to invade our pack lands."

Her eyes narrowed. "Why would they think that?"

"Pack Master, we caught this outsider on the outskirts of the forest." James dragged a scraggly wolf behind between him and another. His shirt was torn and dirty. Searing wounds were slashed across his chest and thighs and cuts along his face. The stranger put up quite a fight with his wolves. They threw him down to his knees. Luke grabbed the wolf's head and yanked it up. He curled his nails and was about ready to take his head.

"Wait. I know him." Elijah stepped forward.

Luke looked up. "How did he end up here? Is he in on this? Are you?"

Sadie put a hand on Luke's chest. "Stop this. All of you. I'm not in on this. Neither is Greyson or Elijah." Her gaze swept over the elders and Luke knew they were also affected by her power. He saw the fight in their faces as they tried to resist. She put a hand on the intruder's head and he looked up. The fear in his eyes calmed. Luke could see he already worshiped Sadie.

I hope he's not another mate. I don't know if I can deal with another one. Luke didn't want to think about having to share Sadie with another man. He bathed in her calmness and let himself relax. As Luke did, Sadie released her hold on him. She flashed him a smile as the stranger leaned against her leg like a frightened puppy.

"Who are you?" Cedar asked the man.

He looked up at Sadie who nodded to him to answer. "Rocky. Elijah is my Pack Master. Sadie is his mate and my alpha. My mate and I were coming to meet up with Sadie. They are friends. Something happened."

"What do you mean something happened?" Sadie asked. Her panic filled Luke's mind.

"I tried. I swear. They were waiting for us. They took her. I tried to get her back. They had silver. Please help me get her back," Rocky begged Sadie and looked at Elijah and then at Luke.

"What is he talking about?" Hector asked.

"Let's go inside where we can talk and tend to this man's wounds," Kade suggested.

"Good idea. Come with me." Luke led them to a large building in the back of the compound.

They walked into the heart of the pack. Those inside looked up. Most were the younger members of the pack. A large kitchen was in the back. Sizeable tables and benches with a few scattered seats lined the hall. In another wing were rooms for those in the pack who needed a place to lay their head or who wanted to live on pack land. The building had been one of his father's better ideas. Luke had helped him build it. His father had actually listened to him and taken some of his suggestions into consideration. A few of those wolves moved from their benches to give them some space. Elijah sat next to Sadie. Luke sat across from her and the elders sat next to him. He could feel their emotions through the bonds of the pack he shared: intrigue, disbelief, uncertainly. The one who seemed to believe Sadie was Cedar. She was one of the older generation who had been around in his grandfather's time. Luke considered her to be more middle-aged than old. Wolves, under the right circumstances, could live for several hundred years.

Once they settled, Kade worked on Rocky as he took off his tattered shirt. Kade wiped away the blood, but the wounds were still angry. Some of them had turned black around the edges. Silver flowed through Rocky's bloodstream, killing him from the inside out. Luke shivered as he remembered the burn of it from when he had been exposed to it. Kade shook his head as though he could read Luke's thoughts that he couldn't do anything for him.

"Sadie, I know you're weary, but his wounds are beyond my skills. Would you be able to heal him as you already healed so many of the pack and your mates?"

Kade asked.

Sadie turned to the shaman and looked at Rocky. A look of fear passed over her face. Elijah rested a hand on his arm. Greyson touched her shoulder also reassuring her. She glanced at the other wolf. Something had happened between them. She seemed more comfortable with the strange man than she had before, and yet there was still some apprehension.

"Can she heal him? No one can heal silver poisoning. Your leaves can only do so much or calling upon the ancestral spirits. No offense, Kade," Hector grumbled.

"None taken, but you might want to eat your words. You haven't seen what this woman can do. A new dawn is coming. We must band together. Sadie is the most sacred thing we have. She will keep the storm from breaking over us," Kade replied.

"We shall see," Justice answered.

Luke didn't know where Justice stood. The elder had been from the time of his father. Luke never much liked the older man. Justice liked to cling to the older ways of the pack and thought a male-dominated clan was the way to go. He was against Luke joining with the other packs. Right now, Luke needed all of them on his side and to support his mate. He might have been the leader and held sway over the pack, but they had friends in other packs and had influence. He needed them, as much as he hated to admit it. Sadie did seem exhausted. After everything, Luke understood why. He had to help her back to his cabin after she had cared for those exposed to the silver. All Luke wanted to do was hold her and protect her, but the Pack Master in him knew he had to find the ones who had disgraced his pack and defiled his sister. He took her hand. She gave him a smile. After this he was taking her back to his cabin and they were going to be alone. Luke needed time with her. His hands ached to touch her. To breathe in just her scent.

"Okay." Sadie placed her hands on Rocky's chest. The other man whimpered a moment. Sadie closed her eyes. Luke saw a heatwave around her shimmer the air and flow like liquid down her arms and into her hands. Rocky moaned from the pain. The elders next to him gasped as the wounds on Rocky's chest closed. The black lines from the silver retreated. A fine sheen of liquid silver seeped like tears from the injuries. Kade dabbed at the liquid with a cloth until Rocky's flesh was clear and no more infection remained in him.

"It's a miracle," Cedar said. "How do you feel?"

"Fine, but it's not me I'm worried about. Please, Mistress, they have Nari. We have to get her," Rocky implored her.

Sadie slumped against Elijah. "After all she's done, she needs to rest." Elijah looked at him.

She waved him away. "Let him tell his story. Then I'll go lie down."

Luke shared a look with Elijah. They both agreed Sadie needed to rest and they could deal with whatever Rocky had to offer. He didn't want Sadie in any danger. Neither did Elijah. "Fine."

"Rocky, what happened after you left with Nari?" Elijah asked.

Someone came over with a tray filled with glasses and water. Greyson filled them and handed one to Sadie and Elijah. She took a sip. He stood behind them and didn't say a word as Rocky began to tell his story.

"Greyson had said he was healed by a bear shaman. I know a couple. With her being Fae, she took me with her. The whole sleuth of bears had been slaughtered. Parts of them had been taken. Silver. You could smell the burn and see it on the bodies. Narissa handled it better than I could because of her mixed blood. Once we touched the bodies, they almost disintegrated, sending silver dust into the air. I've never seen anything like it. We went to the other sleuth and warned them. They didn't want to believe me until Nari convinced them with whatever her power is. They started to reach out to other alphas to warn them something is coming. I asked about Greyson. Their shaman knew him. Said he had appeared on their land. He stayed a few months until he was well enough to leave."

"What happened when you were attacked?" Elijah asked.

"Where were you attacked?" Luke asked. He didn't like the idea of a whole sleuth of bears being murdered. It also meant this was not an isolated incident. Once they spoke, he was going to reach out to the other wolf packs he knew and the other shifters. He would suggest the same of everyone at the table. He knew Elijah had massive list of contacts.

"Nari brought me back to the mansion. And --" Rocky looked between Luke and Sadie. His face paled. The horror of whatever he had seen played across his face. He looked down and his lip trembled.

"What happened?" Sadie encouraged him to continue.

Rocky shook his head and his voice cracked. "I-I can't. I didn't like them really, but they were my pack."

"What happened?" Elijah whispered.

"Everyone at your house. Dead. The same as the sleuth. Silver poisoning. This time Nari and I interrupted them," Rocky told them.

"Interrupted them doing what? Who are they?" Cedar asked.

"I don't know who they are. They were dressed in white suits that covered them from head to toe, like ones you see in the movies where there is a disease. There were a dozen of them or more. I don't know. They had these tanks on their backs like diving tanks for air and smaller guns in their hands they were aiming at the pack.

I caught the burn of silver in the air. We were in the kitchen when they noticed us. We fought them, but there were too many. I couldn't hear what they said, but they took her. She used the last of her strength to send me to you and said to use the drum."

"How do we know you're not making this up?" Hector asked.

"Narissa is his mate. He wouldn't," Sadie growled.

Elijah gripped her shoulder. Luke felt whatever the man experienced, and it nearly tore him open. Sadie felt it too because her eyes welled up with tears. Elijah dropped to the floor and howled. The sound echoed in the hall. Luke went over to his co-mate. He stared at the elders. "He's not making it up. This is more widespread than just Denice and Nick. Whoever is behind this has knowledge of shifters. They are targeting all of us. Reach out to the other packs and groups you know. Find out who is still with us. Tell them we're gathering." Luke looked at the elders and made sure they followed his command. They were still his pack and had to follow him.

The three got up and nodded. Luke sank next to Sadie as she tried to comfort Elijah. "What are we going to do?"

"I don't know."

"You use the drum as your friend said. Call together all the shifters. This group hunting us won't stop until we're all dead. This is what you're meant to do. Lead us against them," Kade said to her.

Luke didn't want her leading anything, but with her abilities he had to agree she was here for a reason. "I think he's right, Sadie. All our messages pointed out you were special. We already know you can do things that no other wolf can. For whatever reason that is, it brought Greyson back to you."

"Please, Mistress Sadie, you have to get her back," Rocky insisted.

She looked up at Luke while she held onto Elijah and nodded. "I know, but later. I need sleep and right now he needs us."

"I agree. Elijah, come on. Kade, will you…?"

"No need to ask. I'll reach out to those I know. Take care of one another. Rocky and Greyson, why don't you come with me?"

"I'd rather stay with Sadie," Greyson replied.

"Not now, Grey. Please go with Kade," Sadie told him.

Greyson didn't reply, but Luke saw the look he shot Sadie. Whatever was between them, it wasn't going to be worked out today. He left with Kade. Luke helped Elijah up and led the now silent wolf back to his cabin and got him inside. Sadie threaded her fingers through his. He didn't seem to respond. Then again, Luke didn't know how he would react if he lost his pack.

"Elijah, they're not all gone. Not everyone was at your mansion. A lot of them had already left," Sadie told him.

The look in his eyes changed from vacant to one of rage. Elijah got up so quick he had Sadie on the floor. Luke sensed the animal in him more than the man. "You did this."

Sadie remained calm and didn't fight Elijah. "I'm here for you. I feel your pain and their loss as well. Let it go."

"We're both here for you. I know how you feel. The rage. The loss. The hole where they were. They might not be my pack, but I share your agony. We're all bound together. Don't let their loss bog you down. We need you level-headed right now. Please. Turn the rage into the thought of what we're going to do to them once we find them," Luke tried to calm him down.

Elijah released Sadie and sat back on his knees. "I'm sorry. I --"

"There's nothing to forgive. We're both worn out and drained. I need to rest before I take on whatever this is I have to take on. I suggest you do, too. I'm here with you. Always. We both are." She kissed him, making Luke feel a stab of jealousy, but he understood Elijah needed this right now.

"Listen to her, brother. Get some rest. We will talk about this in the morning. I'll send someone back to the mansion and help to take care of the bodies."

Elijah offered Luke his hand. "Thank you."

Chapter Nine

"The storm you must face has come. You must be the breaking wall the waves crash upon."

Sadie found herself standing before the still pond she had seen within her mind's eye. The woman seemed tired and her silver hair streaked with black. The once tranquil pool now reflected the thunder clouds overhead. The wind shrieked and Sadie could feel the desperation in the air.

"I'm supposed to go up against this nameless force threatening the shifters."

"It is not just the wolves or the bears. If this force goes unchecked, then all the shifters will be lost. You're the only weapon I can send into the world of men. The Fae once swore allegiance upon the ring you wear to the silver wolf. The tribes and clans of those who shift their shapes were bound into the drum. Each gave a little piece of themselves once upon a time to be woven into the instrument so all would hear its call. That's why it is kept in the realm of the spirits and watched over by the great ancestors. The same with the ring. It will return to Fae when it is no longer needed. Muster your courage. The gray one was sent to protect you. He did not want to part from this realm, but I had a special friend in the Fae who was able to put him back together with a little bit of an enchantment. He's bound together by silver and immune to it as you are."

She knew the woman was talking about Greyson. "Why chose him? I have two other mates. He was already dead and gone. He should've remained with the dead."

The woman touched the pond, sending ripples through it. Sadie almost felt a vibration from the gesture. "He had a tie to you. Having a triad is what was called for. You needed the support to become what you were meant to be. I know you're scared. You are their strength and they are yours. Rely on them now. All of what you are will be tested. Use the drum. It will call the tribes and reveal other secrets if you know how to listen."

Sadie wanted to find out more, but her eyes opened and her heart pounded. She found herself snuggled up to Elijah. He was sleeping peacefully, but his hurt from losing members of his pack cut him deep. He was only filling the hole until they could find out the true damage these enemies were bringing to the shifter community. The first rule of being a shifter was not to reveal yourself to a human unless you figured they could be trusted or eaten. At least that was what Elijah had told her. She got up but didn't see Luke anywhere. She didn't sense him. In the kitchen, she found Greyson making pancakes and bacon. The drum was on the table. He looked over when she came into the room.

"You look better."

"Thanks. I feel better. Healing everyone really did me in. Where's Luke?"

"Some of the other clans have gathered. They're in the hall talking about what they should do. It's a little too full for my taste. I figured you'd be hungry once you got up and might want some pancakes. You always liked it when I dipped the bacon in the pancake batter." He gestured to the pan on the stove.

"I did. Something you just remembered?"

"Among a few things."

Sadie snagged a strip of pancaked bacon and took a bite. She hadn't had this since Greyson last made it the day before they went on their camping trip. Greyson broke off a piece and ate it. He watched Sadie as she finished eating and then slipped his arm around her waist. The feel of his hold was familiar and comforting in the middle of all this chaos. He smelled like wolf and syrup. Greyson ran his fingers down her back and made her shiver. Her wolf still hadn't reacted about the idea of him being her mate as well. It was clear the guys didn't like it. He hugged her to him. Sadie closed her eyes and listened to the steady beat of his heart. It reminded her of simpler days when she knew Narissa as Melissa who was her eccentric rich best friend who doted on her. She and Greyson were planning on a wedding in the spring. His hands slipped from her back and entwined with hers. She looked up at him and he swept her across the kitchen floor. She stumbled on her feet and giggled as he twirled her and caught her in a dip. She saw nothing of the strange wolf he had become, but of the man she had loved for so long and was going to marry. He brought her up slowly. Sadie tried to catch her breath, but each time she breathed in his scent, all she could think about was how intoxicating it was. Sadie stood on tiptoe and kissed him. Greyson took the invitation and deepened the kiss. The gesture made her want more of him. He was her mate. What the woman said in her dream meant he was there to protect her, and he was a part of her life. She needed all three of them to be complete.

Greyson broke the kiss and ran his nose along her cheek. "We thought about taking dance lessons for the wedding, but I think you talked me out of them."

She giggled. "No. You wanted them because you wanted to do some silly mashup of the Monster Mash and the Macarena. I never really understood that."

"I think Tom talked me into it. How is he? Mom and everyone?" Greyson separated from her. She could see memories flashing across his face. He gripped the counter and she led him to a chair. "Shit. I can't go home. I can't believe I forgot my own brother and family."

"Everyone's fine. I saw them at a few months ago at April's birthday party. She's gotten so big. She's seven now." Sadie told him about his niece and his family. She remained close to them and they still invited her to parties. It was nice to be included after what happened.

"I'm glad they're doing so well. God, I miss them. Do

you think there's any way I could go back?"

She shrugged. "They had a memorial service for you. Ester was a wreck, but she always believed you were still alive. We didn't have your body. I... Well, it was a dark time for me. Narissa pulled me out of some very bad slumps where I wanted to kill myself. I barely held onto my job. I had horrible nightmares of the beasts that attacked us. I didn't know what they were at the time."

"Were the ones who attacked me also the ones who turned you?" Greyson got up and placed a few pancakes on her plate along with some more bacon.

Sadie waited to answer while she took another bite. "No. I was left with some scars on my back. When I met Elijah, I was attacked again, but I still didn't turn. Everyone thought it was very odd. I didn't turn until I was actually ready to become a wolf. Elijah and I had a rough road getting together."

"He seems to make you happy. I mean... shit. Does he make you happy?"

"He does, but there's something you need to know about Elijah."

"What does he need to know about me?" Elijah asked.

She looked up and realized he had come into the room and woken up. He came in and snagged a piece of regular bacon and glared at Greyson sitting next to her. Elijah put his hand on her shoulder making it very aware to Greyson she was his. "I was going to tell Greyson about the night we went camping."

"It's the night I realized Sadie was my mate," Elijah answered.

Greyson looked between him and her. The confusion on his face was something she caught. "What do you mean?"

Sadie slipped her hand along Greyson's and squeezed it. "Elijah and a friend of his attacked us when we went camping. Turns out we were on their pack land and never knew it. They killed you. I tried to get away, but Elijah caught my back with his claws and flipped me over."

"I heard her screams, and it brought me back out of the hunger of the wolf. I didn't know at the time she was my mate. That didn't come later until she showed up at my retreat. I smelled her blood and thought I wanted to devour her, but it took me being an asshole to realize it."

Whatever humanity was in Greyson's eyes faded. Under her hand, Sadie felt hair sprouting and his nails turning into claws. He got up so quickly the chair slammed back into the sink. His form shifted so she could see the man and the beast mixed together. He was about ready to lunge at Elijah when she stood up and got between them. The power she had to wield over other wolves welled up. She lashed out and took control of him.

"Greyson, you will not hurt Elijah." Her voice lowered as she wrested to control the creature before her. "You will get a hold of yourself and turn back into a man. This thing between you two has to stop. If you hurt him, then you hurt me. Do you understand?" The power slipped from her grasp as the intelligence returned to his eyes. He growled something and backed off.

"Good. Now sit down so we can talk about this like people." Sadie didn't use her power but left it more of a request. Elijah sat across from her, and Greyson settled back into his human form. Sadie dug into her pancake as silence enveloped the kitchen.

"Damn, I really need to know what happened. You can cut the tension in here with a machete." Luke came into the kitchen. He gave Sadie a quick kiss and helped himself to some breakfast. He took the empty chair and dug into his food. Luke looked tired and his plaid shirt and jeans were rumpled. The circles under his eyes told her he had been up all night. She could detect the scents of at least a dozen different shifters on him.

"Did you find out anything?" Sadie asked.

"In twelve hours, we've called or contacted all the different clans, packs, groups of shifters we have contacts with. Some of their leaders haven't responded which makes us think they won't ever reach out. Some've come here with only half their groups with silver poisoning. Kade is doing what he can for the wounded, but I'm sure he could use your help to heal them if possible. I wanted to let you sleep because I know you were beat. Think you'll be up for going at it again?"

Sadie nodded. "Of course. Anything I can do to help."

"The clan leaders want to meet you or at least see you in action. We haven't gotten much more information other than it seems the same type of thing has been happening with the other shifter clans. A member will go missing. They find the body and when they do it exploded with blood and silver getting into the air. Those closest are the worse affected. Others have said something similar to Rocky. They walked in on men in white biohazard suits spraying silver, killing anyone who was in their way. It seems they want to eradicate all shifters. White vans. No plates. Nothing to would distinguish them."

"Wonderful," Elijah muttered. "I'll get my people on it."

Greyson chuckled. "Your people. What are you, Bill Gates?"

"Not exactly, but I'm richer than he is."

"Is this guy for real? Is that why you chose him to be your mate because he's wealthier than God?" Greyson mocked.

"Grey, you know it doesn't work that way. No, I don't care about the money. It's nice, but Elijah knows I don't like to be bought."

"Learned the hard way. Look, I'll make some calls now I'm a bit more coherent. Excuse me. I need some air anyway." He got up from the table and walked out leaving her with Luke and Greyson.

"Guess he took that well." Luke dug into his pancakes. "These are good."

"Thanks." Greyson began pouring more batter onto the griddle.

"You need to get some sleep," Sadie told him.

"I can sleep when I'm dead. I need to figure out who these people are. Even with all Elijah's money and contacts, I don't think he's going to make any headway."

"I agree." Sadie ran her fingers over the surface of the drum. The power rode up her fingers and settle into the ring on her finger. The woman had said it was time she called everyone together. Maybe she could use the drum and the ring for more than gathering everyone together.

"Grey, when you heard the drum? What called you?" Sadie asked, trying to understand what his reaction had been.

He shrugged. "I felt it in my chest. Deeper. In my soul, I guess. It almost like it had a voice. The compulsion was there to follow it no matter how far it took me. I knew my answer was at the other end. Why do you ask?"

"Something I have to do. I was wondering if I might use it to heal the others. Something from my dream. If this power works on vibration, then maybe the healing energy also does. I don't know. It's a theory. No matter how many clans are here or how many people Elijah calls, we all need to be together. What if they are also doing this in other parts of the world? How far can the drum reach? People have to be warned." Sadie thought back to her dream where the woman had touched the water and felt the ripples of the power from with it.

"Finish eating and I'll take you out there," Luke told

her as he took a piece of bacon.

Sadie finished her breakfast and splashed some water on her face. She held her hair back and looked at her reflection. Many things had changed in just a short time. The human part of her was still wondering if she was dreaming. A surge of confidence and strength filled her from her wolf. *"I'm here with you. We can do this. We'll figure out who took Narissa and who is harming all the others. This is what we were chosen for."*

"I know. I'm just scared. Three men. I don't know how to handle all of them."

"I like Greyson. He was chosen for us. Give him a chance. You already love him, and I have no objections."

"You ready?" Luke asked.

Seeing the strong man standing there gave her some courage. She slipped her arms around him and breathed in his scent. He hugged her and then she gave him a quick kiss. "As I'll ever be."

He led her out of the house and back to the main hall. This time it was brimming with other shifters. The frenetic energy of all the people hit her and she could feel the different types of shifters among them. And she could also feel those who were sick. Those were cornered in one part of the lodge. Kade and a few others were attending to them. The leaders all looked weary as they came over to Luke. Several of them went to one knee before Sadie and all went quiet. The power of their minds pressed upon hers as they all wanted to speak to her alone and get her counsel. A tall, silver-haired woman looked up with eyes of different colors. One was ice blue and the other was completely black. She was mixed blood and strong.

"You are the silver wolf. I have seen."

"I am. Who are you?"

"Ora. I'm the leader of the largest Parliament of Owls east of the Mississippi. We group together. All different types of owls. M-my daughter was stolen from me. We tried to track them, but they used silver to drive us off.

They knew about us. When Luke called, I knew you were going to help us. All our wings are yours. Please, you have to find my daughter." Ora took her hand.

"I'll do my best. Tell me something, is your daughter pure owl?" Sadie asked as a hunch formed in her mind.

"No. Dara is half owl and part Fae. How did you know?"

"Just wondering. Thank you. We'll talk more later." Sadie glanced around the rest of the hall. She caught Rocky's gaze and felt the hole cut into his soul from losing Narissa. She tried not to think about it. However, her friend did say she had been called back to Fairy because something was going on. Sadie wondered if this was all tied together. There was only one way to find out. She had to use the drum.

"You okay?" Luke asked.

"Yeah. Just thinking. Do me a favor, ask Kade if he can ask among the other tribes if any of their loved ones have any Fairy blood in their recent lineage."

"I'll ask, but it may not be something they know."

She touched his face. "I know, but I think it's important. I'm going to see what I can do for everyone." He kissed her palm and led her to the stage.

Sadie felt the eyes on her as she sat down. She tried to ignore the whispers in the crowd. She'd never been one for getting up before a big group of people and speaking. She couldn't sing, so with all eyes on her she felt self-conscious. The agony of those around her reached her more. Their aches and the burning of the silver echoed in her body as did their fear and sorrow. Everything in her wanted to take the agony away. It didn't matter if not everyone was a wolf. Her fingers ran over the surface of the drum. Power was already flowing through it, ready to be used. Her hands grew warm as they had before. She envisioned the warmth as a light wrapping around the drum. Sadie put all her energy into wanting to heal and thought back to the ripples on the pond and then hit the drum. A vibration left the instrument. Gasps filled the room. Some of the pain lessened.

Sadie kept focused on healing until she couldn't feel the pain any longer. When she opened her eyes, all those in the hall were staring at her. She didn't feel as tired as she had when healing all the pack one by one. The drum had helped to spread her abilities and bring it to more people. Others wanted to say something to her, but when her eyes met Rocky's she knew there was one thing left to do. She had to reach out and call the others to her. She thought about the Fae and the other shifters. She didn't know how many of them there were or if they were all over the world, but they would hear the call of the drum. Sadie placed her palm flat on the stretched skin until the power from the instrument waited to be used again. This time the silver ring burned against her skin. It would give her the ability to get her message across to the Fae realm. Maybe even Narissa would hear it. She closed her eyes and thought about what she wanted to say. However, she let herself relax and her fingers flared with power. The drum throbbed under her fingers and the ring nearly burned her flesh.

All her doubt washed away. Her fingers worked over the surface as she found the beat. There was something to it. All she needed to do was let go. Make those she summoned come together. They were bound to the drum and to the ring. They promised once upon a time to help her. Not the current incarnation of her, but the one who had been here before. Sadie could feel the memories in the back of her mind, but they remained veiled. Her nails scraped the surface and the rumble went out, like nails on a chalkboard to get everyone to stop and listen. They all needed to listen. Sadie took in a breath and focused beyond all the scents in the room. All the noise around her was drowned out. The silence in her mind was vast.

"Danger."

She hit the drum hard but with a steady rhythm. As the tempo increased, the message radiated farther than she could fathom. She felt minds latch onto the communication and to the beat.

"Enemies are coming with silver."

With another hit on the skin, a flare of power beat out like a big pulse, nearly knocking her over. She hit the drum again, pounding the messages out again. Even if the shifters getting this were registering it on a conscious level, she wasn't sure if they would answer. Sadie needed more. Sweat trickled down her forehead as the warmth poured through her. The ring seared her finger. She thought about Narissa. All those years of them together and how she was practically her sister.

"Come!"

This wasn't a warning. This was a command. They had to come. All of them. Those who couldn't come needed to the heed the warning. The silver of her ring sent out a pulse. In her mind's eye, Sadie could feel the different energy mingling with the drum. It felt the power of the Fae as it came up with Narissa's mark on her. She drew on the power through the bond she had with her friend. With a breath, she forced the power outward and heard something shatter. It was more in her mind like a brick being thrown into a heavy pane of glass. She hit the drum again with the same power and heard the same shattering. On the third time, the pulse came from the ring. She heard and felt the barrier between this world and Fairy break. The ring glowed and disappeared from her finger. The message had been sent. All the tribes who had once bound their magic to make the ring had been summoned.

The drum still beckoned. She sent out one more demand to come. Once the power left her, exhaustion washed over her.

Chapter Ten

Greyson worked his way toward Sadie while everyone in the hall remained transfixed by the first beat of the drum. The energy wave hit him, but he didn't need to heed its call. Keeping Sadie safe was what mattered. Everyone stopped what they were doing and turned to look at her. Sadie sat on the stage focused on whatever it was she was doing with the drum. The beat washed over him like a crashing wave and went with the current. He heard her voice in his head. This made him stop and listen.

Danger. Enemies were coming. A heavy silence filled the room for a few moments. He took advantage of it and made it to the stage. Greyson hovered in the wings in awe at the woman who sat in the chair. This was not the woman he met as a man. She was so much more. The memories of them together lingered on the outskirts of his recollections. She had grown into something so much more. He loved her all the more for it.

The command came.

Come.

He fell to his knees before her. Greyson glanced around at all those in the hall. They were all on their knees. Some were even trying to crawl to her. They couldn't resist the directive no matter what species they were. Even Luke was on his knees. Greyson saw Luke stripped down to his barest. The wolf loved Sadie. Elijah did as well. She seemed happy with him. If they were to be mated, then Greyson wasn't about to hurt the wolf anymore.

The command left him. However, Greyson found the will to stand before she hit the drum again. The silver ring on her finger glowed as though it was a halo caught on her finger. Sadie hit the drum three more times. On the third time, the ring shattered into pieces of light. The drum slipped from her fingers as she slumped in the chair. Greyson grabbed the instrument and went to Sadie. The others were coming out of their stupors. He felt her cold and clammy skin. Whatever she had done had drained her. Luke rushed toward the stage and lifted Sadie up.

"We need to get her out of here," Greyson told him.

"The others will want to talk to her. Did you feel all that?" Luke asked him.

"I did. She needs to be in a place where she can recover. She needs to be with all of us."

"You're not her mate," Luke growled as he carried her outside.

"Maybe not officially, but it's coming. I'm not leaving her side."

"We'll see."

Greyson felt his wolf bristle and the need to back down. He thought about the woman he loved. "I'm not trying to step on your toes. I know you love her."

"Just because you have a history with her doesn't give you claim to her now."

Luke stopped outside his cabin. He tried to get the door, but Greyson beat him to it and opened it. He followed Luke to the bedroom where he put Sadie down on his bed. She seemed peaceful in the sleep she was in, but it was clear whatever they had done had completely exhausted her. She would need her strength for whatever or whoever she had summoned. Luke moved the hair from her face and brushed his lips across her forehead. A stab of jealousy struck Greyson's heart. He wasn't going to let this alpha scare him away. The other wolf left the room and went into the kitchen where he got a beer out of the fridge, hesitated, and then held one out to Greyson.

Luke gestured for him to sit at the table across from him. Greyson took the offer and sipped the beer. He nearly choked at the first sip and had to put it down. Luke chuckled.

"Not a drinker?"

Greyson shook his head. "I've spent most of my time as a wolf. It's hard to adjust to being in human form for this long. It's taking a while to get used to being on two legs and getting the taste for things again. If it wasn't for her, I wouldn't be this far. I'm sorry if I went at you before at the mansion. I was more wolf than man at the time."

Luke took a long swig before he set the bottle down and eyed him. "Greyson, I haven't known Sadie long. It's been one rollercoaster ride since I found her feverish and out of her mind wandering along the side of the road not far from Elijah's precious resort. She was so out of it she was walking on a broken leg from where my sister bit her. I cared for her through her change. When she woke up, she made it very clear I was her mate. It didn't faze her. My wolf knew the moment he scented the wolf in her. It took me a moment to catch up. Finding out she was mated to Elijah Dane, pain-in-the-ass billionaire who thinks he can rule all the packs in the area, wasn't something I wanted to hear. But if I hurt him, then I'm going to hurt her. I feel for the guy. From what Sadie told me, he put her through the wringer in more ways than one. You know he's the one who bit you?"

"I know. He told me. I wasn't too happy about it. I wanted to hurt him back but doing so would hurt Sadie."

Luke nodded. "And hurting you would hurt her, too."

"I don't want to step on your toes here, but like you said, your wolf scented her and knew she was your mate. It's the same with me. I've been around other wolves and my beast has never been as excited to be with anyone other than her. She was my life before and she is my life now. I'm here to protect her." Greyson stopped and looked at his hands. His nails remained sharper than they were before with a silver sheen to them. "I can protect her from any shifter who would get in her way. I have silver running through me and I'm immune to it. I can hurt another badly. You saw what I did to Elijah."

"What about if you get pissed off again at one of us or at her? You could hurt her."

Greyson tapped his nails on the side of the bottle. "I could never hurt her. She's immune to silver. I can't promise I won't piss you off. I'm not an alpha like you two are. I don't know where I'd fit or if I would ever fit into a pack, but I'm hers. She just hasn't claimed me as her own. I think we'll get there, though. Could you live with me being in the picture?"

"I'm not going to have a choice if she chooses you as a mate. You love her. I can feel it through the bond we share. I can't say the pack will accept you, but I'll see if I can make an exception. You do have a different feel to you. Maybe it's the silver and you can't help it." Luke rubbed his beard and held out his hand. "Truce."

Greyson studied it for a second and contemplated what the Pack Leader said. It would be nice to be able to fit in somewhere even if he wasn't a full member of Luke's pack. But to be among other wolves and not alone anymore put something in him at ease. He took his hand. "Truce."

"Good. Look, I have to go back to the hall and watch over those who are there. More leaders are coming. I can feel it. Watch over her. She's more special than any of us realize." Luke ran his fingers along the drum. "Without her, none of this would be possible. The clans would be wiped out. We both know it in our bones."

"I agree. She's one of a kind."

Luke left the cabin. Greyson finished his beer and put the empty in the sink. A few moments later, the door to the cabin opened again. Elijah walked back in. He didn't have a great look on his face. "Shit. Where're Sadie and Luke?"

"Luke went back to the hall to check on the rest of the incoming shifters. He said more would be coming. Didn't you feel the power of the drum?"

"You're not a part of this. You should be dead."

"I should be and yet here I am. Look, Elijah, I'm not exactly thrilled to find out you were the one who turned me into this beast. I had this conversation with Luke. I'm not going anywhere. Sadie is my mate just as she is yours and Luke's and this has nothing to do with my being engaged to her in the past. That was before," Greyson said to him.

Elijah's face grew red and the veins in his neck bulged. He was going to say something, but Greyson beat him to it. "If you hurt me, then you hurt her. Luke and I came to a truce. I won't blame you or be resentful of you for what you did to me, if you promise to butt out of what happens between me and Sadie. I think it's a good deal."

"Fine, but stay out of my way," Elijah growled.

Greyson felt the command from the alpha. However, Greyson resisted the urge to show any deference to Elijah. If they were going to be together, then they had to learn to deal with one another. Three male wolves all mated to the same female would be tricky.

"Fine, but don't pull any alpha shit on me. I don't need to be bowing down to you because I stepped on your sensitive toes. Luke's right. You are a jerk." Greyson got up as the wolf in him wanted to swat at Elijah once more. This wolf was going to be an issue. He walked into the small living space and took in a few deep breaths. As he did, he heard Sadie stirring in the other room.

Greyson found her standing in the doorway, shaking. Elijah had her in his arms. She pressed her face into the other wolf's shoulder. "What's the matter?"

Her eyes were red and swollen. "It's Nari. I had a dream about her. She's being held captive and they're torturing her."

"We will do something, but you can't run off into the woods or steal Luke's truck. We don't know who is coming and who else is out there. Right now, you're safe. I know you want to keep your promise to Rocky, but we have to focus on what's in front of us."

"I know. Grey, will you walk with me?" Sadie parted from Elijah.

A surge of pride went through him. He most liked the murderous look he got from the other wolf as Sadie left Elijah's embrace. Sadie wrapped an arm around his waist, and they walked outside. She led him into the woods away from all the people. He felt better being away from everyone. Once they stopped, he leaned back against a tree and took in the sounds of the forest. The aroma was more familiar than anything else. It brought his wolf closer to the surface and he welcomed the beast. He licked his lips and felt his teeth had sharpened some. Sadie pressed herself against his body and he shivered. Her female scent filled his nose and her sweet form felt right in his arms.

"Sadie, what are you doing? I thought you were worried about Narissa."

"I am, but I'm not the one driving this. The wolf woke up with a clear agenda on its mind. I can't fight this even if I wanted to. She was going to let me choose for myself about you, but I think she decided it was best to have you on our team." Sadie ran her nose along his neck.

Greyson shivered and his wolf salivated with the idea of being with her. He recalled many of the times they had been together, but this was different because he was different. Her fingers slid along his sides. Her nails pushed through the thin cloth of his shirt and raked along his skin. Each movement made his cock hard. The scent of her desire was so strong it took all of him not to rip her clothes off.

"You already know I'm on your team." Greyson

captured her lips. He kissed her with a ferocity to match her own. He wanted to taste all of her.

"I know you are, but I can't stop her right now." Sadie pulled off her top and tugged at his shirt. When he didn't get to it fast enough, she began to rip it open. He grabbed her hands and took a step back. It took all his strength as he caught the wild look in her eye. She was right, the wolf was in control.

"What do you really want?" Greyson trailed his thumb over her bottom lip. She turned her face into his palm and nipped at his thumb.

"To claim you for our mate," she groaned, "and fuck you while I do it."

Greyson tugged at her pants as the words filled him with satisfaction. Sadie pushed him down to the ground. She stepped out of her jeans and he shimmied out of his pants. She was on him before he could be ready for her. She kissed and nipped at his neck. Greyson groaned at the pleasure of being with her after picturing this moment. He tried to reach out and feel her, but she grabbed his wrists and pinned him to the ground. She growled. All he saw was the wolf and not the woman. Either way, he knew they were both behind this. They both wanted him. He would have a place. He struggled against her and got her lips, yearning to feel her breasts in his palms. She growled again as she kissed his torso and nipped on his nipples. He couldn't take it any longer as he got caught up in the mating frenzy.

"Sadie." He felt a howl building in his throat.

She slipped his cock inside her and began to ride him. Her grip on him eased. Greyson buried his face between her breasts. She tasted of cloves and sweat, but it was wonderful. Her arms encircled his neck as she made up the tempo between them. Her tongue ran along the side of his neck down to the curve of his throat. The warmth of her body drove him over the edge. He couldn't hold on much longer as she moved with him. As his pleasure rose, a sudden pain shot up his neck. Her mouth latched onto his throat for a moment. Greyson howled at the same time. He heard Sadie whisper in his ear.

"I claim you for my mate."

He sucked on the side of her throat and bit her as well. His mind whited out as he tasted her blood. Something in him seemed complete. He could feel her mind brushing against his. She held him tighter as she cried out.

"My mate," he forced out.

"Yes," Sadie moaned. She moved a little bit more on top of him until she settled on his chest. He slid his fingers through her hair and kissed her. The frenzy had worn off and her eyes returned to normal. A light blush splashed her cheeks.

"That was different."

"Sorry. I didn't mean for it to go that way. I had hoped we could be in a bed like old times. She just had control and I couldn't fight it. God, you taste good." Sadie kissed him again and licked his Adam's apple. She sucked it up and he felt himself stirring once more. She started to move with him once more time. Greyson put his hands on her hips.

"We can't."

"Why not?"

"Because your other mates are waiting for you." Greyson motioned with his chin over to the edge of the clearing they had stopped in. Elijah and Luke stared at them. Elijah's face showed his conflicted state. Luke seemed like he was tired and expected what they saw.

"Shit," Sadie muttered.

Chapter Eleven

Sadie sat at Luke's kitchen table staring at the empty bottle of the beer she had just drunk. All three of her mates had said nothing as she had left the clearing and made her way back to Luke's house. The beer helped to clear her head and drive the wolf back. After waking up from her dream about Narissa, all her wolf wanted to do was cement the bond between her and Greyson. It didn't matter what she needed to do, she was going to mark him as her own. When it was over, she wasn't expecting the other two to be watching. The way they looked at her filled with anger and yet desire at the same time made her feel guilty and aroused. It was a strange feeling. Elijah was the angriest at her. Greyson stood behind her and didn't say a word. He set his hands on her shoulders to give her comfort.

"Elijah," she tried to say something to him, but the words died in her throat.

"Why, Sadie?" he asked.

"Because Greyson is my mate the same way you and Luke are. It just had to be this way before all this happens."

"Before all what happens? You know, Sadie, I've put up with a lot of shit with everything that you are. I-I don't want --" he lifted his arms and shook his head. The link between them flared and she could feel the edge of the pit he hovered over because he couldn't make sense of what she was and all that was happening. This wasn't something he had signed on for.

She got up out of the chair, slid her arms around him, and held him close. She rested her head against his chest as his arms closed around her. Elijah hugged her. His sense of losing of her crippled him more than she had ever thought it would. *"You're not going to lose me. I'm right here. I'm not going anywhere."*

"First there was Luke and now Greyson. Has he come back

to haunt me by making my life a living hell? Am I not enough man for you? Not enough wolf?"

Sadie placed a hand over his heart and kissed him. *"You are more than wolf and man for me. My having two other mates has nothing to do with us. I love you. You're part of me. This is just how it is. I can't explain it. I know you've been through a lot. I'm not trying to fuck us up. When this storm has passed, you can have me all to yourself."*

"For how long? You have Luke and Greyson now to satisfy your needs."

"They aren't you. Follow our thread and see what I do? Feel how much I love you."

Elijah let out a huff of air. His wolf paced in his thoughts wanting to get out and show her how cranky it was. He stretched out along their link and all she could think of was soothing his fears. She pictured them together. Running his hands along her body. Touching and kissing her until she could feel her desire. She shared it with him. The time she first met him and how she loved how his ass looked in his expensive pants. How scared she was when she saw him as the wolf. And yet how gentle he was in his wolf form and didn't hurt her. How he saved her from the others.

"I would never take any of it back. I love you, Elijah Dane. Even if you did eat my fiancé. I'm yours."

"And you're theirs too. I can't compete with both of them."

She squeezed his hand. *"I don't expect you to compete with anyone. You haven't lost me. You haven't lost your entire pack. Some of them are still alive and need you. I've called them when I called the others."*

"How do you know?" The surprise in his voice made him want to believe her.

She showed him what she felt about the rest of his pack. She could feel their connections through him. *"They are coming."* A sense of relief and awe went through him.

"Thank you for showing me this."

"You're welcome, love. Will you try with Greyson and Luke?"

He kissed her. "Yes," he said out loud.

She returned the kiss and felt the gulf between them healing. "Good." She turned to the other two men. "I need to know if you're good with all this. I need you together now."

Luke sighed. "I'll figure it out. I'm not going anywhere if you're worried."

"You already know I can deal with them," Greyson replied.

"Good. Now sit down. We need to talk about what's coming." Sadie felt the strength of the wolf return as the tension eased between her mates.

The creak of chairs on the floor sounded as they all sat down. She told them about what happened while she was on the stage as well as with the fairies coming. She didn't know when they were all get there, but they were answering an old summons none of them could ignore, shifter or Fae.

"Do you have an idea who might be behind all this?" Luke asked.

"No, but I've been thinking. Nari told me some things before I went up to meet Elijah at the resort before your sister bit me."

"What did she say?" Elijah asked. He squeezed her knee under the table to reassure her. The calm look on his face belied the storm of emotions swirling in his mind. He didn't like the idea of sharing her, but after this was all over she planned on making sure Elijah knew how much she loved him. Even if he could be a brooding asshole at times.

"She'd been gone for six months and we were having lunch to catch up. She said she had been summoned back because they were finding dissected fairies. Fairy shifters. Nari said there were a handful here and there of Fae who were shifters also like her. She's in line for the throne so they accused her of being part of it, but she said they had the stench of humans. She thought she had things worked out."

"Seems like she didn't," Greyson commented.

"You think the attacks on the other shifters and the fairies are related?" Luke asked.

"I think so. It'd make sense," Sadie replied.

"But the Fae don't interact with humans. They lock themselves away in their own realm," Luke told them.

"How do you know?" Elijah questioned the other wolf.

"They are between this world and the spirit world. Sometimes, when I do vision quests or mediate, I can see into their realm. It's like a quick shimmer and then it goes away. I've heard them hunting. The thundering of their horses' hooves on a moonless night in the middle of the forest where the rips between this world and theirs are thin," Luke explained.

"How are they and the other shifters connected?" Greyson asked.

"Ora said her daughter was half Fae. Nari is a Fairy who was bitten by a shifter. What if that's the connection? Maybe whoever is doing this, are experimenting on those with Fae lineage or Fae shifters?" Sadie didn't know if her theory was correct, but it had to be something to start with.

"It wouldn't mean they would outright attack all shifters," Elijah growled.

"It might actually." Kade came into the kitchen and grabbed a beer from the fridge. He popped the top and threw it into the sink. It clanked around until it settled. "I asked around with the other shifters, as you requested, about anyone with Fae heritage. All of them said those with Fae connections were kidnapped. Then the attacks came on the pack a day or so after the half-Fae ones had gone missing. Someone has told the humans about us."

"Who would do such a thing? It's instinctual not to show ourselves to humans unless we know we can trust them," Luke asked his shaman.

"You know how humans can be when they don't understand something. They want to destroy it. Who knows the real reason why they're doing this? But we have a theory we can work on," Kade replied.

"Even with a running theory, we need to make sure the others are protected," Elijah remarked.

"They'll be protected now they've been alerted to it," Sadie told them. The image of Narissa strapped to a table and being tortured came flooding back. She grabbed her bottle and threw it against the wall.

"Whoa! What's this about?" Greyson asked.

"Sorry. My dream about Nari. She needs me to help her. I don't how because I don't know where she is." Sadie put her head in her hands.

Greyson rubbed her shoulders. "Hey, we'll figure out a way to save her and get the others back."

Someone knocked on door. Luke got up and came back into the kitchen with Rocky. "You should come outside. They are asking for the silver wolf."

They all looked at Sadie. She got up to followed him outside to confront whoever was asking for her. A sea of all different types of creatures lingered outside. Some appeared human, but she could see underneath the illusions they cast to blend in with society. There had to be almost a hundred. Five stood before her.

"You are the silver wolf?" one of them said. His voice was more of a whisper caught in the wind.

"I am. Who are you?"

The five of them each held up a small piece of silver that used to be part of the ring. "We are the descendants of those who pledged to answer the call when needed. Your plea was heard all the way in Fairy. We came as requested and we're glad of it."

Many others gathered around her. They were all frightened of something. Sadie motioned for the five to follow her away from the gathering crowd. She wasn't sure how the other Fae would react to the shifters, but she had to figure out how they played into the equation. Her mates, Rocky, and Kade all stayed behind her as they went somewhere they could talk.

"What are your names?" she asked.

"Our names don't matter. I answer for all the tribes. I am Septia." The Fairy towered over the rest of the crowd and even her mates. He must have been at least eight feet tall. He didn't bother to hide behind a glamour to blend in with humanity. His chalk-white skin made him appear to be almost living stone. The only thing lifelike about him were his deep black eyes.

She stuck out her hand. Septia took it and gave her a weak handshake. "Thank you all for coming. Can you help with what's happening among the shifters here?"

"A plague has descended upon us. Many of our kind have been kidnapped, tortured, and then returned in pieces. We have bonded together looking for help. Now our queen as gone missing."

"Wait, who is your queen?" Elijah asked.

"Narissa," Septia answered him.

"Did you know about this?" Elijah turned to Sadie.

She shook her head. "Not at all. Seems like she's been keeping secrets."

"She has not been our queen long. She did not wish for the title, but she was the strongest among us. The best fit especially after all the unrest in Fairy. The five tribes chose her. She has the royal lineage. If she hadn't been bitten, she would've been second in line to take the throne. You carry her mark. I can see it now. You're the silver one who is meant to help free her and stop this genocide," Septia told her.

Sadie held up her hand to take in all the new

information. Her best friend was now queen of the Fae shifters and she was missing. "The ones who are taken -- are they pure-blooded fairies? Or are they mixed?"

"Mixed."

"How are they being taken? Nari spoke about finding remains stinking of humans. These same humans are also killing shifters in our realm and snatching those with Fae lineage."

"Lata, tell her what you told me about your encounter." Septia motioned toward a slight woman who appeared to be in her mid-thirties. Under the enchanted mask, Sadie saw green skin and blue hair. She was only three feet tall with black eyes. Her three fingers were long and looked like twigs. The woman didn't look up. She kept staring at her fingers.

"They took my daughter. We were gathering fruit. This shimmer started. It was like the portals we create to move between the worlds, but it was so much stronger. It smelled funny. I tried to stop her, but she's so young. A being dressed in a white suit came through. I tried to snatch my daughter away, but they shot her with something and she went limp. They saw me and tried to get me too, but I escaped. They took her. Please you have to help her." She threw herself at Sadie and wrapped her arms around her.

Sadie put her hand on Lata's head to calm her. "I will. I promise. Nari is my friend and I can't see her suffering either. We don't know who is behind all these kidnappings. They are like you said. Dressed in white suits. Driving white vans. No one has been able to track where they go." She hugged the slight Fairy who pulled away and wiped her eyes.

"Thank you."

"Of course. Luke, can you help find accommodations for our new friends," Sadie asked her mate.

Septia shook his head. "Not necessary. We will stay

in the forest along the outskirts of this village. You will hardly know we are here. We don't trust humans even if you are shifters. Our queen marked you so we trust you and your men."

"Okay. Well, I'm here if you need anything," Sadie told them.

Septia motioned for the rest of his tribe to follow him. They melted back into the forest. Sadie was sure they were even there, they blended in so well. Sadie and her wolf sighed. This was all getting so complicated. She needed was to feel normal again. She needed her mates. Sadie glanced at the group and saw the worry in their eyes that she felt in her heart. More shifters were coming. Maybe even more Fae. She didn't know. She glanced at the sky. The moon had risen. She hadn't realized it had gotten so late.

"Kade, can you keep an eye out for the other shifters who will be arriving? Make sure everyone is comfortable. Keep Rocky busy."

The shaman squeezed her shoulder. "I can do that, but I'll need Luke later on."

"I know, but right now, I --" She wasn't sure the shaman would understand about her wanting to be in the arms of the men she loved. Of needing some sort of normality with her three mates. If they were going to face some foe, then she needed to be in the arms of those who could protect her.

He brushed his lips along her cheek. "I understand. All will be well for tonight. Go and be with the ones you love."

"Thank you."

Kade went over to Rocky and dragged him away. Once they were alone, Sadie went to Elijah and slipped her hands over his chest and kissed him. He returned the kiss with a little bit of hesitation. She kissed his throat and nipped a little. She threaded her fingers through his and tugged.

"Will you come?" She felt his arousal. The scent of his wolf helped her to forget the awful things they were all involved in.

"You don't have to ask," he replied.

"I really do. I need all of you. If you can't accept this, then…" She hoped he wouldn't turn her request down. Having all three of her men together in one bed was going to be tricky, but she needed them. Her wolf needed them.

Elijah caught her wrist and pulled her into him. He slipped his tongue along her bottom lip, kissing her with a passion that reminded her of the first time he kissed her. Like he would eat her up. Sadie dug her nails into his back and scraped them down his shirt. He pulled away and hissed. "I need you. Right now. I don't care if they watch or if they want to join in, but you're mine first."

"Yes," she whispered.

He nipped her throat, marking the spot where he once bit her to claim her for his mate. "Luke, how big is your bed?"

Sadie glanced at the other wolf. "Big enough for what we have in mind." Luke grabbed Sadie up in his arms and molded her to his body. His cock pocked against her stomach showing her he was already ready for her. He thrust his tongue inside her mouth and she met him stroke for stroke as he kissed her and pinched her ass. Luke scooped her up and threw her over his shoulder. Greyson's smiled widened as she looked at him. Elijah went ahead and got the door. Greyson followed as Luke went into the cabin. She heard the lock click so no one would disturb them. Luke tossed her down on the bed and pulled his shirt off. She felt the bed depress behind her. More hands slid under her shirt and cupped her breasts. They twisted her nipples until the pain of it brought her pleasure. She moaned. Sadie leaned back into the wolf behind her and found Greyson. He flashed her a smile.

"*You are so fucking beautiful,*" Greyson said to her through their newly formed bond. "*I don't care who I have to share you with. Even the other two if they desire it.*"

She gave him a strange look. "*This is new.*"

"*I'm not the same man you remember.*"

"*Clearly.*"

"*Remember your promise to me,*" Elijah said to her. He joined them on the bed, naked.

Elijah guided her lips over to him. Sadie found herself already drowning in the yearning they all felt. She was already wet for them. She ran her fingers over the tops of his thighs, feeling the strong muscles. Elijah trailed his fingertips along her cheekbones. Once their mouths connected, she was in heaven. Her whole body relaxed, and it felt like she had come home. Elijah's arms slipped around her, drawing her closer until her breasts pressed against his chest.

She ran her finger over his torso and along his sides. It was hard to believe this man was at her mercy if she truly wanted. What he didn't understand, what they all didn't understand, was she was at theirs. She straddled Elijah. Sadie feathered her fingers along his neck and slid her fingers through his hair. Elijah dragged his nails along her back until the points bit into her skin. She broke the kiss and cried out. Her wolf howled within her mind wanting more. Wanting all of them.

She sucked his bottom lip. Her nipples pushed against her bra and shirt, which made the extra garments uncomfortable. It would be so much better to have their naked bodies entwined together. Her wolf kneaded at the confines of her mind. Elijah took in another breath. His muscles tensed. A vein throbbed across his forehead. The tempo of his heart thundered in her ears.

With a small movement, she slid herself along his erection. Her mate's eyes widened as Elijah shifted in an attempt to put a little room between them. She could feel the desire of her other mates as it played along the ties they shared. Sadie nearly slid along their thread, but she wanted to satiate her longings with Elijah first. She had promised him. She claimed his lips in a slow kiss as the other's gazes burned into her soul. He swept his thumbs over her pert nipples. He thrust his tongue between her lips until their tongues touched and entwined. She touched his chest. Elijah grabbed her wrists in an iron grip and a devilish smile appeared on his lips.

"Teasing me now?" Sadie asked.

"Of course. I nearly forgot what this was like," Elijah replied.

"Then I haven't been doing my job. I'm a terrible mate if I made you forget all about me."

Elijah released her. He cupped her breasts and feathered his fingertips over her nipples. A bolt of pleasure hit her from the soft caress. She slid her hands over the fine silver scars on his stomach. Elijah pressed his lips above her heart and dragged his mouth over the top of her left breast before taking the nipple into his mouth through the lace of her bra. She held his head there for a few seconds. Her nerve endings came alive with the raw excitement Elijah enticed in her. His free hand wandered down her stomach, undid the button of her jeans, and then slipped over the fabric of her panties. When Elijah found her buried nub, she cried out. He pushed the thin material aside and fondled her.

He ran his other fingers along her moist folds. All she wanted was him inside her. Elijah sucked on her nipple, and that sent bolts of ecstasy through her, combining with his caresses. Elijah pushed against her nub one final time, causing her to arch her back. The warmth came and she was so close to letting the orgasm flash through her. He stopped. Elijah slipped his free hand from her breast, around her back to undo her bra strap. All the heavy petting and kisses had brought her to the brink. If she waited any longer, she would explode. Her bra strap came off with a snap. The back of it dug into her flesh, but Elijah slid the first strap down over her left shoulder and kissed every place where the fabric had touched. His lips burned a trail along her flesh, warming her skin. Once he got one off, she held the lace triangle over her breast. He gazed at her and went for the other. Elijah sucked in the skin of her right arm until he took the other strap off. He drew in her middle finger and wrapped his tongue around it. She gasped from the sudden wetness and grasped his cock rubbing it more until he released her and then backed away.

"I need you," Sadie cried out.

Elijah stood up and took off the rest of his clothes. She did the same and stood before him in only her panties. She bit her lip and sat back on the bed. Sadie trailed her fingers over her thighs. She glanced at him and beckoned him closer. His smile widened, which gave him a boyish appearance.

Elijah sauntered over and slid his knee between her legs, opening them farther. He pushed her down on the bed and pinned her between his hands. "You're all mine now to do with whatever I want."

She wrapped a leg around his waist. "Promise?"

He slipped his hand over her stomach, moving farther down until he grabbed the fabric of her panties and tugged on them, ripping them away from her body. Sadie pulled him down to her body and held him above her chest. Elijah clutched her breasts and squeezed until his grip hurt. But the pain felt good. When he stopped, he bit her swollen nipple and gave her another look. The devilish gleam in his eye only turned her on more. She reached for him, and a small noise of wanting slipped from her lips.

His smiled widened. Elijah slipped his hand between

her already wet folds and found her core. He thrust his fingers deep inside her pussy. He pumped them inside her for a few strokes until she grabbed his wrist. Elijah brought the fingers to his lips and sucked off her juices. She wrapped her other leg around his waist and locked him to her. Elijah licked a line from her chest and up her neck until he tugged on the end of her earlobe.

"I nearly forgot how you taste," he whispered to her.

"I think the others might say the same," she replied and glanced over at Luke. He pulled off his shirt. Greyson's eyes were already wild with need. It seemed he would break out of his skin if he didn't get a chance to be with her.

"They can wait their turn. Right now, I want my cock inside you as you promised," Elijah told her.

Sadie hugged her knees tighter around him and then guided him into her pussy.

Elijah moaned when he entered her. He clutched her shoulders and pushed his lips onto hers as he plunged inside her. Greyson's mind opened to her. His raw wanting amped up the union between her and Elijah. Her nerves were on fire. Elijah drove into her again and shoved his tongue into her mouth to taste her once more. She raked her nails down his back, feeling the skin underneath her fingers. Sadie closed her eyes and gave herself over to the building ecstasy inside her. She ran the soles of her feet over Elijah's hard ass. Her toes curled from the heights he brought her to. Each time he pushed back into her pussy, he hit her clit and the world crumbled. Elijah plunged into her one last time, cried out, and came. Sadie clutched him to her, not wanting to let him go. He still remained buried inside her and when he moved once more, she came as well.

Elijah kissed her one more time before letting her go. "I guess the other two can have you now."

Her lips twitched into a smile. "So now, I'm just

being passed around. I see how it is."

"That's not what I meant."

She poked his chest. "I'm teasing. We all need to lighten the mood right now." Sadie glanced at Luke. He had the same ravenous look on his face as Greyson did, but his mind was more controlled. It was obvious from his firm cock pointing at her, Luke couldn't wait to claim her. Hunger burned in all her mates' eyes. Their shared desire wrapped around all of them. Sadie got up and pressed herself against Luke and stood on tiptoe so her breasts pushed against his chest. Luke growled.

"You're very naughty for making us watch the display with you and Elijah."

She shrugged. "I promised him. Besides, it just made the wait even better. Don't you think?"

Luke nodded as he picked her up and threw her back down on the bed. Sadie got to her knees and stroked Luke's cock, already wet with the idea of him being inside her. Greyson's weight was added to the bed. Greyson's body warmed her back as he ran his fingers along the curve of her spine to make her shiver. His hands were softer than Luke's, and he was gentler. Greyson's lips pressed against her shoulder. His tongue dragged along the line of her collarbone while his hands wandered lower until they slid around her chest and cupped her breasts.

"Don't forget about me. I love you, Sadie. I've never going to forget again how much you mean to me," Greyson crooned in her ear.

She turned her head to face him. She pressed her lips to Greyson's and pulled away. "I'll make sure that never happens. I want all of us to be together. I want you both to fuck me."

"Your wish is our command." Greyson slipped his arms through her elbows and pulled her back into his chest and held her.

Sadie started to protest, but Luke slid his hands along her inner thighs and spread her legs. He ran his tongue along her inner calf, to the bend in her knee where she started to scream, but couldn't escape the prison of Greyson's arms. Luke discovered a ticklish spot because he hovered there, flicking his tongue over the spot until she squirmed. A cry escaped her lips. He continued his trail along her inner thigh until he stopped at her folds. Sadie took in a breath and held it. Greyson took the opportunity to start kissing her neck and sucking on her skin. He nipped here and there. Luke resumed his onslaught of the sensitive flesh of her inner thigh. He bit there before extending his tongue along her wet slit. She jumped when Luke plunged his tongue into her pussy. Once his mouth enclosed her clit, she arched her back only to meet Greyson's burning gaze. He flashed her a small smile, then his lips descended onto hers. The pleasure of Luke's attentions engulfed her. She moaned into Greyson's mouth. His tongue wound around hers. Greyson twirled her nipples until she cried out. Her nerve endings came alive as Luke continued to suck on her clit. Luke's fingers delved inside her pussy, pressing upon her inner walls until she writhed on the bed. The passion Elijah had awakened inside her from their lovemaking spread like lava along her veins until she wasn't sure if her reason had left her and this was all some marvelous dream. Greyson squeezed her nipples again. Sadie broke the kiss feeling the oncoming tension of the orgasm. Luke plunged his fingers inside her and drew her throbbing nub between his teeth. She pushed her hips into his face.

"Don't stop," she cried out.

Greyson slid his fingers down her stomach and threaded them through Luke's hair for a moment. Luke glanced up quickly and then redoubled his efforts. Greyson's cock poked into her ass. The tips of Greyson's fingers dug into the top of her thighs. Sadie's heart picked up a few beats. Luke flicked his tongue over her swollen nub one last time, until the electric charge of the orgasm race along her nerves. When she stopped quaking and opened her eyes, she saw Luke stared at her with a shit-eating grin on his lips. "You taste wonderful." He walked his fingers along her stomach and then trailed them over one of her breasts. "But we're not done with you yet."

"I'd hope not, because I want another turn," Elijah replied, she could hear the lust in his voice.

"You already had your fun with her. Now she's ours," Greyson growled.

Sadie freed herself from Greyson's grip and studied all three of them. The hunger in their eyes hadn't died. She scooted back on the bed until she hit the headboard. From there, she motioned the others to come closer. "Elijah might have had me earlier, but there's plenty of me to go around. But first, I want Luke to come here."

Luke crawled to her on the bed. Sadie put her hand out and stopped him. He gave her a questioning look. "Lie down." She stroked his erect cock before straddling him.

"What are you going to do with me?" Luke asked.

She smiled. "Fuck you, of course. The others are going to join in, too. But I'm on top."

"As you wish." Luke guided his length inside her pussy.

"Where do you want me?" Greyson whispered into her left ear.

"What about me?" Elijah asked from her right. He ran his hand along the curve of her breast.

Their rising lust pumped through her. Greyson was barely holding onto his control as it was. Underneath her, she could feel Luke's muscles rolling. They had to do this before any of them were overcome by their urges.

"Greyson, take my ass."

"I want to be inside you, too." Elijah kissed her

cheek.

She met his lips and trailed her fingers down his chest until she twisted one of Elijah's nipples. "You already have. Give the others a chance. Besides, we've only just begun."

Greyson ran his hands over the mounds of her ass. "So soft. You sure? This could hurt you."

"Fuck me. I can deal with pain."

"If you take her ass, then I take yours." Elijah growled to Greyson. She looked behind him, surprised to hear the statement. Greyson looked between the two of them. Sadie felt their mutual desire swell. It seemed Elijah was caught up in it. Greyson grabbed Elijah's chin and pulled him down to Greyson's lips in a sloppy kiss. Seeing that only made Sadie want them all more. She felt their burning passion and wasn't going to let it stop them. The need to be all connected, to feel like they were together. The world wasn't going to end and they never got the chance to show how much they all meant to one another. Even if that meant just discovering it at this very moment. Elijah grabbed Greyson's cock and stroked it before he went behind him.

"This is going to be fun," Sadie purred. She closed her eyes and focused on the links between them.

She threw her head back. Luke gripped her arms and held on while she rode him. In the middle of pulling him inside her, Greyson caught her around the waist and stopped her. She growled. Greyson spread her ass cheeks. She jumped at the cold wetness before he slipped his cock between her mounds and slowly claimed her asshole. The sudden stretching and pain she experienced was pleasurable. When she moved with Luke, their minds were both overcome with the bliss of their union. They began to move together, Greyson impaling her a little more until he was completely inside her. Luke pushed into her and strained to pleasure her. Greyson clutched her breasts while she held onto Luke's shoulders to stay steady. And then Greyson groaned, and she felt the added weight of Elijah. They began again with their dance, but with each individual push, their combined bliss was building.

Sadie felt herself slipping away as their individual consciousness's merged. Stars formed behind her eyes. Each of her mates was breathing heavily. The scent of their sweat permeated the air. Greyson's heart thundered in her ears. Luke's vibrated against her skin. Together they were building to the pinnacle she had never reached before. The muscles quivered in her stomach like butterflies trying to escape from her skin. "Harder, my loves," she cried out.

Each of them did as she asked. They moved together. She lost herself until she slid into Elijah's mind. He didn't care who he was fucking. Being close to Sadie was what mattered. Elijah had opened himself to her link and could feel her delight. It reflected and rebounded along until it seemed all her mates had formed a mate bond between themselves. They were all one big ball of passion experiencing the pleasure of one another's bodies. Sadie couldn't figure out where they ended, and she began. As each of them rose to higher heights, the world fell away in a chorus of howls.

A little while later, Sadie opened her eyes. She was somehow in the middle of their bedroom twister. All of them snored. The heat of their bodies warmed her. She never thought this was something in her future. Sharing her bed with three men. They all made her body sing in different ways. When she saw Greyson snuggled up to Elijah, it was a miracle to think Greyson had come back to her. The wolf inside her was contented. She felt the same contentment and for once knew she could take on whatever came to her. She inhaled the scents of her three mates. Each of them so distinct and all wolf. The newly forged bonds between the men vibrated in her mind. She could trace each one as they crisscrossed and wove a web. Somehow they had all gotten connected. It showed she didn't have to worry about them ever hurting one another again. They might not like it, but they had to share everything now. Luke snorted and pulled her close in his sleep. She snuggled against him and knew all was right in the world.

Dangerous Game (Billionaire Werewolf 4)
Crymsyn Hart

Sadie desperately wants to rescue her friend Narissa from the clutches of the humans who kidnapped her, but before she can find a way to their hidden lab, humans capture Sadie for their evil experiments. Elijah, Luke, and Greyson -- her mates -- will stop at nothing to get her back. As the wolves search for a way to keep themselves and their packs safe, something even darker lurks in the shadows.

They don't have one enemy, but two who are out to destroy all the shifters, be they human or Fairy. Will her mates rescue her in time? Can they overcome the threat and save not only themselves, but also set all shifters free from fear?

Chapter One

Sadie snagged Luke's shirt and pulled it on. The top clung to her curves but hung to her knees. The aroma of his wolf lingered on the fabric. She took a large inhalation, and the fleeting image of the first time she caught his scent warmed her insides. Sadie recalled opening her eyes after she awoke from her turning fever. The musky fragrance coming off him had intoxicated her, and her wolf knew Luke was her mate. At the time, Sadie didn't understand what it truly meant to have a mate. Shapeshifters were still a new thing for her. The fear of them had lingered in her bones until she accepted she wanted to be one. All because she fell in love with billionaire Elijah Dane.

She hovered in the doorway and glanced back at the mishmash of limbs as her three mates slept on the king bed. Luke's feet hung off the mattress and he snorted. She chuckled at the sound and let her gaze rove over the two other men. Greyson snuggled against Elijah filling in the hole she once occupied. Her heart hitched at the thought of Greyson. After being gone from her life for so long, he had returned.

Her stomach growled again. She snapped herself away from the memories threatening to pull her under. Sadie walked to the kitchen, opened the fridge and took out a few slices of cold bacon. She savored the greasy taste of the meat and the quiet in the house. The energy of her wolf mates lingered along the outside of her mind as they slept, wrapped in dreams. If she extended her awareness outside the cabin, Luke's pack and other shifters -- who had come at her behest -- made an uncomfortable rake along her aura. All of them struggled to find a safe place where they could mourn their losses while others plotted their revenge. All of them were victims of those who were hurting the packs and clans of shifters with silver.

Her appetite turned at the thought of all the carnage. She was supposed to be some super wolf to save all the shifters. Sadie didn't understand why she was chosen. She certainly didn't fit the role of a superhero. She tried to relax, but her mind spun imagining what the next step might be. She stared out the kitchen window and searched for solace in the woods. A white shimmer rushed past the window. She jumped back. Someone rapped quietly on the backdoor. *This is the part in the horror movies where the serial killer bursts in and slaughters everyone in the cabin.*

Her wolf shifted within her mind. *"It's not a serial killer. Open the door."*

"You sure?"

The beast didn't answer, but she could internally feel the creature roll its eyes.

Sadie pulled the door open. A creature stood outside waiting to come in. She appeared nearly human. Small white horns hugged the sides of her head right above her ears. Black hair hung like a curtain of ink down her back. Intense blue eyes examined Sadie. A long purple gown covered her female form. The creature outside was a Fairy. A female she hadn't seen in the group before when they arrived earlier.

"May I enter your home so we can speak?" she asked softly.

"Who are you and what do you want to talk about?"

The Fairy let out a breath through her nose and black flame curled around her nostrils. Sadie felt a moment of fear but held her ground. "My name is Narin. I'm Narissa's sister. I have information about who took her. Please, she's in so much pain. You're the only one who can help her."

At the mention of Narissa, Sadie's heart dropped. Her best friend had been taken by the same people who were after the other shifters. Her friend's agony had come to Sadie in a dream. It was the driving force she needed to call together all the shifters and those Fairies who had pledged themselves to help the silver wolf.

"How do you know about her being kidnapped?" Sadie asked, keeping the Fairy outside the house. It could be a ruse. Everything in her jumped at the tidbit of news. However, she couldn't believe her without proof. "How do I even know you're Nari's sister? She was shunned in Fairy because she's a shapeshifter."

"You have every right to be wary of me. I love my sister even though our father decreed her not worthy of the royal line because of her tainted blood. The other Fae who came here, the shifters, hate my father as much as I do. Many of his subjects do not approve of his actions and working with the humans. Please let me enter and I'll tell you what I know."

"Swear to me no harm will come to anyone in this house or the other shifters in this compound. Prove to me you're Nari's sister, and I'll let you in." Sadie knew from her friend to get a Fairy's word before agreeing to anything. Then they had to honor it.

Narin glanced around the outside and stared into the woods where the Fairy shifters had taken refuge. "I swear I'm not here to hurt you and I mean no harm to the others. I swear it on my sister's mark upon you. I'm here in peace." The Fairy drew out a silver locket from under her dress and opened it. Inside was a picture of Narissa and Narin. "This was our mother's. Narissa is my twin."

Sadie held the locket and studied the images. The paintings shared a resemblance to one another. The sisters weren't identical. The silver was cool against her palm and didn't burn her like it would have any other shifter because of her immunity to it. *What do you think? Can we trust her?* Sadie asked her wolf.

"She seems distraught, and she swore not to harm anyone. I say we let her in. I'm as worried about Nari as you are."

"Come in, but please be quiet. I don't want my mates waking up."

The Fairy slipped inside. The door closed on its own and locked. No sound came from it. "I put a sound dampening spell over the room so they won't hear us."

"Great. You said you had some information about who took Narissa."

"Yes. She and I have always had a telepathic link because we're twins. Sometimes we can communicate between this world and Fairy. We've had the ability since we were kids and hid it from our father. He wouldn't understand. It's how I knew to come to you. She sent me."

Sadie rubbed her arms at the sudden cold encompassing her body. Then she realized it wasn't a draft. Thin lines of frost spread outward from where Narin stood along the tile floor. Faint ice crystals formed around the Fairy's body and floated to the ground like snow. "Can you turn off the ice? I might be warm-blooded, but I can't deal with the cold you're putting out."

"Sorry," Narin let out a breath. "I lose control when I'm stressed." She closed her eyes and the cold in the room retreated. More ice grew around her feet.

"It's okay. I understand. This whole situation is stressful. Who took Narissa?"

"Humans. Scientists. They're..." Narin broke down into sobs.

Sadie drew Narin into her arms to soothe her. She had to suppress a shudder from the cold as she touched the Fairy. After a few moments, the woman pulled away. Sadie's shirt had frozen where the tears had fallen. Narin sank down into one of the kitchen chairs.

"These scientists. Do you know where they are, Narin?"

"Not the exact location, but I've gotten glimpses from Nari. She's shown me the small white room they've kept her in. The table they've had her strapped down on while they torture her. There is a woman. She has red hair and glasses. She's the main one who hurts her. This scientist wears a white coat with the letters STI on it. Narissa's visions are coming to me less frequently as she grows weaker. I fear she won't last much longer."

Sadie ran the information over in her mind, but nothing rang as familiar. STI could be anything. She had to look it up and see if anything came up on a Google search about it, but she figured even if she did, nothing would come up. "It's more than I've gotten. Thank you for coming to me with the information. I'm going to do everything I can to find Narissa. She's like a sister to me."

Narin smiled. "She's talked about you a lot. She marked you, which is a big deal for a Fairy. It must have changed your life."

"It did, but in the end I didn't really need it because I had Elijah, and then the others came along."

"It can be a burden. Do you think Narissa did it to you to make your life trickier than it was?"

Her eyes narrowed. "Why do you ask?"

"Sorry, I picked up on a fleeting thought you had. I didn't mean to stir anything up."

She crossed her arms over her chest. The thought had run through her mind, but Sadie pushed it aside. "Once upon a time, I thought because she had given me her mark it might've turned me into what I am. However, I know it isn't true. Nari did what she did because she wanted me protected. I love her for that. Is there anything else you can remember about where they're keeping her captive? Any little detail might be helpful. All we know is they drive white vans, wear white suits, and can weaponize blood by lacing it with silver and make it airborne. All those kidnapped shifters have Fairy ancestry or they are outright Fairy shifters. The humans are using whatever they have learned to target regular shifters to wipe them out."

"I'm sorry. I didn't know about that. I've told you what I know." Narin got up to leave.

"Wait. You said many of the other Fairies don't approve of what your father is doing. How much do they know?"

Narin ran her fingers over her hair, pushing some of the black strands behind her white horns. "Your summons was heard all throughout Fairy. The five tribes who pledged themselves to the silver wolf eons ago aren't just shifters. They make up all of our ranks. My father would have heard it, too."

A spear of fear hit Sadie. "Are you saying you were followed or the other Fairy shifters were?"

"Maybe. I don't know. I don't know how much knowledge my father has given the humans. It's because of him they are able to do what they did with the blood of the shifters and the silver. Mixing magic and technology. My father doesn't want the mixed bloods in Fairy at all. Many of my kind don't share his wishes, but they are afraid to stand up to him."

"Do you know what information or magic he has given the scientists?"

Narin grabbed Sadie's hand. "I don't know."

The hair stood up on the back of Sadie's neck. The wolf's hackles rose in her mind. "Shit."

Someone banged on her door. Lights flashed through the windows. Narin grabbed her arms and shoved her against the wall. Sadie tried to move but found she was frozen in place. Narin put a finger to her lips to stay quiet. Sadie couldn't make a noise even if she wanted to. The Fairy had turned her into a frigid statue. Sadie closed her eyes and willed herself to be calm. If this corporation had followed Narin, then every one of the pack was in trouble.

"Luke, Elijah. Greyson!" she cried along their link.

The door splintered around the lock as a shotgun

blast took out the deadbolt. It didn't sound as loud as it should have. The sound dampening spell remained around the room. Narin pressed against the wall as a large man in a white suit came into the kitchen as though stepping into a germ-filled environment.

Static clicked over a black radio he had in his other hand. "Report."

"There's no one here," he replied.

"They should be there. He said they would be." Sadie could make out a female voice on the other end of the radio.

"The whole place is abandoned." Another male voice chimed in on the radio.

"It's where the Fairies' trail ended."

The man who came in ripped open the suit. He appeared to be a normal, unassuming man whom she would have passed in the street. His dark eyes peered around the room. Whatever spell Narin had cast kept the sounds in the kitchen muted so her mates hadn't woken from the shotgun taking out part of the door. "I know they're here. They must've used some kind of glamour to camouflage themselves. Keep looking."

He walked around the kitchen and stopped at the door to the hallway listening for any sounds. He disappeared into the shadows of the house.

"Luke, are you awake?" Sadie asked through their link.

"Yes," he answered her.

"The others?"

"Yes," Elijah and Greyson replied at the same time.

Relief swept through her, but they weren't off the hook yet. The intruder walked back into the kitchen and stopped by the sink as he stared out in the woods.

"What's going on?" Elijah asked.

"Long story. They found us. I don't know how, but they did. For some reason they can't find anyone here. I'm stuck in the kitchen with Narin."

"Who's Narin?" Greyson inquired.

She hadn't realized all three of her mates could hear her at the same time. *"Narissa's sister. She came to give me some information about where Nari's being held captive."*

"I'm coming out there," Luke growled.

"No. Stay where you are. We don't want the spell to be broken," Sadie told all of them.

"I can't hold this much longer. I'm sorry," Narin whispered.

Sadie could feel the spell holding her against the wall weakening and warmth returning to her body. The intruder slowly walked back toward the door. Narin whimpered. A blast of warm air hit Sadie as the spell dropped. A slow smile spread over the man's face as Sadie became visible to him. Dread filled her.

"I knew someone was there. Fairy bullshit. Where's the other one holding the glamour?"

"Go to hell," Sadie whispered. She tried to run around him, but he stepped in front of her.

Narin dashed for the door. Another shot shattered the kitchen. The explosion made her ears ring. Sadie tried to get into the hallway to her mates. The man grabbed her arm. Her heart slipped up into her throat as the fear of what this man would do to her overcame her. She couldn't get her emotions under control.

"You're a feisty one. You smell different than the others in the lab. Maybe it's the taint of the Fairy around you. Didn't think they worked with any of the shifters. I hear they hate your kind as much as I do." He ran his hand down the side of her face. "You'll make the others very happy. Maybe you can tell me where the rest of your pack is, and I'll spare you the pain of what they have in store for you."

The strength of her inner wolf surged forward. Before she could think about what she was doing, her foot connected with his balls. He grunted and caught himself on the chair. It gave her a window to run for freedom. Sadie glanced back. Her mates lingered in the shadows of the hallway. Sadie had to draw the man away from them. As she raced outside, the night energy called to her. She went lower to the ground and moved more swiftly on four legs than she had on two. The wolf seemed to know where to go. As she went toward the woods, headlights turned on and blinded her. All she could make out were silhouettes as men got out of their vehicles and had her penned in with their trucks.

She caught glimpse of other shifters moving in the woods away from the vehicles. Her inner sense told her the other shifters and Fairies were escaping. She had to keep the humans occupied so they wouldn't notice the exodus. Sadie growled as one of the men came into the circle. Her lip raised off her teeth, and she snapped at those who held her captive.

"Sadie, we can't get to you. We killed the one in the house."

"Don't come out here. Stay where you are. The others are getting away."

One of the men came at her with a long stick and hit her. She yelped at the sudden pain and felt her leg buckle underneath her. Sadie tried to shake it off, but something hit her shoulder and she barked at the jolt. The world darkened. She felt the link between her mates and sent one final message to them.

"Run."

Chapter Two

Luke paced in the kitchen, torn between the urge to go after his mate or check on his pack. Both ate him up inside until he slammed his fist down on the counter, taking a chip out of the wood. He grabbed the toaster and threw it into the wall. The scent of the intruders lingered in the air. He didn't think it would ever come out. His door was in shambles. The Fairy who had helped Sadie stayed in the corner near Greyson. Luke raked his nails through his beard. "Fuck this. I'm going after her."

"Doing so would be a bad move," Kade said as he stood in the doorway. He was dirty and out of breath.

Luke glanced at the pack's shaman and growled. "Why?"

"Because then her sacrifice would be for nothing. You would put the pack at risk, all the other shifters, and the Fairies who came here for our protection," Kade told him.

"We have to go after her," Elijah commented.

Through their link, Luke could tell Elijah was also pissed about what had gone down. Even Greyson, whose energy remained calmer, wanted to save Sadie. Luke had to also listen to the advice of his shaman. "They all came here because Sadie called them and promised them they would be safe. They followed her." Luke lunged at Narin.

Greyson pushed the Fairy behind him. "This isn't her fault, Luke."

"What deal did you strike for bringing those men here?" Luke swiped at her, but Greyson covered Narin to make sure the Fairy wasn't hurt.

"I didn't do anything. I came here to tell Sadie what I knew about where my sister was being held. I didn't bring them. I hid Sadie the best I could. I made sure you were also hidden so they didn't see you. I can only do so much magic, and the strain got to be too much. I-I didn't want to reveal her either. Narissa loves Sadie."

"If you protected us, then how did the others get away right under their noses?" Greyson asked.

"The other Fairies banded together and cast a glamour to make sure everyone was able to get out safely. I called upon our pack ancestors to assist as well. It seemed the humans were more focused on your house than anywhere else," Kade stepped inside the kitchen. "I led everyone deeper into the woods where the ancestors said they'd be safe. They're still there until I give them the all clear. The other Fae are keeping a lookout to see if the humans have all gone or if they have a few stragglers."

"I don't think they'd give up so easily. If they came here looking for us, then a good bet is they're going to be back," Greyson stated.

Narin came out from behind Greyson. "They won't be back."

"Did you bring them?" Elijah asked.

"No. I swear. I glimpsed them through Narissa's eyes. Narissa could hear the attackers talking in her cell, and they were coming for Sadie." Narin shook her head and tears ran down her cheeks. "They tracked me or the other Fairies. That means my father told the humans."

"I'm sure you didn't mean to lead them here," Kade said to her.

"Didn't mean it or not, they took our mate away," Elijah replied.

"We need to find a way to get her back. Narin, can you help us get into the facility where they're holding Narissa?" Greyson asked.

Luke couldn't understand how he remained so calm. Elijah barely kept it together from what he felt along their link. *How am I able to sense what Greyson and Elijah are feeling?* Luke was used to being connected to his pack because he was the leader, and with Sadie because she was his mate. Being linked to the two other men was a new development in their relationship. He loved Sadie with all his heart, but she had become something out of legend and was here to save all the wolves and other shifter clans from impending danger. He witnessed her ability to command his whole pack. Then she could heal silver poisoning. Then what she did with the drum... Luke shook at the thought of the way her luscious body moved and how she fit against him when they made love. Losing her would be like pulling his heart out and stomping all over it.

"I've told you everything I know," the Fairy told them.

"I might be able to help with finding them," another voice said from the doorway.

A woman stepped inside. She was only three feet tall and looked to be more bird than human.

"Who are you?" Luke asked.

"I'm Pricilla. My mother was one of the ones taken. My sister was in the trees when they took her. We flew together and followed the vans, so I know the way. They caught my sister, which allowed me to escape." Pricilla looked more like a child than an adult. Luke knelt down and took the smaller shifter into his arms.

"I'm so sorry to hear that. If you can lead us to where they took our mate, then I'd be forever grateful," Luke said to her. A sense of relief flooded him as he saw some light in the dark pit in which he found himself. He glanced at the other men. They nodded, feeling the same way. If this little slip of a thing could lead them, then they had some hope of getting the woman he loved back.

"I have no home anymore. For repayment for showing you this, would I be allowed to stay with the wolves and not be considered a midnight snack?" Pricilla asked.

"Of course. You can stay here."

"Or even with my pack, or what's left of it," Elijah replied to her as well. The other wolf laid a hand on

Luke's shoulder.

"Thank you. Then I will show you where this place is. Silver lines everything. It's even in the dirt and in the air. It affected my sister when she flew over the building. It was so large -- like three football fields long and wide. It's surrounded by woods in the middle of nowhere."

"Get us there first and we can figure out how to deal with the silver," Luke told her.

"We can't run in there without a plan. We have to figure out when we are going to do this. Luke, I know how much you want to get Sadie back, but you can't go running off half-cocked when there is the pack to take care of. The pack and the other clans are looking to you three now that Sadie is gone." Kade leaned against the counter.

Luke didn't like the shaman's comment, but he knew it was true. He needed to assess what the damage was to their sanctuary. The burden of all the responsibility landed on his shoulders. He scratched his beard and nodded. He got up and looked over at Pricilla. "Stay with us for the rest of the night. After a few hours of sleep, we can figure out what we're going to do. Sound good?"

The little bird shifter nodded. Kade motioned for her to come with him. Luke waited for them to leave before he slumped down in the kitchen chair. Elijah took the other chair beside him. The history between them only made it unlikely they would ever get along. Here they were, forced together by fate. It took Luke's sister, Denice, to bite Sadie and turn her into a wolf for them to come together.

Luke thought back to his sister's laughter when she was a little girl. He missed everything about her. Now would be the time Denice would say fuck everything and charge into battle. She had always defied the rules. He had been the levelheaded one. Now she was gone and so was his mate. *Sadie isn't dead. I have to stop thinking she is.*

Their connection vibrated with life. He tried to follow it and hit a wall. Greyson slid his hand over Luke's and squeezed. The outpouring of love he felt from the other man overwhelmed him.

"We'll get her back, Luke." Greyson put the other hand on his cheek.

Luke nearly pulled away. This bond between him and the attraction he felt for Greyson was still too new, even if they had shared a bed and a mate together. "Thanks, Grey."

The other wolf leaned in and brushed his lips across Luke's. The small gesture sent a jolt of pleasure through Luke. For a brief moment, Luke leaned into the kiss before he pulled away. "You're welcome. She's still alive. She's a fighter. Even back in the days when we were both human, she fought for what she wanted. It was what I loved about her in the first place. Sadie never saw it for herself, but her inner strength pulled me to her. Being a wolf, it's come out. She won't give up. We can't give up on her."

"Of course we won't," Elijah chimed in. Dark circles rimmed Elijah's eyes. "She's strong and sassy. It's what made me want to help her the first time I met her."

"You mean after you ate me," Greyson replied.

"Yes, after I ate you, and before I knew you were back from the dead. She was arguing with the bellhop at the front desk of my resort. Narissa had made reservations there, not realizing we had a gathering of werewolves coming in. The clerk didn't know she was human at first." Elijah sat back in his seat and chuckled. Luke studied the billionaire werewolf. The man before him was broken. He had lost most of his pack and the woman they shared. Something inside him had snapped and he held on by a thread. Luke understood the feeling. He suffered the same.

"When I found her wandering on the road deep into

the turn fever, delirious, I knew I had to take care of her. Her system fought against the turning. Something inside her finally decided to come to terms with it, because she quieted. When she opened her eyes and looked at me, I knew she was something special. My wolf knew she was the one for me. Sadie claimed me for her mate without truly knowing the consequences. She's a marvel." Luke looked at both men and held Sadie's image in his mind. Together they would find her. They had to.

Elijah stood up and threaded his fingers through Greyson's. Elijah slid his hands along Greyson's face and kissed him. The act roused Luke's passion. He shouldn't be thinking of anything else except Sadie and checking on the rest of his pack, but if he desired, he could sink into the safety and loving arms of his other mates. He sat back in his chair as the thought settled in his mind.

"*Did you really expect them to be anything less after we've shared ourselves with them and the bonds were forged between the four of us?*" his wolf chimed in. It didn't seem as frantic as he did about finding Sadie.

"*I didn't know what to expect, considering what Sadie is. Fuck, I don't know. It isn't in my nature to be into guys, but...*" He thought about Greyson and Elijah and felt the pull toward them. It wasn't so much about their physical sex, being male, but he felt the same lure toward them as he did to Sadie. To be around them and see they were pleased.

"*Sometimes our nature changes because of the situation. They're connected to Sadie. We've taken on her feelings for them through the new ties she forged between all of us. We will get her back, but we have to work together.*"

Luke couldn't run off and leave Elijah or Greyson behind. He got up and touched Elijah's back. He expected the other wolf to flinch, but instead Elijah smiled. The small gesture lightened Luke's heart as though Sadie were looking at him. Elijah held onto Luke's hand and rubbed his thumb across the back of it.

"We'll get her back and make sure the fuckers pay. This is more than saving her. It's also about getting justice for all those who died and what they did to them. They killed my pack. I can't let this stand. Everyone here will say the same thing. If humans know about us, then we have to be ready for the next time. Destroy all the information they've gathered and whatever else we find," Elijah growled.

"We will. We need a plan and some sleep. I know you want to go after them. Believe me, I do, too. You heard what Pricilla said about them having silver everywhere. You'd be doomed once you got near their facilities. I'm the only one who is immune to silver," Greyson told them.

"Are you saving we should stay here like cowards?" Luke snarled.

"You know I'm not. I'm stupid to think you won't come with me or that Elijah is going to sit back and not want to get his claws dirty. I'm stating a fact. How about we try and get some sleep? Kade can hold down the pack and other shifters until morning. Then, Luke, you can address everyone. We can't do anything for Sadie if we're exhausted," Greyson explained.

The shaman came back into the kitchen. "He has a point, Pack Master," Kade replied. "I'll make sure everyone is okay for the night and get them fed in the morning. Once everyone has gathered, then you can address the clans about what you plan to do."

"Thank you, Kade. I appreciate it more than you know." Kade squeezed Luke's shoulder and then left the house. Luke tried to close the door the best he could, but it still didn't shut all the way because of the damage done to it. The hinges were twisted. He would have to replace the door, but he would deal with that much later when it was more important.

Greyson got up and Elijah followed. "Come back to

bed, Luke."

"I'll be there in a minute," he told the others.

He sat in the silence as he listened to the night sounds. The bed creaked from his other mates slipping into it. He could hear the faint whispers of Pricilla and Narin in the spare bedroom. All he wanted was to feel Sadie next to him and have her hands running along his chest. She would breathe on the back of his neck and tell him it was all going to be okay. He slid his mind along their tether and prayed she would be okay, but he was met with the same darkness he felt before. It only meant she was still unconscious. Anything else to think about would drive him crazy. Luke scrubbed his face once more and tugged on his beard. He shut the light off in the kitchen and headed back to bed.

Elijah hugged the edge of the bed and Greyson was in the middle leaving room for Luke on the other side. As he slipped under the covers, Greyson wrapped his arms around Luke. He inhaled the lingering scent of Sadie on the covers. His eyes teared up. Greyson pulled him close. Luke let the other man comfort him as best he could as the tears spilled out at the loss of the one they all loved.

"It's okay. It's going to be okay," Greyson crooned and rubbed his back. Luke let out the rest of his pent-up emotions. When he did, he tried to turn away and wiped his eyes, but Greyson touched his cheek and smiled. He looked into the eyes of the other wolf and saw love and compassion. Luke brushed his lips across Greyson's and felt like he could face the coming day.

Chapter Three

Sadie opened her eyes. Everything hurt. They had put her on a cold floor and dressed her in light blue scrubs. She rubbed her arms to warm up, but nothing helped. When she let out a breath, it came out in a cloud of vapor. The light in the room was wan and yellowed. Taking in a breath, she tasted something metallic on the tip of her tongue. Silver. At the end of the room was a stainless steel toilet. Sadie looked for a door but found only a clear wall with a woman staring at her, studying her as though she were a lab rat. Sadie got up and walked toward the glass. The woman scrunched her eyes behind her glasses. Her red hair was piled on top of her head into a bun. Sadie glanced across the hall at another room. She couldn't see into it because of some dark screen they had on the cell window.

Before she could figure out what they were doing to her, a tapping started on the glass. It drew Sadie's attention back to the woman. "I see you're awake now. There are a few things I'd like to discuss with you."

"Fuck off."

The woman gave her a sly smile. She let out a yelp. A quick jolt dropped Sadie to her knees. A sharp pain vibrated up her legs. Sadie glanced at the woman who held something in her hand. It appeared to be the size of a garage door opener. Sadie wanted to growl at her, but the redhead's pink-lacquered fingernail tapped over the small device. She held her tongue.

"You learn quickly. I guess you're not a dumb animal after all. I couldn't tell when they brought you in here. Then the miracle happened where you turned from the wolf into the woman before my eyes. We dressed you but with the slight modification you just experienced. Are you shocked?"

"Do you plan on cutting me up and dissecting me the way you have with the others? Or maybe injecting me with silver and then dumping my body back where you took me from so you can infect the others?"

"You're clever. Although not what I expected. We have other plans for you. Your friend has been some trouble. All we got out of her is that you're some super wolf."

"What have you done to Narissa?"

The scientist glanced behind her. "See for yourself. She's quite entertaining. We can't dispose of her. It's part of the deal. As long as we keep her breathing we're not in violation of anything." The woman hit another button on her little device and the white wall next to Sadie lifted to reveal another cell. In the center was a metal table angled on its end. Strapped to the table was Nari. Her limp form looked ready to pool off the metal if she hadn't already been pinned down. Dark black and yellow bruises fanned across her arms, legs and torso. Purple circles accentuate the hollows around her eyes. This didn't look like the stubborn woman Sadie knew who always got what she wanted.

"Nari, what have they done to you? Why are they torturing you?" Sadie touched the wall. Narissa's eyes fluttered slightly. It gave Sadie some hope. Something pressed upon her mind, and it felt like Narissa.

"Don't react. We can talk more later. Go along with what they want you to do or they'll hurt you. They can't know you're immune to silver."

Sadie tried to keep her face calm from the warning she had gotten from Narissa. She agreed she couldn't let any of them know about her silver immunity. If they could pull the immunity from her, then who knew what they would do to her. What the scientists said about not being able to kill Narissa piqued Sadie's interest. Knowing they had to keep her best friend alive gave her some hope. Her mates would come looking for her. Sadie had to get them a message before they decided to barge in and get caught. She figured the facility was wired up to the hilt with cameras and technology to alert anyone coming and going.

"Are you satisfied your friend is alive?" the scientist asked.

She turned back to the woman who held her captive. Her lab coat had an STI logo stamped into it. She scrutinized it and made out the name underneath the letters. Silver Tech Industries. "Even if I was, it doesn't mean anything. You're showing her to me because you want to gain my trust. You're the god while you hold whatever device that's going to shock me again whenever you deem I'm doing something bad."

"You're right. I am the god here. I say who lives or dies. If you eat or if you sleep. It all depends on if you're good. Why don't we stop the chitchatting and get down to business. I'm going to ask you a series of questions. If I feel you're bullshitting me, taking too long to answer, or if I simply don't like your answer, then you get shocked. Understand?"

"Yes. I understand," Sadie said through clenched teeth.

"Good. I'm coming into your cell. If you try to run or hurt me, then you're going to get something even worse than the little jolt I gave you before. Now back away," she told Sadie.

This bitch is going to get it when I get out of here. Sadie backed away from the glass. As the scientist opened the door, someone brought in a chair for her to sit on. A blast of cool air hit Sadie and so did the screams of others in the facility with her.

"Sit on the floor."

Sadie waited.

"Do it or you're going to drop to the floor."

Sadie gritted her teeth and went slowly down to the floor. The scientist adjusted her glasses and glanced over her clipboard of questions. Sadie took in a deep breath and ran her fingers over the stiff scrubs they had dressed her in. She glanced around the room. Besides the door which led into the hallway, a window too high for her to get to let in a little bit of light. It was no bigger than a shoebox so she wouldn't be able to fit through it even if she tried.

"Good, girl."

"I'm not your dog."

A sharper jolt ran down her arm and then into her chest. She hit the floor and the breath was pulled from her lungs. The second time it enveloped her entire body. Sadie curled up in a ball and bit her lip to keep from crying out. After moment, the pain evaporated. When she caught the gaze of her captor, it was a triumphant smirk.

"You are what I say you are. You should keep learning fast and being a good bitch or you might find your friend gets more punishment. I'm sure you don't want to cause any suffering to her. Do you?"

Sadie glanced through the cell to where Nari remained immobile. Her friend didn't look so good. Anything to cause her any pain would only make Sadie feel worse than she already did. "No."

"Good. Now answer my questions and you'll get a reward if I like your answers. Would you like that?"

"Yes," she whispered never feeling more humiliated.

"Do what she asks. We'll play along for now. You have my strength to get you through this," her inner wolf relayed to her. A rush of strength bolstered her confidence. She could get through this ordeal the same way she had dealt with being bitten by Denice and losing Greyson. She would endure.

"Let's get down to business. What's your full name?"

"Sadie Lynn Matthews."

"Good. How old are you? Tell me your true age including being a shapeshifter."

"I'm thirty-two."

A zing hit her, but not as painful as the last shock.

"Again. How old are you?"

"I'm thirty-two. I've only been a shifter for a few months. If you don't believe me, you can drag it out of Nari." Sadie panted as another sharp jab hit her shoulder. Her heart thumped against her chest as though it would drive itself out of her ribcage.

"Hmm… okay, I'll take it for now. Why are you so important to the Fairy? She said you were some kind of super wolf."

Sadie shrugged. "Narissa's my best friend. I've known her since college. She's helped me through a lot of rough times after the death of my fiancé."

"Ahh, yes… tell me about your past with her."

She picked at a thread in her scrubs. "Not much to tell. My fiancé and I were camping. Late in the night I went into the tent to get some sleep. He stayed outside. I woke up to hear him screaming. When I went outside, two monsters were attacking him. One had him around the neck and the other one had its mouth buried into his stomach. I screamed. A beast attacked me. It flipped me over and scratched across my back. I don't really remember much after that except waking up in the hospital. They never found his body. I spent two years mourning for him, barely able to get up in the morning. Nari got me through it all."

"Don't those who live through attacks turn at the next full moon?"

"It's what I've been told. I should've, but it didn't happen then. Nor did it happen the next time I was assaulted two years later."

The scientist gestured for her to continue.

"I went to a hotel to get my head on straight and take a vacation. I was out by the pool at night relaxing. When I opened my eyes, two large wolves had me cornered. I tried to get away, but one of them scratched me. Left a large scar on my thigh. It was pretty deep. The doctor at the hotel was able to fix me up."

"I hope you got a free stay at the hotel."

Sadie shook her head. "I haven't gone back."

"Did you turn after that?"

"No."

"Did you know then what these beasts were that attacked you the second time?"

"I had an idea even though I didn't want to believe it. Who wants to believe in shapeshifters? It's like believing in vampires or the Loch Ness Monster."

"Yet you ended up becoming one of them. When did this happen?"

"A few months ago, I was out walking and got ambushed by two wolves. One of them turned into a woman. Told me I needed to take a walk on the wild side. She turned back into the wolf and bit my leg hard enough she broke it. I don't really remember much until I woke up in a strange man's cabin. He said he found me on the side of the road wandering around. Once I came out of the change fever, he gave me the quick rundown of what happened to me and then set me back on the road so I could figure it all out."

The woman tapped her gadget. Sadie waited for the woman to press it, but she seemed satisfied with the answer. "Sounds like you've been through a lot. Your friend tells me you're some kind of super wolf."

"I have no idea."

The next shock made her scream. Sadie landed on the floor and felt her body convulsing. Her wolf lent her the strength and she found herself unlocked from her body. Instead, Sadie stood in the place within her mind where she went when she needed to find her inner wolf. The beast sat at the edge of the pond.

"You can't tell them anything about being the silver wolf. It's like Nari said, we can't let them know who and what we are," her wolf told her.

"I know. I don't intend to, but the pain..." She peered into the pool and could see her body still twitching. The scientist touched her. She couldn't hear what the woman said, but it seemed like she wasn't happy about it. She exited the cell, leaving Sadie unconscious.

"You come here to deal with the pain. That is the beauty of being able to come here. There's something else." The wolf dipped her nose into the water.

Sadie glanced into the pool and saw the kitchen in Luke's cabin. They sat around the table eating. She couldn't hear what they were saying, but she could see they were all getting along. Elijah sipped at his coffee and Greyson had his hand on Elijah's knee. *That's new.* Seeing them getting along together made her heart hitch.

"I really wish they could hear me."

"They can. Bonds have been formed between each of them. They are all mates now as they are mated to us," the silver wolf said. She looked at the beast, still not believing this magnificent creature was something she turned into.

"They'll want to know we're still alive."

"They know we're alive. The connection between us would be severed if we passed on into the other realm. Reach out as we normally do." The wolf bumped her head into Sadie's shoulder and wanted her head scratched.

A flutter of nervous emotion went through her as she looked at her mates. *"Elijah,"* Sadie said to him.

Elijah dropped his fork on the plate. The other two men stopped. They looked at one another and then back at Elijah. He shrugged.

"Sadie?" Elijah asked.

The outpouring of love she felt from her mate overwhelmed her. *"Yes, it's me."*

"Where are you? Where did they take you?" Luke asked.

His frantic emotions filled her up as did his love. *"I don't know where they took me or where I am. They have Nari and some other shifters are here. I'm in a room. They can see everything. They have Narissa strapped to a table and have been torturing her. They've put some kind of shocking device in me. When I don't answer their questions the way they like, they jolt me."*

"I'll kill them," Luke whispered.

"We'll all kill them," Greyson replied. *"We're coming to get you, love. We have someone who can lead us to the place they're holding you. Stay strong until we get there."*

Sadie nodded more to herself since they couldn't see her. *"They have this place lit up like a Christmas tree. I can taste the silver in the air. It's faint, but it would affect you."*

"We're working on a plan to get you out," Luke told her.

She sent a current of love along their bonds. Her vision grew fuzzy around the edges. *"I know you are. Be careful. I love you all no matter what happens. Take everyone to the resort. They won't look for you there."*

His brow scrunched. *"How do you know that?"*

"Call it a hunch. The counselor there will give you more detail." The silver wolf butted her head against Sadie's hip. Sadie glanced down into the pool. The vision of her mates faded as did her connection to the glade she found herself in. *"I love you -- all three of you."*

Their love came through in one big surge. It lit up her insides and kept her holding onto her sanity as the glade faded away.

She opened her eyes and found herself staring back at the scientist who tortured her. The hatred she had in her heart darkened into fury. For the first time, Sadie knew she wanted to rip off this woman's face.

"There you are. Now you're back, we can begin again. This time, I hope your answers are better."

Elijah stared back at his plate of food, his appetite lost over what he'd heard. The disbelief on the other wolves' faces told him they had heard Sadie. She was alive. Hearing her voice gave him the hope he needed to keep going. Elijah was losing faith they were going to get her back. What she said about bringing everyone to the resort made sense, but he didn't understand how this company wouldn't come looking for them there. They had found his house and attacked those there. He had to trust her, though.

"That really happened, didn't it?" Greyson asked in a whisper.

He glanced at the other wolf. His gray eyes were lined with tears. The look on his face was one of disbelief and relief at the same time. The emotions roiling within Greyson thrummed along the newly formed link Elijah shared with Luke and Greyson. Elijah didn't know what Sadie did to tie them all together, but in way he was grateful for it. Having the connection to the other men made him feel not so alone. The comfort they had in one another's arms gave him an anchor so he wouldn't dip under the sea of the depression he felt within him for the space where those in his pack used to be. The ones who had not been affected by the silver poisoning at his mansion were here. They had responded to Sadie's call for safety. They mingled with Luke's pack. He wasn't sure about the Fairies, but they had also responded to Sadie's summons.

Elijah didn't know how she accomplished it. All he knew was when she used the drum, the beat of it sliced through his mind and soul. He didn't have any will of his own. He could do nothing about it except obey her command. Her voice echoed over and over again in his mind. Even now he could hear the command in the back of his mind. She was all that mattered. Elijah wasn't going to let some organization that had a hard-on for killing shifters get away with taking her captive. He needed to get her, but as they had discussed, they had to take precautions. One of those was getting all the other shifters who had come to this place to safety. If taking them to the resort was what it had to be, then that was what he was going to do.

"It really happened. We all heard and felt her," Luke said. The alpha got up and slid his hands over Greyson's shoulders to help quiet the other wolf down. Once Luke touched Greyson, Elijah could feel the calming touch as if it were on his own shoulders.

When he looked at the other men, Elijah wanted to see them safe. He wanted to protect Luke and Greyson and make sure they were happy as though they were his primary mates. He no longer felt the deep jealousy he had had for Luke or Greyson. When Sadie told him Greyson was also her mate, Elijah didn't understand how she could want the attention of three men. Adding Luke into the mix was bad enough. Then Greyson showed back up in his life. That was how he'd first met Sadie. He thought he wanted to eat her, but he stopped when she screamed. It wasn't until years later when he ran into her again at his resort that Elijah realized she was his mate.

All the changes that came with being with her had opened his eyes and his heart to things he never thought possible. One of them was feeling love for the two other men. "Her words felt like she was right in the room with us. You all heard what she said."

"They're torturing her," Luke stated simply.

"We can't think about it," Greyson shook his head. "We have to focus on how to save her. Luke, you need to address the pack here. Elijah, what was it Sadie said about the counselor at your hotel… that she would know it's a safe place? Can you call her?"

"Yeah. I can do that. The psychiatrist. Dr. Maran, is a

little different. She's a snake shifter. Older than you and I combined. She's been there for as long as I can recall. I'll give her a call, but you're right, Greyson. We need to get our shit in gear. Pricilla said she would show us the way to the facility, but we can't get near it because of the silver they have around the place," Elijah responded.

"I can go. I'm immune to silver. Luke, you have responsibilities here. Elijah, you have to set up your resort. So that leaves me," Greyson replied.

Elijah tossed the idea around in his mind. It did seem to be the only logical explanation. His gaze darted to Luke. The other wolf reminded him of a mountain man, someone who never came out of the forest, with the long beard and his never-ending supply of jeans, work boots, and plaid shirts. As Luke stroked his beard, Elijah wondered when Luke would cut it. Sadie wasn't partial to lots of facial hair. He'd had a beard when they first met. Over time she'd hinted it wasn't her favorite thing so he shaved it off for her.

"You're right. Sadie would want me to take care of my pack. I guess that leaves Greyson to go and rescue her," Luke replied.

A knock came on the door. Elijah looked outside to see Kade waiting with a tense smile on his face. Luke motioned for him to come in. Behind him were a few other people Elijah recognized from the other night as the leaders of some of the other packs and shifter clans. "Luke, they want answers. They want to talk to Sadie, but I've told them all I know. Everyone else is in the hall eating breakfast. This is a good time for you to fill in all the others on what happened last night. Many of the clans don't feel safe here."

"Kade, we're working on it. Elijah has a plan. He was about to make a call and set everything up," Luke answered.

Elijah stood up. "I am. If you'll excuse me." He

walked into the bedroom to have some privacy so he could call Dr. Maran and see what Sadie meant about making the resort safe for everyone. He had to trust his mate. If the reserve was going to be a haven for shifters, then so be it.

He grabbed his cell. The phone rang and he was almost ready to hang up when she answered.

"Good morning, Mr. Dane. I had a feeling you'd be calling."

Her background was a mystery even to him, except she was good at what she did. "You know why I'm calling?"

"I've already alerted the staff. I made them stay once I heard about the attacks on all the shifters. I heard the call from Ms. Matthews and knew it was time I acted. I brought in all the families I could. Many of them are here waiting for word on what will happen next."

Unbelievable. He couldn't understand how this woman had acted ahead of time, but it would make sense if she'd heard Sadie's call like everyone else. They had no idea of how far the scientists could reach. "Sadie told me to send everyone up to the resort. It's a safe place. She also said to ask you about it because you would know. They found the pack at my mansion. How come they won't attack the resort?"

"Simple. I have a spell around it. The enchantment will keep those here safe. It disguises the nature of the shapeshifter and makes them appear human. It will last until I need to fortify it again. I'm working on something to help you rescue Ms. Matthews as well. Get everyone here. Don't attempt to rescue the damsel by yourselves. It has to be a unified effort. It's the reason the three of you were brought together."

He sighed. "Great. I get to share the woman I love with two other men because it was destiny."

"Mr. Dane, don't sound so down. You'll get your

woman back."

"You sound like you know for sure. Many things can occur between now and then."

The therapist chuckled. "I know a little something about everything. I've been around a very long time, Mr. Dane. This isn't my first round with the silver wolf. We've tussled in the past."

"You knew all this was going to happen?" Elijah asked, not sure what to make of the snake shifter he employed.

Silence lingered on the other end of the line. He almost wondered if she had hung up on him. "I don't know the future the way you think I do. I can't see visions. I get a knowing of things. Impressions if you will. When you get everyone settled in, come and see me with the other two and we'll talk. Bring the bird and the Fairy with you. I'll see you soon." Dr. Maran hung up the phone leaving him wondering how much she really knew.

"Elijah, do you have a minute?" Greyson asked.

He turned back and saw the other man in the doorway. Greyson seemed a little more content than he had been before in the kitchen. He smiled and slipped his arm around Greyson's waist. It was an odd juxtaposition for Elijah to feel the attraction to want to bed the man and not eat Greyson the way he had first done. He slid his fingers along Greyson's neck over the scars where Elijah had attacked him so many years ago. If he thought back, he could remember the terror in Greyson's eyes as a human. That was in the past when he hunted humans from time to time and ate them. However, he no longer ate human meat, although there were a few in the pack who still did. He didn't have any laws about them not hunting humans. Some packs forbade it. After all this, he figured something might have to change. All the clans and different species of shifters needed to come together.

They needed to band together if they wanted to survive. The scientists knew about them. He needed to make sure the humans would never hurt any shifter again. Greyson slid his hand over Elijah's on his neck. The small touch made him come back to the present.

"You okay?" Greyson asked.

"I'm fine. I was thinking about how we first met."

Greyson winced. "Yeah, something I don't really like to think about."

"I didn't mean to bring back the bad memories. I was thinking how things had changed between us. I never thought you and I would be mates. I care for you the same way I care for Sadie. It's still blowing my mind. The same way it does when I do this." Elijah pressed his lips to Greyson's feeling the roughness of stubble brushing along his chin.

Greyson slipped his tongue along Elijah's lips and squeezed Elijah's ass. A small moan came from his throat as Elijah deepened the kiss. He ran his fingers down Greyson's thighs and felt his firm cock. The other wolf broke away from Elijah. "We can't be doing this right now."

Elijah hung his head and ran his fingers through his hair. "I know. I'm sorry. I find this new attraction between the three of us a little harrowing. Even though I'm... we're... dealing with all this, it's like the new bond I had with Sadie. All I wanted to do when I first met her was fuck her."

Greyson leaned back against the wall giving them some space between them. "I know. I feel the same way with you and Luke. Although Luke is more standoffish when it comes to me showing him affection. He seems to be getting used to the idea of the three of us being together as well."

"Yeah. Luke has a lot on his mind."

"We all have a lot on our minds. Speaking of, Kade

and Luke wanted us all to go into the main hall there so we can give an update on what we're doing. Did you get through to your hotel?" Greyson asked.

"I did. Everything is going forward. Let's go talk to them." Elijah followed his mate out of the bedroom and into the kitchen. Luke stood with the shaman. They left the kitchen and went toward the hall where he could see a line had formed out of the door. From the smell, he could pick up bacon and eggs on the breeze. They moved into the main room. Before they went up on stage, Luke pulled him aside.

"Is everything set?" Luke asked.

"Yeah."

"Good. I didn't want to get up there and make a fool of myself."

"I wouldn't make you look like a fool. Ever," Elijah told him.

Luke squeezed his shoulder as he climbed up on stage. All the shifters in the main lodge stopped eating and looked up at him. Elijah's gaze drifted over those in the building and he found Rocky sitting at a table with a few other wolves Elijah recognized. Rocky and the others gazed up. The remnants of his pack had come. When he closed his eyes and concentrated, he could feel their lingering links. Seeing them together made his eyes tear up. When he felt the great loss of the pack before, he didn't think he could recover from the emptiness that loomed in his soul. Sadie had reassured him, but he didn't believe her. They were alive and he had to stay strong for them.

Luke stood at the center of the stage and raised his hands. All talking ceased. "Everyone, I know you're worried about what happened last night. I've been talking with Kade and some of the other elders of the clans. We have a plan in place to get everyone to a safe place."

"Is anywhere safe?" someone asked.

Elijah went up next to Luke. "Yes, we have a safe place for all of us to go where we don't have to worry about there being a lack of space. Luke has been gracious enough to let everyone be here. None of us were expecting the attack last night."

"Where is this safe place? How did they find it? What happened to the woman who called us here?" Another woman stood up. Elijah couldn't get a sense at what she was, but he did feel she was an alpha if not the leader of her clan of shifters.

More murmurs erupted in the hall. Luke put up his hands again to quiet everyone. It took a moment, but they did.

"I own a resort. It's a few hours' drive from here, but we can get everyone there. There's a spell around the land to make sure the scientists and whoever else is looking for our kind won't find us. We don't know how they found this place. We do know Sadie is alive, and she was the one who told us to go to my resort. I trust her with this. These scientists are out to kill all shifters. It doesn't matter if you are bear or bird, wolf or otter. No one is secure while these humans are using silver. Once we are settled in, we plan on going to rescue Sadie and shut down the humans," Elijah told everyone.

"If they are using silver, then how will you get to her?" one of the members of his pack asked.

"We're going to have some help from the Fairies," Greyson said.

A few of the people laughed. Elijah could see the disbelief on their faces. No one wanted to believe in Fairies. For some of the shifters it was difficult for them to believe in werewolves or other were beings because they were regular humans until they were bitten or turned into whatever they had become now. He knew that from Sadie. It had taken her a lot of time to being comfortable with the idea of wanting to join him as a wolf. Fairies were another thing altogether. He never believed in them until he met Narissa and started dating her many years ago. When she revealed what she was, a whole new world opened to him.

Narin came up on stage. No one seemed to react to her as if she was any different. A moment later hushed whispers circulated through the crowd as she dropped the glamour. "Many of you don't believe in the Fae. We've kept it that way on purpose. For many years, our worlds have been separated. Some of my kind has been bitten by shifters. They still exist in our world although not looked at favorably. Like the many of you who have been affected by the silver and the kidnappings, they happened in our realm first. Humans found and abducted our kind and butchered them. My sister is one of these victims. She's best friend to Sadie and I swore I'd help get her back."

"We need to get going," Luke commented.

Elijah nodded. "Everyone finish your breakfast, and then we'll head out. Follow me or Luke. We know the way to the resort."

"Should we be going by car?" someone asked.

Kade stepped forward. "Already got that covered. I made a few calls. The buses are outside. We have enough for all."

Luke motioned for them to come off the stage. Elijah followed them back outside. "Do you really think it's going to work? We can get there and it's protected?"

"Yes. Dr. Maran needs to talk to us about Sadie," Elijah told him.

"I hope this counselor of yours knows what she's doing," Luke commented.

"I trust her with my life. Let's get our stuff and get everyone on these busses so we can get going. The sooner we get there, the less anxious I'll feel. We don't know if the scientists have us under surveillance," Elijah told them.

"They don't. I've checked," Kade interrupted. "I have a few tricks up my sleeve. The Fairies helped to conceal everyone when they came last night. The scientists focused on Sadie. Someone has to know she's special. We owe the Fairies a lot. We owe Sadie a lot because she tried to create a distraction so we could all get away."

"We're going to get her back. I don't care what it takes. When we do, I plan on ripping those fuckers' throats out," Greyson growled.

Elijah nodded his agreement. Soon. They would get her soon. For now, they had to keep calm and get the rest of the shifters to safety.

Chapter Five

The bitch had finally eased up on her questions and left Sadie alone. Every part of her hurt from the torture they had inflicted upon her after the incessant barrage. Her ears rang from the woman screaming at her. No matter how many times they shocked her, she wasn't going to give them any information about who and what she was. The pain got so bad, she went to the place in her mind to be with the wolf. It helped for a while until she had to come back to her body. Sadie didn't know where the implant was because each time the shock came from a different part of her body. They kept asking her questions about what her abilities were and why she was so special. She didn't give them any answers the bitch liked. Now they were giving her a break, but it didn't matter because they were watching. She pulled herself along the wall and stared into the next cell to keep an eye on her friend.

Nari hadn't moved during the session of questions and torture. Sadie knew she was saving her strength. She closed her eyes and reached to her friend. Knowing she was alive gave her some relief even though they had to figure out a way to get the hell out of the facility and destroy it. Sadie wasn't going to wait around while this organization decided it was going to eradicate all shifters.

"Nari, are you awake?"

"Of course, I am. I never could sleep through your screaming. Remember those days in college when you brought Ian back to the sorority house? I could hear you screaming his name two doors down. Those were the days, weren't they?"

Sadie held back a laugh. She hadn't thought about Ian in a long time. He did make her scream in a good way. *"That man certainly knew how to use his tongue, but that was about all he was good for. Nothing else existed between his ears because all his blood went to his dick."*

"Yeah. You're right about that. I had a go at him after you broke up."

"You bitch. You never told me that."

"I wasn't sure how you'd react. You were insecure about everything. Besides, I made him realize what a catch you were."

"I can only imagine what you did to him," Sadie said. She couldn't help the smile that pulled at the corners of her mouth.

"Last time I checked, he was a balding used car salesman in Anchorage."

"You kept tabs on him?"

"Not on purpose. I heard about it at one of the house reunions."

"I don't know why you insist on going to those things. How many times have you been to college and studied for another degree? At first, I thought I was your pet because there was no reason why we should've been friends."

"There you go again, putting yourself down. Don't you know how much fun you were? I knew there was something special about you. That was the reason I decided to hang out with you when I first met you. Now you're some super wolf who is immune to silver."

Sadie ran her hands over her knees and opened up her eyes. *"Yeah, some super wolf who can't get us out of this place. I don't even know where to begin."*

"It'll be okay. Your men will come and rescue us."

"That's what I'm afraid of. These scientists knew where I was, Nari. They know I'm some kind of super wolf. What did you tell them? What happened after they took you from the mansion?"

Nari opened her eyes and stared at her. *"First tell me Rocky made it?"*

"I thought you didn't like him. The way you reacted when you found out he was your mate…"

"Is he alive?" Nari demanded.

The desperation in her voice made Sadie stop. She had never heard Nari sound like this. *"Yes. He made it. Some of Luke's pack found him and brought him to us. He was the one who told us how you were kidnapped."*

"I know what I said about him being my mate. After we left the mansion to go to look for the sleuth of bears Greyson had been healed by, we crossed through Fae. My father's guards were waiting for me. One of them tried to kill me, but Rocky jumped in front of the energy bolt. He saved me. I felt it then. He would do anything for me. I couldn't get his scent out of my nose. I still can't. The thought of him has been one of the only things that's gotten me through what they've done to me."

"He's alive, I promise you. Nari, tell me what's going on. I know these guys are only taking shifters who have Fairy lineage or those Fairy shifters. Before I was taken, the five tribes came to the Luke's land and said they had made you their queen."

"Some queen. Sadie, I'm so sorry. It's all my fault. I told the humans about you. It slipped out when they were torturing me. I couldn't help it. They were asking me questions about other shifters. It hurt so much."

"It's fine. The scientist told me they can't kill you because of some deal they made. Narin came to me and told me she was your twin. You never told me you had a sister."

"I only get to see her on occasion. Our father thinks I'm less than nothing because of my mixed bloodline. Sadie, he's the one behind all this. He told me when they had us surrounded. He said he was going to make sure my polluted bloodline didn't exist anymore. Any tainted Fae who had shifter blood in them would be wiped off the Earth. He's the one who made the deal with the humans. Gave them the access to the Fairy realm so they could do their experiments. He gave them the secret on how to make the blood a weapon once it hit the air. It's all because of me. I'm so sorry."

Sadie sighed. "You didn't ask for this. You never asked to get bitten by the wolf who infected you. You didn't make the hate grow in your father's heart. It all has to do with him and his shortsightedness."

Nari shook her head. "If only that were true. I was to inherent the throne. He wanted the perfect strain of Fairy to take after him. By using the humans he's given them leave to take out any Fairy who is mixed. They tortured me and you slipped out. I said you were going to save us. I don't know how *they found Elijah's mansion or Luke's place. I swear."*

"*I believe you, but you can't give up hope. The guys are going to get us out of here. Whatever these humans have learned, we're going to destroy it too. I'll deal with your father.*" Anger bubbled up inside her from the thought of what the king of the Fairy was doing to his own people and those of mixed heritage.

"I see you've recovered quite nicely from our little chat earlier." The door to her cell opened and the scientist stepped inside.

Sadie glanced at the window in her cell and saw the sun had gotten lower in the sky. When she glanced back at Narissa, several workers stood around her. One of them attached and IV to her arm. "What are you doing to her?"

"Trying something new to see if we can get the animal out of her. That was what her father wanted us to do in exchange for all the wonderful information he's bestowed upon us. Never did I believe in such a thing as Fairies until he walked right out of the fog and told me such a whopper of a story. It was hard to believe at first until he showed me his magic. I guess I was in the right time at the right place."

"It sounds like you're in love with him."

The woman gave her a cold smile. "Admire. I wouldn't say love. He's too cold for that."

The air around her grew colder. She rubbed her arms and looked around. Veins of frost slid over the glass from Narissa's cell. The glass splintered along each line of frozen cold. It creaked and cracked as though it would explode at any moment. Nari screamed in the next room. Her friend convulsed as they pumped a purple liquid into her body. Sadie rushed at the glass hoping to break through. Before she could get to it, pain dropped her to the floor. Green boots stepped out from the glass. The agony eased and Sadie looked up at a slender man dressed in darker shades of green as her gaze traveled up.

His hair hung down to his waist. It was whiter than even the purest snow, absorbing the light and reflecting it at the same time. He didn't look old enough to be a father to anyone let alone to all the siblings Narissa had told her about. His completely black eyes were a stark contrast to the paleness of his skin. His flesh was transparent enough she could make out the network of veins underneath. The aura that came from him pulsated with power.

"Setep, I wasn't expecting you this early," the scientist told him.

Sadie stayed on her knees to regain her breath from the sudden shock. The glass to Nari's cell returned to normal. Her friend screamed again, but Sadie wasn't about to let on she had recovered.

"Your Majesty will suffice, Nancy. We're not behind closed doors. I don't need your staff hearing you calling me by such a personal name."

"Forgive me, Your Majesty. I didn't mean any disrespect. I'm not sure you want to --"

"Don't interrupt me again, Dr. Cooper. I wanted to check on the progress you'd made on my daughter. There have been some disturbing ramifications to what you've been doing. Those ingrates made her their queen. Others have heard about it and are starting to gather. They're siding with her."

"It sounds like you have a civil war unfolding on your side. I thought your people were with you on eradicating the animal taint from the Fairy bloodlines?"

"What you have done at melding your science with our Fairy magic is good with these human shifters. You've started to wipe out even the humans and I applaud that. These animals shouldn't be allowed to live in case they infect others of my kind. They need to be eradicated. Have you shared the research with others yet?" the King of the Fairy asked.

"As I was trying to say before, maybe you don't want

to be talking about this right now?"

"Why not? This animal isn't going to be around for very long. She can't get out. Why haven't you started your experiments on her yet? I was hoping I might peer inside one of them and see what makes them tick. I know you've gotten a few of them while they're in different stages of change and kept them... on ice as you say. Quite an enjoyable sight. What are you doing to be doing with this one?"

"Your Majesty, this woman is the super wolf your daughter's spoken about in some of our sessions. Although, we don't know much more than they are friends."

"This frumpy human is the one who my daughter values enough to give her the mark of our people? I find that a little unbelievable my daughter would stoop so low. She might be of mixed blood, but she's also a royal and has more sense." The Fairy King's boot poked Sadie's side, nudging her to see if she was still alive.

"It's true."

"Have you gotten anything else out of this creature from your sessions?"

"No."

"Maybe I can do better. Why don't you leave me with this super wolf so I can get some answers of my own?"

"I'm not sure that'd be a good idea. It's against protocol."

The king grabbed the front of Dr. Cooper's lab coat and pulled her to him. He pushed his lips onto hers. The woman melted against him. Sadie watched the Fairy King kissing Dr. Cooper until he threw her backward into the door. Her face was flushed. She was ready to melt into a pool. The king sneered as the woman straightened her lab coat and her glasses. She slid out of the cell leaving Sadie alone with the Fairy King.

"You can sit up. I know you've been faking as I've been talking to the good doctor. I have questions for you."

Sadie got up slowly and looked at the King of the Fairies as Narissa screamed. She glanced over at her friend and cringed at her being in pain. They would pay for what they were doing to her friend and the torture they were putting her through. "How could you let them do this to your own daughter?"

The king smirked and glanced at Narissa. "She's always been a problem child even when she was little. Narin was unexpected, but I made Narissa flawless. Her mother was chosen on purpose for her beauty and the purity of her bloodline. I used every spell I knew to make sure she would be perfect. I sacrificed to the old gods that she would be the one to rule after me. For years, she grew into her beauty, and then she was attacked by some filthy animal. I went to a few of the ancients to have them remove the taint from her. They said it had wrapped around her so tightly they were unable to banish the curse from within her."

"So you cast her out, cut ties with her family, and everything she loved. Great thing to do for a father who claims he loves this daughter."

A sharp sting went across her face, the blow turning her head to the side until she thought her neck would snap. Stars appeared before her eyes. Sadie waited for her vision to adjust before she rubbed her jaw and could feel the bruise already forming along her cheek. Her anger welled up, but she bit her tongue to make sure she didn't say something to put Narissa in more jeopardy. She had to make sure she and her friend got out alive.

"Why she chose to give you her mark of protection is beyond me. You're nothing special. Don't think I don't know who you are, Sadie Matthews. I might've banished my daughter to your realm except for the occasional time when she passes through ours, but I've kept tabs on her. She's always had supporters on her side. Here they go and make her queen of their twisted tribes. It's all your fault!"

Sadie scoffed. "My fault? I never believed in Fairies or shapeshifters. How do you think I felt when I lost the man I loved to a werewolf? I never suspected your daughter was a Fairy until she told me. You're the one who sided with the humans. You're the one causing her all this pain. Get them to stop. You can't take out the shifter DNA with whatever Fairy magic and science you've given these people. You're going to kill her."

"All this is so she will be cleansed. In the end, she will be my true daughter once more. You'll be nothing more than a bad memory to her. Your kind will be wiped off the face of the Earth like cockroaches. Sometimes things have to be done for the greater good. I consider revealing myself to these humans as a good thing. Soon you'll be gone, but first I want to know what all this means about you being a super wolf?"

She rolled her eyes. "Go fuck yourself. I'm not telling you anything."

The Fairy King smiled. "I think you're going to tell me everything I want to know. The pain you've endured is nothing compared to what I can do to you." He waved his hand and Sadie doubled over in pain.

It felt like she'd been hit in the stomach and worms were crawling through her veins. Sadie screamed. She fell to her knees and curled into a ball. It took a few moments for the pain to fade away so she could respond. "What the fuck did you do to me?"

The king chuckled. "You might have gotten all the good things that go along with my daughter's mark of protection, but she didn't tell you, someone more powerful than her can influence it. She is of my flesh. I am her king. Narissa will never have my kind of power."

"I don't think it's the power that matters to her. It's the fact that the only father she has cast her out. Being different doesn't mean you love your kid any less. You really are an ass."

He squeezed his fist together. It felt like her heart was being torn from her chest or being shredded. She wasn't sure which. Even with the strength her inner wolf lent to her, it didn't stop her from writhing on the floor. Her wails joined with Narissa's. The king knelt down and stabbed her chin with his fingernail and made her look into his black eyes. The white lashes that framed the completely black orbs only made them seem more fake. His twisted smile made her realize he enjoyed doing this to her and hearing his daughter scream. It hit her what he said about making Nari perfect. The thought turned her stomach.

"I'd be more courteous to me if you want to survive the night."

Sadie laughed. "They're going to kill me anyway. It doesn't matter what you do to me. What you want to do with your own daughter is disgusting."

The king's eyes narrowed as he ran his fingers down Sadie's cheek until he grabbed her chin and nearly crushed it. "What you think you know and what you actually know are two different things."

"Really? You wanted perfection with a little bit of humanity mixed in. You got that. I've seen Narin. Is it her horns that make her unacceptable for you to fuck? Are you another inbred creation of the ones who came before you?"

"Choosing the right partner to keep the bloodlines pure has been done for centuries in human royalty. The pharaohs did it. The kings and queens of England did it so they could remain in control. Why is wanting my offspring to be untainted any different? I'd contemplated keeping her the way she was until she came into Fae with that animal of hers who claimed to be her mate. I made sure he was marked and followed her trail backward."

"You let the scientists know where Elijah's mansion was. You tagged him so they would find Luke's pack territory."

"None of that means anything to me except, yes, I gave Dr. Cooper the means to track the male. When I learned they had taken Narissa instead, I made sure they knew what to do with her. Why do you think I let them experiment on the other Fae? They needed test subjects so they could find the right combination of potions in order to strip the animal from her blood. If the ancients can't do it, then your humans should be able to. They're close. I can feel it. Once they're done, then she won't even care about this other wolf. She won't care about anything except doing exactly what I say. Even you will be a distant memory to her."

"You won't be able to brainwash her."

"I'll do anything I want to her, including making sure she kills you as her first act of showing me her love. I have plans." The Fairy King leaned in close. "Once they figure this all out and eradicate all the shifters from the world, I'm going to make sure this place burns to the ground. The humans will no longer have any knowledge of Fairies or even shapeshifters. This place and your kind mean nothing to me. Even if you are some super wolf, you won't survive this."

A surge of strength went through her as her wolf joined with her. That power she used to force all the other alphas and the wolf pack to do her bidding came through her. It gave her the strength to stand up straight and face the King of the Fairies. "That's what you think. No matter what you do to me, you won't get away with this."

The Fairy King's mouth spread into an even wider smile showing off his black tongue. "I think I will."

"Then you should tell that to the doctor you're

fucking because she thinks she's going to be your next queen."

"Never happen. She's a human and impure."

"Tell her after she tells you about the child she's carrying. Your child."

"Lies."

Sadie shook her head and realized she was right. The woman was pregnant. She was also in love with the Fairy King. That was plain to see. "I don't think so. I can smell it on her. Why don't you go take a whiff and tell me I'm wrong?"

The Fairy King let her go and gave her a strange stare. "What are you?"

"Wouldn't you like to know?"

Chapter Six

Greyson stayed in the background and helped where he could while they got the endless stream of shifters settled into their rooms at Elijah's resort. Greyson took in the marbled floors and the ten different kinds of water with various fruits and vegetables floating in it. Actual crystal tumblers sat on trays next to the decanters. Even the air smelled different inside the large hotel. Elijah talked to the manager. Luke and Kade assisted everyone to get where they were going. Greyson leaned against a pillar and watched all the shifters with haunted looks on their faces as though they had gone through some sort of disaster. In a way they had. All their lives had been rocked by learning they were no longer safe in their homes. Their lives had been uprooted and their loved ones were being killed. Since he'd lost Sadie, and his whole world was turned upside down.

Now he had feelings for the other two men he shared mate bonds with. Greyson wanted to make them happy. Without Sadie he felt useless, as if he wasn't anchored to anything. Part of him wanted to run back into the woods, without any cares in the world except finding his next meal and a good place to sleep. That was his old life. Now he had a purpose.

"You're the gray one."

"Excuse me?" Greyson asked the three-foot-tall woman who stood in front of him.

She gave him a sly smile and adjusted her glasses, making her already big eyes seem even bigger behind the frames. Something about her screamed she had power. He couldn't sense what kind of shifter she was, but the hair on the back of his neck bristled. He held in a growl as she came closer. She would eat him if he got on her bad side. She patted his hand and wiggled her finger for him to follow her. Greyson didn't at first. The woman turned back around and motioned for him to come once more.

This time he felt a force weigh on his mind and the urge to go along came over him. This shifter was an alpha and nudging him to come. Greyson wove through the throngs of people and outside. The woman stopped in front of a cabin and then waited before the open door.

As soon as he stepped in, a wall of power hit him. It pulsated like a heartbeat. Something was alive inside the building. Herbs hung from the rafters and swayed in an invisible breeze. The scent of the air smelled like silver and sage all rolled into one. It made his skin crawl. He darted toward the door, but she stepped in front of it.

"You feel it, don't you?"

"I feel something and I don't like it."

"Good. You'd be the most sensitive to it because you straddle both worlds. I can see how the Fairies put you back together using silver to make your spirit adhere to your flesh, binding you to this plane. They did a good job, although it cost you a lot until you found her again. She is a strong woman."

"You're talking about Sadie."

"I am."

"Who are you?" Greyson asked this strange woman.

"I'm older than most by a lot of years and yet younger than many who have lived in other realms. My kind knows how to see between the dimensions. Some things you don't need to know about me except I know more about the realm of Fairy and the world of shapeshifters. I've learned from both and spent time among many. That's not what you wanted to ask me. You wanted to know what's going on in this house and who I am. How do I know your mate?"

Greyson nodded. She had read his mind.

"I'm Mistress Maran or Dr. Maran. I first met Ms. Matthews when she came here two years ago looking for help from the deep depression she lingered in over your death. Mr. Dane needed someone to talk to, as well. I'm the psychiatrist they keep on staff here. You still have this need inside you to figure out why you were brought back. I think you know it was because you were needed to help with Sadie. She needed a reason to rally, even with the other two here."

"We're finally joined together as we should be. I'm worried about her. I should've gone out there and saved her, but I was frozen in the other room along with the others."

The counselor laid a hand on his arm. "You have nothing to be ashamed of. Everyone wants to get Sadie back. No one wants the humans kidnapping or injuring any more shifters or Fairies either. Getting everyone safe is the most important thing. Now they are here, you can be sure they are. Didn't you feel the difference when you stepped off the bus and came into the building?"

"It feels like my skin is crawling. What did you do in here to make it feel this way?"

"I'm glad you finally asked. Come with me." Dr. Maran opened a door and motioned for him to stop at the threshold.

Silver lines writhed around in a circle. Upon closer inspection, he saw they were silver snakes. Three touching, nose to tail. As they went around, they began to eat a little bit more of one another until it seemed they were one whole snake. A purple glow emanated from the center of these snakes. The waves of power made him want to step away from the cabin and go outside.

"What is this?"

"The center is the resort. The snakes represent the barriers around the land. This protects all the shifters on the property so anyone will think they're human."

"How long will this last?"

"As long as the snake keeps eating itself."

"That can be forever."

She smiled. "It could be, but I don't intend it to go on

for long. It'll serve another purpose as well. We don't need the humans figuring out a way to take us down. They've already been meddling with the natural order of things by working with the Fairies. I don't know how they did it. I'm sorry. I'm rambling, but I wanted to show you this so you'd understand I'm here to help. I have a way for you and the others to get into the scientists' facility without being detected. It will also make your mates immune to the silver the humans pumped into the atmosphere around their facility."

"What is this great solution you've come up with?"

The therapist grabbed his hand. Greyson struggled to get away. Instead, he was forced to kneel by the circle as the snakes slowly slithered around. One came by it was so quick, he barely saw it, but he felt it. The fangs dipped into his flesh. Pain burned along his hand and raced up his arm. His whole body tingled. The woman released his hand and he shook as he tried to get feeling back into it. Around the fang marks, he could see a silvery sheen.

"What the hell did you do to me?"

"Gave you some of the magic surrounding this place. You don't need the silver immunity, but you do need the ability to blend in. Any human at this compound will think you're one of them. It won't matter if they scan you with technology. They will only see you as human. If you come across a Fairy, you might be in trouble, but I'm not sure. I tried to include them in this part of the spell, but I can't be completely sure since there are so many different types of Fae who have various spell casting abilities."

"Great. How long is this going to last? I need to get Luke and Elijah over here so they can..."

"Dr. Maran, are you in here?"

"Speak of the devil," Dr. Maran chuckled.

"Yeah," Greyson muttered.

"Mr. Dane, I'm in the back. Why don't you come in

here? I was explaining to Greyson about the spell I've cast around the resort to get everyone warded and how you were going to be protected when you go and rescue Sadie." She motioned the other two wolves into the room.

Elijah gave Greyson a look. *"What's going on?"*

He shrugged. *"You need to have her tell you. I'm not sure I understand all the finer points of her magic."*

"Okay."

"What are Narin and Pricilla doing here?" Greyson asked.

"They're here because I asked Mr. Dane to bring them. They need to go with you to at least be there while you're in the facility," Maran said to Greyson. "If you don't want anyone to hear your private conversation, then you need to learn to guard your thoughts better, Mr. Greyson."

Luke laughed. "She got you there, Greyson."

Greyson flipped his mate the bird. The psychiatrist told the others what he already knew. They didn't seem to believe it, but when the little woman took each of their hands he had to hold back a laugh. The big, bad wolves didn't want anyone to think they had been overpowered by a three-foot-tall woman. Whoever she truly was, she had a vested interest in saving them. After both of his mates were bitten, then Narin and Pricilla were also bitten by the snake. Their pale skin was also flushed pink as though they weren't taking to the spell. Then again he didn't think any shifter would be taking well to having a little bit of silver pumped into their veins.

"How long is this going to last?" Elijah asked.

"Long enough for you to get there, get in, and get out. I'd say twenty-four hours, give or take."

"It will take nearly twelve hours if we fly to get there," Pricilla told them.

The doctor smiled. "That's where both of you come in. You're the sister, right?"

Narin rubbed where she had been bitten. "Yes.

Narissa's my twin."

"Good. As a Fairy you have the ability to part dimensions so traveling to one place in this reality shouldn't be much trouble."

Narin smiled as she seemed to be catching on as to why she had been asked to come. "Not at all, but I can't get there without knowing where we're going. I've only seen inside the facility through Narissa's eyes."

"That's why you need the little bird. Pricilla can show you the location from a bird's eye view. Shouldn't take much out of you to transport all of them. Are you able to read minds from other entities who are not Fairies?" Dr. Maran asked.

"Yes. Most Fairies can. It's one of the reasons we practice keeping a wall up around our thoughts," Narin told them.

"Good to know. It's been a long time since I was in Fairy and didn't know if you had changed any."

"Great, so we have this all worked out on how long the spell is going to last and how to get there. We have no idea where Sadie is when we get inside. How we are going to get her and Narissa out of there?" Luke inquired.

Dr. Maran patted his hand. "I'm sure you'll figure it out. You're a resourceful bunch."

"Sure you don't want to come with us?" Greyson asked.

"If I did, then no one would be here to keep an eye on the shifters who've come here seeking refuge. Besides, I need to keep an eye on the spell I cast. It might have the ability to last forever, but it drains my life force. I don't want to leave this place unprotected. I want this taken care of as quickly as you want Sadie back. I like Ms. Matthews. Maybe when you get back, the four of us can have a counseling session."

Elijah's face went pale as did Luke's. "There's nothing we need to talk about in our relationship."

Her eyebrow lifted. "Are you sure about that? Maybe it doesn't have to be about how the three of you are getting along. I'm known to run a wonderful sexual therapy course and how it plays into relationships."

"Okay, thank you for your help. Ladies, Elijah, Greyson, I think we're done here. We need to plan our next move as to when we are going to get Sadie." Luke motioned for them to leave.

Pricilla and Narin held back their laughter. Luke threw them a dirty look as he walked past them. Once Greyson stepped outside, he felt ten times better. Elijah ran his hand through his hair. Greyson could feel his apprehension and the anxiety he felt about whatever was going to be planned. What was planned?

Luke paced. His pent-up energy ran over and spilled into Greyson. All of them chomped at the bit to rescue the woman they loved.

"Do we know how we're going to get Sadie?" Luke asked.

"The doc expects us to walk right in and blend with the scientists. How is that possible?" Elijah asked.

Greyson touched Elijah. He nearly pulled away from Greyson and growled at him. "Hey, it's going to be okay. We have to figure out what we're going to do."

Elijah nodded. "Right. Sorry."

"Do you have any weapons?" Pricilla asked.

"I won't be able to transport you if you bring weapons. Nothing man-made or with iron in it. It has to be you and nothing else," Narin told them.

"Okay, so we go with what we have on." Luke leaned against a tree.

"Are you guys okay?" Greyson asked. His head buzzed with energy from his mates as it combined with his own.

Elijah raked his fingers over his face. "I have all this energy and I don't know what to do with it all. The spell is working through us. I'm surprised you're not feeling it either."

Greyson looked down at his hands. "I didn't get the energy boost you did, but I'm feeling it through you. Why don't we try and contact Sadie to let her know we're coming? She might be able to give us an idea of where they're keeping her."

"That's the smartest thing you've said all night," Narin replied.

"We need water," Luke said.

"Why do you say that?" Elijah asked.

He shrugged. "Why does Sadie say half the shit she does and it ends up being right? I'm going with this one."

"Water will be good. It will help me transport you. It makes it easier to part the worlds. It helps conduct energy," Narin told them.

"Everyone follow me." Elijah motioned for them to follow him.

Greyson stayed at the back. As he walked after his other mates, he noticed the place was deserted. They wound through the paths and emerged into a long corridor of a hedge maze. In the center of it was a large pool. A trickle from a fountain poured into the pool. It barely sent any ripples across the pool's surface. They sat at the edge of it.

"Sadie," Elijah called out. Greyson and Luke each put their hands over Elijah's so it touched the surface of the water.

Their bond electrified. The water rippled and the reflection changed so they could see Sadie. She was doubled over and in pain. Someone else stood over her, another man he didn't recognize.

"You need to stop," Narin whispered.

"Why?" Luke asked.

Narin grabbed their hands and pulled them back from the water. "The man you saw was my father. If he got wind of you being able to look in on Sadie, then he might figure out we're coming."

"Why would your father be in the cell with Sadie?" Elijah asked.

Narin looked down at the water and sniffled. "Because he sided with the scientists and taught them how to use our magic. It was an exchange so they would stop hunting other Fae. That's how it all started until they struck up a bargain."

"What bargain was that?" Elijah asked again.

Greyson could feel his other mate's temper flaring. He squeezed Elijah's shoulders and glided his hands over Elijah's chest, trying to calm him until Elijah touched Greyson's hands, and he did feel Elijah quiet down.

"He'd show them some magic to incorporate with their science. They would use all their technology to drive the tainted part of Narissa out. He always wanted her to rule, but I think there was more to it."

"We have to get them both out of there," Luke said.

"Pricilla, can you show Narin where the facility is?" Greyson asked.

The little bird shifter nodded. Narin placed her hands on her head. She smiled after a moment. "I got it. I can get you there. Get back to the woods as soon as you can. I'll leave the gateway open as long as I can."

The three wolves got up and followed Narin to the hedge wall. She placed her hand on the holly leaves. They shimmered. A cold blast of air hit Greyson. It felt like he'd been sent into a blizzard. The leaves froze over and turned white. When the foliage fell away, they revealed a small archway enough for them to fit through.

"Thank you for doing this," Luke said to her and stepped through the gateway.

She nodded. "Get Narissa back here safe."

"We will," Elijah said as he went into the opening.

Greyson was about to step through when Narin

pressed something into his hand. "If you run into my father, stab him with this."

"Okay. I thought you said you couldn't send anything through man-made?" he asked her.

She smiled. "This wasn't made by the hands of man, but by Fairy."

Greyson shook his head as he entered the gateway and emerged standing before a large building. He glanced at his other mates and he knew what they were thinking. How were they going to walk in there, spell or not, and find the woman they loved?

Chapter Seven

Sadie let her head fall back against the wall. The Fairy King finally retreated as did the pain he brought to her. Whatever he was doing was worse than the little gadget Dr. Cooper had used to shock her. Narissa stopped screaming from whatever they injected into her while trying to get the shifter genes out of her. Whatever they tried, even if it was mixed with Fairy magic and science, was not going to stop her friend from being a shifter even though she was also a Fairy. The thought of the purpose of the pure bloodline the king wanted to create turned her stomach.

She took a breath and glanced outside the window and saw it was night now. Where had time gone? The constant hum of the electronics and the lights grated on her nerves, but she had to stay positive. Her eyes went over to the cell next to her. Narissa remained strapped to the table. It seemed as though she still sleeping, but she turned her head slightly.

"Hey, stranger," Narissa said. Her internal voice was nearly a whisper.

"You don't sound so hot," Sadie replied.

"Better than you when you went out with Tommy Watson after your pledge party into the sorority. How many drinks did you have?"

She rolled her eyes. *"Stop trying to make me feel better. You sound like shit. Are you okay?"*

"I don't know. I don't feel so hot. Whatever they pumped into me is doing something. I can't feel my wolf. Fuck, I can't feel my feet so I'm not sure what that means."

"Your father told me why he's doing this."

"Did he give you the same perfect breed speech he crooned in my ear?"

"It's not funny. He wants to make you his queen so he can have perfect children. Your father is a bastard."

"I could've told you that. You didn't have to meet him to know that. I never thought he'd take it this far. He must be

desperate to want to have a worthy heir."

"Stop talking and focus on getting better," Sadie told her.

"But it's so much fun trying to think of ways to rip his throat out."

"I think you should have the honors, your highness."

"Don't call me that. It wasn't my decision to be named queen of the ragtag bunch of Fae shifters, but they were all behind it."

"Your father doesn't like it. Nor did he believe me when I told him you're going to have another brother or sister?"

"Shit. I knew I smelled something on that bitch. Yeah, he's not going to claim the kid."

"Well, maybe someone can come and replace -- Nari!" Sadie looked at her friend, who had started convulsing. Sadie dashed over to the cell wall and banged on the front of it to get the attention of her captors. One of the male attendants pressed something and a small buzz came across an intercom so they could speak.

"What do you want?"

"She's having a seizure, dickwad. Go help her or you're going to get some serious shade from your boss and her boyfriend." Sadie pointed toward Narissa.

An alarm sounded in the building. The lights dimmed and more attendants scrambled over to Narissa's cell. They pulled her out on a stretcher and wheeled her away. The lights remained dim during the commotion. At the same time, the door to her cell opened. Sadie glanced at the cell door and couldn't believe what she saw -- Elijah and Greyson with lab coats over their regular clothes and no one seemed to take any notice of them.

"Are you going to stand there and stare or are you going to get your fine ass out here?" Elijah asked.

"You don't have to tell me twice." Sadie walked out of the cell. She resisted the urge to hug them because the cameras were everywhere.

Greyson pulled a hood out from his pocket. "Put this

on and shut up." Then along their mate bond he said, *"I'm sorry, love, please play along."*

"Give me your hands," Elijah demanded.

Sadie gave them her hands. Greyson slipped the hood over her head blocking her vision. Elijah cuffed her wrists and pulled the restraints tight. She hissed in a breath and Greyson pushed her. Sadie slipped and went down to the ground, so they had to pick her up under her arms.

"Get moving, mongrel," he told her.

"Let me go, assholes." She struggled to try and get away from them. They both held her tight.

"I thought you said you had her," Greyson said. *"Act like we've sedated you."*

"If you won't cooperate, we'll drug you," Elijah growled.

"Do what you gotta do," she muttered.

"Now," Elijah told her.

She grunted and let her weight drop so she hung between them while they dragged her through the hallways. Her heart hammered in her ears. Questions pinged through her mind as to how they got into the building, not to mention how they weren't reacting to the silver in the air. The tops of her feet hurt from where they hauled her. They finally stopped and she tried to stay as relaxed as she could. Had to keep up the ruse she was drugged and by covering up her face they must have known about the cameras. How did they get in there? Why weren't any alarms going off? How did they find her?

"Where do you think you're taking this one?" a gruff male voice asked her two mates.

"Research lab. They want to see what makes her tick."

"Where's the transfer order?"

"Fuck, Gary, did you forget them again?" Elijah barked.

"Sorry, Ralph. It got kinda hectic there with that other bitch seizing."

"Come on, man. Don't make me walk all the way back there. You know how heavy this mongrel is? Can't we get them and bring it on the way back? It's the end of my shift. Cut me some slack," Elijah pleaded with the guard.

"Look, it's protocol."

Sadie mumbled as though she were coming around. She shook her head and made it look like she was convulsing. "Fuck protocol. She's having a seizure. I need to get her to research now. Move out of the way or you tell the Doc why this bitch died on your watch."

"Fine. Get the fuck out of here. If anything happens it's not going to be on me. I don't get paid enough for this shit." A door buzzed and they moved again. She continued to shake until Greyson poked her.

They kept going until she heard a door slam behind her. They released her so she was on her knees and the hood came off. Greyson helped her up. Sadie hugged him and kissed him before turning to Elijah and doing the same. Seeing their faces sent relief and great joy through her, knowing they were okay. The jaundiced light in the stairwell made them look strange. A silvery sheen surrounded them.

"How the fuck did you get in here?" she asked.

"Long story. We need to get you out of here. Luke's going after Narissa. He should be along soon," Elijah told her.

"Fine. Answers later. We need to make sure this place goes up in flames."

"We're not going to have time for that," Luke said, nearly out of breath as he carried an unconscious Narissa in his arms.

"He's right, we have to go."

They ran down four flights of stairs and then out a

fire door. As soon as they got outside, Sadie expected them to be surrounded by guards, but nothing. They raced across the field that separated them and the chain-link fence surrounding the whole facility. Part of the fence had been sliced wide enough for a person to get through. Elijah went first. Luke shoved Narissa through the hole, and Elijah took her unconscious friend. Luke came through. The door burst open from the facility and guards poured out. A loud alarm bell sounded. Shots hit the dirt around them. A silver tube with a small orange puff attached to the top of it. A tranquilizer dart.

"Guys, run," Sadie screamed.

They didn't need any more urging as they led Sadie toward the forest. As they got toward the line of trees. Something pinched her leg. She staggered but kept on running. Her mates were before her. Another hit her shoulder. She felt herself slowing down. Her vision blurred. Her eyes told her the men ran into the trees and disappeared. The air rippled where they entered. Greyson went through with Nari. Sadie kept pushing herself, tripped though the gateway, and found herself face-first in a pool. There was more commotion. When she looked back, she saw guards coming at them. Elijah hauled Luke through the gate. As soon as his prone form was through, the doorway collapsed and they were looking at the hedge. Sadie's head swam. It felt like she was drunk. When she saw Luke's back, he had been hit with eight tranquilizer darts. He had taken the brunt of them for her.

She tried to stand up, but Elijah caught her and led her over to the bench. He pulled out the darts and then smoothed the hair from her face. "How are you?"

"I'll survive," she whispered as she tried to keep her eyes open. Even the rush of adrenaline was wavering from her system. "Nari and Luke."

"Luke will be fine. I'm not sure about Narissa. We will need your healing skills when you're up for it."

She half nodded. "Get her to the snake lady. She can..." Before she could finish her sentence, Sadie slumped down into darkness.

* * *

Sadie opened her eyes and felt like she had the worst hangover ever. She glanced around and found herself in bed. Greyson lay curled up on her left side. Elijah had his arm draped over her right side. Luke snorted, but he was passed out in a chair across from the bed. She recognized the penthouse suite they resided in at the resort. She had shared this room with Elijah many times. The last time she was human had been in this room.

"I know that smile. What're you thinking about?" Elijah whispered next to her ear.

She snuggled closer to him. The musky scent of his wolf made her sigh. Sadie rested her forehead against his. "I was thinking about the last time I was here when you were about to fuck Denice and how much of a dick you were to me that night."

"I didn't want you to get hurt. I thought my turning you might result in you resenting me after you woke up from the turning fever. I didn't want to lose you. My wolf didn't want to put you in any danger. I was mistaken."

"Damn right you were. How long was I out?" Sadie asked him.

"Six hours give or take. Luke is still out of it. How are you feeling?"

"Like I got hit with a semi. Everything hurts. How is Narissa?"

"Snake Lady is taking care of her for now."

"Snake Lady?"

Elijah chuckled. "Dr. Maran. You don't remember calling her that?"

"Not at all. I remember getting through the portal. The rest is a blur. How did you get in there? How did you get us out of there without being affected by the silver and no one catching on to what you are?"

"Dr. Maran cast a spell around the resort and used part it to make sure we could get in there undercover. Narin helped us get there. We got you out. Nothing else matters."

Sadie shook her head. "We have to make sure the facility is destroyed. We have to go back and --"

"It's something we've planned on doing. Right now, we have to make sure you and Narissa are okay. I thought I'd lost you. After everything else happened, I wouldn't know what I'd do if I lost you." Elijah kissed her lightly on the lips.

Sadie returned the kiss with urgency because she felt the same way. She thought she had lost all her mates for good. After all that pain and torture, she hadn't known if she'd ever get out of the place alive. His hands traveled down her sides and raked the top of her thighs. His need for her flared along their link.

She pulled away. "I need to take a shower to wash the grime off me. Want to wash my back?"

"You don't need to ask me twice. What about the other guys?"

Greyson snored and Luke remained laid out on the chair. She shimmied off the bed and walked into the bathroom. The bed springs groaned as Elijah followed her. He hopped on one leg as he tried to pull his jeans off and get into the room. She bit her lip to keep from laughing as he finally got naked. He closed the door and locked it. He turned the water on in the shower and grabbed a washcloth. The steam filled the bathroom. She stepped into the shower, under the water, and felt the deep aches in her body. Elijah hissed in a breath when he stood before her.

"What did they do to you?"

"I'm okay."

"No, you're not. These bruises should've healed by

now. Tell me."

Sadie shook her head. She wasn't going to tell the man she loved how she was tortured by the Fairy King and the other scientists. "It doesn't matter now. It's over."

Elijah trailed his fingers over her side. She winced at the sudden pain. He went around to her back and gasped. "Love, I knew they hurt you. I could feel it, but I didn't think it was this bad." He touched her back. She shook both in pleasure and with the echo of the pain she had endured. She closed her eyes at the fresh recollection of the Fairy King making it hurt worse than anything she ever experienced. Elijah touched her once more and she jumped.

"Sorry," she muttered.

"You don't ever have to be sorry, but you can talk to me. What did they do to you?"

"Nari had mentioned that I was special to the scientists. They didn't like my answers about who I was and how was I so special. The Fairy King wanted to know why I had such an influence on his daughter. He wants Narissa pure to breed perfect children. He drove all the other Fairy shifters away. As I said, he didn't like my answers. Every time he or the scientists hurt me, I went to place in my mind where I could talk to my wolf. It helped for a little while until the Fairy King realized what I was doing. I'm not sure what he did, but it hurt."

"I'll kill him."

"Others are standing in line waiting to do the same thing. Including me. Let's not worry right now. If we have this time, then let's use it. I need to know you're here with me."

"You know I am."

She walked her fingers down his chest and flashed him a smile. "Then prove it."

Elijah grabbed her up in his arms and pressed her against the wall. His solid body molded to hers. Her body would heal. The agony of the torment would fade. Her mates would help her through it. Elijah turned her around.

"I thought you were going to rock my world?"

"I will, but I promised to wash your back first." He ran the cloth lightly over her flesh until he came to the base of her spine. "They put something inside you."

"The scientists used it to shock me. They probably put a tracker in it too."

"Then they are going to be coming here looking for you."

"Yes, but we'll be ready for them when they come. They are human and have underestimated us. They think silver will stop us, but they'll be wrong." The words came out before Sadie had time to think about what they meant, but their meaning lingered in the back of her mind.

"Another bit of prophecy?" Elijah muttered and kissed her neck.

"Something like that. Will you do me a favor? I need you to dig out the module they put in me."

"Sadie, it'll hurt you."

"It'll be fine. Go ahead with one of your claws."

"Sadie."

"It's okay, love. Trust me. The pain I've suffered being held captive is nothing compared to it. I need you to take it out of me. Please."

Elijah didn't answer her, but pain sliced her flesh where the implant was. She held onto the shower bar and bit her lip while a small groan came out. He dug around with his finger, and then she felt a tug. He ripped the implant from the small of her back. He held it out to her so she could see. A small piece of metal the size of a quarter covered in blood and flesh lay in his palm. The water washed over it. She tossed it outside the shower. She felt his tongue covering the wound where he had pulled out the device. It tingled because she could feel her body starting to heal. She had a sense something inside the gadget had also made it challenging for her to heal. She was starting to feel like her old self. Elijah flicked his tongue over the place on her lower back, and then he slipped his fingers over her ass cheeks. He placed kisses on each cheek and then touched her clit. Sadie felt her knees buckle from the quick jolt. She sucked in a breath as he rubbed her slowly.

The steam from the shower made her skin damp and she was starting to sweat from the heat. It felt good when he moved to her front and his fingers replaced his tongue on her buried bud. She slipped her fingers through his silky hair. He didn't halt his onslaught on her clit until she groaned and the orgasm ripped through her. When he stopped, he looked up with his amazing eyes and his love encompassed her.

"You still have to wash my back," she said trying to catch her breath.

"There's still a lot I have to do."

Elijah took the cloth, rolled it slowly over her breasts, and touched each of her nipples until they were so firm they hurt. She moaned as the desire to have him inside her pounded through her. It was then she realized someone pounded on the door.

"I know you're in there with Sadie. I know what you're doing. I want to come in, too. It's not fair you're keeping her all to yourself, Elijah," Greyson growled along their shared connection.

"Does he have to?" Elijah asked her under the roar of the water.

"Go let him in," she said.

"I thought you wanted me all to yourself. Wasn't that what this was all about?"

Sadie closed her eyes and thought about the love she had for Elijah and all the times he brought her pleasure. She focused it along their link and touched his stiff cock.

Elijah fell into her and cried out. Sadie grabbed his chin and kissed him quickly. Elijah thrust his hips into hers. His cock poked against her. She worked her hand along his dick. Sadie concentrated all that feeling and desire into him. He broke the kiss and thrust against her one more time until he stopped moving.

"What the fuck was that?"

She gave him a wicked grin. "Did you like it?"

He nodded. "You cheated, though. It's nothing like being inside you."

"Whatever you did, I want in on it. Fuck, Sadie, let me in." Greyson banged on the door again.

Elijah kissed her. Their tongues touched and he finally backed away to let Greyson into the room with them. Grey was already naked and stepped into the shower. His relief at seeing her well hit her like a brick. His eyes watered even with the steam. He brought her into his arms and hugged her. "I thought we'd lost you. I mean when you were taken, I didn't…"

She wiped his eyes and felt hers burning from the emotions pinging between the three of them. "It's okay. I know what you meant. I was afraid I wasn't going to see any of you again at one point. I didn't give up hope of us not being together again. I had to figure out a way to get me and Narissa out of there. You beat me to it. It's okay, Grey. You don't have to worry. We're safe now."

Elijah slipped a hand around Greyson's waist. He hugged Greyson to his chest and kissed the side of his throat. Greyson's eyes fluttered shut. Passion raced along their bond and Sadie felt herself getting caught up in it. The water kept coming out hot, but she wanted to be in their arms. However, they seemed to be in their own little world. She enjoyed watching them as it made her curious. She slipped under the water and lathered her hair. Greyson backed Elijah up against the wall and kissed Elijah with a force she felt and enjoyed. Elijah raked his hands down Greyson's back. Greyson went down on his knees and took Elijah's dick into his mouth.

Elijah stared at her as he cried out in ecstasy from Greyson working his cock. The water washing over his defined muscles made her hot. She slid back on the seat in the shower stall and spread her legs as Greyson kept working on Elijah. Sadie glided her hands over her nipples and then let her fingers find her clit which she massaged while her two mates pleasured one another. Elijah thrust his hips forward and he came. Sadie cried out as her orgasm hit her at the same time. Greyson looked over at her. The grin on his face made her shiver. Elijah stood under the spray as Greyson kissed her throat and nipped on her flesh. Sadie wanted him inside her.

Greyson sat next to her and patted his lap. He seemed to sense what she needed. Sadie straddled him as Greyson slid his cock inside her slowly so she could feel every small detail of him in her pussy. He kept his thrusts slow. He licked the water from her throat and sucked on her nipple. Sadie cried out when he bit down and rolled his tongue over the firm bud. Sadie needed more. When he was human, he was always gentle with her. They weren't human any longer.

"Don't hold back on me, Grey. Fuck me like you want to," she cried out.

"When we're some place more comfortable. Being inside you, knowing you're here is the most important thing to me. Fuck, you feel so good." Greyson gripped her ass as she rode him. Greyson threw his head back and howled as he released inside her. He slid his hand between them and fingered her clit until she Sadie couldn't take it anymore. The wolf needed more of him. Before she could think about what she was doing, she bit into his shoulder. Greyson held her as they rocked together coming down from the orgasm.

Sadie slid off him and sat on the seat next to

Greyson. Elijah sat on the other side of her. They laid their heads on her shoulders. Each trailed their fingers over her breasts and her thighs. The water washed over her as Greyson kissed her and slid his fingers inside her. She arched her hips when Elijah worked her clit. Her body already hummed from the pleasure each had brought Sadie. She didn't know if she could withstand another onslaught. How could she resist her two men? She grabbed hold of their thighs as another orgasm claimed her.

"Come for us, love," Elijah murmured next to her ear.

"Call out our names," Greyson said in the other.

Sadie tried to hold back the tide of emotions swirling inside her. The heat slammed her heart into her chest. She arched her back and whimpered. Elijah wrapped his lips around her firm nipple and sucked on it. Greyson took the other one and pumped his fingers faster inside her. Or maybe it was Elijah. She lost all sense of self as they both took her. Sadie grabbed their dicks and rubbed them, at the same time trying to keep them in her hands as she writhed until finally it felt as though they were blending together. She lost herself in their connection and they lost themselves in hers. It was too much to bear and they all came at the same time.

The water ran cold when she stepped out of the shower. Greyson wrapped a towel around her. Elijah helped to dry her hair. Her body sang at being with them.

"I think we needed that," her wolf said to her.

She rolled her shoulders. *"Yes, we did. What was the bit about what we told Elijah he called a prophecy?"*

The wolf shrugged. *"Even I don't know all the answers. We need to talk to the therapist. She'll be able to help."*

"How long do we have?"

"Not sure. Right now, I want us to go check on Luke."

"Glutton for punishment."

"Not for sex. Just to kiss him and check on him."

Greyson and Elijah sat on the bed and patted the empty spot. "Are you going to come back to bed?"

"In a minute." She moved the hair from Luke's forehead and brushed her lips over it. The gesture satisfied her wolf. Her mate snored, but he seemed fine. Sadie didn't sense anything was wrong with him she needed to heal. Her body felt heavy. She threw the towels down and then slid between her two mates. As the bodies touched, she felt more secure than she ever had before.

Chapter Eight

Luke opened his eyes. It took him a moment to realize he was staring at a large, unmade bed with no one in it. The aroma of food made his stomach growl. His head felt like it was filled with gauze, but he recalled everything before he passed out. Luke got up slowly and followed the scent of cooked meat. Sadie and his mates sat around a large table laden with food. Seeing them together made him realize how much Greyson and Elijah had grown on him. Sadie made his heart swell because she was so beautiful and strong. She had put up with so much and had come out the other side. She looked up and smiled. His world brightened. She had given him strength and saved him. He looked at Elijah and Greyson and realized she saved them too in her own way.

"You're awake." Sadie got up and threw her arms around him.

Luke scooped her up and held her. His lips found hers in a kiss. Her scent invaded his brain and the warmth of her body hardened his cock. Sadie broke the kiss and rubbed her nose along his neck. "If you do that, then I'm going to fuck you with the other two watching."

"That's not fair," he teased. "They've already had their turn."

"You were out, and there was no waking you," Sadie nibbled his neck.

Luke's stomach growled. He wasn't sure which desire he wanted to satiate first. His hunger or his need for her. His stomach rolled and the smell of the food won out. "Well, we'll have to do something later. I need food."

"There's plenty. The kitchen's working overtime to make sure everyone's getting fed," Elijah said to him.

Luke sat down. A long silence filled the room as he ate. He kept glancing at Sadie to make sure she was okay after the ordeal she went through. Questions built up in his mind. She slid her hand across his.

"I'm fine. Promise. Once we're done here, we're going to go check on Narissa. Narin's been sitting with her while we slept, so I know she's safe. Thank you for bringing her back. I know it wasn't easy."

"You know about the spell around this place and how we got into the compound?" Luke asked.

"Greyson and Elijah were filling me in on what happened to get you to the facility when you walked right in. I'm curious to talk to Dr. Maran about the spell," Sadie told him.

They finished their breakfast and headed outside. The whole place bustled with life with all the different shifters on the grounds of the resort. They made it to the psychiatrist's cabin. Before they could knock, the door opened.

"You've come in time. I've exhausted all my efforts to keep her from fading, but she is beyond my handiwork." The therapist's wide eyes drooped from exhaustion. She took her glasses off and rubbed them on her shirt.

Luke felt Sadie's panic as she rushed past him and into where they were keeping Narissa. Narin's eyes were the bloodshot from crying. Sadie sat down next to her, but he couldn't hear their conversation. The little woman tugged on his shirt and motioned for him to follow her. The other two wolves came with her.

"You were successful in rescuing Sadie and the Fairy shifter, but you didn't destroy the facility. Now they'll come here. I pulled this device out of the Fairy." She took a small round contraption the size of a quarter out of her pocket and held it out to them.

"Sadie had one in her back, too. She had me dig it out of her. They tortured her. Narissa's father did something to her as well. Sadie didn't want to talk about it," Elijah told them.

"Why didn't you tell me about this earlier?" Luke

growled, hating the idea the woman he loved was put under such horrible treatment.

"I'm sure she will when she's comfortable enough to do that. After you guys both collapsed from the tranquilizer darts, we kept watch over her. She had some nightmares," Elijah told him.

"Boys, enough of this. Argue later. We need to worry about our next move and how we're going to keep the scientists from attacking all of us," Dr. Maran snapped.

"You said you had the place protected so they'd think we are all regular humans," Greyson said.

"I do, but it's not an impenetrable barrier. I could maybe create one on a smaller scale, but there is a lot of land to cover. I'm not all powerful."

"Sadie said something earlier about she wanted to talk to you about your spell," Elijah said.

Luke felt more confused than ever. It seemed he missed more while he was unconscious. "You all have it out. I'm going to check on Sadie."

He walked in the room. Sadie's hands were Nari's chest above her heart. The Fairy's skin glowed. The luminescence showed off the outline of her heart and lungs. Even her veins were lit up. He watched in awe as the light tried to reach farther down into her veins. Sweat beaded on Sadie's forehead. She sucked in a breath and shook her head. Narissa trembled on the bed. Sadie lifted her head and opened her eyes.

"What is it?" Luke asked.

"Whatever they did to her at the lab, it's really messed up her insides. She said she could hardly feel her wolf. I can barely feel it. I've been trying to heal her, but it's slow going, like pushing a boulder up a hill. I get a little bit, but then it pushes back against me. I don't know."

"I'm sure you're doing your best. Is there anything I can do to help?" Luke asked.

"You're doing it by being here. I'm not sure how to reverse what they did. Healing silver poisoning is one thing. I've pulled that out of her already. Whatever the humans used in their cocktail altered her somehow."

"What about your drum? Would it help? You used it before at the lodge to heal all the others who had been affected by the silver," Luke asked.

"Maybe. Do you have it?"

"It's back in the room. I'll go get it. Keep doing what you can for her." He gave his mate a quick kiss and headed back toward the room. As he entered the elevator, Kade came in after him.

"Hello, Pack Master, you're awake. How is Sadie doing?" Kade asked.

"She's good. Better. I think she's getting back to her old self. Although I'm not sure about Narissa. Sadie doesn't know if she can heal her or not. I was on my way to get the drum. I figured it might help to focus her power. Not that I have any idea how it all works with her."

"Let me come with you. I might be able to help with the healing."

Luke nodded. They retrieved the drum and headed back to the doctor's cabin. When they got to the door, they heard screams. Luke rushed in to check on Sadie. Greyson and Elijah were holding Narissa down. Narin had her feet. The therapist held her head. Dr. Maran's lips moved as though in prayer. Sadie had her hands over Narissa's heart. The glow he had seen before emanated farther outward around her lungs. Sadie had healed her a bit more. Narissa thrashed around. The other wolves strained to keep her in one place.

"What's wrong with her?" Kade asked.

"They've been pumping her full of some kind of serum trying to separate the shifter DNA from her Fae DNA. I've gotten all the silver out of her, but whatever else they did, it's fighting me with everything I've got. Did you get the drum?" Sadie didn't look up as she kept up her onslaught.

Luke held it up. "Right here. What do you want me to do?"

"I can't take my hands off her or everything I've done will be lost. Kade, take Narin's spot. I need you to hold her and concentrate your energy into her the soles of her feet. Luke, hit the drum. I need to feel the vibration from it."

Kade took Narissa's ankles. Luke stood against the wall by Sadie. He took a deep breath and glanced at his mate. She nodded at him. He held the drum against his knee and hit the skin. Luke didn't so much hear the noise it made -- he felt it. The sounds moved through him. His wolf winced. It felt like his ears hurt, like hearing a dog whistle, but there was no sound. The other winced as well. He hit it again. Sadie glanced at him and nodded, letting him know he had gotten it right on the second time. This time he didn't wince. It felt as though it was a second heartbeat, and he could breathe with the beat of the drum.

He struck the instrument again. As the vibration hit him, Luke found himself standing out of his body, watching the scene as it unfolded. A silver glow around Sadie nearly blinded him. It moved down her hands and into Narissa. Where her fingers met Nari's chest, they were black, as though they were burning away something inside Narissa. The blackness threaded through every part of her except where the golden light in her chest and lungs were. The silver light from Sadie's fingers pushed against the darkness. As Nari's heart beat, it forced the silver energy into her veins, burning away the infection. Luke looked at his other mates. The same lines connected Sadie to him and them to Sadie. Each had a different light around them. Greyson was blue. Elijah was dark green. A rainbow of light danced around Kade. Pink bathed Narin. He was red.

Luke struck the drum again. Power flowed from it. The silvery light from her hand pushed farther into Nari. The blackness flickered from the vibration. Whatever Sadie was doing, however she used the device, her ability fused with the drumbeat and drove it into Narissa.

The drum kept him anchored. Luke didn't know how long they were all in the room until he heard someone pounding on the door. He couldn't make himself react to the noise. Narissa ceased thrashing. Rocky burst into the room. As soon as he touched Narissa, Luke was thrown back into his body. Elijah and Greyson removed their hands from the woman on the bed. Narissa hadn't stirred. Sadie pulled away. Her hair was plastered to her head. Luke could feel her fatigue.

"You can't go away from me. Not when I've found you. Sadie, you promised I'd have a mate. Please, you have to do more," Rocky pleaded with Sadie.

She shook her head and sniffled. "I've done everything I know how to do."

"Don't be ungrateful, son. Sadie's done more than any healer could ever have accomplished. The humans poisoned your mate to the point she's barely even a shifter anymore. She must wander the path and find her wolf again. Stay with her, let her know you love her. Give her a fighting chance to come back from wherever she is," Dr. Maran told Rocky.

Rocky glanced at the therapist. "Will she be the same if she comes back?"

"Will you love her any less if she's no longer wolf?" Elijah asked.

"No."

"Then you don't need to ask questions," the doc said. "Why don't we let the two of them have some time together. Sadie, you need to rest and eat before you fall over. The natives are getting restless. Elijah, take Kade and let them know everything's okay."

Elijah took the shaman and they left. Luke and Greyson remained behind with Narin. Sadie stood up but wobbled on her feet. Luke caught her and led her out of the room. He sat Sadie on the couch amidst a bunch of plants and sat next to her. Dr. Maran came back in with something to drink.

"This will restore your energy. What you did in there was remarkable. I've never seen anything like it."

"I'm not sure I did anything. I don't think I got all of it. It's like she's not there. I hope Rocky can bring her back."

Luke squeezed her hand. "You did what you could. I saw it while I held the drum. Your energy went into her and burned away the blackness. At the very end there was only a little bit left. You gave her a fighting chance. You've done miracles."

Sadie pushed the hair from her face and rested her head against Luke's chest. He felt complete as he wrapped his arm around her. "Thanks."

"Where's Greyson?" Luke asked.

"He went to keep Narin company and get her something to eat. Sadie, when you're up for it. I think we need to discuss what we're going to do about the ones who are coming. We don't have a lot of time," Dr. Maran told her.

Luke didn't like the sound of that.

"I know. I wanted to get a second wind. Give me a few minutes with Luke."

"Of course. Take all the time you need. You know where to find me when you're ready." She left the room.

He kissed her forehead. "You're amazing."

"I wouldn't say that."

"No. I mean it. You've been through a lot in the last couple of days and yet you're working on saving your friend and not facing any of the stuff you've gone through."

"It's easier to keep going forward than to stop and think about all the shit that's happened. There are too many people counting on me to make sure they are kept safe. Shit, I never signed up for the gig."

He trailed his fingers along her cheek. "I don't care what you say. You're amazing. What I saw and what I know you can do. Do you even know what you're doing as you're doing it? Some of the things you say, it's like you can predict the future..."

Sadie shrugged, and he sensed her uneasiness as they talked about who and what she was being the silver wolf who was supposed to save all the shifters. "I don't know. As I say things sometimes, I realize they're going to be true. Sometimes I get flashes in my mind or a knowing I can't explain."

"Intuition."

"Can we not talk about this right now?"

"Sure. What do you want to talk about?" Luke asked.

"Nothing. I want to lie here and listen to your heartbeat. Feel you breathing and taking in your smell. When all this is over, I want some alone time with each of you."

Luke ran his fingers over her back taking in her curves. He liked her way of thinking and before long he felt her slip away into dreams.

Chapter Nine

Sadie opened her eyes and felt a little more rested after her nap. She found herself on Luke's lap. He stroked her hair while he closed his eyes. Feeling his familiar warmth made her relax even though she knew there was much to do. The wolf within her stirred. She got up and stretched. Luke opened his eyes. "Is it time for you to go already?"

"'fraid so. I need you to come with me." Sadie got up and entwined her fingers with Luke's and led him to Dr. Maran. She was sitting cross-legged in the room where the enchantment originated. A silver reptile circled around itself and ate its tail. Sadie could see the spell was attached to the woman somehow.

"Glad you could make it. They will be here soon." Dr. Maran didn't open her eyes when Sadie sat down. Luke remained in the doorway with the drum.

"I know. I need you to help me with what I want to do," Sadie told her. The inklings of a plan worked on the inside of her brain.

"I will do what I can. What did you have in mind?"

"You gave my mates silver immunity for them to rescue me. I need you to help me do that with all of the shifters at the resort."

That got Dr. Maran to open her eyes and laugh. "What you ask is impossible."

"It's not. Greyson and I are immune to silver. With my blood and his mixed with the power of the drum it can work."

"How do you know this?"

"How did you know to do the spell and send them to me? We've worked together before. The last time when you were young, and in Fairy."

Dr. Maran's expression fell. "You remember?"

A foggy bit of memory floated back to Sadie when the woman was younger and some conflict was happening in Fairy, which was why the silver wolf had been called. They had partnered together to deal with the threat. "Parts of it, but it's not clear. I remember it only because it's important. And you needed to be reminded what you think is impossible is really possible."

The older woman nodded. "We did work together in your other life, and I've gotten complacent in my old age. What do I need to do?"

"My blood and Greyson's will give you the boost you need for the silver immunity. The drum has to go back to the spirit world because it's served its purpose. We use it in the spell to return it until the next time it is needed."

"How will the others get their immunity? Luke got it through the bite of the snake."

"That is where the drum comes in. Whatever gives us immunity to silver, it's going to work with vibration of the drum."

"Sadie, what happens if they come with tranquilizer darts to kidnap more shifters," Luke asked.

"They won't be coming to take any shifters. They're coming to kill. Whatever they did to Narissa, it's about as perfected as it can get. I'll need Narissa's blood too, because it'll have the Fairy element. That will affect the Fairy shifters."

"If this all works, what do you expect to happen after all of this is done? Will they retain the silver immunity?"

"That's the plan," Sadie told them.

"Are you going to tell everyone that?" Luke asked.

"No. I'll tell them it will stop once the threat is done. Then they will carry the immunity to their children. It will spread slowly from there," Sadie told them. Her inner wolf agreed it was time to take advantage away from the humans.

"I think it's a smart plan. You know it's going to work?" Luke asked.

She saw the hopeful look in her mate's eyes. "I don't know at all, but I know this is what has to happen. Will you go get Greyson? Have Kade and Elijah gather everyone together and bring them here." Sadie pointed to an area that was to the left of the glow coming from the center of the spell.

"That would be the golf course. The second tee, I believe," the doc said.

"Fine. The scientists will expect everyone to be hiding and scattered about. They won't think everyone will be gathered in one spot."

"Won't it make everyone a sitting duck, easily to pick off?"

Her canines felt sharper. Her lips curled up in a smile as the hunger to taste blood welled up in her. After everything they had done to her, Sadie wanted revenge. She wanted the humans to understand they shouldn't mess with her or any of her kind. Once a upon a time, she would have balked at the idea of wanting to sink her teeth into someone because of the memories it brought back of Elijah chowing down on Greyson. That was before she accepted who she was. Sadie wanted to wrap her jaws around the Fairy King's throat and rip it out. He wasn't going to leave this place alive.

"It won't be easy. We'll have the advantage. The energy of the drum will keep them away. Once the spell ends and the drum is destroyed, we'll be vulnerable to attack."

"We need to get started," the doc said.

"Will you be able to stay focused and keep the spell going? You know what will happen once the drum is destroyed."

The snake shifter nodded. "I know. I've figured it was coming when I met you again. I have things in order. I have lived a long time, and I am ready for the end."

"I'll get what I need and be back in a few minutes."

Sadie got up.

"I'd suggest getting blood from all three of your mates. They've all had contact with my spell and play a part in your life. It will strengthen the enchantment."

"Good idea." Luke followed Sadie into Narissa's room.

Rocky lay alongside her. "There's no change."

She glanced at Nari. As much as she wanted to stay and work on Narissa, she had to use her energy on those who were coming. She took her friend's hand and squeezed it. No response. Sadie let her nails grow and sliced Nari's palm. The blood gathered onto the drum. Once it hit the skin, it was absorbed into the instrument.

"What are you doing?" Rocky asked.

"Long story, but I need her blood for the spell we're going to perform." Sadie used a small bit of her power and healed the cut. "Stay with her."

"I'm not going anywhere."

She called to her mates along the link they shared. *"Elijah and Greyson, I need you to meet me, and then I need you to get everyone over to the golf course. It's where we are going to make our stand."*

Luke said nothing as she waited for the two other men to meet her. Their questions bubbled in their minds, but she held up her hand. "I know you want answers. Luke can fill you in. Right now I need your blood. Hold out your hands please."

All three of them held out their hands. She slashed all of them in one stroke with her sharpened nail. Sadie held the drum underneath the wounds as the blood flowed. It did the same as Nari's had and soaked into the instrument. The power building in the drum rubbed along her palms. She got back to the cabin and Narin paced outside.

"They're almost here. What do you want the Fairies to do?" Narin asked.

"You mean the shifters who are Fairies?"

"No. I've told all those who will listen about what my father did to Narissa and you. Narissa was well liked, even though she was in exile because of what she was. Many knew of your friendship. It's easy to see her mark upon you. They're with you now and wish to see him abdicate the throne."

Sadie hadn't expected this. "Having help from the Fae would be wonderful. Is there some way I can speak to them?"

"No need. They're all around you, and those who aren't will get the message a few seconds after you say it."

"Okay. It'd be a big help if they can distract the humans who are coming for us. We're weaving a spell to give us an advantage. I don't know if it will affect any of the Fairies who are not shifters. However, we can use all the help we can get. And… I've done all I can for Narissa after the damage was done. If your healers can try anything, it would be appreciated, but please take into account her mate is with her. He's a wolf and is very protective. I've tried my best with her."

"I know you did. I watched you even if you couldn't see it."

Sadie gave the Fairy a smile. "You said you wanted to see your father abdicate the throne. I'd see him put to a more permanent solution. Would you be opposed?"

Narin's expression remained blank. "No."

"Good. One other thing. The scientist your father is involved with. She's pregnant. Find her. Have the others pull her away from her people and keep her captive."

"You have plans for her?" Narin asked.

"I do. She needs a taste of her own medicine."

"And the child?"

"The child is an innocent and will be your brother or sister."

"Do you plan on biting the scientist?"

"I never said that," Sadie said. "I haven't made up my mind. Although, it'd serve her right to become what she's experimenting on. Keep her away from everyone else."

"It will be done."

"Thank you." Sadie returned to the Dr. Maran. The snake shifter sat deeper in a trance. The energy in the room pressed upon Sadie. The woman didn't open her eyes. The purple glow in the center of the circle turned golden. The silver serpent's scales flashed red and green as it kept eating its tail and being reborn all at the same time.

"Once you place the drum within the glow, the spell will begin. You have to add your blood to it. They've gathered at the golf course. I'll keep up the spell for as long as I'm able. The enchantment is tied to my life force. I'll give it all to give you some time. Once the spell dies, so do I. It was good to cross paths with you again, silver wolf. One day, I think we will meet again."

Sadie sliced her palm and held it over the drum. She let more blood flow from the wound until the drum skin turned completely red. Sadie felt the power in it throbbing as though it were trying to escape. She set the instrument into the glow in the middle of the spell. The snake eating itself took a quick moment to hiss at her as she broke the line of the circle. It reached up and bit her. She figured she deserved that, but it went back to eating itself. She set the drum into the center of the circle. It took a few moments, and then it ignited. Energy blasted against Sadie and it chased her from the room.

The heat from the enchantment raced along her veins. It started in the center of her chest and radiated outward. Sadie got to the green and couldn't count how many people were gathered at the tee, but it was several hundred. Purple haze glittered over them.

"What's happening?" someone asked.

Sadie stood before them. "Those who killed your loved ones are coming. They aren't here to take us hostage or do more experiments. They will exterminate all of us. The one behind this is the Fairy King."

"Why am I burning up?" Someone else asked as Sadie felt panic starting to spread.

Sadie let her power loose. She didn't know if she could influence everyone without the drum, but she was sure going to try. All of the shifters had all different auras. Some were alphas. Many were not, but she had to calm them. "I know you're scared. You came here looking for protection because I called you, and then they took me away. Every one of you has the right to feel as though I haven't lived up to my word. I feel as though I haven't been able to give you what I promised. The heat you're feeling is making everyone immune to silver forever. You will carry the gift down, and it will spread through the generations."

"Is this true?" one of Luke's pack's elders stepped forward. "That's an impossible feat. We have tried in the past and nothing's happened."

"She speaks the truth," Luke told all of them.

"You say because she's your mate," the elder sneered.

"Would you say I'm lying?" Kade asked them.

"You're part of this, too," the elder replied.

"I'm here to make sure everyone gets out alive. Sooner or later the humans were going to figure out what we are. We don't know the extent of the damage the human scientists have done when it comes to other shifters around the world. If we don't make a stand here, then everything Sadie's done -- and all the suffering of the ones who have been kidnapped or killed -- will have been in vain."

"Why has all of this happened?" another asked.

Sadie sighed. "The Fairy King decided he didn't like

any of his kind being of mixed blood, being able to shift their shapes into animals, when it's not natural to their regular states. His daughter was bitten by a wolf many years ago. He partnered with the humans and gave them access to Fairy magic. They combined it with their science to stamp out the shifter gene within her. In the process, the humans discovered a way to weaponize blood by infecting shifters with silver and sending them back to your clans. Once their blood hit the air, the silver in the blood became a weapon. All those from your packs who were kidnapped had some Fae lineage. He bade the humans to destroy all of us they could find. They tortured me. I saw the serum they've developed to wipe out what makes us shifters. For some of you, maybe it's what you want, but you'll never truly be human again. Even if they did offer it, it'd kill you in the process. I'm not going to stop anyone from walking away and choosing their own path. The humans are here, being held off by the Fairies who have sided with us. Stay and fight with me or run off. Make your choice now."

Sadie pushed her will into as many as she could so they would feel an echo of what she felt while she was being tortured. Tears ran down her cheeks as she relived it. A few looked at the others and some raced off into the trees. The majority stayed. Sadie's wolf twitched. It wanted to face their attackers. The breeze carried the sweaty scent of the humans who had come to kill them, and she could smell the humans as they were getting closer to them.

Greyson pulled out a knife and grabbed Elijah's hand. He sliced Elijah's palm and held it up for all to see. The wound didn't turn black around the edges where the silver touched. The blood ran red and the gash closed within a few seconds. "This is what she's doing for you. Trust her or not. Take revenge for the ones you love and the ones whose lives were taken." Greyson threw the knife down and pulled his clothes off. His shape twisted as he became a half wolf/half man. Balancing on two legs, he was a monstrous thing standing seven feet tall. He threw back his head and howled. Elijah and Luke shifted into their wolf forms. Their howls joined Greyson.

The heat of the spell and the battle lust rushed through her. Sadie pulled at her clothes as the wolf pushed against her flesh to break out. The snake shifter had been as good as her word. Sadie could feel the power reaching its peak. She raced toward the front of the resort. A shot rang out and a puff of air went by her shoulder. It had come from the right. Another shot came from the left. They had broken past the Fairies. More shots came from above. She couldn't see where they were coming from, but there was no plane or helicopter. She glanced up and saw something hovering above.

Drones.

"Any bird shifters, I need you to take out those drones." A screech sounded overhead that she figured was the answer to her request.

Sadie kept her eyes forward as shadows appeared out of the darkness. Other shots came at them. All the others fanned out and were taking down humans. She couldn't worry about them. Greyson stayed to guard her. He took a few shots, but he kept on going as though they didn't affect him. Sadie caught the odd scent of the Fairy King. It wasn't quite human and yet the aroma of humanity clung to him like a bad perfume. His guard surrounded him to fend off any shifters. Her eyes were set on him.

"I'll clear a path for you," Greyson said to her.

"Thanks, love. Be careful, they have swords."

"I'm not afraid of bullets or flitting things with wings who think they can harm those who I love. Rip out his throat for me."

Elijah jumped and landed on top of one of the humans who had come to exterminate them. All he could see was red. All the fury, loss, and hatred he experienced from losing his pack welled up inside him. Anything that wasn't a shifter was his prey. Shots rang out around him. A sting and a burning pain hit his shoulder. These weren't tranquilizer darts, but real bullets. By their metallic smell he could detect the silver.

Another wolf jumped to his side. He recognized Rocky. *"Pack Master, let me help you."*

"I thought you were with Narissa." Elijah glanced at him as he caught the scent of another human.

"The Fairies are working with her to help her come back. They told me they'd call me if they needed me. She's alive and I need to feel like I'm useful somewhere."

"Good. There's a concentration of humans in the hotel itself. We need to flush them out."

"I've called the pack together. We're here for you."

Elijah looked behind him and saw what remained of his pack. Of the original five hundred wolves, the number had been cut in half. Once Rocky had been his enemy, but now he cared enough to show up with backup. Elijah howled. His pack answered. It filled him with a renewed sense of strength. The wolves were his family along with Sadie. It didn't matter if he had all the money in the world. Without them, he was nothing. Without Sadie he was nothing. Hearing them bolstered his confidence, and he ran toward the main building watching as other shifters -- large lions down to the smallest sparrow -- massed upon those who had come to attack them. As they ran more shots rang out, but his pack broke off to take out the threats, protecting him as well. A human stepped out from behind tree dressed all in black and raised a weapon at him. Elijah jumped on top of the guy before he could get a shot off and made sure he would never rise again.

They made it to one of the employee areas near the back of the resort. Two of the goons guarded the door. He transformed back to human form, but kept his claws sharpened. They looked at him stunned, not sure what to make of a naked man coming toward them.

"Hey, fellas. My girlfriend stole my towel and swim trunks. You think you could let me in?"

They glanced at one another. One pressed the earbud in his ear and was about to say something, but Elijah swiped his claws across the man's throat. Before the other one could get a shot off, Rocky had brought him down. Elijah opened the door and motioned for several of his wolves to enter. A camera watched over the entrance. He hoped it wasn't working.

Elijah stayed human while more of the pack guarded the entrance. The heavy scent of male sweat mixed with something with a slight chemical burn like bleach sat on his tongue when he inhaled. He followed the aroma to the security room. He recognized the guard from the facility as he watched the security monitors. This room gave access to most every part of the resort and the outer areas farther away from the main building. His wolf wanted out so he slipped back onto all fours so they could both have vengeance.

"Let's go in there and rip his face off," it barked.

"Patience. Listen."

"The bullets aren't having an effect nor is the aerosolized silver. I thought you said they had a weakness for it?" the leader of the human guard replied to whoever was talking into his ear.

Elijah strained, but he could hear the other person on the end of the earpiece.

"They're supposed to. I don't know what is going on. Doc said she wanted a few of them alive for more testing. Fuck what she said. Take out all the freaks."

Elijah snarled. The man grabbed his gun. Elijah leapt

at him. The man screamed as he knocked him to the ground. Elijah tried to lock his jaws around his neck. All he got was a mouthful of body armor. The man struggled to get free from underneath him.

"This isn't over. We're going to wipe out all of you mutants. We're not the only ones who have this information. There are other facilities. Others will come."

Elijah pulled back his lips and kept the information to tell Sadie. She would want to know. All the other facilities would have to be destroyed. No more shifters needed to suffer the same fate as his pack.

The man twisted again. His movements gave Elijah enough room to lock his jaws around his prey's throat. He bit down and the man's life ended. It was all too quick for him, but there were others he had to take care of first. Elijah licked the blood from his muzzle. Rocky and a few of the others were waiting on him, guarding the security room.

"Search the rest of the hotel. They shouldn't be in the rooms, but if you find an open one, flush them out. Make sure they don't leave the hotel. I have a bone to pick with the bitch who did this." Elijah recalled the head scientist's smell and caught it on the head of the security guard's uniform.

He looked at the cameras one last time. Many dead bodies littered the grounds. Humans and shifters. Elijah studied the monitors and found what he wanted -- the female scientist being led farther back near the woods in the far east corner where only a few trails winding deeper into the wood existed.

The creatures who surrounded her weren't human. Fucking Fairies. Elijah raced toward them in case they decided to bring her into their world and keep her forever.

Rocky caught up to him. *"Pack Master, where are you going?"*

"To get the one responsible for all of this. That bitch who kept Sadie and Narissa locked up."

"Then I'm coming with you. I owe this bitch a piece of my mind."

Elijah grunted in agreement. Rocky stayed at his side and a little bit ahead of him to ward off any shots. When they got to the scientist, the Fairies stepped out in front of them with spears.

"No one passes here."

Elijah took to human form once more. "Sadie sent me here. I need to talk to the woman."

"Not possible," the other guard said.

Rocky tried to get between them. They knocked him backward. He yelped but got back up as a human. "She is the one who hurt my mate."

"Even so, Sadie asked us to guard until she comes to claim her. We know you are the mate to our queen, which is why we'll not hurt you. Whatever agenda you have here, it must come from Sadie and your personal feelings will have to wait."

"Help me, please!" the human woman screamed as she struggled to get away from the Fairies.

"Quiet. We have not hurt you beyond a few bruises from you struggling to get away from us. Be thankful we are loyal or we'd throw you to these wolves."

The Fairies wouldn't give up the woman. Elijah had to wait for Sadie. "Fine. I'll be back. I --"

A sharp pain sliced through his shoulder. He grabbed his left shoulder to see what had gone through the flesh, but he came away with no blood. A scream split his mind. He cringed at the pain and grabbed his head. This wasn't his pain. *Sadie.* Elijah followed the link and sprinted to where he sensed his mate. He howled. Greyson and Luke responded.

He caught a glimpse through her eyes and saw the koi pond at eye level. She was on the ground. When she looked up, a white-haired man with a shit-eating grin on his bloodied and scratched face had a sword pointed at her. Another slice hit Elijah's side. He limped and screamed again as Sadie was wounded.

"I won't let you die. We're coming. Hold on." He worked through the pain and raced to save his mate.

Chapter Eleven

"You really thought you could kill me? That's adorable," the Fairy King sneered. "Your silly spell to make your shifters immune to silver to fool the humans didn't fool me. I've faced worse enemies than you. Pathetic. I know what you are. We met before in your other incarnation when my father ruled. Back then, he worked with your kind so we could rid Fairy of the evil infecting it. You are a pale shadow of what you used to be. You took my daughter away from me. You'll suffer for all you've done." He raised his sword again and pierced her right shoulder.

Sadie screamed again.

She had gotten a few good swipes in before he brought out his sword. She thought she had him. The spell gave her strength. The heat in her heart had diminished, letting her know the incantation was fading out. The enchantment had worked. It made her proud knowing the shifters would be immune to silver even if meant she would not see the end of the spell.

The Fairy King ran his finger along the edge of the blade to gather her blood. He brought it to his lips, grimaced, and then spit it out. "Even your blood tastes foul. I'll be happy knowing humans drove out the taint in my daughter. She *will* be whole once more. You can't keep her from me."

"That's what you think. You haven't driven the wolf from her. She will never give you a perfect race."

The Fairy King growled and swung at her again. This time Sadie rolled out of the way. She tried to get up, but the wound to her leg made it impossible to put weight on. She crawled back, away from the Fairy King, and grabbed hold of the holly hedge and forced herself to stand, gritting her teeth against the pain. The strength of her wolf surged forward and she faced the Fairy King.

"You think you're going to slay me. You and your

mates are nothing. I won't stop until all of your kind is dead. The humans might not help me any longer, but my Fairies will wipe out all the shifters there are. Mark my words."

"That won't be happening. You'll be the one who won't be making it back alive." A brush of fur swept past her leg and pounced on the Fairy King. Luke had him pinned, but the Fairy King fought him off. Another gray blur, bulkier than the last one came by loping on all fours, then it stood straight up. Greyson in his wolf-man form. The Fairy King threw Luke off him, but Greyson matched the king move for move.

"The knife in my pocket." Greyson gestured to his torn pants. "It will kill him."

Sadie limped over and took the knife from his pocket. The last to come into the small space was Elijah. His sides heaved from running. He growled at the Fairy King and blocked any way he could escape.

"You think these beasts or your little silver blade will stop me?"

Sadie gripped the weapon tighter. It had the same power she felt from Narissa. The knife was not man-made but forged by a Fairy. Elijah jumped at the Fairy King and grabbed his arm. The king screamed and dropped his sword. Luke took hold of his other hand. Greyson swung his claws and caught him in the chest, which brought the Fairy King to his knees. The look of pure hatred on the king's face fueled the anger in Sadie's heart after everything he had done to her. He struggled to get away, but he wouldn't escape her mates.

"It's more than silver. Your daughter gave it to us. Narin seemed quite adamant it'd kill you," Sadie told him.

His terrified expression betrayed his arrogance. "Y-you're lying. She'd never give you such a weapon and betray me."

"Guess you're going to find out." Sadie plunged the blade up to the hilt into his heart. Her mates released him. The Fairy King stumbled backward into the koi pond.

Sadie lost her footing as the pain of her wounds and her blood loss caught up to her. Greyson caught her and held her to him. Elijah returned to human form and ran his fingers along her cheek. "You did it. He's dead."

"Get his body and bring it. The others will want to see he's dead. Get me to where they're holding the doctor," Sadie stammered as she felt herself starting to lose consciousness.

"Hang on, love. You'll be okay."

Sadie clung to Greyson as she slipped in and out. His pelt was warm as he carried her. The pain of the wounds receded some. The heat from the spell evaporated. Dr. Maran had given her word and the drum no longer resided in the physical world. Her mates got her to the human woman who'd kept her captive. The Fairies guarding the doctor straightened when they saw her.

"We've kept her safe as requested."

"Thank you," Sadie told them.

"One of your mates tried to get past us and get to the human," the other guard said.

She glanced at Elijah who shrugged. "I was pissed. Still am. What can I say? She needs to pay for what she's done to everyone."

"What are you going to do to me?" Dr. Cooper asked.

"Luke, show her and them what happened to the king," Sadie instructed her mate.

Luke laid the corpse at the woman's feet. She wailed and sank down. Dr. Cooper touched the king. Sadie could see the woman loved him. "How could you? He said..."

"He said a lot of things." Sadie knelt by the scientist. "He was never going to let you keep the child. If he did, he certainly wasn't going to claim it as his own. You were a means to an end. Now, he won't be here to protect you."

The woman looked up at her. "Why would I need protection?"

"Because the bastard growing in your belly isn't welcome in our land. Anyone loyal to the king will be shown no justice. We've held you here because she asked us to." Sadie looked up at her friend. Narissa stepped out from the woods.

Rocky stood by her side with a proud smile on his face. Narin was at her other side. Behind her were the Fairy shifters. Nari glanced at Sadie and smiled. The Fae guarding the human went to one knee and bowed their heads before Narissa.

"Your Majesty, what is it you wish?" one guard asked.

"Will you all be loyal to me without question even though I'm a shifter?" Narissa asked.

The head guard looked up. "You have already been named queen by the five tribes. Those tribes encompass all of our kind. It doesn't matter if you can shift your shape. You are descended of royal blood. The king was once placed on the throne by the five tribes. We follow the old laws."

Narissa had a cold look on her face, and yet she was as regal as Sadie had ever seen her. "You cooperate with Sadie and her mates or I'm going to cut the child from your belly. What do you say?"

"I told Sadie if we watched this woman that no harm would come to the child," Narin spoke up.

"It won't if she agrees to assist us," Narissa said.

The doc's hand went to her stomach. "What are you going to do to me? What do I have to do?"

Sadie felt her teeth grow. With everything in her she yearned to make the woman pay for what she had done, but knowing she was pregnant, Sadie couldn't hurt the baby. Her feelings were conflicted. It wasn't in her to hurt an innocent even with all her anger. Before she could say anything else, Rocky grabbed the woman's arm and sank his fangs into Dr. Cooper's flesh. Narissa made no move to stop her mate. Neither Elijah nor Sadie stopped him. The woman screamed and tried to get away.

Sadie glanced at Narissa. "She shouldn't be a problem now."

"What did you do to me?" the woman spat and held her arm trying to stop the bleeding.

"Now you'll understand what you've done to the innocents here. All the children you've killed along with the others. You brought it upon us because the man you loved was a twisted fuck who wanted to make a pure race," Sadie told her.

"You lie," she spat. The woman began to weave on her feet.

Narin placed her hand on the woman's head. "She doesn't. I've heard his conversations. See what he had planned."

Whatever Narin did, Dr. Cooper's eyes teared up. "No. He loved me. He showed me things. He --"

"He lied. My father was good at it. He gave you enough to get you hooked so you'd do whatever he wanted. Now you see the truth. Soon you will be one of us as will your child. Take some time to think about it." The scientist collapsed as the fever took her.

"Rocky, take her to Kade. He'll look after her." Narissa's mate picked up the woman and left. She gave Sadie a long hug. "I don't know how to thank you. You risked everything to save me. You healed me and brought my wolf back to me. I'm forever indebted to you. You've always been my best friend and my sister in all of this. What can I ever do to repay you?"

"I'm glad you're better. You command all the Fairies, right?" Sadie asked.

"I do."

"Ask them to find the other facilities. Tell them what's been going on so they can work on stopping them. I don't expect them to get hurt, but anything they can do."

Narissa smiled. "Already planned on doing that. How about we discuss all of this later? I have those who will clean up the mess. Make sure no human or shifter is left behind. If that's okay with you, Elijah."

The wolf nodded.

"Good. My people want to have some kind of payback in this. I'll let you have the information once I get it. Go be with your mates, Sadie. It's time to celebrate. We'll make sure all the other shifters here are taken care of. Trust me on this one. We've got this. You've done what you're supposed to do." Sadie glanced at the other Fairies and they nodded. She looked at Narin, who smiled. She could feel the other Fairies flitting around too fast for her to see and her mates wanted to get her alone.

"Thanks. Elijah and Luke, please tell your packs what's going on. If they wish to stay, we can talk to them tomorrow, but everyone can get some sleep. Thank them for all they've done. We are free and the enemy is dead," Sadie told her mates.

Howls and roars sounded in the night so she knew the message had been passed on and they were celebrating. Greyson ran his muzzle along her neck and made her quiver. He scooped her up and held her to him.

"I can walk on my own."

"I like it better this way, and you're still healing. I want to be sure you're protected until we get back to the room. Besides, I get first dibs on you," Greyson said to her.

"I get all dibs on all three of you," Sadie told them as Greyson carried her into the hotel and back up to the penthouse suite. Once they got there, Greyson returned to human form and slipped off his pants. Luke and Elijah also became men once more.

"I can't believe we did it." Luke swung her up in his arms and crushed her to him.

"We did. Thank you for rescuing me from the Fairy King. I thought I could take this on myself, but you were all my wolves in shining armor."

"We're alive because we worked together," Elijah said to him.

"We did. Dr. Maran gave her life to help with the spell. We prevailed because we all worked together. This will look different in the morning." She rolled her neck when she felt hands slide down her shoulders. When she looked up, Greyson smiled at her. The lust and the pride in his eyes warmed her. She glanced at her other mates and felt their pleasure as it rolled over her mind and body. "We need to celebrate. I want to make sure you're okay."

"I'll be happy to show you." Greyson kissed her throat.

Luke guided her lips to his in a slow kiss until she pulled away, breathless. "I can assure you, we're all okay."

Elijah nibbled at her throat and tugged on her ear. "We're okay because we have you. Now let us worship you to show you how much we love you."

Sadie couldn't say no to her mates. Instead she fell into their embrace and knew the threat had passed and they would all be okay. Elijah bit a little harder over the spot he originally bit her to claim her as his mate. Sadie couldn't hold in the moan that slipped from her lips. Their combined passion ignited the mate bonds between them. It burned inside of her until her body hummed. Her mates' pride and love infused her. Elijah's hands roamed over her body and cupped her breasts. He squeezed her nipples as a gush of wetness warmed her thighs. Sadie didn't want to lose herself just yet. They had the whole night to enjoy themselves. She wiggled away from Elijah and went to the bed. All three men came at her, but she put up a hand to stop them.

"Greyson called dibs on me first, if I recall correctly." She smiled.

"You're really going to make us wait?" Luke asked as Greyson went over to the bed.

"For now. You can watch," she said to them.

Elijah growled. "That's not fair."

Sadie chuckled at his frustration. "I think it is. Besides, I want to watch you and Luke. That's a fair trade, don't you think?" she asked Elijah.

Her mates glanced between one another. They thought only about having her, but not about having one another. Luke pulled Elijah to him quickly and kissed him. Sadie watched as he stiffened and then relaxed into the embrace from the other man. Sadie felt Elijah let the passion of their joined bond take over him. He hesitated for a moment and returned the kiss. Elijah's hands slid down Luke's back and squeezed the other wolf's ass. Sadie groaned.

Elijah stopped kissing Luke to look at her and flash her a smile. "You felt that?"

Sadie nodded. "I did. I can feel how difficult it is for you to hold back your pleasure." She closed her eyes and turned into Luke. "Luke, you want to bite into Elijah's ass. Your wolf is on the edge. It wants to take Elijah and then me." Sadie caught a bit of the wildness from Luke's inner wolf through their bond. It brought hers out as well. Her teeth sharpened and the animal instincts in her began to take over. She couldn't fight the sudden urge. The build-up of feelings from the battle and their win, along with their combined emotions was too much for her. She grasped the feeling and spread it out along their thread so they would understand. Even as she did, their feelings reflected back on her creating a loop between all of them.

Greyson huffed and kissed Sadie hard enough his

teeth caught her bottom lip, drawing blood. She returned the kiss as Luke's howl split the room. She looked over and he had Elijah up against the wall kissing him and raking his hands down Elijah's chest. Sadie felt the slight pain of it and Elijah's pleasure before Greyson ripped her attention away from them. He nipped the other side of her throat.

"I need you. I don't know what the fuck you did, but I need to be inside of you."

"Then fuck me," she groaned.

Greyson grabbed her and flipped her over onto her stomach. He took her hips and dragged her to the edge of the bed. A sharp sting hit her ass as he bit her. Sadie squealed. Luke cried out in pain and pleasure. Sadie felt Elijah bite into him and tasted blood on the back of her throat. She closed her eyes and dug her fingers into the blankets to hold on as Greyson slid his cock inside her. He took a hold of her hips and thrust himself into her pussy. One hand slipped over her stomach and grabbed her breast. Sadie moved against him, but he moved so quickly. It was easy to let him claim her. She held in a groan as his finger found her clit. The sudden massaging of her buried bud made her forget herself. It made her forget everything except the ecstasy merging them all together.

Elijah moaned. The building bliss within him mounted with hers. Luke pounded into him while Greyson pounded into her. Sadie moaned as she neared climax. "Harder."

Greyson obliged and fucked her harder. Sadie shut her eyes and let the joy wash over her as her body trembled. She raked her fingers over the bed and had the sudden burst of pain when Greyson bit her again as he came. He slumped on top of her for a second before he rolled back onto the bed. Sadie nestled in his arms for a moment as she tried to catch her breath. However, she could barely draw breath when Luke's orgasm hit her. She writhed on the bed. Greyson caught one of her arms and pulled one of her fingers into his mouth. A light touch ran along the inside of her thigh. She looked up. Elijah licked her flesh up toward her inner thigh.

"Did you think pairing me with Luke would make me stop wanting you?" Elijah asked.

"No, but it was…"

Elijah planted more kisses until his mouth found her clit. His tongue stroked the swollen bud until he pulled it between his teeth. Luke took her breast into his mouth. She looked over at him and saw the cocky look in his eye. His lips grazed over her nipple. She reached for his cock, but he pinned her arm down. Greyson had her other arm so she couldn't move while Elijah lifted her leg and draped it over his shoulder. His tongue continued to swirl around her clit. Her mates had her in their grasp and wouldn't let her go.

They might have captured her body, but she grabbed the threads of their minds. Sadie pushed her pleasure along their links. Luke kissed her harder. Greyson bit her breast. Elijah moaned but worked her faster, his fingers delving inside of her. Sadie pushed against all three of them, unable to hold back any longer. Bursts of light lit up her insides. Her wolf howled within her mind, but then she realized the sound came from her. As she howled, her mates joined in until the sound came together in unison. Together. They would never abandon her. They would always be together no matter what.

* * *

Sadie opened her eyes and found herself in the meadow of her mind where she first encountered her wolf and the woman who claimed to be the mother of them all. The pond reflected a tranquil scene of the moon above and the sunrise off in the distance. Her wolf stood by her side instead of by the woman. Sadie felt a calmness and tranquility she hadn't felt before in this place inside her mind.

"Why did you bring me here?"

The woman smiled. "Because it's time for me to bid you farewell. I'm no longer needed. You've done well and weathered the storm."

"Thanks. You set me on this path even if I didn't understand it."

"The way of the silver wolf is never over until she takes her last breath."

"Is that a warning or a threat?"

"No. Your job isn't over until it's over. You have many years ahead of you, but you no longer need my guidance. All you need is in your memories and the knowledge you already have. It's one of your gifts, the intuition, of things to know if they happen or not. You've already figured that out. Enjoy your mates. They love you. Enjoy them. Enjoy life."

"Thank you for everything you've given me."

"Thank you for what you've done for all my children. One day we will meet again."

The world faded out and Sadie woke up. When she did, she found her mates snuggled up against her. Their even breathing calmed her. They also gave her strength to know she could face whatever else was coming. They would be there and she would always love them. They completed her in different ways. If it weren't for them, she wouldn't know herself.

Her wolf rubbed along her mind and shared her joy of having them. *"We love them. They love us. There's nothing else to question. Now let's snuggle and forget everything else except bathing in their scent and their love."*

"Yes, wolfie."

"Don't call me that."

Sadie giggled and snuggled back into the arms of her men. *"I like wolfie."*

"Wolfie works," Greyson said.

A growl came from her lips before she could stop it.

Elijah laughed and trailed his fingers along her curves. "Wolfie. Sounds good."

"Told you," Sadie said to her wolf.

It growled again as her mates laughed and pulled her back down onto the bed.

Crymsyn Hart

Crymsyn Hart is a National Bestselling author of over eighty paranormal romance and horror novels. Her experiences as a psychic and ghostly encounters have given her a lot of material to use in her books. Vampires, grim reapers, shifters, and other paranormal creatures tend to end up in her books no matter how hard she tries to keep them away.

She currently resides in Charlotte, NC with her hubby and her three dogs. If she's not writing, she's curled up with the dogs watching a good horror movie or off with friends.

Crymsyn at Changeling: changelingpress.com/crymsyn-hart-a-188

Changeling Press E-Books

More Sci-Fi, Fantasy, Paranormal, and BDSM adventures available in e-book format for immediate download at ChangelingPress.com -- Werewolves, Vampires, Dragons, Shapeshifters and more -- Erotic Tales from the edge of your imagination.

What are E-Books?

E-books, or electronic books, are books designed to be read in digital format -- on your desktop or laptop computer, notebook, tablet, Smart Phone, or any electronic e-book reader.

Where can I get Changeling Press E-Books?

Changeling Press e-books are available at ChangelingPress.com, Amazon, Apple Books, Barnes & Noble, and Kobo

ChangelingPress.com